Survivor

Dean Crawford

ISBN: 149759040X
ISBN-13: 978-1497590403

Also by Dean Crawford:

The Ethan Warner Series
Covenant
Immortal
Apocalypse
The Chimera Secret
The Eternity Project

Independent novels
Eden
Holo Sapiens
Revolution
Soul Seekers

Want to receive notification of new releases? Just sign up to Dean Crawford's newsletter via: http://eepurl.com/KoP8T

"As I looked, behold, a storm wind was coming from the north, a great cloud with fire flashing forth and a bright light around it, and in its midst glowing metal. Out of the middle thereof came four living creatures. And this was their appearance; they had the likeness of a man."

Ezekiel 1:5

I

The cold awoke her.

For a moment she believed that she was already dead, for when she opened her eyes she saw nothing but blackness, as deep as the universe. A chill enveloped her naked body and she shuddered, her skin feeling oily and under pressure from all sides.

She tried to move her head but could not, and swivelled her eyeballs down to seek some sense of where she was. She could hear her own breathing, muted as though she was underwater, and she realised that she was confined to a tiny space barely bigger than she herself was.

Like a coffin.

The cold bit deep into her bones, touched her skin as though ice was being pressed against it. She shivered and her heart began to race in her chest as panic rose like a dark wave inside her.

She tried to scream.

No sound came forth, choked back somewhere deep inside her throat, and her lips touched cold metal as she moved them. A slight pressure on her nose and on her forehead, cold and hard, and she realised that her head was encased in some kind of metallic mask. She blinked, and felt her eyes sting briefly before she realised that she was not only totally enclosed but also completely immersed in a fluid. A word flickered through her mind: per–fluorocarbon, used to preserve life and oxygenate for long periods of time.

The panic rose up again and threatened to consume her, but then her eyes caught on something.

Light.

The faintest glow appeared just above her eye line as though it were the most precious thing in the universe. She fixed upon it, willed it with all of her heart to grow, and grow it did. The faint light swelled in intensity, broadening into a warm orange orb. She saw it illuminate geometric patterns and an intricate web of lines interconnecting with each other in a blurred miasma. It took her brain a few moments to realise what she was looking at.

A screen, not much bigger than her face and encrusted with ice that had formed beautiful spirals and whorls. The light cast a brief but blessed warmth upon her face as it drifted past on the far side of the screen.

She tried to move her arm to wipe the fogging from the screen, but she could not. She looked down and in the glow saw her naked body strapped inside the tiny capsule. Ice crystals blinked like distant stars as they caught the light, sparkling weakly through the amber fluid.

Closer to her, a small panel attached to the interior and frosted with ice crystals cast a weak light of its own. Upon it was a single word.

SURVIVAL

The light burned bright and cast shadows through the fluid filling the capsule, but then it began to fade again. Her eyes snapped back to the screen and she almost cried as the light faded away until she was pitched into absolute blackness once more.

She began tugging at her restraints, her limbs aching and feeling sluggish as they moved inside the dense and viscous fluid. Something tugged at the insides of her arms and she realised that tubes were inserted into her veins. Creeping dread clawed at her as she fought to release herself from her bonds in the darkness, her fingers and toes already numb and her limbs twitching and trembling.

Breathe.

She closed her eyes and forced herself to calm down, controlled her breathing until it settled, the fluid moving slowly in and out of her lungs. She opened her eyes again and curled her fingers back toward the insides of her wrists to feel the restraints there. The rough inside surface told her that they were not metal but merely an adhesive of some kind. She began working away at her right wrist, twisted it and levered it up and down as she tried to force the adhesive apart. The coarse material scoured her skin but she felt the restraint give a little.

The light returned, swept across her field of vision to illuminate her tiny prison once more with a brief but wonderful warmth and brilliance. She worked harder as the light vanished again and heard a faint tearing sound as the adhesive began to give way. Moments later her right wrist slipped free of the restraint and she lifted her arm for what felt like the first time in a hundred years.

The tube inserted into her vein pinched as she lifted her hand through the fluid surrounding her to the screen in the darkness. She touched it, cold and hard, the ice sticking her fingers to the surface. She pulled them back and then scratched at the ice, trying to rub it away as the light returned to drift across the screen. It rapidly grew in intensity and suddenly flared as bright as a thousand suns even through the per–fluorocarbon.

Through the tiny screen she saw a star burning, flaring as it breached the vast curved surface of a planet in a brilliant halo.

She realised that it was not the light of the star that was moving, but her own capsule as it tumbled end over end in the bitter emptiness of space. She saw the sun's light flare past the screen, saw the surface of the planet through the thin sheen of ice coating the screen, blue oceans flecked with countless cloud formations glowing pink and orange in the light of a beautiful sunrise being cast somewhere far below, saw deserts and forests and lakes and then the plunging blackness again as she was spun over and plunged once more into shadow.

She worked her left wrist free, shivering uncontrollably now and her liquefied breath coming in short, sharp gasps. The light spun once again into view and illuminated the depths of the capsule right down to her bare feet. She saw the panel with its single word, and she reached down and wiped the last ice crystals away from its surface to reveal the entire panel.

SURVIVAL PROTOCOL: ACTIVATE?

With a muffled cry of desperation she pressed the surface of the panel, and the touch–screen blinked green as a tiny beep sounded out in the darkness. She heard a faint hum from somewhere on the capsule's exterior, a vibration across her back as some kind of device activated, and then the capsule suddenly began to warm.

She recalled that the liquid–ventilation system incorporated a membrane oxygenator, pumps and a heater to circulate the fluid. With the heater activated and the oxygen flow accelerated to provide sufficient metabolism for movement, she felt her limbs come alive.

Tears formed in her eyes as she felt blessed warmth flood the tiny capsule, saw the light of the star drift past once more as she tumbled through space. The ice crystals melted away, some of them floating like tiny spheres of chromium on the surface of the screen as the fogging vanished and she could see more clearly.

The planet revolved back into view once again, bright sunlight searing her eyes. She raised a hand up to shield her view and saw around her chunks of debris spinning in the blackness: cables, twisted metal, fragments of glass sparkling brightly as they caught the light of the star and then vanishing into absolute darkness as they tumbled away from her.

All at once the debris field resolved itself in brief flashes as her capsule tumbled through it. Bigger chunks of machinery floated further away from her, some of them spewing crystalised gases out into the absolute cold of space, spinning end over end into the void. Below her she could see in the distance brief but bright flares and streaks of fire as debris entered the planet's atmosphere and began to burn up as the planet's gravity pulled them ever closer and ever faster to certain fiery doom.

Fresh panic swept her as she turned to her control panel.

There were few instruments. A small display revealed the amount of fuel on board, which was now being used to keep the interior warm, a small amount of oxygen which was keeping her alive, and a digital clock that was counting down:

7.46

There was no doubt then.

She had just over seven minutes to live.

She watched as the planet and its star revolved past her screen, taking in more detail each time. Clouds of metallic debris, and among that debris another slim black capsule nearby, its glossy surface flashing as it caught the light of the sun. A thought flickered through her consciousness along with conflicting emotions of relief and anxiety.

I am not alone.

Even as she considered this, she saw the capsule suddenly emit a burst of gas into the blackness that instantly turned to ice crystals in the frigid vacuum. The capsule righted itself, its endless tumbling arrested as a small blinking light began flashing on one end that she recognised as an anti–collision beacon.

She looked down and in the fragments of illumination provided by the sunrise she saw two small handles embedded into the interior wall. She grabbed them and yanked them this way and that.

A hissing sound filled the capsule and she felt its rotation change, twisting awkwardly sideways and slowing a little. Her brain rapidly orientated itself to the controls and she saw her oxygen supply diminish slightly faster as she fired controlled bursts, venting the precious gas out into space.

She ceased rotating and sunlight filled her vision. She turned the capsule, rotating it enough to shield her from the star's blinding flare, and scanned the debris field. There, amid the tangled wreckage, she saw numerous other glossy black capsules spinning and rotating in the silent void. As she watched, several of them began emitting bright flashing lights from their bases and firing jets of gas.

She looked at the timer on her control panel: *6.27.*

The wreckage around her tumbled in a mass of colliding fragments and her capsule shuddered as a chunk of debris slammed into it. She fought for control, wasting more precious air as a twisted girder of metal floated past, flashing as it reflected the sunlight.

6.09.

Out of the screen she saw a flare of white light, a reflection of the nearby star's light off something larger than a chunk of debris. Through the clouds of wreckage she saw something looming, cast half in shadow by the harsh starlight. Big. Intact. Sanctuary. Suddenly she recalled what the vessel was: a prison.

On an impulse she fired her capsule toward it, just as several of the other capsules around her did the same, their puffs of crystalised gas sparkling behind them.

***

II

Her capsule began to move, drifting through the chaotic cloud of debris as she sought a course toward the vessel. She aimed for a gap between two large chunks of hull plating drifting left to right in front of her when something slammed into her capsule with a dull clang.

She looked out to her right as she saw another survivor collide with her, and for a brief moment she saw a face staring out at her from within: twisted with malice, shouting something at her, pink mouth agape and eyes poisoned with fury.

She spun down and away from the impact, rolling and tilting so that she could no longer see where she was going. She fired her controls and heard the gas hiss from exhaust vents, saw the planet revolve back into view just as her capsule slammed into the hull plating. The impact caught the top of her capsule, the edge of the hull plating smashing into her screen with a sharp crack that fractured it in jagged splinters.

She tumbled end over end and she glimpsed the other capsule being hit even harder and blasted back the way it had come, spinning violently as the man inside fired wild blasts of gas to try to regain control again. She saw the blasts suddenly fade away, could make out the face of the man trapped inside screaming and beating his hands against his screen as his capsule, emptied of oxygen, tumbled away toward the void of space.

Her screen made a tiny cracking sound and she felt her guts turn to slime as she saw the fractures begin to spread cracks from the point of impact. They splintered outward from the centre, the fluid pressure inside and the perfect vacuum of space outside conspiring to bring about her demise.

She aimed once again for the vessel outside the debris field and fired another burst of gas. She began to move painfully slowly forward again but several of the other capsules were now far ahead of her, trailing sparkling crystals as they accelerated toward salvation.

Her capsule rattled as tiny fragments of debris peppered its surface like rain drumming on a window, and she saw the angular fractures on her screen jerk outward to the sound of tiny cracks. The warmth inside the capsule was now an enemy to her, the contrast with the freezing vacuum of space liable to make her screen ever more brittle.

She glanced at the timer: *5.12.*

Half a dozen capsules ahead of her were streaking toward the vessel as they broke free of the debris field that she could see was trailing from the vessel itself, the stern a mess of metal girders ripped and twisted as though by some kind of explosion, the hull plating torn open like a giant metallic flower.

She gauged the distance to the hull and the position of the other capsules, and with a renewed sense of dread she realised that she could never catch up with them.

From the large vessel something flashed. She saw a bright plume of blue flame and then a trail of vapour as something streaked toward the onrushing capsules, a ball of fearsome blue–white energy. Plasma charge. The object flew into the centre of them and detonated with a bright flash of light. She squinted, turned her face away as the explosion radiated outward and felt her capsule shudder as the shockwave slammed silently through the debris field.

To her horror she saw several of the survivors ahead of her spinning out of control as they spewed gas from countless punctures, the metal capsules melted by debris from the blast. The capsules spun past outside of the debris field, their occupants either already dead or in the process of freezing to death as their blood boiled in their veins, their faces twisted with the rigor of agony.

A capsule tumbled past, its screen shattered and a face staring out at her, white as a sheet and with globules of blood pulsing from its eyes, ears, nose and mouth in gruesome red fountains that froze instantaneously in the vacuum.

She eased past it as another plasma charge was launched from the vessel ahead. Capsules scattered to avoid it before it detonated. She remained inside the debris field, sheltered from the blast that thudded into her capsule as the shockwave sent chunks of metal spinning around her.

Her screen cracked loudly and she saw fine, hair–like tendrils of per–fluorocarbon escaping out into the void.

4.05.

Debris smashed into her but she did not make any attempt to correct her orientation. She felt two more thumps reverberate through the tiny vehicle as detonations smashed through the leading capsules and sent their fatally wounded occupants spinning into oblivion.

She turned slowly and she glimpsed the vessel ahead of her, looming large now. A bulky, ugly secondary hull with the damaged stern tethered to what looked like a frigate ahead of it. She let herself drift as though dead, surrounded by the shattered remains of other capsules destroyed by the weapons. Faces twisted in agony screamed silently as they died, or stared lifelessly through frozen eyeballs as they spun past, streams of per–fluorocarbon spiralling in frozen amber globules from them.

3:28.

She waited, feeling the warmth slipping away from the capsule as it began to run out of fuel. The survivor protocol was obviously a last–ditch attempt to preserve life, and such a small capsule could not provide a long reprise for its unfortunate occupant.

Her capsule slipped out of the debris field and into plain sight, its beacon still flashing.

She saw the bright flash of the plasma charge as it left the vessel and accelerated directly toward her. She grabbed her controls and fired herself directly toward the damaged rear section of the hull, toward the gaping flower of shredded metal, and she kept her finger on the trigger for several seconds as a blast of gas pushed her clear of the field.

She accelerated away and then glanced at her timer.

1:17.

She released the trigger and braced herself as the onrushing plasma charge zoomed to the edge of the debris field where she had been just moments before and detonated. The blast rocked her capsule and it tumbled end over end away from the shockwave as she heard shrapnel hammer on its surface like hail on glass. An alarm sounded and she saw her screen fill with cracks and splinters as she was catapulted forwards and a sloshing, sucking sound warned her that the hull of her capsule was breached and that her per–fluorocarbon was leaking into space.

She saw the hull of the vessel looming before her, its darkened interior black and dangerous. She grabbed her controls as a terrible cold filled the capsule, the icy grip of space itself creeping in to freeze her to death. She fought to orientate the capsule as the last of her precious air supply was used up.

0:32.

The giant hull was bare metal, scratched and stained, its markings eroded away as though by relentless weather on an endless journey through the cosmos. She guided the capsule with the last of its fuel as it plunged toward the hull's surface, and instinctively aimed for the coffin–shaped holes lining its side.

As she closed in she spotted amid the darkened tangle of twisted metal a searing blue–white light, as though a star had become trapped in the web of wreckage nearby. She looked at her timer.

0:12.

The hum of the generator and pumps on her capsule faded away as the last of her fuel was expended and the oxygenation of her per–fluorocarbon ceased.

The nearest blackened hole rushed toward her and she felt herself suddenly accelerate as something pulled it in. The screen gave a last ear–piercing screech of tortured glass and then it was torn outward by the intense vacuum and she felt the touch of absolute cold freeze her skin and yank at her eyeballs as in a terrifying rush all of the remaining warmth was sucked from the capsule as the screen failed and shot away from her.

The protective amber fluid around her was sucked violently out in a rush that pulled her head toward the vacuum, the dense fluid freezing instantly as it exited the capsule and tumbled in frozen chunks to bounce off the cold metal hull.

Her eyes clouded for an instant as though she was enveloped in fog as her eyeballs began to freeze and then a thud reverberated through the capsule as it slammed into the side of the hull, pulled in by powerful magnets that ringed the hull's receptacle. Total darkness consumed her, and then a hiss of pressurisation filled her ears and air was pumped automatically into the capsule. Her lungs convulsed and she coughed out a thick bolus of per–fluorocarbon that spilled like syrup into the interior of her mask and drained slowly out across her chest.

Raw, cold air filled her lungs for what felt like the first time and she coughed and wretched, barely any sound escaping past the mask as though she were still entombed in the fluid. Her eyes watered and she shivered in the cold air washing across her skin, as though she were a new born plucked from the womb of a damaged mother.

The capsule's surface clicked loudly as latches came undone under automatic guidance. More clicks as the lines into her arms were retrieved automatically and suddenly the capsule opened wide and the lid fell slowly away and hovered above a black–tiled floor slick with water and foam.

She hung there for a moment, still strapped in and with blood dripping from the crooks of her arms. Her limbs twitched and her chest convulsed as she sucked in huge breaths of air and pressed the wounds on her arms closed to prevent the blood from pooling in the veins as she looked around.

She was inside a containment unit, probably a storage depot of some kind alongside the engine bays. Magnetic trolleys were scattered across the floor and metal boxes of all kinds were strapped to racking that lined the walls. That there had been a raging fire was obvious, much of the plastic and metal scorched or even melted around her and the air thick with the smell of smoke and electrical fires. Automatic fire–retarding systems had come on–line sometime during the blaze, blasting the fire with chemicals that now floated in globules on the air in the zero–gravity conditions.

Her hair hung damp and thickly bound in per–fluorocarbon, plastered across her mask as she parted it with her fingers and took in the scene around her. Emergency venting doors had been closed, probably after the blast that had destroyed the rear of the vessel: during fire, which was as lethal in zero–gravity as it was under planetary conditions, the usual practice was to evacuate the air from the affected sections of the ship, thus starving the fire of oxygen. Then sprinklers cooled any remaining electrical fires before the damaged hull was sealed off and air re–introduced to parts of the hull affected by the fire but still stable, allowing for repairs to begin.

She could see that the fire had burned out quickly and the remains of any people caught in the blast would have been vacuumed out into oblivion as soon as the hull was breached or the air evacuated through the blast doors, which were now sealed shut.

Now, scoured of life and all but emergency power, the interior of the hull was a mess of floating water and foam and shapeless tendrils of smoke. High on one wall a single red light blinked on and off, scarlet light interspersed with complete blackness.

She coughed again, no sound breaking free from her dry lips. Her body shook from the cold, her skin raised in bumps as she reached down to her waist and loosened the straps holding her inside the capsule. They dropped slowly away and she held on to the capsule's frame as she crouched down and pulled her ankles free from their restraints.

She made to step out of the capsule but her legs failed her.

But she did not fall. She floated free of the capsule, hanging limp in mid–air as she willed her legs to respond. Her thighs quivered, her ankles jerking spasmodically as she tried to control them. Her muscles began to twinge and tingle as the life began to flow back into them, her blood oxygenating them and long–neglected nerves and tendons twitching as they tried to convey messages from her brain.

She floated amid the clouds of foam, swatted them aside from her mask as she tried to seek a source of warmth. The sound of creaking braces echoed through the superstructure around her as she drifted slowly through the storage unit, a few feet above the floor. Sealed off from the ship, the damaged section would have only minimal life support, enough to sustain anybody who was trapped inside for long enough to effect a rescue.

She was about to move when a loud clang echoed through the hull around her. Moments later, she saw an automatic door hiss open on the opposite side of the unit, and then the cover of a survival capsule fall slowly down to thump onto the floor as per–fluorocarbon fluid spilled in amber spheres onto the air.

A man floated free of the capsule, thick–set and with his torso smothered in webs of scars and tattoos that denoted both gang kills and prison slayings. His big, craggy bald head swivelled to look her naked body up and down as a grim smile spread like an infection across his face.

She pushed herself against a broken computer terminal that was floating lazily amid the foam, sending it toward the rear of the storage unit and propelling herself toward the sealed access hatches. The man shoved himself free of his capsule and drifted toward her, flying through the air with his arms outstretched.

Her body was shivering violently as she drifted through the debris. The bald convict floated toward her, both of them converging toward the hatches. She reached out to stop herself at the bulkheads. The metal was cold to the touch and slick with retardant foam, her hands numb with cold as they slid down its surface. She knew that within minutes she would succumb either to the bitter chill or her pursuer's grip.

A heavy looking bulkhead door, sealed from the other side, blocked her way as she dragged herself down to hover in front of it, her feet barely an inch off the floor. A small glowing red light told her that power was available to it and she searched for an input panel.

She glanced over her shoulder to see the man almost upon her, a guttural laugh spitting from his twisted lips and his manhood already standing proud of his body like the rudder of some disgusting, pale–skinned ship.

A small box on the wall alongside the door attracted her attention and she reached up for it. It opened and she saw a red lever fixed in the *locked* position.

She grabbed hold of the lever, pinned her knees against the bulkhead and pulled hard.

The lever snapped down and the bulkhead shuddered as its locking mechanism deactivated. She pulled herself down and turned the sealing valve anti–clockwise until it spun freely in her grasp. The bulkhead door hissed and she scrambled to gain purchase on the greasy floor as she leaned her shoulder into the heavy door and pushed against it.

The door inched open and she reached out to grab the edge of the frame and haul herself through.

A hand grasped her ankle like a vice and she turned to see the man gripping her as he dragged himself along the slippery floor, his other hand reaching up instinctively between her legs. She twisted her body as she held onto the edge of the door and raised one foot to smash it down toward the man's face. Her heel smacked across his nose and crushed it in a spray of blood that splattered across his face and flew upward in shimmering globules between them. The man growled in pain, his thick fist still gripping her ankle as she hauled herself through the doorway, her leg stretched out behind her.

She turned and pushed her free foot against the door as she hauled her other leg through the bulkhead, dragging the bulky man's arm with her. He reached out for the door to pull himself through, his eyes fixated upon her naked body.

She braced herself, grabbed the side of the bulkhead frame and then pulled his arm through after her and slammed the bulkhead door with all of her might. She heard the man growl in pain as the heavy door crushed his wrist between the door and the jam and his grip on her loosened.

She slammed the door again, the bulky man unable to find purchase on the slippery floor to oppose her. Her ankle, still drenched in per–flourocarbon, slipped free of his grasp as his hand shot out of sight. She heaved the door closed and slammed her arms down on the manual security locks and held them in place with one hand to prevent the convict from opening them again.

The man's bloodied face appeared at the observation window, poisoned with rage as he slammed his big fists against the glass. She spun the sealing valve back into place and then looked to her right. There, an active computer terminal set into the wall flashed warnings at her:

HULL BREACH: EVACUATION PROCEDURE?

She looked at the man's twisted, screaming face, and then she reached out and pressed the evacuation button.

A distant alarm sounded as she watched and then the blast door seals inside the storage unit were automatically released. The blast doors hissed open, a whirling cloud of vapour rippling around their edges as the atmosphere was vacuumed from the storage unit.

The man screamed again as he was dragged away from the door, his legs pointed toward the widening vacuum and his eyes wide with horror.

Evelyn watched in silence as the man's face turned even paler, his eyeballs frosting over and blood spilling from every orifice in his body until he was yanked out of sight by the vacuum.

***

III

She drifted down onto the floor of the gangway, her legs folding without resistance beneath her as she listened to the sirens fade away and felt warmth slowly creep back into her exhausted limbs. Clearly, this section of the ship had not been breached and the temperature was relatively comfortable. Her breathing echoed against her metal mask, heaving through her throat and rattling in her chest as the last of the per–fluorocarbon was ejected from her lungs.

She pushed her long, damp hair away from her mask once more and peered down the empty gangway. Bare metal walls, no markings, ceiling lights evenly spaced leading into the distance that flickered erratically. The floor felt cold against her skin and she dragged herself up onto her feet once more, her body feeling as light as air and yet still as heavy as all eternity.

She tried to call out, but the mask was preventing her from speaking. She coughed, a tiny sound that seemed to echo away down the gangway into the distance.

And then it drifted back to her, as though the sounds had reached her from afar on an errant wind. A whispering, like voices but too faint to understand. She stared into the distant reaches of the gangway, both afraid and hopeful. The soft whispering haunted the air and then faded like a ghost.

She shivered and hugged her arms about her body.

She was already covered in bruises, and a little blood had trickled down her arms and smeared her skin. Conscious of hurting herself further, she aimed herself down the gangway and pushed off the bulkhead door. She drifted silently along in the zero–gravity, listening intently for the sound of voices but hearing nothing except the low rumbling and creaking of the vessel's hull around her.

The gangway continued through bulkhead after bulkhead, all of which were open. She recalled the shape of the hull of the vessel that she had seen from the outside when she had first awoken, a bulky cylinder of ugly grey metal, and surmised that she was travelling along the port flank.

The lights continued to flicker and blink erratically around her as the power surged in and out. She sailed on through the groaning, empty vessel, a wake of per–fluorocarbon globules trailing behind her. Her ears twitched of their own accord as she heard again the faint whispering, as though the vessel were haunted. Her skin tingled and a shiver rippled down her spine as she drifted through the silence and looked behind her.

The gangway was empty.

Finally she reached another bulkhead, this one turning right. She reached out to stop herself from banging into the metal wall as she sailed through the bulkhead, and looked to her right.

A narrow passage opened out before her onto what looked like some kind of vast chamber. She edged forward and reached a gantry that looked down upon a broad hall lined with tiered ranks of heavily barred cells, all of which were open. All were filled with debris and slick with foam and water where fire had ripped through them.

The prison had been scoured of life, left filled with a silently floating miasma of debris like dirty clouds drifting in a metal sky, and amid the debris floated the bodies of the condemned men who had once suffered here.

She could see that few of them had burned. Most, judging by the colour of their lips and the grotesque expressions on their faces, had suffocated. They drifted like ghosts through the prison, many of them surrounded by a halo of their own stomach contents that had voided in undignified clouds around their corpses.

She saw one body floating nearby and she moved forward to the edge of the gantry and reached out for it. Her fingers brushed against the sleeve of the convict's orange prison overalls and she pinched the fabric and pulled him in to her.

He was about her height, shorter and stockier than her and probably no more than twenty five years of age when he had died. His eyes were rolled up in their sockets and his cheeks were scarred where somebody had driven a horizontal blade backwards into his mouth, slicing through the flesh of his face and leaving him with a gruesome, bloodied and permanent grin.

She unzipped the one–piece uniform from his corpse and slipped into it, then removed his prison–issue socks and boots and pulled them on. They provided a little extra warmth and covered her nakedness.

She pushed the dead convict's corpse away from her through the cloud of debris, high over the tiers below. She turned and looked into the nearest cell on the gantry. Amid the mess she could see a bed with restraining straps to prevent sleeping convicts from floating about in the zero–gravity conditions, along with a sink and toilet likewise adapted for the conditions.

On one wall was bolted a steel mirror.

She stepped into the cell, only then seeing the corpse of its former occupant floating against the ceiling, eyes white and his swollen purple tongue hanging loosely from an open mouth. She gently eased her way past beneath him and then stopped in front of the grubby mirror.

Her heart skipped a beat in her chest.

The mask completely covered her face, its surface covered in slits that allowed her to see and to breathe more easily. Made of plain, unadorned metal, her eyes peered back at her from within the dark, narrow slits. Atop her head, the full–face mask became two metal plates that extended down the back of her head and connected to a metal collar around her neck. Her hair, thick with the syrupy per–fluorocarbon, hung lank across her shoulders or floated upward in tangled tresses.

But that which scared her most was the metal probe that protruded from the upper lip of her mask and into her mouth, hugging the roof of her mouth and extending down into her throat. She coughed and her eyes watered as he saw for the first time what was preventing her from speaking. She reached up and pulled at the mask, but it would not budge and the pressure caused her throat to spasm. She gagged and coughed again, managed to swallow and bring her breathing under control as she stood up and looked at herself again.

She remembered the man in the storage unit. He had not worn a mask and nor had the other men in the capsules who had died, and they hadn't as far as she knew been wired in with intravenous lines. She realised that she must have had them to provide her with nutrients of some kind, and wondered how long she had been incarcerated inside that tiny capsule.

She turned in the cell to look up at the dead convict floating above her. He wore no mask, had no tubes in his arms. She looked down at the rubbish floating around her in the cell and saw morsels of food among it. She reached out and grabbed some, throwing them into her mouth.

The food tasted stale and dry, and she struggled to swallow any of it. What she did manage to get down immediately made her thirsty. She moved across to the sink, reached down for the tube floating from the sink edge and put it in her mouth before twisting the tap.

A feeble trickle of cold water spluttered into her mouth and she swallowed it gratefully until the flow vanished. She made her way out of the cell and froze as she heard voices drifting again through the cell block. Distant, vague, ebbing and flowing as though heard from the last recalled remnants of a dream.

She forgot herself and tried to call out again, coughed as a result.

She blinked tears from her eyes at the strain on her throat as she heard the last ghostly whispers fade away into the silence around her. She looked to her left, down the cell block. The four tiers of cells ended at a control tower set into the towering walls and festooned with thick glass windows, arc–lights and automated cavitation weapons: the tools of crowd control, of non–lethal response systems.

One of the tower's windows was shattered and one of the cavitation weapons twisted at an awkward angle on its mounts. As she scanned the block she realised that the prisoners had escaped, perhaps run riot. They had overwhelmed the tower, maybe murdered any officers monitoring them. Perhaps then the emergency override had been activated, and the prisoners suffocated in their own cells to protect the rest of the vessel…

But then, where were the rest of the crew?

What was in the rest of the vessel?

She glided along the gantry, pushing debris and floating corpses out of her way until she reached a flight of steps that descended down toward the floor of the block. There, she saw the body of a correctional officer lying flat against the base of the steps.

His uniform was soaked in blood, his face battered to an unrecognisable pulp of torn flesh and bone and his legs broken at awkward angles where they lay against the metal steps. She pulled herself down the steps toward the corpse, which was dressed in heavy black boots and dark blue uniform. Nearby lay an equally heavy looking helmet and face–shield that had been torn from the officer's head before he had been beaten to death.

Unlike the prisoners, the officer's body did not float in the air. The fabric was filled with micro–filaments of positively charged iron. The effect upon the wearer, as the uniform and boots attracted themselves to the negatively charged filaments in the vessel's deck, was to replicate gravity.

Upon a prison vessel, enforced zero–gravity resulted in the convict population losing muscle mass, their weakened bones and reduced strength making them compliant and easy to control. The prison officers wore gravity suits, their muscles under the same load as planetary conditions and thus becoming far stronger than those of their unruly charges.

She reached down and yanked from the dead officer's belly a four–inch shank, fashioned from the sharpened end of a fork handle, the pronged end of which had been encased in a sheath of thickly–wrapped medical dressing. The blade made a sucking sound and left a gloopy string of blood floating in mid–air as she dragged it free of the unyielding flesh.

She heard whispers just over her shoulder and she whirled, waving the scarlet–stained blade before her as a chill rippled across the back of her shoulders. A breath of sound, soft and gentle, carried like distant music on the cold air. She pushed off the edge of the stairs and drifted across the block to the guard tower.

The access door at its base was locked, so she pushed off the ground with her legs and floated up to the shattered window high above, careful to avoid cutting herself on the jagged remains of the smoked glass as she reached in and pulled herself inside.

The tower control room was deactivated, probably from elsewhere when the riot had begun. She realised that the situation had been sufficiently bad for the monitoring officers to have been abandoned to their fate inside the cell block.

The corpses of two dead officers and at least half a dozen convicts drifted through the control room, gently bumping into each other in an endless slow dance of death, their eyes staring into nothingness and ribbons of spilled blood, black and cold, lacing their bodies.

She eased her way between the corpses and heard once again the whispering voices, clearer now as she moved into the control room. She tensed, listening, and heard somebody speaking.

She turned toward the voice and saw the body of a convict slumped across a control panel nearby. She drifted toward him and pulled his body off the panel.

Instantly, she heard the voice speaking, distorted and garbled as though coming through intense interference.

'....designator Nine–Nine–Four–Delta... major hull breach... is there anybody there...?'

She reached for a transmit button on the control panel and then hesitated. She could not speak through her mask.

She stared impotently as the voice continued.

'... Nine–Nine–Four–Delta, please respond... repeat, you are severely compromised... everything has gone... will be forced to cut loose...'

And then a new voice replied, stronger and clearer than the first.

'Nine–Nine–Four–Delta's inactive, cut them loose. Repeat, no survivors in the high–security wing. Cut loose immediately, hold Atlantia Five on the tethers only...'

She stepped back from the control panel and glanced about her.

From somewhere in the distance she heard the sound of huge collisions that reverberated through the vessel's hull as though giants were hammering at the hull plating. She felt the vessel shift around her as she floated just above the control panel, a shuddering motion and then a deep silence.

She pushed off the control panel and pulled herself down a spiral staircase that descended down through the control tower, passing the tangled bodies of correctional officers and convicts locked in duels to the death, their long–dead faces twisted with pain and fear.

She reached the bottom of the staircase, where two doors awaited her. One, which was locked, led out into the cell block. The other, also locked, led from the tower into the rest of the vessel. She turned and drifted across to the nearest correctional officer's corpse, searching through his pockets for access passes, keys, anything that might unlock the door.

Her hand rested on a large pistol, gripped in the officer's cold hand. She wrested the weapon free and shoved it inside her suit before foraging further.

She found a passkey and turned, floating across to the tower door and swiping the card over the locking mechanism. It opened out onto the cell block with a hiss of released pressure. She turned and tried the other door, out of the cell block tower and into the rest of the ship. A display flashed a request at her.

BIOMETRIC SCAN: PLEASE COMPLY

She cursed mentally and turned, grabbing the nearby officer's boot and dragging his corpse toward her. She spun him over, grabbed the back of his head and shoved his face toward the sensors. A bright green laser–line swept down the officer's face and the sensor beeped in recognition. Then, another request flashed up.

AWAITING CONFIRMATION

She pulled the pistol from her suit and left it hanging in mid–air near the security door, then she pushed back and away from the door and out of the tower. She looked up to where, above her on the walls of the cell block, several observation spheres swivelled to point at her, unblinking glossy black eyes staring down into hers.

From the control panel up in the tower, she heard a voice ring out loud and clear in the otherwise silent block.

'We've got a live one!'

***

IV

She floated just above the floor of the cell block, surrounded by clouds of debris, corpses and spilt blood as she gazed up through her mask at the cameras.

A long silence ensued as she awaited a further response. When it came, it echoed around the cell block to haunt her.

'It's Alpha–Zero–Seven. It's her.'

She heard a flurry of broken conversation in the background, panicked voices fluttering back and forth.

'How the hell did she survive?'

'What do we do with her?'

'She's maximum security, we can't deal with her.'

'Cut her loose!'

More silence as the microphone was abruptly cut off. She waited, staring up at the cameras but not moving or making any attempt to influence any decision they might make.

The microphone crackled again.

'Hey, Alpha? How did you escape?'

Escape. Something about the way the man behind the microphone used the word sent a ripple of anger fluttering through her guts. She remembered the weapons that had been fired at the escape capsules.

She reached up and pointed to her mask.

'She can't speak,' a voice in the background uttered. *'And look at her, she's tiny. She ain't nothing.'*

A flurry of angry responses were cut off as the microphone was again silenced. She waited, glancing around her at the cell block and it's hundreds of corpses. Slowly, a dawning realisation that there may not have been an accident after all began to creep into her mind, and with it a rage that seemed familiar and yet muted, distant, as though all that she had been as a person had somehow been scoured from her mind, an entire history erased.

The microphone clicked again.

'Alpha, we got a deal for you.' She remained still, looking up at the camera. *'We'll open the security door for you, but we want something in return.'*

She let the silence draw out and gave no indication of any emotion.

'We got needs, y'know? Men got needs. You understand?'

She stared up at the camera for a moment longer, and then she reached up and began unzipping the convict's suit she was wearing. She kicked off the thin boots and let the correctional attire slip away from her shoulders. The cold air touched her skin once more, pale and soft as she stared up at the camera, her features hidden behind the mask.

She heard a strangled muttering on the speaker and then a loud click echoed through the cell block and the security door inside the tower rattled as electronic seals were opened. The heavy door squealed as it slowly opened on hydraulic rams.

She pushed herself forward off the floor of the cell block and glided through the air back into the tower and to the door, pushed it open further as she slipped through and grabbed the pistol as she went.

A corridor, devoid of retardant foam or scorching, led away from her. The lighting was not flickering here, the power supply more stable. She could tell that she was still in a prison vessel, the harsh metal walls scarred with years' of neglect, the smell of unwashed bodies and lousy food filling the air.

She pushed the security door shut behind her and locked it manually before turning and floating down the corridor. The air was still cool but it had lost some of the chill of the cell block and the bumps on her skin settled as she floated along.

Ahead she could see two barred gates set twenty feet apart, security against convicts escaping that also allowed for weapons to be discharged through the bars. Each gate was mounted into heavy beams that crossed the ceiling of the corridor. Floating between the two sets of gates she could see the bodies of two more correctional officers, their backs shredded with wounds.

She heard a bang and a squeal as a solid security door was opened on the far side of the gates. She slowed, turning her body so that her feet touched the floor a few cubits away from the first barred gate, and waited.

There were four of them. They walked through the security door, their heavy black boots thumping against the floor of the corridor. Magnetic suits in graphite grey, bearing the markings of maintenance crews, weighed them down and allowed them to walk almost normally in the low gravity. Each man carried a pulse rifle at port arms.

She knew that they were not maintenance. One man had a shock of blonde hair from which dangled numerous tags, coloured ribbons signifying gang kills. Another man was missing the flesh from half of his face, tattoos carved off in retaliation for turning against a former prison crew, the savage injury healed into a mass of twisted scar tissue. The other two, tough looking men who were tanned despite years inside, were almost certainly pirates or mercenaries of some kind. Both wore tattoos on their necks of roiled dragons that she recognised, their allegiance to a gang whose leader was known as Tiamat.

What they differed in appearance they shared in expression, all of their gazes fixed upon her as they walked toward her down the corridor. She stood in silence, naked and small behind the bars as they reached the first set of gates.

She saw their eyes caress her naked body for a few moments.

'Alpha Zero Seven,' one of them said, the shorter of the two pirates. 'Heard of you.'

She remained still.

'We should kill her, right now,' said the blond convict with the tags. 'She's bad shit, man.'

'You ever known shit to be good?' asked Scarface.

'Man, they don't put masks like that on without a damned good reason,' replied Tags.

Scarface's one good eye twisted upward in delight as he smiled with half of his teeth. 'It's so they can't bite back. I want me a piece of that.'

The stocky pirate stepped up to the gate.

'You good with that, Zero Seven?' he asked her.

She did not move, just stared at the pirate through the slits of her mask. He stared back at her, and looked her up and down for several long seconds. She saw him lick his lips, his eyes drawn to the cleft between her legs.

'All smooth,' said the taller pirate, 'just the way I like 'em.'

The shorter pirate slung his rifle across his shoulder and from his pocket withdrew a blocky metallic key. Difficult to copy and implanted with a holographic identity chip, such keys provided more security than any biometric scan. He inserted it into the first gate and turned it. The gate creaked open and he moved through, the other pirate right behind him.

'Stay here,' he ordered Scarface and Tags.

'Don't you cut us out,' Scarface growled. 'We agreed, the dice decide who gets her first.'

The pirates did not respond, their gazes fixed on hers as she watched them approach the second gate and insert the key into the lock. It turned, and she stood her ground as the gate swung open and the two men stepped through it.

'Now,' said the stocky pirate, 'you be a good girl and give us what we want and you'll be just fine.'

He smiled, gold teeth interspersed with black ones that gave him a predatory appearance. She stared at him in silence, her arms hanging limply by her sides as the taller pirate, his rifle still aimed at her, jerked the barrel of the weapon upward a couple of times.

'You know the drill,' he growled. 'Get 'em up.'

Slowly, she raised her hands and placed them behind her head. The movement caused her breasts to lift and both men's gazes drifted down to them. The stocky pirate reached out for her as he stared at her breasts, and one rough–skinned hand cupped her between her legs and squeezed.

She kept her hands behind her head as the pirate smiled again.

'Man, am I lookin' forward to tasting every inch of you and…'

She unfolded the pistol from where she had coiled it in her thick hair as she grabbed the pirate's arm and pulled herself into him, pinning his rifle beyond his reach and his hand between her legs. She aimed the pistol around his shoulder and fired, a deafening crack as the pistol shot a bright blue–white ball of plasma that punched through the taller pirate's face in a hiss of sizzling flesh that echoed down the corridor as a huge flower of blood blossomed outward from the back of his head.

The second shot went into the side of the stockier pirate's head even as he tried to push away from her, a blast of blood, brain and bone splattering the wall of the corridor amid a blaze of plasma particles as a frenzy of shouts went up from Scarface and Tags. They aimed their rifles down the corridor at her as she pushed off the floor of the corridor and shot up to collide with the ceiling behind the beams.

A deafening clatter of rifle fire rang in her ears as she hugged the ceiling behind the shelter of the beam, saw pulses of energy smash against the ceiling close by to scorch and dislodge tiles, heard the convicts shouting at each other as they fired in a confused frenzy of accusations.

'I told you!' Tags shouted. 'Let's get out of here and shut the gates!'

'Shut up!' came Scarface's response.

The shots ceased. She remained in place, waiting.

Scarface called down the corridor. 'You got a pistol, missy, but we've got two rifles and hard dicks. It's your choice. You either come to us willingly, right now, or we kill you and use you anyway while you're still warm.' He chuckled manically. 'Ain't no use in...'

She poked her pistol below the beam in the direction of the voice and fired twice.

A scream of agony shrieked down the corridor as Scarface took the full impact of her shot, the fearsome energy pulse searing his flesh and burning his uniform with it.

A broadside of shots peppered the beam beside her, sparks of plasma showering past and the smell of scorched metal singing her nostrils as she huddled out of sight.

'Kill her!' screamed Scarface in a tortured, keening cry. 'Kill the bitch!'

She peeked her head out and saw Scarface lying on his back in the corridor and being dragged away by Tags, who was trying to aim back at her while pulling his injured comrade away from danger and into shelter.

Bad move.

She swung her pistol down, took aim and fired before Tags could even aim back at her properly.

The shot hit Tags in the chest and blew half of his lungs out of his back in a scarlet spray, his face bulging with agony as he toppled over backward and slammed to the deck, his suit pinning him there as smoke puffed from his chest.

Scarface screamed again, still tearing at the smouldering wound in his right thigh.

She fired again and Scarface fell silent and still, his jaw skittering across the corridor in a trail of blue smoke.

She pushed down off the ceiling toward the stocky pirate's corpse, grabbing his rifle and security key as she propelled herself through the open gates. Tags and Scarface's smouldering bodies wreaked of burning flesh as she glided over them and hit the security door at the far end of the corridor.

She slammed the key into the locking mechanism and turned it, the heavy security door swinging open as she pushed through and aimed the pulse rifle down the corridor ahead. Nobody was waiting for her so she pinned it open and then floated back to the bodies of the dead convicts and rifled through their belongings.

Knives. Prison 'scrip. Ammunition.

Working fast, she stripped the stocky pirate of his uniform and boots, pulling them all on. She hauled herself to her feet, feeling as though she weighed a hundred tonnes, and in a laborious gait she ran to the security door and slammed it shut behind her. She turned the key in the lock and then turned and faced the corridor.

She checked the rifle over. Each could only carry around thirty rounds per magazine, and the two idiots at the security gates had loosed off at least fifteen between them. Each charge contained a dense, pressurised container of plasma, which was ruptured when the weapon fired: the released energy propelled the charge out of the rifle barrel at supersonic speed, the velocity turning it into a lethal ball of super–heated energy that spread with distance. She counted how many rounds she had left and then advanced as quickly as she could down the corridor.

As she moved, she saw for the first time a viewing port running along the wall to her left. She hurried to it and slowed as she looked out through the triple layers of polished glass.

The bright flare of the nearby star cast its light across the vast sweeping horizon of a planet. She looked down upon the expanses of ocean, endless forests and deserts, tundra and mountains cast by nature's elegant hand and glowing in the warm light and for a moment her rage was forgotten.

Life goes on.

She gripped her rifle tighter, and moved on.

***

V

'How many hostages do we got?'

Qayin's voice rumbled like boulders from his massive chest, his body a dark–skinned cliff–face of muscle bursting from his prison fatigues, a physique cultivated using improvised resistance devices in prison: the rubber from clothes and flexible plastics. His hair, vivid locks of alternating blue and gold, dangled to his shoulders like the mane of some terrifying beast, and etched into his skin were spiral tattoos that glowed with rippling bioluminescence in the low light.

'Enough,' came the response from his companion.

Cutler was much older than Qayin, grey hair and a short beard framing icy grey eyes that darted from one sight to another like a bird of prey hunting for its next meal. Once the muscle in the prison block, Cutler was a spent force too old to maintain a crew on his own, and had allied himself to Qayin's gang of tattoed killers. Qayin walked down the gangway toward the cell block with strides so long Cutler was forced almost to jog to keep up. The big convict filled over half the gangway, Cutler's voice reaching him from over his right shoulder.

'The prison hull's not looking good. The cell block protected it from the worst of the blast, but I reckon we're leaking fuel and atmosphere.'

Qayin sneered down at Cutler as he walked.

'So you're saying that as we're facing death whichever hull we're in, we may as well stay in prison?'

'I ain't saying that,' Cutler protested. 'But here we rule the roost, whereas over there we'll be under armed guard. So what if they've got the sanctuary?'

'They've also got the food, the water, the power supply and the only functioning engines as leverage,' Qayin reminded him. 'One flick of a switch and they could starve, freeze or drop us into that planet's atmosphere. Apart from that, you're a genius.'

'Was just thinkin' out loud.'

'Don't,' Qayin advised 'Thinkin's not your job.'

Qayin slowed as he reached a small administration block. Four convicts were standing outside the block, their pulse rifles variously slung over their shoulders or propped against the walls. They took one look at Qayin and abruptly jerked to attention.

'Did we get them all?' Qayin asked.

'All the survivors, right back to the engine room,' Cutler confirmed. 'There ain't nobody else alive on the block but us and them.'

Qayin nodded and pushed open the door to the administration block.

Inside were several small offices and one larger, central office. In the centre of the larger office, sat in a circle with their backs to each other, bound and gagged, were fifteen uniformed correctional officers. They looked up at Qayin, the fear already etched into their features deepening as they took in the hulking convict's immense size and uncompromising expression.

Qayin walked into the office, slowly circling the captive officers like a giant black shark watching terrified minnows. He glared at them, making eye contact with them one at a time, sensing their fear like blood in water.

Amid the group, one captive stood out. Her long, auburn hair was distinctive enough for Qayin to recognise her instantly and he turned and looked over his shoulder at Cutler. The old man smirked in delight.

'Thought you might like that,' Cutler said.

Qayin turned back to the woman and squatted down in front of her.

'Meyanna Sansin,' he said. 'Welcome to the new order, doctor.'

The woman tried to speak through her gag. Qayin reached up with one giant hand and pulled the gag free.

'This isn't going to work, Qayin,' she said. 'They'll drop you all into orbit and let you burn.'

Qayin raised an eyebrow, his thick gold and blue braided hair swaying as he shook his head.

'And you with us?' he mocked her.

'I'd happily go to hell if I could drag you with me,' she spat.

'Now that's no way for a doctor to speak,' Qayin chided her. 'You got the whole crew to think of now, because what the good captain does will affect what happens to you, right?'

Meyanna smiled grimly. 'He's got the stones to stand up to you, Qayin, because win, lose or draw, he's the captain and you're not.'

Qayin grinned broadly and shoved her gag back into place before he stood and surveyed the hostages. Four of them wore not the uniforms of correctional officers but the black fatigues of marines, assigned as back–up in the event of prison riots. Heavily armed and well trained, a number of them had died when the block had been evacuated of air. The rest had been captured by Qayin and his men, hopelessly outnumbered and unable to retreat to the Atlantia when the governor had followed procedure and sealed the hatches.

Qayin moved to face the soldiers.

'Names?'

All four of the men refused to make eye contact with him, following their training and staring instead at the floor or their boots.

'No matter,' Qayin said. 'The captain will know your faces when we slice them off and send them to him, one at a time.' He turned to Cutler. 'We'll start with them, as soon as communication is established.'

'What about the wife?' Cutler asked.

Qayin looked at Meyanna Sansin for a moment.

'Save her for now,' he replied. 'If the good captain has the stomach to watch his troops tortured and killed, we'll need to step up to the next level.'

A convict's running boots echoed down the corridor outside and a young, tanned face laced with purple tattoos poked his head into the office.

'Qayin, you've gotta see this.'

*

The prison hull's control centre was clouded with a swirling miasma of blue smoke curling from the tip of a thick cigar clasped between Qayin's teeth. He strode in behind the tattoed kid and sprawled in a command chair that had once been occupied by the prison governor, Oculin Hayes. Hayes' severed head was now propped against a console like a discarded toy, fat purple tongue hanging from fat purple lips against fat purple jowls.

'What is it?'

'She's out,' came the reply. 'She's killed them all.'

Qayin pulled the cigar from his teeth and his bioluminescent tattoos flared and shimmered on his face. He stood up as the control centre fell utterly silent. Dozens of convicts, all sat at control stations around the dimly lit centre with their faces glowing in the light of their monitors, watched as Qayin strode down off the command platform and peered over the shoulder of one of his men.

A screen showed a corridor deep in the prison complex, and through it strode a uniformed and armed person wearing a metallic mask. Qayin smiled, his teeth bright white against his dark skin.

'Like death does she wander,' he whispered as though quoting a verse.

The control centre was hexagonal, computer terminals occupying each wall except for a single access door, currently sealed shut. Dark and filled with glowing lights and control panels, it served as a secondary nerve centre for Atlantia Five, the prison hull. The primary control centre was the frigate's bridge, currently sealed off from the prison hull. For the purpose of security the prison hull was tethered to the Atlantia rather than directly connected, preventing any form of access by the prisoners in the event of an outbreak. Four temporary passages were available to transfer personnel coming on and off duty from the prison hull, and at any time only one was connected and heavily guarded.

Qayin spoke, his voice heavy and deep enough that it seemed to reverberate through the room.

'How many of you want to live?'

The silence grew heavy in the room until one of the convicts, a spiky-haired youth with eyes sunken from substance abuse replied. 'She's only one person, one woman. What's she going to do to us?'

Qayin turned his head. Slowly, he strode across the control centre to where the youth sat at his station. The kid's bravado vanished like an errant thought as Qayin loomed above him, the muscles in his neck sheened with sweat in the heat. He glanced around him at the watching convicts.

'You want to know why you should fear her?' he asked, looking each of them in the eye.

Silence replied, the convicts watching and waiting.

Qayin swung back to the seated youth, the blade in his hand appearing as though by magic as it flashed in the light. It slammed into the kid's head behind the ear with a dull crunch, the metal sunk to the hilt as it punctured the kid's brain. His eyes flared wide and then the life vanished from them and he slumped in his seat, the weapon poking from his head.

Qayin stood up to his full height. 'You should fear her because *I* do.'

The convicts watched Qayin for a long moment and then one of them raised a furtive hand.

'Who is she?'

Qayin turned away from the dead youth and strode back to slump into the governor's chair. He put the cigar back between his lips and drew deeply upon it, exhaled a billowing cloud of smoke onto the air as he replied.

'She is death,' he said. 'Wherever she goes, chaos follows. There were over a thousand convicts upon this vessel. Only four of them were forced to wear those masks. Three of those had killed over a hundred men between them, and they wouldn't come within a hundred cubits of that woman.'

'What's her name?'

Qayin turned to the man who had spoken and then he laughed loud enough to make several men closer to him flinch.

'Her name?' he echoed. 'She is by far the most dangerous person aboard this vessel and you give a damn about her name?'

A long silence followed until a convict asked: 'What shall we do about her?'

Qayin removed the cigar from his mouth again and rubbed his temples. 'How long since last contact with the bridge?'

'Two hours,' came a quick response. 'They're calling us every sixty seconds.'

Qayin looked up at a series of monitors, several of which had been attuned to cameras outside the vessel. They looked for'ard, beyond the prison hull's ugly surface to where a giant frigate was illuminated by the glow from the nearby star. Huge engines were mounted vertically on strakes either side of a long, slender hull burnished by long exposure to deep space radiation and countless micrometeorite impacts. Qayin could see her name emblazoned upon her stern.

ATLANTIA

'Put them on loudspeaker,' Qayin said.

The sound of a man's voice echoed through the control centre, the transmission broken and scratchy.

'*... we cannot submit to your demands... too many lives at risk and we... ... no time left... please respond...*'

'It will be some time before the Word arrives,' Qayin said over the transmission, 'if at all. Right now all we have to worry about is the power supply and Alpha Zero Seven.'

'Or the captain dropping us into the planetary atmosphere,' said an accusing voice. 'In which case we'll all be toasted and none of this will matter.'

A weariness infected Cutler's expression.

'I didn't ask you,' Qayin snapped back.

'That's the problem,' Cutler replied. 'You've got yourself backed into a corner and there's no way out.'

'Says who?' Qayin shouted as he stood and pointed one huge, muscular arm at Cutler. 'You?'

'Me,' Cutler replied without anger. 'We've already lost half the rear of the hull, a thousand or so souls and now we're hanging on to the main section's hull by nothing more than the tethers and a single pressure hatch. Threatening them with annihilation by dragging them down with us toward that planet isn't exactly a great bargaining chip, Qayin.'

'They're sweatin' on it,' Qayin snarled back.

'So are we,' Cutler countered. 'If the Word arrives while we're all stuck here, then we're all dead.'

'We got this far,' Qayin said.

'Only because somebody blew up the damned cell block!' Cutler wailed. 'You didn't have anything to do with that, so it must have been arranged by somebody aboard Atlantia. It's only dumb luck that any of us got this far. Much longer and they'll cut us off themselves.'

Qayin shot the old man a dirty look but did not respond.

'How long will our own power last?' asked a convict.

Cutler shrugged. 'Who knows? The fusion core must have been damaged from the blast. If it shorts or blows then we either freeze to death up here or burn to death down there.' Cutler gestured to the monitors trained on the planet far below them. 'Either way, we're dead.'

'We were dead before this happened!' Qayin snarled as he paced up and down in front of the governor's chair.

'You were dead the moment you cut off the governor's head,' Cutler pointed out.

'He disrespected me,' Qayin growled.

'You overreacted.'

Qayin stormed down off the platform and loomed over Cutler, his fists clenched. 'How 'bout I overreact again?'

Cutler held his ground but did not reply. A voice cut across the confrontation. 'She's almost here.'

Qayin scowled at Cutler, then turned away and looked at the monitor.

'You should kill her,' Cutler said to him, 'before she kills all of us.'

Qayin stared at the monitor and then shook his head. 'No. We need to turn her. She might be our only way out of this.'

'How the hell do you figure that?' Cutler asked.

'Fear,' Qayin replied. 'We've got to force the captain to bargain for the lives of the hostages.'

'Because of her?' Cutler asked. 'How is she going to threaten them?'

Qayin unclipped the pistol holster he wore at his belt. He dropped the holster and weapon onto the governor's seat.

'Being here should be about enough,' he replied.

'I think you overestimate her.'

'You know how many times the Word has used those masks on people?' Qayin asked rhetorically. 'Fifteen times in a hundred years.'

'So? She's a real bad dude. It's just another reason for them to keep us pinned down in here.'

'No, it's a reason for them to keep her silenced,' Qayin replied. 'Those masks were used to stop people speaking. The Word doesn't want people to hear what they have to say, that's why they put them on.'

'Why not just kill them?'

'Too easy,' Qayin said as he strode toward the security door. 'You know what else the Word used to do before they put those masks on? They wiped their memories, so I've heard.'

Cutler turned as Qayin opened the security door.

'So you're just going to let her walk on in here, just like that?'

'Just like that,' Qayin said, 'because it's the last thing the captain would expect us to do.'

***

VI

Captain Idris Sansin strode onto the Atlantia's bridge and surveyed a scene of controlled chaos.

The bridge consisted of a raised platform that held the captain's chair and control panel, all facing a viewing platform that looked out over the front of the Atlantia. All around the circular bridge were control stations manned by twelve sworn officers, the captain's command crew who could, in principal, perform any action across the entire vessel without ever leaving the bridge. The Atlantia, his ship, his pride: now crippled by a blast that had freed hundreds of convicted criminals. The Atlantia, once a front–line frigate of the Colonial Fleet, now light years from home, barely able to support her military and civilian compliment and dragged down by the ugly grey hull being dragged along behind it.

The crew were fully engaged in an attempt to stem the tide of a series of tremendous calamities that had befallen the vessel. He surveyed them, his craggy features illuminated by the endless banks of lights and screens in the otherwise dark bridge.

'Control status?' he asked.

'We've lost all command functions to the prison hull and what's left of the high–security wing has been detatched to burn up in the atmosphere,' came the desperate response from Lael, a woman barely out of her teens, her dark hair cropped short. 'Still no communication from the prison hull.'

The captain strode up to his command chair and turned to look at several screens behind him, each relaying visual information from cameras mounted outside.

The Atlantia's hull stretched away behind the bridge for almost half a mile. Behind that was the bulky, angular prison hull, enveloped in a cloud of debris and escaped gases frozen in the vacuum of space.

'What about us?' the captain asked.

'The blast has severed fuel lines and power conduits across the stern,' came a response from Jerren, the ship's tactical officer and youngest member of the bridge crew. 'The prison's still got power but it's coming from us via the tethering lines – her own fusion core is either ruptured or off line.'

The captain glanced across a bank of instruments before him on his own control panel that relayed vital information regarding the ship's status. He didn't like what he saw there.

'Hull integrity?'

'Ours is fine sir, but the prison hull is severely compromised in several quarters.' Jerren turned to look at the captain. 'She's dragging us down toward the planet's surface, sir.'

The captain turned to face the ship's port cameras, and saw the looming surface of the planet and the bright star rising majestically across its horizon.

'Can we cut them loose?' he asked. A hush fell over the bridge as the crew stared at the captain. 'Can we cut them loose?!' he roared again.

Jerren nodded, struggling to speak. 'Yes sir, we can, but... we still have at least fifteen staff unaccounted for.'

A man ran onto the bridge, bearing the shoulder epaulettes of a senior officer. Bra'hiv was a soldier, the commander of a company of marines who had found himself aboard the Atlantia with a contingent of less than two hundred men when everything had gone to hell in the colonies. His shaved head was sheened a gun metal grey, the lines of his face hewn by years of military service, his jaw square and expression always severe.

The captain turned to him. 'I want to know everything.'

Bra'hiv gave his report as though he were a computer spewing data in orderly lines.

'There was a blast of some kind between the security wing and the main prison, captain,' he replied. 'Not sure of the cause yet: maybe power lines, maybe sabotage. The security wing is lost to us, with all aboard presumed dead.' He drew a deep breath. 'The blast started a fire in the aft wing of the prison cell block and damaged many of the cell gate controls. The prisoners got out. As far as we can tell they've taken control of the block, the tower and the governor's command centre, and are moving forward through the prison hull right now.'

The captain turned away from Bra'hiv and stared at the screens behind him.

'Casualties?'

'Unknown sir, but the fire protocol engaged when the temperature exceeded two hundred units.'

The captain turned back to the general. 'The block was evacuated?'

Bra'hiv shook his head. 'Not of people, sir. The riot prevented any coordinated action. The prisoners were still in their cells or fighting on the tiers when the air was evacuated to choke the fire.'

A ripple of murmurs drifted across the bridge as the captain realised just how awful the tragedy had become.

'There were over a thousand men incarcerated in there,' he gasped. 'Who gave the order?'

'Hevel,' Bra'hiv replied, 'Councillor Hevel.'

The ship's political officer. Hevel was responsible for the ship's prison and its governor, Oculin Hayes. As a military captain Idris could not intervene in civil matters, even those that threatened the safety of the Atlantia and the hundreds of people aboard her.

'How many survivors?' he asked.

'Estimates are that less than a hundred convicts have survived.' Bra'hiv hesitated as he looked at the captain. 'Your wife is also unaccounted for, sir.'

The captain turned away from Bra'hiv and his hands wrapped around the metal guard rail that ringed the centre of the bridge. His wife Meyanna was the ship's chief physician, charged with the care of both the crew and the prisoners. She had been performing her duties aboard the prison hull when the blast had occurred.

'The shuttle?' he asked.

'Not an option while the prisoners are in control of the hull,' Bra'hiv replied. 'If they were to get aboard here…'

Before the captain could even consider what would happen if a hundred lethally dangerous convicts with nothing but their lives to lose got aboard the Atlantia, a voice called out from across the bridge.

'Sir?'

'What is it, Jerren?' he asked.

'Our main propulsion units have been damaged by debris from the blast,' Jerren replied, 'multiple power lines fractured, several exhaust ports blocked and…'

'Conclusion!' the captain demanded.

'We're sixty per cent down on power,' Jerren replied. 'It could take days to repair the damage and we're in low planetary orbit.'

It did not take a student of physics to explain to the captain what that meant.

'How long?' Bra'hiv asked before the captain could.

'No more than a few days, sir,' Jerren replied. 'Our orbit will decay to the point where we will strike the planetary atmosphere and burn up.'

'And if we jettison the prison hull?' Bra'hiv pressed.

'It won't save us,' Jerren replied, 'but it might give us enough time to repair the damage and escape the planet's gravitational pull under our own power.'

The captain sucked in a deep breath of air and stood up straight again, reasserting control over both his own wildly swaying emotions and his crew.

'Focus on re–establishing communication with the prison hull. The more we can find out about the situation there, the better. Make a full account of everything that is known about what happened. If we're ever found it will prevent a repeat occurrence.'

Bra'hiv nodded. 'And the prison hull?'

The captain glanced at the screens showing the ugly grey hull behind them, many of the immensely strong tethering lines torn and frayed.

'We wait,' he said. 'As long as we can.'

'Understood,' Bra'hiv replied, and turned to leave.

The captain hesitated as a large figure strode onto the bridge. The tall, bulky frame of Hevel barged his way onto the command platform. His size was not intimidating to the captain, consisting more of slack fat and tissue, Hevel's dark skin sagging beneath his chin and his stomach. His sharp little eyes scanned the bridge without blinking, his skin lightly sheened with sweat in the heat.

'You should cut them loose, right now,' he insisted, moving to stand before the captain.

Behind him followed a diminutive, exotically dark skinned woman named Dhalere, Hevel's legal secretary.

'Noted,' Idris replied without looking at Hevel and then nodded to Bra'hiv. 'As you were, general.'

Bra'hiv left the bridge.

'That could be costly,' Hevel said. 'The longer we stay attached to it the less time we'll have even once we cut it loose.'

'I'm aware of that, Hevel,' the captain said and turned to Jerran. 'Assuming we lose the prison hull and we manage to repair the damage to our own hull and engines, what are the chances of us standing up to an attack with our current compliment of weapons and Raython fighters?'

Jerren's features paled as he apparently considered this for the first time. He scanned his instruments intently and then his jaw sagged as he turned back to face the captain.

He shook his head slowly. 'None, sir.'

The captain managed to prevent his shoulders from sagging. He turned to look at the planet far below, ribbons of cloud glowing orange in the sunrise above endless blue oceans.

'What about that planet?' he asked. 'Could we acquire what we need from down there, use the shuttle to transport materials back up here?'

Dhalere spoke for the first time, her voice silky smooth and calm in contrast to Hevel's.

'There are protocols to observe when entering the atmosphere of a foreign planet, both for its indiginant species and for our own safety.'

Hevel nodded in agreement.

'Polluting a foreign world with our presence would violate the Word's instructions on contamination of...'

'Do you want to live or die, Hevel?' the captain snapped.

Hevel fell silent as the communications officer, a young blonde haired woman named Aranna, replied to the captain.

'The planet has everything we need,' she said. 'There are signs of intelligent life but its population density is low, pre–industrial civilisations, some agriculture, nothing major. We could get down there and move about without them being aware of us. Mostly we need water sir, for consumption and for hydrogen fuel. We're leaking both at an alarming rate.'

The captain nodded, and peered at the screen showing the planet below them.

'What's that?' he asked, and pointed to a towering pillar of dark smoke marring the perfect blue of an ocean.

'Volcanic eruption,' Aranna replied. 'It's threatening a large region of the land below our position in geo–stationary orbit. It would be wise to recover any supplies before it erupts, captain.'

'First things first,' he said. 'We control the prison situation. Then we seek to repair the engine and pull us out of low orbit before we end up becoming permanent residents here.'

Hevel leaned closer to the captain.

'The prison hull is a scourge,' he snapped, 'a stain on our populace. We should cut them loose now, before it's too late.'

'Is that why you gave the order to evacuate the air from the cell block?' the captain asked outright. 'To give you a reason to run away even faster?'

Hevel sneered at the captain. 'They were as much a hindrance then as they are now. We should never have brought them with us, thieves, liars and criminals that they are.'

The captain nodded. 'I feel the same about politicians, Hevel.'

The councillor smiled without warmth. 'The people follow me, captain. They need me, and they don't appreciate being ignored while you and your crew bend over backwards to protect a group of savages who have rejected the lives that we hold dear. How long, do you think, before they reject you as their leader?'

'I am not their leader,' Idris snapped. 'I am their protector.'

'Then protect them, captain, and forget about the damned convicts.'

A voice cut across them from nearby.

'Captain, you need to see this.'

'What is it?' Idris asked.

'The maximum–security wing,' came Jerren's response, 'one of the prisoners survived.'

***

VII

Alpha slowed as a door ahead shuddered and the locking mechanisms were released.

The corridor in which she stood was painted white, the aged paint crumbling and flaking to reveal patches of dull grey metal, but the panel lighting was working normally overhead and the air was warm. Her hair still felt thick and cold on the skin on the back of her neck, drenched in per–fluorocarbon that had stained the shoulders of her uniform, and her stomach was rumbling with hunger.

She brought her rifle up, aimed it at the door as it swung open and an enormous man stepped into the corridor, stooping to fit through the hatchway. Gold and blue hair fell in dense braids to his shoulders, his skin the colour of burned wood and flecked with shimmering tattoos, his borrowed uniform stretched to its limits to contain his bulky frame.

The man locked eyes with her and slowly held his hands out to his sides, showing her that he was unarmed. He was so large that he could not fully extend his arms without touching the opposing walls of the corridor.

'Easy now,' he said, his voice rolling like boulders toward her down the corridor. 'I just wanna talk.'

She watched him, kept the rifle pointed at him as he shut the security door behind him and stood in the corridor. His eyes seemed bright white against his dark skin, clear and steady as he watched her.

'I know that you can't talk,' he said as he took a pace toward her, 'so this is going to be a one way thing.'

She tensed, pulled the rifle into her shoulder and gently squeezed the trigger. The pulse–chamber hummed as it activated and the big man froze.

'Okay,' he said, 'it's still a two way thing.'

She gestured with the rifle barrel, jerking it down twice. The big man slowly got down onto his knees, his hands still held out to his sides. She moved closer, focusing on the man's face, then stopped moving and waited.

'My name's Qayin,' he said finally. 'You're Alpha Zero Seven, out of the maximum–security containment facility.'

She jerked her head over her shoulder, and Qayin nodded.

'The stern section of the prison hull,' he said, 'reserved for the most dangerous convicts. Looks like somebody decided one of you was a bit too dangerous, put a bomb in the hatches between your wing and ours. It went off a couple of hours ago, severed the wing from the rest of the ship and sent it into the atmosphere of that planet we're orbiting.'

She kept the rifle pulled tight into her shoulder, looked over Qayin's head to the security door.

'Got fifty of my guys in there,' Qayin said, 'fifty more up front in case the hatches to the Atlantia open. Our cells were closest to the blast, aft of the cell block. The damage ruptured some of our cell gates and we got out before the fire really got goin'. Fought our way into the control tower and got out just before the governor ordered the entire block evacuated, an' I don't mean of prisoners.'

She looked at Qayin, seeking any hint of deception, but the big man's gaze was steady.

'They flushed the cell block,' Qayin went on, 'bled out all the air. Most o' the guys died where they were, fighting or bleedin' out. We made our way up here, got as far as the command centre before the Atlantia cut us off. The prison hull fusion core's been compromised, no power comin' from it. Cell block's connected to the Atlantia by a single passage, and all our power and life support is comin' from them too through the tethers. One wrong move and we're all history.'

She remained still as Qayin spoke, the big man gesturing with a nod of his big head to his right.

'Nice lookin' planet down there, somewhere to start over, some are sayin'. We've got the captain by the balls, took hostages in the fight. Whole ship's losing orbital velocity and droppin' toward the atmosphere. They don't give us what we want, we'll drag 'em down to hell with us.'

She raised her head slightly, a questioning gesture.

'Freedom,' Qayin said. 'They let us aboard the Atlantia, we'll bring the hostages with us and they can cut the prison hull loose. Everybody wins.'

She watched him for a moment longer, thinking hard.

Qayin was a convict, for sure, and from somewhere in the deepest recesses of her mind a phrase sprang to mind, something that she remembered. The big man's glowing tattoos signified his gang or crew: the *Mark of Qayin*.

'You don't remember me, do you?' Qayin said.

She took a paced closer and let the rifle drop slightly. She shook her head once.

'You want in?' Qayin asked her.

She looked at him for a moment and then turned her masked head slightly and looked up at the black eye of a camera high up on the wall of the corridor.

'Yeah, we saw everything you did to the pirate crew,' Qayin said. 'They got what they deserved.'

She turned slowly back to Qayin, and he appeared to sense rather than see the rage concealed behind her featureless mask.

'They's fools,' he said, 'shoulda known better. Right now this ship is doomed so we all gotta watch each other's backs, right? Or there ain't none of us getting out alive.'

She watched him for a long time. He could see the shape of her breasts rising and falling beneath the fabric of her uniform and he was clearly forcing himself to maintain eye contact with her, to fix his gaze on the thin slits in the metal mask. She knew that nobody on the block had seen a woman in years. It was probably just their damned luck that the one who did show up was the most lethal person on the whole vessel.

'You in?' Qayin asked again.

She slowly lowered the rifle and pulled it in to port–arms. Qayin lowered his hands and got to his feet.

She was tiny compared to him, the top of her head not even reaching as high as his armpit. It appeared hard for Qayin to believe what she was capable of, what she had done, so hard was he scrutinising her. Qayin gestured with a thumb over his shoulder.

'Fifty men in there an' none of 'em seen a woman in years. You ready?'

She turned her head to look at the security door behind Qayin, and then she shouldered the rifle. He saw something bright and sharp flicker in her right hand, a blade or shank of some kind that had been concealed inside her sleeve.

Qayin turned and banged on the security door.

'Open up, we're good!'

The door clunked and then swung open again and Qayin stooped inside, hiding his discomfort at having Alpha Zero Seven immediately behind him with a concealed weapon in her grasp. He strode toward the governor's command platform and turned as she made her way inside.

The silence in the control centre deepened as the men around Qayin got their first close–up look at her. A live current seemed to flicker across them, volatile emotions of desire and uncertainty about the newcomer and her featureless mask.

The security door was pushed closed behind her by one of the convicts, who sealed it and then turned to look at her from behind. Qayin saw his eyes drift down to her ass and legs, and then the convict stepped forward and one hand settled on her ass.

She moved with remarkable speed, spinning around as the back of one forearm swiped up and under the convict's jaw and spun him sideways and over onto his front against a control panel. She grabbed the convict's wrist with one hand as the other, the shank flickering in its grasp, flashed through the air and drove the weapon straight through the convict's palm and deep into the plastic control panel.

The convict let out a scream of pain and two of his closest companions moved toward Alpha Zero Seven. As Qayin watched they backed away again as she smoothly unslung her rifle and charged the pulse–chamber, the faint hum filling the control centre.

'Are we done assaulting our guest?' Qayin asked.

The convict pinned to the control panel groaned in agony as he tried to pull the shank from his hand. Cutler walked across to him, reached down and yanked the weapon out to a fresh yelp of pain. The convict slumped to the floor, cradling his bloodied palm as Cutler turned and handed the shank out to Alpha Zero Seven. She reached out and snatched the weapon back, flipped it over and it vanished up her sleeve as quickly as it had emerged.

'Are we done here?' Qayin asked again.

The other convicts relaxed, their eyes off the woman and back onto Qayin. He turned to a convict manning the communications terminal.

'Contact the bridge,' he ordered. 'It's time to end this.'

Qayin turned to see Alpha standing on the edge of the platform, her back to the convicts lower down. She was either entirely fearless or psychologically adept: none of the convicts moved toward her, and the man she had injured was still whimpering as he bound his wound with strips of grubby clothing torn from his fatigues.

'Bridge, this is cell block.'

The convicts listened and waited. They didn't have to wait long.

'Cell block, bridge.'

Angry. Uncompromising. Probably a senior officer, Qayin guessed, trying to maintain the hard line. The Word. Qayin pressed a button on the governor's chair and the communications link opened up onto loudspeaker as he replied.

'It's time to negotiate,' Qayin said.

'There will be no negotiating. The Word does not...'

'The Word is irrelevant here,' Qayin interrupted. 'You have a choice. Either you allow us access to the Atlantia or we pull you all down to certain death with us.'

'You seem to have forgotten that we can send men out to cut you away at any time we choose.'

'Then why haven't you?' Qayin asked. 'Is it, perhaps, because you left a few people behind?'

A long silence echoed down the communications channel.

'How many of our people do you have?'

Qayin's grinned.

'The only way you'll find that out is if they walk across with us, or we finish sending all the pieces of them.'

'How many?'

'Several,' Qayin said. 'We will bring them with us provided you do exactly as I say.'

'I want proof of life.'

'You want?' Qayin asked, smiling broadly. '*You* want. Do we have somebody here important to you?'

The channel clicked and a new voice appeared. Captain Idris Sansin's brittle, rough tones were clearly audible over the link.

'Now you listen to me, scum. We give the orders here. The Word will decide what happens.'

Qayin did not respond. He put his fingers to his lips as he looked around the control centre. Nobody made a sound.

'Do you hear me?!'

Qayin made a cradle for his chin from his interlinked fingers and listened for a moment.

'I'm talking to you, scum! Do you have any idea what will happen to you when the Word finds us and...'

'If they find us, captain,' Qayin replied, 'which won't happen before we're all pulled down into the planet's atmosphere. Do you want to live, or die?'

A long silence and then the gruff voice replied.

'I'll do whatever I have to do to ensure the safety of my passengers and crew.'

'Including murder?' Qayin asked. 'Surely, that would make you no less criminal than us. I'm surprised we have so much in common, captain.'

A ripple of low chuckles wafted around the control centre.

'We have nothing in common, Qayin,' came the reply.

'We are in danger,' Qayin shot back. 'We are in crisis. None of us wants to die. We have much in common and we must work together. We don't like it. You don't like it. Our hostages sure as hell don't like it but it's happening.'

Qayin stood up and strolled across to Governor Hayes' grisly severed head. He picked it up by the hair and carried it across to one of the observation monitors, gesturing to one of the convicts as he went.

'Open the feed,' he said.

The monitor flickered into life and Qayin thrust the decapitated head into view. A gasp of disgust whispered down the channel.

'You're animals,' came the captain's response. *'You don't deserve to live.'*

'That's what the governor thought when he cleansed the cell block,' Qayin replied as he tossed the governor's head aside and beckoned Alpha across to him. She walked across the platform to his side. 'Got somebody for you to meet. You don't give us what we want, we'll put her to work on the hostages.'

Qayin stood to one side and Alpha moved to stand in front of the screen. Another gasp of disbelief.

'Her? They were terminated!'

'All but one,' Qayin replied. 'And she's already killed four of my men. I'd like to say I control her, but in truth, she's got her own agenda. You did fire plasma charges at her escape capsule, didn't you captain, after the blast? We saw them.'

Another long silence and then Qayin spoke loudly.

'You have one hour, captain, or I'll broadcast what she does to the hostages live across the whole damned ship.'

***

VIII

Captain Idris Sansin sat in the commander's chair on the bridge, watching the surveillance monitors arrayed before him. Two showed the tattered remnants of the tethers between the prison hull and the Atlantia, two more the only intact passage which was currently guarded by twenty of his best marines on permanent rotation under Bra'hiv's command.

'Status report?' he asked his first officer.

Andaim, a young lieutenant and fighter pilot upon whom Idris had found himself relying in these troubled times, called out his reply from across the bridge. 'All life–support systems active, repairs ongoing to the hull, but we can't access the prison hull from here. The only way in would be via shuttle, maybe through the damaged stern section.'

The captain dragged his weary frame out of his chair and strode to the aft section of the bridge. There, a spiral staircase led up to a viewing platform, a smaller room surrounded by windows that afforded the captain a broad view of his vessel.

He climbed the stairs and stood inside the platform, examining the spectacular panorama arrayed before him.

Below him was the Atlantia's main hull, a long and angular construction typical of ship–of–the–line frigates of Colonial design. Strictly speaking the Atlantia was an out of commission warship assigned to the prison service, stripped of many of her weapons and with a large portion of her hull given over to accommodation for the families of both military and correctional officers attached to her. Almost three hundred men, women and children lived in the sanctuary, protected by a hundred or so sworn military officers. Another hundred or so correctional staff carried out their duties in the prison – or rather, they had done until the blast that had caused such terrible carnage.

The Atlantia's hull was almost half a mile in length. At its bow was a vast scoop that drew in the hydrogen that floated in immense yet tenuous quantities throughout the cosmos, obtaining fuel sufficient to provide light and heat for the entire vessel. Those scoops also fed the enormous ion engines attached to either flank of the Atlantia on vast wing–like structures, although the frigate was incapable of atmospheric flight.

Further, retractable scoops slung beneath the Atlantia's keel were used to skim the atmospheres of planets or even the tails of comets to extract other essential elements such as oxygen, nitrogen and various ices. All of these valuable chemicals were then used to sustain life in the sanctuary as well as more general life support.

Once a large storage area for weapons, stores and maintenance, the Atlantia's core hull was now a place of such beauty that far from having to be cajoled into joining the colonial prison service officers virtually fought each other for a place. Such were the rewards required for men to spend long months away from home. Forested, with an illuminated sky powered by the vessel's central fuel core, the sanctuary represented a near–perfect copy of home, complete with isolated abodes for the crew and their families, all of it perfectly concealed and protected with the vast plated hull.

Idris lifted his head to peer beyond the Atlantia to where the angular, ugly black and grey mass of the prison hull trailed it. Apart from blinking anti–collision beacons there was little to see. Unadorned grey metal hull plating, all of it surrounded in a halo of debris from the blast. Atlantia 5 was his charge, his responsibility, and now likely his doom.

Behind the ship loomed the planet, filling the captain's field of view and far too vast to take in at a single glance.

'Captain?'

Andaim had ascended the staircase behind the captain and stood with his hands behind his back.

'What is it, lieutenant?'

'Sir, we have calculated that the vessel can only remain in a stable orbit for a couple of days before the prison hull drags us too close to the atmosphere. If we sink too deep into its gravitational well we will...'

'I know,' Idris replied, cutting his first officer off as he looked up at the colossal planet. 'Our engines won't have sufficient thrust to push us out of the planet's gravitational field.'

For a frigate the Atlantia was enormously powerful, but she was designed for deep space operations. Her engines were designed not for bursts of immense thrust but for the gradual building of the tremendous velocities required to traverse the vast expanses of interstellar space in reasonable amounts of time. Once those velocities were reached the engines were shut down; the ship's inertia and the negligible resistance in the vacuum of space meant that no further input was required until she reached her destination, upon which she would reverse her orientation and begin the deceleration to orbital velocities.

Those same engines were no match for the gravity of a planet, even a small one such as that which they orbited.

'We're already accelerating and sinking fast, sir,' Andaim added.

The captain eyed the planet's sweeping horizon for a moment, his practiced eye calculating angles.

'There's a fair chance we could use the increased velocity to skim the planet's atmosphere and break orbit across her horizon.'

'Calculations suggest the risk is too great,' Andaim countered. 'Once we're that close, there's no escape if you're wrong.'

Idris pinched the corners of his eyes between finger and thumb. 'How did this happen?'

'We still don't know sir. All we're certain of is that the blast came from within the high–security wing and that it was deliberate. The fires that came after and destroyed the prison wing were secondary features, not a planned…'

'I get the picture, Andaim,' Idris snapped. 'Do we have any idea who did this?'

'Not yet sir.'

'What about the survivor?' Idris asked.

'We have no idea how that was possible, sir. All of the convicts incarcerated in the high–security wing perished either in the blast or immediately afterward when their escape capsules were….'

'Destroyed,' the captain finished the sentence for his officer. 'Councillor Hevel has much to answer for. And yet, despite everything, there she is.'

He pointed to a monitor, one of several that lined the observation platform to relay imagery from the bridge to those above it. The monitor was filled with a still–image of the masked convict, Alpha–Zero–Seven, her metal face staring into the camera.

Andaim shivered. 'Who is she?'

'Her file is almost non–existent. No criminal record until five precessions ago, when she apparently murdered her family,a crime serious enough to silence her and send her out to Atlantia Five to permanent isolation and biological stasis.'

'Castaway protocol,' Andaim nodded. 'Only heard of one other case in the history of the Word.'

'My guess is that she's somehow behind all of this,' Idris said. 'I don't pretend to know how, but she got herself out and she's on the rampage. You saw what happened. Qayin and his thugs didn't have a clue what to do until she showed up, probably didn't have the guts to start torturing hostages. But this one, she's capable of anything and they know it.'

Andaim swallowed, and the captain could see the fear leeching from his pores as he spoke.

'I don't suppose…'

'We're on our own out here and we need to think out of the box,' Idris replied, wondering whether the lieutenant would suggest what Hevel had.

Andaim tensed, then lifted his chin and with it his resolve. 'What would you have me do, sir?'

Idris offered his first officer a warm smile. Fact was, Andaim was afraid and Idris could see it as clear as the bright star flaring in the heavens directly above them. Yet he was ready to do his duty, or at the very least willing to give it a try.

'The convicts want out of the prison and into the Atlantia, specifically the sanctuary. I think that it's fair to say we cannot allow that to happen.'

'Then we must liberate our people by force,' Andaim said.

'Oh, how I wish we could,' Idris said. 'But the risks of a close–quarters fight against an armed and numerically superior enemy turn the odds against us. The warders in the prison could not hold out against a small portion of the convict population. How would we fare?'

It was not Andaim who replied, but Hevel as he mounted the stairs to the observation platform, Dhalere alongside him.

'Then we have no choice, captain.'

'No choice?'

'We must prioritise those that we can protect at the expense of those we cannot.'

Idris turned to face the councillor. 'Are you again advocating abandoning the hostages?'

'I'm not advocating anything,' Hevel insisted. 'If we do not act soon we shall sit here and watch Qayin and his thugs start slicing our people into chunks. Do you have any idea how much panic that will cause here, among the crew, among the passengers?'

Andaim jabbed a finger at Hevel's chest.

'Do you think being seen to walk away from our own officers, at a time of great need, will shed us in any better a light?'

'They do not need to know,' Hevel said in a whisper, glancing down into the bridge to ensure that they were not overheard. 'The hostages will succumb far faster if we cut them loose than if they were left to Qayin.'

'And if you were there?' Idris challenged. 'Would you be so ruthless?'

'I would do what had to be done.'

'Would you?' Idris uttered. 'Somehow I doubt that. Those men over there are not just correctional officers. They are husbands, sons, fathers and brothers.'

'We know well who they are, captain,' Dhalere purred smoothly. 'This is not an action that anybody would choose lightly.'

The captain ground his teeth in his jaw.

'Every person aboard this vessel will know well the kind of man you are, Hevel, if word of this conversation ever got out.'

'I will deal with that when the time comes.'

'How?'

Hevel appeared uncertain, and Dhalere spoke for him.

'I don't know,' she said. 'What we do know is that the prisoners are ruthless, cruel and self–serving – it's why they're imprisoned in the first place. They won't bend to our will. The choice is not ours captain, it's yours, but act we must.'

Idris scowled and turned, his old eyes scanning the monitors. 'We don't have much time here.'

Hevel stepped forward, his gaze firm. 'Then we must begin, now, before they start hurting people. What are we going to do, captain?'

Idris stared at the image of Alpha Zero Seven, and made his decision.

*

'Open a channel to the prison.'

Idris took his seat in the centre of the bridge, heard Lael open the link. A wash of static filled the bridge as the link was put on open speaker, and then Qayin's voice boomed through the speakers.

'Captain, you have decided to open the passageway to the Atlantia,' he announced, as though it were ordained.

Idris gripped his seat tighter as he spoke. 'No, Qayin, I have not.'

A long silence followed. Hevel leaned in close to the captain. 'You're doing the right thing.'

The captain did not reply. Qayin's voice, brooding and cruel, reached them from the speakers.

'Then your people shall pay with their blood.'

A screen in the bridge flickered into life as the prisoners reattached the camera links, and Idris flinched as he saw a young marine strapped tightly into a chair that was floating inverted in the prison block amid the corpses, his body naked and shivering, his eyes darting left and right, poisoned with fear.

'No!'

Idris turned as Bra'hiv, standing at the entrance to the bridge, recognised the face of one of his marines.

'That's C'rairn!' he yelled. 'Let him go!'

Qayin grinned into the monitor.

'Your captain doesn't want me to let Officer C'rairn go,' Qayin sneered at Bra'hiv. 'He wants to leave him to die.'

'There will be no bloodshed,' Idris insisted. 'There are other ways.'

Another monitor flickered into life, Qayin's dark features filling it. 'How so, captain?'

Idris kept his features impassive as he spoke. 'We shall organise a rota for your men to travel to the Atlantia. Two days a piece, four men at a time and…'

'Shut up!' Qayin bellowed into the camera. 'You will open the passage to the Atlantia or I will send small pieces of C'rairn over one at a time until you do!'

Idris closed his eyes and shook his head.

'That can never happen, Qayin,' he replied. 'If you do not release our people in the next hour then we will be forced to follow the Word.'

Qayin frowned on the screen. 'You don't have the guts.'

'We will forcibly detach the prison wing from the hull,' Idris said, 'and save those whom we can.'

Qayin's dark features rippled with suppressed rage and then he suddenly laughed into the camera, spittle flying as he pointed at then captain.

'I take it back, you got the stones for this game,' he laughed, and then that laugh died away and Qayin's eyes burned into the camera, his tattoos shimmering like rivers of magma coursing down his cheeks. 'But so do I. You condemn us, I'll broadcast my people tearing yours apart, all the way down.'

Qayin pulled away from the camera and looked at somebody off screen.

Idris saw Alpha Zero Seven move into view. In her hand was what looked like a welding torch.

'Do him,' Qayin ordered. 'Take your time over it.'

***

IX

Alpha Zero Seven glanced at the screen where the captain's tired old features stared back at her. That he was helpless to recover control of the situation was clear to her. The command of Atlantia Five had probably been his last before retirement and he seemed to lack the resolve needed to stand up to Qayin.

She turned, the torch in one hand as she strode out of the prison's command centre and down the passage outside toward the cell block. The air felt colder once again and the uniform still unwieldy and heavy as she moved, passing through the now open gates. Nobody from the command centre followed her. Despite their bravado she knew that even hardened convicts were still human beings, and despite their reputation few had much stomach for torture.

She forced her weighty boots to keep moving against the magnetic forces pulling them toward the floor, her heart beating a little faster from more than just the exertion of walking down the passageway.

She reached the cell block control tower, the door now propped open by Qayin's men. She walked through and saw the marine floating upside down in his chair, his hair flowing like blond water in the zero gravity, his young body smooth and virtually hairless. Officer C'rairn.

He turned his head and his handsome features crumbled as a tiny sound of fear escaped from his lips.

'Don't do this,' he whimpered.

She turned and kicked the prop from the door so that it closed almost completely behind her, just the prop preventing it from sealing them both in. The door clunked against the metal, the sound echoing through the haunted cell block.

She turned back to C'rairn and approached him.

'Please,' he blubbed, tears filling his eyes. 'I have a baby daughter, please.'

She held the torch up in her hand and activated it. A fierce blue light flared into life, crackling and snarling at the end of a finger–length metallic probe.

'Do him, now!'

Qayin's voice snapped over the communications link up in the control tower.

She reached out, the officer's hair floating as she grabbed it and yanked him toward her. 'Please, no,' C'rairn begged, his tears floating upward in rippling spheres of liquid as they broke free from his eyes.

She stared at him through the slits of her mask and then pushed the torch hard toward him.

*

C'rairn's hellish screams broke out of the speakers and soared through the Atlantia's bridge. Idris winced as he glimpsed a shower of blood spilling out around Alpha's body as she worked on the officer, whose inverted seat blocked the view of the horrendous injuries he was suffering.

'Shut it off!' he bellowed across the bridge.

Jerren cut the feed off. The screams of the officer seemed to echo through the bridge long after the screen went blank, and Idris realised that Qayin had a monitor playing the same scene in the governor's command centre that could still be heard over the intercom on the bridge, the dying officer's strangled cries of agony drifting away into silence.

Qayin tutted and shook his head as he glanced at the unseen monitor and its gruesome images. 'She's a fearsome animal, isn't she? I wonder what she'll do once she really gets warmed up?'

Idris jumped out of his chair and pointed at Qayin as he shouted.

'I'll have you pay for this, Qayin! I'll have you torn limb from limb and fed to your men!'

'Now you're talking like a captain,' Qayin sneered at the screen.

'Cut them loose, now!' Hevel snarled at the captain. 'Before they murder anybody else!'

Idris seemed to shake on the spot as though tremors were rippling through his entire body, fresh rage encased in a shell of old age. Then he whirled and pointed at the communications officer.

'Open a channel, all frequencies, open speakers!'

Aranna obeyed as Qayin chuckled at the screen. 'There's nobody else out there to help you, captain.'

Idris grinned cruelly at the image of Qayin. 'No, so I'll just have to help my damned self.'

Dhalere stepped forward. 'Captain, what are you going to do?'

'What needs to be done.'

'May I remind you,' Dhalere said, 'that you are by law required to conform to the standards of the colonial district...'

Idris turned his back to Dhalere and looked at the communications officer, Aranna, who nodded.

'The channel is open, captain, to the entire prison hull.'

'Gentlemen,' Idris said loudly, 'of the prison ship, I have an offer for you, for any man strong enough and smart enough. I offer a full amnesty, on my word and on that of my officers and command, to any of you able to liberate my staff and bring them safely home here to the Atlantia. And Qayin with them.' Idris smiled grimly. 'Dead or alive.'

*

Qayin whirled, one hand flashing to the pistol at his belt as he drew it and aimed at the nearest man to him. He fired without a moment's hesitation, before the hapless inmate had even realised what was about to happen, and the convict's head was blasted from his shoulders by the plasma round in a gruesome mess that splattered across the man sitting next to him.

The blood–soaked man promptly vomited onto his boots, his face plastered with blood and brain.

'Try it!' Qayin bellowed to the convicts around him. 'Any man among you, try it!'

Qayin turned, sweeping the bridge with his pistol and daring any man to move before yelling at the convict manning the communications console.

'Shut him off!'

The link to the Atlantia's bridge was terminated, the captain's features vanishing as Qayin slowly turned, the pistol still pointing out in front of him.

'Let's make one thing real clear,' he growled, his tattoos pulsing with light, 'any man even thinks about crossing me, I'll do things to them that'll make what's being done down in the cell block look real nice, you understand me?'

C'rairn's screams echoed through the command centre and then trailed off into a final, keening wail of unimaginable pain as the sound of the crackling welding torch finally snapped out.

'What do we do now?' Cutler asked, glancing briefly at the headless torso now smouldering in a seat nearby. 'The captain just played us out of moves.'

'We've still got the hostages.'

'So?' Cutler almost laughed. 'You heard the captain, they're willing to walk away.'

Qayin scowled at Cutler, but he did not reply.

Moments later a figure appeared at the door to the command centre. Qayin turned to see Alpha standing in the doorway. Her uniform was caked in a bloody mess, the torch in her hand trailing gloops of blood that drifted in the air, and her mask was splattered with human remains.

'Is he dead?' Cutler asked her.

Qayin cursed under his breath. 'Who cares?'

Alpha stood in the doorway and nodded once. Cutler shook his head. 'That's it then, we're played out.'

'Will you shut up?' Qayin snapped. 'If one of their people is dead it might be enough to make them take us seriously.'

'It might be enough for them to take us out altogether,' Cutler snapped back. 'We should have handled this better.'

'There *is* no we!'

'Again,' Cutler smiled coldly, 'that's the problem.'

A voice from across the control centre called out. 'Orbital velocity has increased by a factor of four. We're sinking real fast here.'

Qayin stared at the monitor where the captain's face had been and then at Alpha where she stood with the bloodied welding torch in her hand.

'Send them the body,' he growled at her. 'Give them something else to think about.'

Alpha turned and stalked silently away down the passage outside the bridge.

'She gives me the creeps,' Cutler uttered.

Qayin watched Alpha leave.

'You and me both, man.'

*

Alpha walked back into the cell block and got to work.

She unstrapped the officer's body from the seat and folded him over, concealing the bloodied mess on his stomach, and then used the straps to tie him up into a neat ball that she then pushed in front of her through the air as she walked back toward the control centre.

Instead of pushing the body through the control centre, she followed the signs around it to the for'ard airlocks, where the prison hull's tenuous links to the Atlantia were. Several armed inmates guarding the hatches saw her coming with her grisly package and they stepped silently out of her way.

Four huge, heavy sealed hatches awaited her. The two outermost hatches were topped with red flashing lights that indicated they were sealed against the vacuum of space, disconnected as they always were. Of the two innermost, one was solid red, indicating an unsafe seal.

Only one was indicating green.

Alpha stopped and looked up at an observation camera, then waited.

Moments later, the airlock door hissed and slowly began to open.

Ahead was a passageway, lined with silvery thermal insulation that led toward the Atlantia. Illuminated only by small panels in the ceiling, she could see at the far end armed marines behind a similar hatch.

They watched her through a screen, their weapons held ready, as she guided the bundled body of the correctional officer into the passage and then pushed him hard. The corpse floated directly toward the far end of the passage, revolving slowly, as Alpha stepped back out and looked up at the camera again.

The door hissed shut as she watched the officer's naked, bloodied body float slowly toward his comrades.

*

Captain Idris Sansin paced up and down his bridge, his crew giving him a wide berth.

'I did *not* see that coming.'

Hevel watched the captain with an expression of admiration as he walked up and down, his hands behind his back and his head bowed as he moved.

'You said it yourselves,' the captain replied, 'the prisoners are ruthless, cruel and self–serving – I just decided to use that against them.'

Hevel smiled tightly. 'Still, it's a very risky course of action and could lead to…'

'Every course of action is risky now, Hevel!' the captain roared, silencing the staff on the bridge around them. 'We have but hours to live!'

'I know,' Hevel uttered, 'and I understand that our choices are limited, but turning them against each other puts our own people at even greater risk and you've already lost one of them.'

The captain stopped pacing and stared at Hevel. '*I've* lost one of them?'

'I didn't mean it like that.'

'Yes, you did,' Idris replied. 'You think that I'm responsible, don't you?'

The silence on the bridge deepened. Dhalere stepped in for the councillor once more.

'I think that we are all responsible in our own way, sir.'

Idris glared at Hevel. 'Would you think yourself more capable in my stead?'

Hevel's back straightened and he raised his chin. 'No, of course not.'

'Good,' Idris said as he walked closer to Hevel, his voice dropping to a whisper, 'because left to you *all* of those hostages would be dead, would they not?'

The captain looked into Hevel's unblinking eyes and saw the repressed shame festering within. The councillor looked as though he was about to say something when Bra'hiv rushed onto the bridge.

'Sir!' The captain and the first officer turned together as Bra'hiv waved for them to follow him. 'You need to see this.'

Idris shot Hevel a final dirty look before he turned and hurried after Bra'hiv, Andaim joining them as they rushed off the bridge and down a long, descending passageway.

'What is it?' Idris asked as they reached a small transport cart attached to a tubular rail system that ran the circumference of the Atlantia's vast hull.

'The hostage, C'rairn,' Bra'hiv replied as they climbed aboard the transport cart and it hummed into motion. 'Alpha Zero Seven handed him over.'

Idris sighed wearily. 'I think that I've seen enough blood for one day.'

Bra'hiv, controlling the throttle of the cart as it hummed along the rail, shook his head.

'You've got to see it to believe it, sir.'

After a minute's travel the cart slowed as it reached the Atlantia's stern and a series of airlock hatches that led to the prison hull. All four security hatches were sealed, all inoperative save a single one with a green light above it. The active door was sealed, however, using hydraulic rams monitored by a dozen armed marines who were now huddled around something on the floor between them. Bra'hiv slowed the cart and climbed out with the captain, Andaim behind them.

Idris slowly approached the group of soldiers, who all stood back to let him through.

Idris drew a deep breath as he saw the first sight of flesh smeared with blood, and then he gasped. He found himself looking down into a pair of gleaming eyes, those of a young man in the prime of his life.

Idris tried to open his mouth to speak but the young officer got there first.

'She faked it,' C'rairn said as tears sprung afresh from his eyes, this time of joy. 'She got me out, sir. Alpha Zero Seven, she's on our side.'

***

X

'Who is she?'

Idris strode as fast as he could onto the bridge, Andaim alongside him and Hevel waiting with a suspicious expression pasted onto his features.

'Who is whom?' he asked.

'Alpha Zero Seven,' the captain snapped. 'Tell me everything.'

'I don't know,' Hevel shrugged and looked at Dhalere. The dark skinned woman spoke from memory.

'High security prisoner, Castaway Protocol,' she said. 'She was sent to Atlantia Five after a closed–door trial by the Word. Full stasis orders, restraining mask, everything. Her file is closed and classified.'

The captain glanced around him. The bridge was a hive of activity as staff worked to find a solution to the vessel's orbital decline.

'How far have we got?' he demanded of his technical staff as they pored together over a series of charts on one side of the bridge.

A tall, thin man with a hooked nose glanced up.

'Nowhere but down,' he replied.

'How long?' Andaim asked.

'Less than two days,' the thin man replied. 'Every passing moment becomes more critical.'

Idris turned to Andaim. 'Then all we have is that woman, Alpha Zero Seven.'

'That's insane,' Hevel snapped. 'She's a mass murderer, a born killer!'

'He's right, captain,' Dhalere agreed. 'Alpha–Zero–Seven is one of the greatest–risk prisoners every carried by an orbital prison. If she is presented with even the slightest opportunity for escape she will kill without remorse, as she has already done in the prison hull.'

Behind them Officer C'rairn walked in, thermal blankets wrapped around his shoulders and his wife holding him through tears and smiles. Hevel and Dhalere's jaws dropped as they stared at the marine. The guards with him guided him to the captain's chair, where he was sat down with a steaming mug in his hand.

'How are you doing, son?' Idris asked him.

'I'll be fine,' C'rairn replied, clearly shaken by his ordeal but rallying fast.

'Good,' the captain said. 'Look, I know it's a bit soon but we need to know what's happening down there.'

C'rairn nodded.

'Fifteen hostages all being held in the office block, everybody restrained using their own cuffs. The prisoners got free from their cells after the blast but before the fires took hold. We tried to fight them off but there were too many.'

'They took the control tower?' Hevel asked.

C'rairn nodded. 'We lost a lot of good men, sir, and the governor's dead.'

'Qayin?' the captain asked.

'He led them,' C'rairn replied. 'They stormed the tower, broke through to the for'ard sections using the captured officer's passes and keys. We were making a retreat under fire when the cell block was cleansed.' C'rairn looked up. 'Did you order that, sir?'

Idris tensed, his jaw grinding as he glanced at Hevel.

'No, I did,' Hevel said. 'There was a danger of breaching in both hulls. We had to end it as fast as we could, once the fires started.'

C'rairn stared at the councillor for a long moment.

Idris kept his expression as neutral as he could. 'What happened next?'

'Qayin offered us terms,' C'rairn replied. 'Surrender and we'd be spared. We had nowhere to run and were both outgunned and outnumbered, with little ammunition left. Qayin disarmed us, then the bastard shot Feyer in the head as a warning to the rest of us not to cross him. We've been locked up in an office block ever since.'

'Until Alpha Zero Seven,' Dhalere said.

C'rairn nodded, his grip on his mug tightening.

'They stripped me, put me in the chair, said that you'd told them they could do what they liked to us, but they'd never get into Atlantia.' C'rairn looked up at the captain and his voice cracked. 'I figured that was a lie, sir, but then she turned up with the torch in her hand and I knew I was done for.'

'Alpha Zero Seven,' Idris said. 'What do you know about her?'

'Apart from the fact that she just saved my life?' C'rairn asked. 'Nothing. All we've ever been told is that she's the most dangerous woman ever to have lived. She's been on permanent lock–down since we left home, on life–support in a survival capsule. Nobody, but nobody, ever goes near her.'

'The mask?' Hevel asked.

'Vocal resonance restrictor,' Dhalere replied, 'it prevents the wearer from biting, spitting and also from speaking. It was fitted to her when we left the colonies.'

Idris rubbed his temple. 'That was two years ago. I though those things were for temporary use only?'

'They are, back home,' Dhalere replied. 'But the Word's orders for her were strict – it was never, ever to be removed. Not even on the day she died. She was to be conflagrated and buried wearing that mask, for all time.'

Idris looked briefly at Hevel. 'Why?'

'Who knows?' Hevel replied. 'The assumption is that she's real bad news and people just stay away from her.' Hevel frowned as he looked at C'rairn. 'How did she survive the explosion? The entire high–security wing was wiped out, no survivors. She may have detonated a device herself.'

'We don't know that,' the captain replied, 'but we'd very much like to find out.'

C'rairn shook his head.

'I saw her, sir,' he said. 'Close up, and I mean right through that mask. The look in her eyes scared me half to death, like an animal, no soul. But she risked her life to get me out of there.'

'How did she do it?' Hevel asked.

'There are hundreds of bodies down there in the cell block, all just floating around. She must have climbed up the control tower and taken off one of their arms or something and tucked it inside her uniform, because when she came back down and I saw her for the first time she already had blood on her. I thought she'd already carved somebody up and I was next, but when she leaned into me she slid the severed arm out and just started hacking it up.'

'We heard you screaming,' Dhalere said.

C'rairn nodded.

'If she'd asked me to sing camp–fire songs I would have done, but she couldn't speak. She just looked at me, and I got it right away. I started screaming, blood was flying everywhere and the seat was inverted so the cameras couldn't quite see anything. Genius, really.'

'Why?' Idris asked. 'Why would she protect you?'

'I don't know. Until today, I'd not been anywhere near her. But she put her hand on my shoulder at one point, squeezed it and winked at me. She knew what she was doing sir. Whatever she might be she ain't no cold–blooded murderer.'

Idris stood back from C'rairn and looked at Andaim. 'She killed four convicts back there, but if they attacked her it would be self defence. We need her if we're going to get those hostages out.'

'We can't talk with her,' Andaim said. 'She can't speak.'

'No,' Idris said thoughtfully as he turned to his communications officer, 'but she can communicate. Arrana, wind back the footage of Qayin talking to us.'

Aranna accessed the video feed and wound back the footage, Qayin's face filling half the screen. Behind him, as he spoke, they could see Alpha Zero Seven standing in silence, watching. Captain Sansin's voice echoed through the bridge from the recording.

'How many of my people do you have?'

Qayin's grinned in response on the monitor.

'The only way you'll find that out is if they walk across with us, or we finish sending all the pieces of them.'

Idris pointed at the screen as he saw Alpha Zero Seven move her hands slightly. 'There.'

Alpha's bunched fist opened to reveal first her index finger, and then she closed it before opening it again to show all five fingers.

'Fifteen,' said Aranna. 'They have fifteen of our people, just like C'rairn said. She took your bait, captain.'

Andaim shook his head. 'No. This was before the captain offered an amnesty to anybody willing to bring the hostages back alive.'

'Yes it was,' Idris murmured, 'which makes me wonder why she would have any interest in helping us. She's a convict in the middle of an insurrection: most of them think that we would shoot them on sight if we could.'

'Wouldn't we?' Hevel asked.

'Alpha Zero Seven, she took down four of the convicts all on her own, is that right?' the captain asked.

'We think so,' Bra'hiv replied. 'Some sort of dispute inside the prison.'

'If she was in the high–security wing during the blast, then how did she make it into the prison hull?' Hevel asked.

'The security wing has a life–preservation policy,' Bra'hiv explained. 'In the event of a major disaster of any kind that compromises hull security, the convict housed there are able to access survival pods and be ejected into space. Their capsules have a short lifespan, enough for them to have a chance of making it back aboard the prison hull.'

Idris nodded.

'Are they all kept in isolation for the entire period of their confinement?' Andaim asked.

'No,' Bra'hiv explained. 'They're in cells, but especially high–risk prisoners are placed in stasis for as long as the vessel is in transit, sir,' Hevel replied. 'They're easier to contain if they're out cold for the journey, but the process is complex and expensive, so it's only reserved for the most dangerous inmates.'

Idris paced slowly up and down the bridge.

'What is it?' Andaim asked.

'And this woman, Alpha Zero Seven, she was the only convict aboard to be masked in that way?'

Dhalere nodded. 'It's very rare, sir. Only psychopaths are fitted with masks, and she's clearly one.'

Idris did not reply, still pacing the deck.

'Sir?' Andaim asked.

'I want a team to go out into the debris field and locate the source of the blast,' the captain announced.

'We don't have time for that,' Hevel protested. 'We're on the verge of being pulled down out of orbit and…'

'I'm aware of that!' Idris growled at the councillor. 'But I feel certain that Alpha cannot have placed the charge that destroyed the security wing. Somebody else must have done so.'

Hevel blinked. 'Why?'

Idris grinned without warmth. 'That's what I'd like to find out.'

'Captain, the last thing we should be doing is worrying about the prisoners. Our own people are in grave danger.'

'Yes they are,' Idris agreed, 'and if one of them were responsible for endangering us all by attempting to blow up half of this vessel, I'd want to know who that person was. Wouldn't you, Hevel?'

Hevel stared at the captain for a moment and then nodded. 'Yes, of course.'

'As soon as you've found the detonation device or identified what it was, I want to open a channel to Qayin,' the captain said to Andaim, 'and give Alpha the chance to communicate with us again.'

Hevel gaped at the captain. 'You want trust the most dangerous prisoner on the entire vessel?'

'She's the only survivor,' the captain said. 'She also can't have tried to blow the prison hull up because she was in stasis the whole time, so she's the only one I can be sure isn't responsible for what happened.'

'The prisoners are ruthless,' Hevel said. 'None of them can be trusted.'

'Can't they?' the captain asked. 'Yes, they're desperate but then so are we. Let's use that against them. If we can get Alpha to communicate then we can maybe figure out a way to get our people out without compromising the Atlantia's security.'

'How?' Bra'hiv asked, his features taut with anticipation.

The captain gestured to the prison hull's ruined stern.

'Why not let us keep them busy at the front while you and your marines go in at the back?'

Bra'hiv nodded. 'That's good enough for me.'

Hevel's eyes narrowed.

'And what if the deception works, captain? What will we do with the prisoners then? I do hope that you're not considering bringing them here to Atlantia?'

'We'll cross that bridge when we get to it,' Idris snapped, and turned to Bra'hiv. 'Take a shuttle and be prepared to leave at a moment's notice to access the prison hull. Twenty men should be enough. The prisoners will be anxious to escape and they might be forced into making a mistake. Get to the hostages if you can, and bring them home.'

Bra'hiv left the bridge and the captain turned to survey his monitors.

'Let's see who's in control now, Qayin.'

***

XI

'You're insane. They'll never do it.'

Cutler watched as Qayin worked, rummaging through discarded weapons damaged in the blast in the prison hull.

The bodies of the dead haunted the silent prison, floating like ghosts in the half–darkness as Qayin unloaded the power cell from a rifle and pocketed the fist–sized magazine. He threw the un–loaded weapon up into the darkness above him, the rifle flying straight up in silence and vanishing into the shadows until it clattered against the distant ceiling.

'They'll let us in,' Qayin said, 'they've got no choice.'

Qayin unloaded another rifle and tossed the magazine to Cutler. The older man caught it easily and stuffed it into his already bulging pockets.

'We don't have enough men to fight trained troops,' Cutler cautioned, 'and what will it achieve anyway if they have enough firepower to cut us off?'

'The hostages will guarantee our safety,' Qayin muttered. 'All we need is the distraction, enough to get us all aboard the Atlantia without them opening fire on us. They can't cut us loose without dooming the hostages, so they'll want to get into the prison and liberate them. We'll use that against them.'

Cutler leaned in close to Qayin. 'And what about Alpha? I don't trust her.'

Qayin yanked the magazine from one last rifle and stuffed it into a pocket. 'If she goes behind our backs, she'll regret it.'

Cutler snorted and shook his head. 'She doesn't care about anybody but herself and…'

'So you all think,' Qayin cut across him.

'What's that supposed to mean?'

Qayin and Cutler strode toward the control tower, pushing floating corpses out of their way as they went.

'The mask,' Qayin said. 'The silence. You all assume that she's crazy enough to do anything: that she's off her head, lethal.'

'You saw what she did to Jehan and his pirate crew,' Cutler shot back. 'She was naked and unarmed. Sixty seconds later, she'd killed them all.'

'I didn't say she wasn't a fighter.'

'What then?'

'I knew her before she got masked.'

Cutler looked across at Qayin. 'How'd you know her, if she's masked?'

'Her eyes,' Qayin replied, 'the shape of what I can see. It's her all right.'

'When did you know her?'

'Back on the colonies,' Qayin said, counting the number of power cells he had shoved into his pockets. 'She weren't no convict back then.'

'What the hell was she then? A soldier?'

'A journalist.'

Cutler stopped walking. 'You're tugging my chain.'

'Visited me in Beya Prison, back in the day,' Qayin explained. 'She was doin' research, wanted to know a lot of details about the man I was sent up for killin'.'

'And?'

'I tol' her what I knew and she listened a damn sight more than my dear brother ever did,' Qayin replied, and glanced across the lonely, haunted prison block. 'I got busted for the murder of an elected official, some up–town suit who'd figured out how the Word first broke out and started infectin' the population.'

Cutler watched Qayin in silence for a moment before he spoke. 'You know how it started?'

'Maybe,' Qayin shrugged. 'My crew was running devlamine street dope out of Ethera's spaceport, doin' a fine trade of it too. Then this guy shows up and stings us, but he doesn't arrest us. Says he's with a government department and that our shipments have been infected with nanobots or something. I told him to do one.' Qayin sighed. 'Two weeks later and half of my buyers are turning up wanting more devlamine, selling their damned houses, can't get enough of it. Real weird, you know, like they were on the verge of overdosing days after first trying it.'

'You have it checked out?'

'I went back to the suit,' Qayin nodded. 'He took a sample, said he'd get back to me. Next day he was found shot to hell down southside under the keel of a merchant ship in the docks. My gen–print all over him, the murder weapon tossed nearby, you name it. How I ended up here.'

'And Hevel never helped?'

'My dear brother tol' me I'd had it comin',' Qayin explained, 'which was probably right. Said it was all excuses, which weren't right. Last time we laid eyes on each other I broke his nose. That kind of ended any legal rep' I could trust.'

'And Alpha?'

'Visited me in Beya, seemed like she was chasing it all up,' Qayin said. 'She figured the drug had been modified to contain nanobots that entered the body and were programmed to stimulate the pleasure regions of the brain. Jus' like a drug, except that there was no downer – people jus' wanted more and more. The bots would build up, and then take over the body and brain. Brilliant, for freaks who like that sort of thing.'

Cutler guessed the rest. 'Same thing happened to her as to you, right?'

'Few weeks later and she's up for a double murder,' Qayin confirmed. 'I never saw her again, until now.'

'You sayin' she's innocent?'

'I'm sayin' she's dangerous to know,' Qayin replied. 'That prison block got blown up because o' her, I reckon. But right now we gotta make allies of our enemies, y'know what I mean?'

They reached the control tower, the seat where Officer C'rairn had been tortured still hanging in the air and splattered with blood, globules of which orbited the chair in gruesome little red orbs.

Qayin slowed down as he looked at the chair, and then he grabbed a convict's corpse and pulled off his uniform before emptying the power cells from his pockets and folding them up in the uniform. He ordered Cutler to do the same and then pointed at the control tower.

'Take these back to the command centre and arm the men, then wait for me there.'

'What are you going to do?' Cutler asked as he tied the sleeves of the convict's uniform around the cells and pushed it through the air toward the tower door.

'I want to check see if there's any explosives in that tower, or maybe some of that crowd–control gas they used to use on us.'

Qayin waited until Cutler was gone and then he looked at the chair hanging upside down in the cell block amid its constellation of dark blood. He turned and looked up at the control tower to see a bulbous black eye staring back at him.

Slowly, he moved toward the chair and leaned down, peering up into the seat through the rippling clouds of blackening blood. The seat where C'rairn had been strapped was unmarked, as expected, but still…

Qayin stepped back from the chair a few paces and examined the cloud of blood surrounding it. The cell block was full of it, mostly congealing on surfaces but often hanging in clouds where severed arteries had sprayed it across the block to hang in grim ribbons. Qayin studied the cloud of blood hanging in the air around the chair, and then he spotted what he was looking for.

A faint trail, a line of blood leading away from the seat. It went past where Qayin was standing, a faint dribble that led into the control tower. Qayin walked into the tower, the line of blood broken now by the passage of Cutler and himself as they had entered the tower minutes before. Qayin stopped near the door and looked up and around him.

He could see no cameras, his body tucked too close to the tower entrance.

Qayin looked around, not touching anything but merely observing the interior of the tower, the control panels that had been used by officers to selectively open cell doors or even whole tiers, the hardened glass windows and the monitors shattered as the convicts, Qayin among them, had run amok in a frenzy of rage and destruction.

The bodies of several correctional officers lay slumped on the ground, weighed down by their uniforms, while the corpses of convicts floated as though underwater. Qayin searched them one by one, turning them over.

It was when he rolled over one of the correctional officers slumped on his front that he realised what had happened. The officer's left arm was missing, the flesh cauterised just above his elbow and the severed limb tucked beneath his body and scorched black by the flame of a welding torch.

'Well,' he muttered to himself, 'ain't you one clever little lady?'

***

XII

'What's he doing?'

Captain Idris Sansin watched along with his crew as a monitor flickered into life, the communications channel controlled by Qayin's men opening up again.

Qayin was walking, facing what was presumably a hand–held camera transmitting from the prison hull. The camera appeared to be floating backwards in front of Qayin as he spoke.

'Captain,' he said with a grand smile, his arms opening wide as he walked as though he were attempting to embrace Idris. 'It appears that you have failed to take me seriously? The hatches to the Atlantia have not been opened to welcome us.'

The captain moved closer to the monitor. He knew that Qayin would not be able to see him, but that the audio channel was open and active.

'Oh, I take you seriously Qayin,' he replied, 'seriously enough to want you taken down, dead or alive.'

'That's not going to happen,' Qayin replied as he walked, gesturing to the convicts following him, the sound of their boots on the deck audible on the transmission. 'My men are loyal, just like yours.'

'Your men are afraid,' Idris snapped.

Qayin's smile withered. 'No, it is the hostages who are afraid. Would you like to see them?'

Idris glanced at Hevel, who seemed mesmerised by Qayin. The rest of the bridge crew were watching the captain with interest.

'I want proof of life,' he said.

'Then you shall have it,' Qayin replied, 'at least, of life at the moment. You see I don't believe that you will free us without another demonstration of our determination to succeed, captain.'

'You leave my people be,' Idris growled, his thick fists bunching by his sides.

'No,' Qayin replied. 'I won't. Not until you release us from the prison. Ah, here we are.'

Idris watched as Qayin was filmed walking through the cell block's control tower, corpses visible floating within, and then out into the cell block. Debris and blood drifted through the air as they walked.

A ripple of whispered profanities and exclamations of disgust drifted across the bridge as the crew witnessed for the first time the ghostly aftermath of the riot in the cell block. Corpses drifted everywhere, blood and other bodily fluids spilled in long glistening trails that hung in the air like gruesome gossamer webs. Qayin's voice chortled over the grim scene.

'Like what we've done with the place?'

'You'll pay,' Idris replied. 'One way or another, you'll pay for what you've done.'

'What *I've* done?' Qayin asked, touching his own barrel chest as though appalled. 'I didn't try to blow up the prison, captain. Makes me wonder who did it and why, y'know? Especially now, seeing as you're willing to cut us loose and all of the hostages too.'

'You give me no choice.'

'You have a choice!' Qayin roared, his face filling the monitor and the image shuddering as he grabbed the floating camera. 'You let us all out or none of us! That is your choice, captain!'

Qayin turned the camera and let the captain and his crew see the hundreds of corpses floating through the cell block.

'This is what happened, captain,' Qayin's voice echoed through the bridge as he swept the grisly scene slowly with the camera. 'This is what your governor did to us. And now you think that I ask too much, to be freed from this place?'

Qayin set the camera in the air before him as he spoke.

'It's time, captain, to make your choice.'

Qayin sent the camera gently flying up alongside him as he scaled steps that climbed to the top tier of the prison block, then caught it and pushed it down the gantry as he walked past the cells. He twisted it so it faced sideways to its plane of motion, the view on the monitor changing to sweep past the cells one by one.

Inside each cell, variously standing at the gates or cowering on the thin mattresses, were the captured correctional officers and marines

'These are your people are they not, captain?' Qayin challenged.

Idris ground his teeth in his jaw but did not respond.

'Fine looking gentlemen,' Qayin taunted, 'honourable, upstanding, Word abiding men.' He chuckled. 'All of them, except one.'

The camera was stopped in front of the last cell on the tier and Idris almost rushed at the camera as his voice boomed out across the bridge.

'No!'

There, in the cell, was a woman. She was sat on the bed with her back to the wall, her legs pulled up against her and wrapped in her arms. Her long auburn hair was draped across her legs, her body covered only by the thin, stained sheets of the bed. From her bare shoulders, feet and arms, it was clear she was naked beneath them.

'Yes,' Qayin replied from out of shot. 'Say hello to your wife, captain.'

The woman on the mattress looked up, her face stained with grime and tears, her hair matted against the sides of her face.

'Meyanna,' the captain gasped, his whole body trembling as he gripped a stanchion for support, his gaze fixed upon the image of his wife.

'She survived, captain,' Qayin mocked him. 'For now, anyway. I have not yet decided how best to use her. Should I have her tortured and killed, like C'rairn? Or maybe I could let the men have their way with her, all fifty three of them.'

The captain's complexion paled as he slumped against the stanchion. Andaim rushed to his side and helped him right himself as Qayin's voice echoed through the bridge.

'And then I had an idea, captain,' Qayin said. 'I thought to myself, let's do all three. Alpha?!'

Idris looked up at the monitor and the image swivelled toward the main entrance to the block. There, walking through the cell block, was Alpha Zero Zeven.

Andaim's voice sounded meek as he whispered low enough to ensure that Qayin would not hear him.

'They're going to use Alpha again. She can't deceive them this time.'

Qayin's voice echoed through the bridge once more.

'You saw fit to ask my men to kill me, in return for an amnesty captain,' Qayin sneered. 'Now I will kill your wife if you don't extend to us all the same courtesy.'

*

Alpha Zero Seven strode down toward the cell block, the arc welder in her grip as she stepped between the corpses floating in the control tower and out into the block proper.

As Qayin had promised, the hostages had been installed into the cells once more, his men accessing the power lines and rigging the cell gates to open and close via the control panels in the tower.

There was no noise, not like the cell block used to be. Once, before the blast and the riot, the cell block had been a constant source of noise on the rare occasion she had passed through under armed guard before the Atlantia had left dock and she had been sent into solitary stasis. Breathing, shouting, swearing, sweating men confined to their cells. It had never been as quiet as it was now.

She walked across to the centre of the block and looked up at the tower, where two of Qayin's men watched her through the smoked–glass windows. One of them pointed up to her right, to the top tier, and she turned and headed for the stairs. She heard the sound of Qayin's voice sniggering out across the lonely cell block as she reached the stairs, and she let her boots fall heavily on the metal steps as she climbed. The steps clanged noisily, each stride echoing back and forth up and down the block until she reached the top tier and turned onto the gantry and listened to Qayin's voice.

'Now captain, I can't speak for myself but I suspect that many of my men, cooped up for so long in here, would like to get to know her much better, don't you? So we'll have to leave something alive for them. They won't appreciate tainted goods now, will they?'

The convicts on the gantry parted for her, their eyes fixed on her metal mask. She saw from the corner of her eye the hostages, incarcerated in the cells they had once guarded, their gazes filled with fear as they watched her walking alive and unconstrained in the cell block.

She reached Qayin, who stood back and grabbed a camera that was floating in the air before him. He turned it and pointed it at her.

'You remember Alpha, don't you captain?'

She heard from the camera's microphone the captain's voice, tinny and small.

'Don't do this.'

'Why not?' Qayin asked with an airy rhetoric. 'You're not giving me a good enough reason not to, captain.'

'If you kill her, you remove the last reason for me to not cut you all loose.'

'The *last* reason?' Qayin asked, his eyes widening. 'So the other thirteen hostages mean nothing to you captain, a mere inconvenience to you, are they?'

'You'll murder them all!' Idris yelled. 'You're a killer, nothing more. You cannot be trusted!'

Qayin grabbed the camera and stared into it. 'I'm a killer,' he agreed, 'and I cannot be stopped.' He turned the camera back to the cell. 'Unless you do my bidding, captain.'

Qayin glanced at Alpha and nodded.

She turned and walked into the cell.

Fear. It had a unique scent, rank and shameful. It poisoned the air in the cell, tainted the body of the woman curled upon the mattress. She could see that Meyanna Sansin's ankles were restrained. Her wrists were likewise cuffed, and a thin coiled–metal binding attached those cuffs to the ones at her ankles.

Alpha approached the bed and Meyanna looked up again as she sensed the approach. Alpha saw pure terror flush pale and sickly across Meyanna's face as she realised who was occupying the cell with her. Alpha heard the cell door slam shut behind her with a crash that echoed throughout the block as Meyanna's sudden, choking sobs filled the cell.

'Please, let me go.'

Alpha loomed over her and activated the welding arc, a fierce blue–white flame roaring into life. Above the sound of the arc she heard the captain's voice on the camera's microphone as Qayin poked it between the bars of the cell.

'Leave her alone!'

Alpha reached down and yanked the sheet aside, hurling it behind her as she leaned down and grabbed Meyanna's arm. She turned to one side so that the camera could clearly see what she was doing and then jabbed the welder at Meyanna's body. The fearsomely bright arc welder clicked and hissed as it hit Meyanna's skin and seared into her body as though it were not even there.

The smell of burning flesh stained the air as Meyanna screams soared out of the cell and shrieked across the cell block, her body writhing in agony.

'All right!'

Alpha barely heard the captain's horrified, agonised plea from the camera. She pulled the welder away and turned as Qayin spoke.

'What was that, captain?'

Meyanna had slumped down onto the mattress, the flesh of her arm seared with a hideous lesion of cauterised flesh several inches long, her body shaking and her sobs muffled as she buried her face into her shoulder.

'All right,' came the captain's voice again, choked with sobs in harmony to those of his wife. 'I'll open the hatches.'

Qayin grinned and turned the camera back to face himself.

'Congratulations, captain,' he murmured. 'For the first time today you're saving lives instead of taking them. You will open up the main hatch from the prison into the Atlantia. I and my fellow convicts will be allowed out first, upon which time you may send men to recover the hostages.'

'No,' Idris gasped, sounding out of breath. 'The hostages are to be released before anybody else.'

'No deal!' Qayin snapped and then looked at Alpha. 'Cut her again!'

'No!'

The captain's voice was both a roar and a cry, sharp and loud enough that Alpha did not move.

'The convicts first,' Qayin insisted. 'No negotiations, captain.'

'Very well,' the captain whispered, his voice scoured of defiance. 'The convicts may leave first.'

'We will remain armed,' Qayin informed the captain. 'We wouldn't want you shooting us all like rats in a barrel once we're aboard, would we now?'

Alpha heard the captain agree and then Qayin tossed the camera casually over his shoulder. It floated out over the cell block, tumbling as it went.

'Get the men ready,' he ordered Cutler, and then shouted across the block loudly enough for the convicts to hear him. 'It's time to leave!'

A rally of cheers soared through the block as Cutler turned and hurried down the gantry and the convicts freed the hostages, yanking them out of their cells and hauling them away with shouts of glee.

Qayin looked at Alpha. His glare bored deep into her eyes and he spoke slowly.

'Nicely done,' he said. 'Patch her up and then move her.'

Qayin grinned broadly and then walked away.

Alpha turned to Meyanna's huddled, rocking form.

She grabbed the sheets and draped them across Meyanna's shaking body and then turned to the cell door. The camera had tumbled out over the abyss of the cell block, spinning as it went, and collided with the corpse of a convict.

Alpha began stripping out of her uniform.

***

XIII

'You cannot do that, captain!'

Hevel was standing on the bridge, his hands behind his back and his pallid skin glistening in the dim bridge lighting.

The captain leaned against the stanchion, dragged a weary hand across his face. 'And why is that?'

Hevel paced toward the captain and dropped his voice.

'Give them their escape and before you know it they'll have the helm. It's suicide to let them in here.'

'And murder if I don't,' Idris snapped back. 'They have my *wife.*'

'You think that they'll let her go once they're aboard?' Hevel challenged. 'They won't give her up. She's their only leverage over us, her and the other hostages. Letting them aboard saves their lives but gives us nothing.'

'Tell that to the hostages!' Idris growled. 'You would have me abandon them all to their deaths?'

'Do you think that Qayin and his thugs won't try to take control of the vessel once they're aboard?' Hevel pressed. 'We have no means of housing them securely and not enough armed troops to contain them. There are murderers among them, thieves. Just what do you think's going to happen when you open that hatch?'

'Fourteen innocent people won't die!' Idris yelled back. 'Tell me, Hevel, would you be so bold were it *your* wife held by those murderers and thieves?'

Hevel stepped back from the captain.

'No,' he replied. 'I would be bolder. I would go in there and take them back.'

'I don't believe that for a moment,' Andaim snapped. 'You do have family in there, don't you Hevel?'

'I don't care to think about it,' Hevel uttered.

'One son a politician, the other a convict,' Andaim said. 'Qayin and Hevel, cut from the same cloth.'

'We are nothing to each other,' Hevel snapped, 'and we share no traits.'

'Yet you murdered hundreds at the flick of a switch,' Andaim pointed out. 'Just the sort of callous act that Qayin was imprisoned for.'

Hevel did not reply, his features twisted in frustration. Jerren pointed up to the monitor nearby.

'Sirs, you need to see this.'

The captain turned and saw the camera moving again on the screen. The mask of Alpha Zero Seven briefly appeared to fill it. Then the camera was turned and showed her naked flank as she glided away from the corpse of a convict floating high in the cell block.

'What the hell is she doing?' Hevel asked out loud.

Nobody answered, every man on the bridge enraptured as the video showed Alpha glide back into Meyanna's cell. The camera swivelled over to point at Meyanna and then they saw Alpha approach her, the arc welder back in her hand, Meyanna staring wide eyed in horror at the naked, masked woman as she toward her.

'Stop!' the captain yelled.

They heard a shriek as Meyanna cringed away from the brightly flaring arc welder, and then silence as the fearsome device sliced through the wire joining Meyanna's wrists to her ankles. Moments later, Meyanna gritted her teeth, her eyes squeezed shut and a muffled cry of agony reaching the camera's microphone as Alpha used the welder to slice through the cuffs on her wrists.

They fell away, bright globules of molten metal tumbling through the air as Alpha tore them free, Meyanna's wrists scorched by the blue–white flame of the welder. Alpha moved to her ankles and moments later they too were free.

'She's cutting her loose,' somebody said.

Alpha turned and let go of the welder. Her masked face approached the camera and stared at it in silence for several long seconds.

Captain Sansin spoke, his voice clear on the bridge.

'I can see you.'

Alpha turned and grabbed the captain's wife, hauling her off the mattress and propelling them both out of the cell. Alpha grabbed the camera and carried it with her as they flew out over the cell block, Alpha pushing off the floating bodies of dead inmates and directing both her and Meyanna toward the opposite tier's access door.

'She's heading for the prison hull's stern,' Idris said. 'What's back there?'

'Storage units,' Andaim replied, 'alongside what's left of the engine bays.'

'What now?' Hevel asked. 'What the hell is she going to do?'

The captain shook his head.

'I don't know, but whatever it is we had better be ready. She wants an amnesty and by the Word I'll give it to her if she gets those people out.' He turned to the security detail. 'Alert Bra'hiv's men in the shuttles!'

The soldiers turned and dashed from their posts as Hevel spoke up.

'She cannot be trusted,' he insisted. 'She is a convict.'

'I know,' the captain replied. 'But we can handle one convict far better that we can control fifty of them, agreed?'

'You were not so adamant about mounting an assault until your wife was presented with a means of escape, captain,' Dhalere purred alongside Hevel. 'Are we to understand that all other citizens aboard the Atlantia are second class when compared to...'

'This is not the time, Dhalere,' the captain snapped. 'I have my hands full enough without accusations of favouritism clouding the waters further.'

'Dhalere's right,' Hevel growled. 'Your wife now has a chance of escape, but what about all of the others in Qayin's hands? They are being taken to the bow, are they not?'

'One thing at a time!' the captain shouted. 'I cannot control everything that happens aboard the prison, but I can remove the most powerful bargaining tool they have.'

'And save yourself from the grief that others may suffer in your stead?' Dhalere asked.

The captain scowled at her and turned to Andaim.

'If Qayin and his thugs find out what Alpha's doing they'll tear her to shreds, and the other hostages with her.'

Andaim, his hands behind his back, tensed a little and raised his chin.

'I can join Bra'hiv. Maybe we could use this to join forces with her and get all of the hostages out?'

The captain nodded. 'Do it, right now.'

'Alpha should be left behind with the rest of them,' Hevel insisted. 'She has no place on...'

'Belay that,' the captain said, and looked at Andaim. 'Do not put my wife's life at risk, but if you can liberate Alpha then please do so.'

Andaim nodded and without another word marched off the bridge.

Hevel, flushed with impotent rage, turned his back to the captain and stared at the monitors.

*

Alpha pulled Meyanna along behind her as they crossed to the aft cell block exit, the same blast door that Evelyn had entered through hours before. She swung her legs out in front of her, her bare feet bumping against the cold metal walls over the gantry

'What are you doing?'

Meyanna's voice was weak and she was shivering, her arms wrapped around her body and her wrists smeared with dry blood.

Alpha said nothing as she set the video camera in mid–air and gestured for Meyanna to go inside. Meyanna hesitated, her eyes wide with fear as she stared into the half–darkness, the lights flickering sporadically and illuminating a dangerous path.

'I don't want to go in there if...'

'Hey!'

Alpha whirled and saw two convicts appear at the control tower entrance, both of them carrying pulse rifles.

Alpha grabbed the door with one hand and Meyanna with the other and propelled her through as she heard the convicts shout again and start running toward them. A salvo of shots blasted out and hit the doorframe near Alpha's head, a shower of searing plasma sparks raining down painfully on her back as she hauled herself through the door and pulled it shut behind her.

The heavy door slammed shut with a deep thump that echoed through the gloomy passage behind her as she locked the door from her side. The faces of the convicts loomed up in the observation window and she heard them screaming at her through the dense glass.

'What the hell are you doing?'

Alpha pulled her uniform from where she had wrapped it around her waist and tied it around the manual security lock, pulling it tight and then tying the legs around the nearest wall brace.

Alpha grabbed the camera and pointed it briefly at the two convicts, hoping that the signal from the device was strong enough to reach the Atlantia's bridge, then turned and pushed herself off the door and sailed down the tunnel straight past Meyanna.

The captain's wife, faced with no option but to follow her, pushed off in pursuit.

Alpha floated rapidly down the passageway, glancing over her shoulder to see Meyanna a few feet behind her. The security door receded into the flickering gloom behind them but Alpha could hear the convicts fighting to release the door from the far side, her uniform preventing them from opening the latches enough to get through.

The bangs echoed in pursuit of them as they floated through the chilly darkness.

'Are you going to kill me?'

Meyanna's voice reached Alpha's ears. The tone suggested that Meyanna was more than aware that Alpha did not intend to kill her, the question born more of nerves than doubt. Alpha did not respond, floating through the flickering darkness and feeling the air grow colder as she reached the security door that entered the storage unit.

The glass was frosted with ice particles on the far side, still chilled to the temperature of deep space from when she had evacuated the chamber of air and killed the murderous convict who had pursued her inside it. Alpha swung her feet to arrest her glide as she reached the door, then moved aside as Meyanna slammed awkwardly into the wall alongside her.

Alpha turned to the external control panel and opened the air–bleed vents into the storage unit. A humming sound reverberated through the darkened corridor as air was re–introduced into the storage section.

A dull, distant blast echoed through the tunnel, and Alpha knew that the convicts had broken through the security door and were heading her way. They had probably blasted it open by shooting one of their plasma magazines wedged into the door. She looked at the security door viewing panel, saw the frosting gradually starting to melt, angular pieces of ice fracturing off the glass and floating away.

Voices echoed down the passageway and in the flickering lights she saw figures running toward them, shouts as they were spotted.

'They're coming!' Meyanna shrieked.

Alpha turned and grabbed the door's manual release, braced herself against the wall and then yanked the mechanism into the open position. The higher air pressure of the corridor prevented her from pulling it open. Meyanna pushed herself off the wall opposite and grabbed the handle with Alpha, bracing herself against the wall and pulling hard.

A rush of air was sucked into the storage unit as the door's seal was broken and it suddenly swung open as the near–vacuum inside the storage unit sucked in a great rush of air from the passageway. Alpha shot through the doorway and tried to maintain her grip on the handle, but she was dragged with too much force and felt her hand wrenched away as she was hurled through the darkness and slammed into the rear of the unit.

Meyanna was sucked through the doorway and tumbled toward Alpha, who pushed herself clear just as Meyanna thumped into the wall alongside her. Alpha pushed off the wall as the last of the vacuum was replaced with air from the passageway and saw the dead convict's body floating high in the unit, his muscular body frosted with ice and surrounded by a grim halo of blood that had leaked from his corpse in the low pressure vacuum.

She pushed off the deck and floated up to the grisly remains, grabbed them as she rotated her body and then pushed off the ceiling toward the open security door.

Two pulses of plasma energy crackled as they zipped through the open door and exploded against the wall near Meyanna as shouts echoed loudly into the storage unit.

'Give it up Alpha, there's nowhere to hide!'

Alpha slammed onto the deck with the convict's body, then reached up and pulled the security door closed. The latches clicked loudly as the manual locks shot into place. Then she lifted the dead convict's body and pushed both of his arms through the locking wheel, jamming them in place as the convicts outside in the passage slammed into the far side of the door.

She saw the grimacing faces of several inmates leering at her and Meyanna's naked bodies as they fought for a glimpse.

'Let us in and we'll be gentle with you bitches!' one of them sneered.

Another, stronger voice broke through.

'I say let's send them out into space.'

Alpha heard Meyanna gasp in horror as an older, heavily scarred convict appeared to sneer at them through the window, his bioluminescent tattoos pulsing weakly.

'You open up,' he said, 'or we'll blow the vents again from here.' He smiled, his teeth stained yellow and black. 'You got one minute.'

***

92

XIV

'We're out of here!'

Qayin strode into the control centre and reached out for Governor Hayes' bloodied head, lifting the bloated and grisly trophy by its thin grey hair and hoisting it aloft to the convicts amassed around him.

'The governor is dead!' he roared. 'Long live the governor!'

The convicts let out a blustering crescendo of ragged cheers as Qayin slung the severed head over his shoulder to hit a wall with a wet thud somewhere behind him.

'I want every single man armed,' he boomed as he lifted a pulse rifle and the uniform filled with plasma magazines. 'If the captain tries anything the hostages get blasted into oblivion, understood?'

Qayin unwrapped the uniform filled with ammunition magazines. More cheers as the men swarmed upon the ammunition and began arming themselves.

'They'll try to herd us in,' Cutler snapped at Qayin. 'Chances are they'll keep closed all but one of the access passages. We'll be funnelled into a holding area and shot like rats in a barrel.'

'Not with the hostages behind us,' Qayin soothed. 'We blow them all away if the captain's troops screw with us.'

'Suicide,' Cutler snarled with a grim smile. 'Better that than be left to rot in here.'

'I like the way you're thinking,' Qayin replied with a wicked grin. 'The captain will want his wife alive and we'll make sure he can't have her. Once we're in the sanctuary she'll be our guarantee of safe passage.'

'Until what?' Cutler challenged. 'What happens if the Word finds us? The captain's lost his stones and won't fight. We should take the bridge and the ship for ourselves.'

'You think that you got a say in this, Cutler?' Qayin snapped.

'It's my life on the line too.'

'Don't worry about it. As long as we've got Meyanna Sansin, everything will be…'

'Qayin!' A convict burst into the control centre, his face flushed with panic.

'What?'

'Alpha! She's got the captain's wife!'

Cutler shot Qayin a look of wild dismay as Qayin stormed toward the convict. 'What do you mean she's *got* her?'

'They're running aft!' the convict said.

Qayin cocked his rifle and turned to Cutler.

'I'll find them. As long as she's still in our hands, the captain won't dare try anything.'

'This is heading south already, Qayin,' Cutler growled. 'It ain't gonna work if we lose the captain's wife.'

'You got any better ideas, old man?' Cutler swore under his breath but said nothing. 'The convicts out first, Cutler,' Qayin went on. 'Keep the hostages behind you so that they can't be grabbed by the captain's marines, understood?'

Cutler nodded and followed the other convicts now rushing out of the bridge for the for'ard hatches. Qayin dashed in pursuit through winding, half–lit passages to the transfer bay at the bow. The convicts were amassed around the hatches and huddled against one wall with the hostages, their wrists bound and rifles pointed at their heads.

'Open the hatch!' Qayin yelled.

A pair of inmates slung their rifles over their shoulders and deactivated the hatch's locks before spinning the locking wheels and pulling the door open. It swung open to reveal the docking tunnel, and at the far end an open hatch leading into the main hull.

The convicts backed away from the door, their weapons once again held ready as Qayin moved to stand in plain view in the hatch entrance. He peered down the tunnel, and glimpsed the movement of marines tucked either side of the Atlantia's hatch.

'We've got the captain's wife and she's rigged to blow!' Qayin boomed. 'And the hostages will remain behind us! Any of you try and pull anything, we'll blow her to hell and take every last one of you suckers with us!'

Qayin's mighty voice thundered down the tunnel. He stared at the amassed troops awaiting them on the far side for a long moment, and then he stood back and looked at his fellow inmates.

'Get in there, all of you!'

The convicts flooded into the hatch, their boots hammering the deck as they plunged into the passageway connecting the two hulls. Whispers of excitement fluttered among them as they ran and Qayin slapped them on their backs one by one as they filed into the tunnel and vanished.

Cutler brought up the rear, his own rifle cradled in his grasp.

'You better bring that bitch back here fast, or this will all be over.'

'Don't worry,' Qayin grinned. 'She'll be aboard before you know it.'

Qayin slapped Cutler on the back, propelling him toward the tunnel as he turned to the cowering hostages.

'On your feet, all of you, now!'

As Cutler entered the tunnel the hostages clambered to their feet, their weary faces lined with stress and their eyes downcast. Qayin turned and looked down the tunnel at the dirty little flood of convicts running toward the troops on the Atlantia's side.

'Unto doom do they flee,' he uttered under his breath.

He saw Cutler running, the old man glance back over his shoulder. Something changed in Cutler's expression, his eyes locked on Qayin's, and in an instant the old man knew. He opened his mouth to shout a warning but it was far too late.

Qayin reached out and with one huge arm he hauled the hatch shut, the heavy door slamming with a boom that resonated through the passage. Through the thick glass viewing panel he saw the troops at the far side of the passage likewise slam their hatch shut, trapping the convicts inside.

The convicts panicked and opened fire, the bright plasma blasts hitting the distant hatch door in halos of wasted energy that spilled onto the tunnel floor. Their cries of panic filled the tunnel as the convicts turned and began running in a horrified mass back toward the prison hull.

Qayin spun the locking wheel closed, sealing it tight. He saw the look of utter disbelief on Cutler's scarred old face that mutated into a grotesque howl of rage. The old man reached the hatch and hammered on the viewing panel, his mouth agape as he screamed at Qayin.

Qayin turned to the hostages and jabbed his thumb aft. 'Move, now!'

The hostages turned and shuffled in the indicated direction.

'Faster!'

Qayin slammed the butt of his rifle into the back of the nearest officer and sent him flying through the exit.

***

XV

Alpha turned away from the door and set the camera in the air to point across to the wall of the storage unit. There, set into the wall, were the two capsules that she and her deceased fellow convict had used to survive the blast in the high–security wing. One was damaged beyond repair, the screen shattered.

Alpha pushed off the wall and grabbed Meyanna, dragging her toward the undamaged capsule.

'What the hell are you doing?' Meyanna protested.

Alpha spun Meyanna around and shoved her backwards into the capsule. Meyanna's face fell as she understood what Alpha was attempting to do.

'No,' she gasped, and then: 'What about you?'

Alpha pulled the restraints loosely about Meyanna's ankles and across her waist and then looked up at the captain's wife. She was older than Alpha but attractive, and had a gleam of intelligence in her eyes that all academics shared. The prison physician, Alpha recalled: she had met her briefly for a routine medical after the mask had been fitted, to make sure that it was not causing her what had been termed *undue discomfort*. She remembered what the captain's wife had uttered without interest after a cursory examination. *She'll live*.

Alpha turned her back to Meyanna and hoisted the capsule's lid up off the floor. As heavy as it was in normal gravity, the lid flipped up easily and Alpha pushed it into place. Still connected to the ship's power supply, the capsule re–activated and the lid sealed shut.

Alpha opened a panel on the front of the capsule, and with a few simple commands had re–charged the capsule's oxygen supply and batteries. She closed the panel and stood back, turned to a larger panel on the wall beside the capsule and entered a launch command.

She heard Meyanna's voice through the capsule window, muted by the thick glass.

'What about you?'

Alpha looked at the capsule and its occupant one last time and then she hit the launch button.

The capsule hissed as it sank back into its docking cavity, and a shield door slammed shut as it sealed the cavity off from the storage unit. Alpha heard a clunk as ejection bolts fired, saw a puff of vapour inside the cavity as the air was sucked out into space, and then saw Meyanna's face shrink away as the capsule was ejected.

Moments later, Meyanna's eyes still fixed on Alpha's, she saw the capsule turn as Meyanna fired the thrusters and propelled herself for'ard toward the safety of the Atlantia.

The security door clanged and Alpha turned as she heard a dull crunch. The dead convict's arms twisted awkwardly and a shard of bone punched through the dead man's skin as his limbs were broken. The door shuddered, then the corpse slipped from its position and the door swung wide and six convicts tumbled into the storage unit, their rifles raised and pointed at Alpha.

*

'She's away!'

Jerren's voice was charged with a volatile mixture of exhilaration and disbelief as the bridge crew watched the capsule being ejected from the storage unit, a tiny white speck shining in the light from the nearby star as it turned and began drifting through space toward the Atlantia.

'She got Meyanna out,' Captain Sansin uttered.

Her turned, as did every other man on the bridge, to the monitor that still showed the footage from the camera in the storage unit. Several armed inmates stood with rifles aimed at Alpha's diminutive, naked form. The masked woman stood her ground, making no effort to conceal herself.

'They'll finish her off,' Hevel said, his face touched with a maniacal hint of excitement.

The captain shot the councillor a strange look.

'Are our troops in position?' he asked Jerren.

'They're manning the hatches now sir, and the shuttles are in position aft of the prison hull.'

'What about the convicts?'

'Most of them are trapped back in the prison hull again sir,' came the reply. 'It worked – they kept the hostages behind them.'

'Where are the hostages now?'

'We can't account for them,' Jerren replied. 'And, sir, we cannot find Qayin.'

'He'll kill them,' Hevel sneered. 'Qayin will kill them all!'

The captain gripped the bridge railings more tightly as he surveyed the monitors. 'Wait until I give the order. Nobody moves until we know where the hostages are.'

*

Alpha stood in silence as the lead convict, his teeth stained yellow and black from decay, edged toward her, his rifle pulled tight into his shoulder and the barrel pointed squarely at her chest.

'Now then, missy,' he sniggered, 'best you lay down on the floor for old Tammer, eh?'

She remained silent and still. Tammer stopped moving, smart enough to keep the barrel of his rifle out of her reach.

'I said down, now!' Tammer screamed at her.

She did not move.

One of the other, younger convicts behind Tammer handed his rifle to the man next to him and walked up alongside Tammer.

'I don't think she's taking to you so well, Tammer,' he smirked. 'Cover me.'

The armed convicts moved to keep their weapons trained on Alpha as the younger man approached her.

'No sense in fighting us,' he soothed. 'Better to play along than be dead, right?'

She kept her head facing forwards, but her eyes swivelled to watch the approaching convict. He reached out and his hand clasped her right arm.

'Easy now,' he said as he reached out for her with his other hand.

Alpha made to move away from his touch, and he jumped forward.

Instantly she jerked her head back and then slammed it forwards into the convict's face, the metal mask smashing his nose sideways across his cheek as a cloud of blood globules spiralled away from him. The convict growled and staggered sideways and then the other convicts were upon her in a frenzy.

She felt herself tumble backwards, her feet off the ground as they all charged in at once and grappled her down onto the deck. She landed hard beneath their weight, the metal deck cold and painful as it dug into the flesh of her back.

She tried to fight, but she was hopelessly outmatched as they gripped her arms and legs and stretched them out, pinning her on her back with her legs spread.

Tammer smiled as he set his rifle aside in mid–air and strode until he was standing between her legs. He reached down and unbuttoned his fatigues.

'Now then missy, you'll thank me for this one day,' he chortled as he shuffled himself free of his prison uniform and knelt down between her legs. 'Hold her tight, lads,' he warned the other convicts with a chuckle. 'We don't want her to miss anythin'!'

She remained still as he leaned over her, one hand supporting himself beside her head as he dropped down and his lips closed around one of her nipples. He groaned as he sucked hard on it.

'Hurry it up, Tammer,' one of his companions snapped. 'We all want some!'

Tammer licked her nipple and looked through the slits in her mask as he pushed himself against the cleft between her legs.

'Say hello to old Tammer, missy,' he breathed.

A shadow passed over Alpha and Tammer, blotting out the light, and suddenly the old man was lifted away from her and he screamed in pain as his hair was pulled rigid against his scalp.

She saw Qayin's towering form loom over them as the big convict reached up with his other fist and drove his knuckles deep into Tammer's throat. Tammer's thorax collapsed with a crunch as the old man gagged and choked. Qayin hurled the old man aside as the convicts released Alpha and leaped away from Qayin.

'We was bringing her to you,' one of them said.

'Change of plan,' Qayin growled.

He grabbed Tammer's pulse rifle from where it hovered and fired it in one smooth motion, the charge bursting from the barrel and hitting the convict square in the chest. A blackened, sizzling cavity smouldered in his body as his face fell limp and he slammed to the deck in a cloud of blue smoke.

The convicts began screaming as Qayin fired again. Alpha turned and grabbed the nearest man to her, then smashed her face mask into his nose with all of her might. The convict tried to pull her hair but she butted him repeatedly and his eyes rolled up into their sockets as his arms fell limp.

She yanked the rifle from his shoulder and turned it on the convicts as they screamed and scrambled to bring their weapons to bear on Qayin.

The last two fell together, their bodies twisting in violent spasms as super–heated plasma charges seared their flesh and they fell to the deck.

Qayin moved over to each of the fallen inmates and fired one last blast into their bodies before he turned and looked at Alpha.

'Did Meyanna get away?' he asked.

She nodded, her rifle in her grasp and pointing at Qayin. The big convict looked down at the weapon and then his dark eyes flicked up to meet hers. Alpha took a pace toward Qayin, and then she flipped the rifle up and deactivated the magazine with a flick of one finger.

Qayin grinned at her and turned, shouting down the corridor behind him.

'This way!'

Alpha stared in amazement as fourteen hostages, their faces drawn and weary and their gaits awkward, stumbled into the storage unit. Most of them shrank away from Qayin, hugging the walls as they spread out. Only the three marines maintained a manly bearing, their faces fixed in defiance. Qayin turned to Alpha, who was staring at him from behind her mask. Qayin's grin faded as he shrugged.

'What can I say?' he uttered. 'I'm a pragmatist.'

'Bastard!'

Alpha turned and saw Cutler charging down the tunnel toward them at the head of twenty or so convicts, his rifle pulled into his hip as he opened fire. She hurled herself clear of the blasts as they exploded through the hatch, flying through the air to hit the far wall as the shots sprayed searing plasma bursts behind her. Qayin fired at the open hatchway but was forced to fall back as the convicts took up defensive positions in the corridor and opened fire en masse, showering the storage unit with blasts of energy.

'Stay back!' Qayin yelled at the hostages as they cowered behind beams and in tight corners.

The big convict fired several more rounds down the corridor and then grabbed the door. His immense bulk hauled the door shut as rifle blasts smashed into it and he slammed the locking mechanism in place.

He turned and looked at Alpha's shattered escape capsule. 'No more of those left?'

Alpha shook her head.

Qayin turned and saw Cutler standing on the other side of the door. There was no longer any rage on his features, no emotion of any kind that Alpha could detect. Instead, there was only a cruel delight.

'Goodbye, Qayin,' he grinned.

Alpha saw Cutler turn to one side and access the control panel that she herself had used to evacuate the chamber. He reached out and put his hand on the evacuation lever.

'You pull that lever,' Qayin said, 'and you'll rot in that prison forever.'

Cutler, the other convicts now amassed behind him, shook his head.

'Like I said,' Cutler smiled, 'suicide is better than surrender.'

He yanked the lever.

***

XVI

The vents in the storage unit screeched as they opened and Alpha saw a halo of frosted air form in billowing clouds around the vents as the air was vacuumed out into oblivion. A freezing chill enveloped her in its embrace and she felt her eyes bulge as the air pressure plummeted and she was lifted off her feet toward the vents.

A vice–like grip clamped around her ankle as she saw Qayin grab her, his teeth gritted as with his other hand he gripped the security door handle, his muscles bulging and trembling under the load. Two of the hostages were yanked from where they crouched and slammed into the vents, screaming as the vacuum of space froze their skin and tried to drag them physically into the vents and out into deep space.

Alpha saw the air crystalizing before her very eyes, felt all sensation drain from her limbs in the bitter cold, and then the rush of air stopped as the vents suddenly slammed shut. The two hostages pinned against the vents dropped onto the deck. Qayin sagged as he collapsed to his knees and with a great blast of noise and flame one of the vents was blasted from the wall and spun across the unit.

Alpha, suspended in mid–air, saw heavily armoured marines tumble into the storage unit, their weapons trained before them, faces shielded and sealed against either vacuum or toxic fumes and their black uniforms weighted at fifty per cent gravity, making them nimble yet subject to the vessel's magnetic quasi–gravity.

'Hands behind your heads!'

Alpha twisted in mid–air as the marines aimed their weapons at Qayin, and with an effort she shielded the big convict with her body and shook her head vigorously.

Another blast and the security door was blown aside as an explosive charge detonated, and through the smoke Alpha saw Cutler and the convicts fleeing into the depths of the prison hull as the troops turned their full attention onto Qayin.

Alpha sprawled her naked body across Qayin's, shielding him as best she could as the marines swarmed around them, weapons aimed down at her. She looked up into the eyes of the nearest man and saw something in his expression. The trooper raised his hand, holding his comrades back, and then he leaned closer to her.

'Hello again,' he said, his voice muffled by his breathing apparatus. 'Officer C'rairn at your service, ma'am.'

He held out one black–gloved hand to her, and she stared at him for a long moment before she reached out for it. C'rairn gently pulled her to her feet. She looked over her shoulder at Qayin, and then at C'rairn.

'Seriously?' C'rairn asked, looking down at the huge convict.

Alpha nodded once. C'rairn shrugged and looked over his shoulder.

'Arrest this man, but don't harm him.'

Qayin was hauled to his feet and manacled as in the distance Cutler's men were chased down by the marines in the nearby passage to the sound of shouts and energy pulses. Another officer, bearing the shoulder insignia of a lieutenant and with his dark eyes fixed upon Alpha's, spoke into a microphone.

'Bra'hiv, cease fire and pin the prisoners between yours and the Atlantia's troops. We need to get them back in their cells, right now.'

The gunfire ceased immediately.

Officer C'rairn reached down to his utility belt, filled with pouches, and from one he pulled a thin silver rectangle of material that unfolded seemingly endlessly into a thermal blanket. He reached out and wrapped Alpha in the blanket, covering her body.

Through the slits in her mask, Alpha watched C'rairn work to ensure that she was properly covered. As he adjusted the blanket on her shoulders, she reached out and grabbed his forearm. She squeezed it once, firmly.

'I hear you,' C'rairn smiled. 'Just be ready. The rest of the crew isn't going to see you like I do.'

*

'I hope you know what you're doing.'

Hevel's whisper was just audible to the captain as he watched the shuttles touch down in the Atlantia's landing bay. The shield doors closed behind them and the bays filled with air and warmth again, the warning claxons falling silent and the bay lights turning from red to white to properly illuminate the two craft.

'So do I,' the captain murmured in reply as several marines opened the access doors to the landing bay.

Idris followed his marines into the bay as the shuttle's rear ramps lowered and the hostages were marched off by Bra'hiv's men. Among them was a masked woman wrapped in a thermal blanket, apparently unafraid of the troops and weapons arrayed around her, and beside her a giant convict, his gold and blue hair swaying as he walked with his huge muscular arms clamped in manacles that seemed too feeble to contain him.

'What the hell?' Hevel uttered in horror.

Captain Sansin watched as the liberated hostages were led quickly away within a protective shield of armed guards, leaving just Alpha Zero Seven and Qayin surrounded by their escort. Beside the captain stood his wife, who had rapidly dressed in a trooper's fatigues after docking her escape capsule and joining her husband.

The marines around the captain did not move, their weapons trained on Alpha Zero Seven as she walked toward them, but he could feel the rising tension as she and Qayin approached. The featureless mask betrayed no emotion and her strides were controlled, fearless beneath the shapeless thermal blanket that was wrapped around her, her bare feet tiny on the metal deck. Alpha Zero Seven, flanked by Officers C'rairn and Andaim, walked to within a few feet of the captain and then stopped. Idris was momentarily surprised by her diminutive size, but the blood stains smearing her mask and the soft skin of her neck reminded him of what she was capable of.

Qayin looked past the captain at Hevel and a grin fractured his features.

'Brother,' he growled. 'I'd say it was a pleasure, but it isn't.'

Hevel said nothing. Idris watched Alpha but she did not move, as though she were a statue, the mask hiding all emotion.

Idris stepped toward her, staring into the shadows behind the mask.

'You seek amnesty,' he said, uncertain of how to speak to this bizarre and dangerous woman.

To his amazement Alpha shook her head, and then turned and nodded toward Qayin.

'You seek amnesty for *him*?!' the captain gasped.

Qayin smiled brightly. 'What can I say? I don't know where I'd be without her.'

'He tortured my people!' Idris protested. 'He threatened my wife and...'

'I *had* to,' Qayin snapped. 'If I didn't make it look like I was willing to kill, then none o' those suckers would have followed my lead. We got your wife out of there, captain. We got *all* of your people out of there. The least you could do is cut us a break.'

Captain Sansin moved to stand in front of Qayin and had to crane his neck up to look the convict in the eye.

'I didn't see any evidence of *we*, Qayin,' he snarled back. 'You would have abandoned her just as you abandoned your fellow convicts in that passage.'

Qayin's right eye twitched. 'What have you done with them?'

'They're back under lockdown,' the captain replied. 'My quandary now is whether to leave them in their cells or just detach the entire linkage and let them sail off into space to die.'

'They're men, not animals,' Qayin said.

'You could have fooled me.'

The captain turned to look at Alpha. 'As for you, I'm at a loss.'

'I'm not,' Meyanna said behind her husband. 'She saved my life. The very least you could do is cut that monstrosity off of her face.'

Alpha's masked head turned to look at the captain.

'I don't know,' Idris said. 'She could…'

'That's not possible,' Hevel interrupted. 'She was masked for a reason, by the Word, to prevent her from corrupting others!'

Hevel lurched forward and reached out for the thermal blanket covering Alpha. He tore it from her shoulders. Alpha stood naked but for the mask sealing her face. The captain looked down at her naked body, tiny amid the hulking marines with their heavy weapons pointed down at her, and for a moment he felt a tremor of pity.

'Leave her be,' he ordered.

'She's a convict!' Hevel shouted.

'And a victim,' the captain growled back.

Hevel scowled but he stepped back from Alpha. The troops too backed away, their circle expanding outward from Alpha as she drifted slightly off the deck. She hovered, entirely naked once again, her features concealed behind the mask and her skin forming pimples in the cold air. She showed no sign of shame or embarrassment as the men stared at her body.

Officer C'rairn knelt down and picked up the blanket, draping it over Alpha's shoulders once more.

'Now,' the captain responded, 'we put her in the one place where she won't want to do any damage. We need to be able to talk to her.'

Hevel looked at the captain. 'You're going to take off the mask? That's an insubordination of The Word!'

Idris nodded as he replied and pointed to C'rairn. 'Take her to the sanctuary! And don't give her any clothes for now. I don't want her able to conceal any weapons.'

*

The troops walked fast, Alpha drifting in mid–air with her hands and ankles bound in steel restraints. Gloved hands, rough against her skin, guided her left and right through various passageways, most of which looked much the same: functional, dull grey metal, harsh ceiling illumination.

She glimpsed more appealing corridors to her left and right from time to time, probably crew's quarters, more comfortable than the course she was being led upon. She figured that they were using service corridors to prevent her from seeing too much of the rest of the Atlantia.

The troops escorted her to a large, heavily armoured door. She waited in silence as two men, rather than open the large door, instead opened a smaller side panel. A tubular, smooth sided tunnel gaped into darkness at her as one of the troopers extracted a concave shaped cradle that fitted smoothly into the tunnel.

'Get on it,' the marine called Bra'hiv ordered her.

Alpha saw in her mind's eye a fleeting image of the capsule in which she had been trapped, and for the first time since she had awoken she hesitated.

'Put her in!' Bra'hiv growled.

Strong arms removed her restraints and lifted Alpha off her feet. She felt herself tilted horizontal and had to force herself not to struggle. The troopers lowered her into the cradle, the plastic surface cold against her skin, and then they backed away as without another word she was slid into darkness and the panel door slammed shut behind her.

It happened in a breath–taking rush. The air was sucked from the shaft in a deafening roar and she opened her mouth to scream as she realised that she was being sucked out into space. Visions of convicts bleeding from eyes frozen solid by the chill vacuum of space flashed through her mind as her scream was trapped deep in her throat and she coughed.

She rocketed down the shaft, sliding on her back as the deep blackness within the tunnel consumed her and she reached out to try to hang on to the surface, but it was slick with some kind of lubricant. A bright light shot into view and she hurtled through the air and plummeted down into a tangle of vines and foliage.

A waft of warmth rushed across her skin, the air fresh and clean, touched with long–forgotten scents of rain and lush foliage. Despite herself Alpha gasped, her chest swelling and her breasts rising as she sucked in a lung full of the wonderful aromas. The sound of rushing water filled her ears, her back wet where it lay on soft, sodden soil as she looked up and saw a bright, perfectly blue sky peppered with white clouds.

She sat up and stared about her, realising that there was natural gravity here.

She was sitting on a large mound of soft soil and grass, probably placed there on purpose to protect the landing of whatever goods were sent down here from the rest of the ship. The tunnel from which she had been fired was in the centre of a soaring cliff, the hatch that sealed it hissing shut, virtually invisible against the rocks.

Alpha got to her feet, felt dampness on her cheeks and was mildly surprised to realise that she was crying. The air was touched with vapour and she looked to her right to see a waterfall plunging from great cliffs above her into a deep, clear pool. The cliffs extended away from her toward what appeared to be a vast, forested valley.

A flock of winged animals fluttered through the sky high above her head, chasing and wheeling through the warm air near a rainbow cast in the vapour from the waterfall, and she realised that for the first time since she had awoken she no longer felt cold.

Slowly, as though she were dreaming and feared that any sudden motion would exterminate the illusion, she stepped down off the grassy mound and walked to the edge of the pool, its surface shimmering in the light from the sky. She dipped her foot into the water, gasped at the warmth and plunged into it as though it were the first time she had felt it upon her skin.

The warmth consumed her, enveloped her in an embrace that drew a broad smile across her lips beneath the mask. She twisted and turned in the water, rubbed her hands across her body and drenched her filthy hair, splashed it up under the mask until it stung her eyes. For a moment, just a blissful second, she forgot about the ship around her, the prison, the hostages and the hellish cell block and let the water cleanse her soul and carry her away from all that she had come to loathe.

'Hello.'

She started at the voice, coughed as the perfect water flooded her throat as she lost her balance and her heavy mask almost dragged her under the water. She spun and saw a man standing on the shore nearby, watching her.

She touched her feet down beneath her in the water but remained submerged up to her neck as she stared at the man. He was taller than most, over six feet, and not more than thirty years old. Glossy black tangles of hair framed a jaw that was perhaps a little too wide, broad shoulders bearing the epaulettes of an officer, probably a soldier or pilot of some kind. He stood with his hands behind his back, watching her quietly.

'The water,' he said finally. 'It feels good?'

She stared up at him, cautious of any response, but she realised that she recognised his voice: the officer who had ordered Bra'hiv's men to stand down and allow Cutler and his fellow convicts to escape. Somehow, something about this man told her that she had nothing to fear.

She nodded, once.

He smiled. 'My name is Andaim. We need to talk.'

***

DEAN CRAWFORD

XVII

Andaim stepped down to the water's edge, his dark blue Colonial uniform resplendent in the daylight and his eyes clear. No hint of deception, no shadow of hubris. He extended one hand toward her, the other holding clothes bundled under his arm.

'Come, please,' he said. 'You can't bathe properly with that monstrosity on your head. If you try to swim you'll sink and I'll end up talking to your feet.'

Now she froze. She heard her breathing against the metallic surface of the mask, felt again the pain where it rubbed, the sore skin where it pinched her head, the things that she had for so long managed to push to the back of her mind now seeming unbearably painful.

Andaim reached out more closely for her.

'Please. Enemy or friend, that horrible thing must come off somehow. Let me help you. Meyanna is waiting.'

She hesitated, watching him through the slits, and in some small part of her mind she realised that she did not actually now know if she wanted to remove the mask. For so long it had been a shield behind which to hide from a cruel and uncaring universe.

'You can't hide forever,' Andaim said, as though reading her mind. 'You'll be better off without it. Or would you wish to be silenced forever more?'

She stared at his hand, and then slowly she reached up and took it.

Andaim pulled her gently toward him and she walked up and out of the water. Andaim's eyes remained fixed upon hers, never once drifting down to her body as she stood on the bank, her skin glistening in the sunlight. He handed her the clothes, a white hooded robe, and politely turned his back to her as she quickly dressed.

'This way,' Andaim gestured, when she was ready.

She followed him, walking along the bank as they skirted the edge of the beautiful pool. More birds fluttered through soaring tree tops as he led her down a winding path through a lush forest. The sunlight cut through the canopy far above in shafts of shimmering gold that dappled the foliage around them, the ground beneath her feet soft as she walked.

'The whole interior of the Atlantia's for'ard hull rotates,' Andaim explained as they walked, 'a shell within the body of the ship. The rotation produces acceleration equal to normal gravity, keeping our feet on the ground.' He pointed up to the sky above them. 'Just as well: the birds would be in chaos otherwise.'

The path led out of the forest and up a hill until Andaim stopped on a ridge. She joined him and found herself overlooking a plain, swaying grasses sweeping across the valley around them, and beyond mountain ranges soaring to untold heights. To their right, the shore of a vast ocean stretched away into infinity. She walked past Andaim and cast her gaze across the beautiful vista, smelled the odour of the ocean and felt the cooler breath of the mountains.

Scything across the plain, a river shone in the sunlight like liquid metal as it drained toward the ocean.

'Impressive, isn't it?' Andaim asked.

She nodded, elated at the sheer spectacle. Somewhere in her mind she knew that it was all an illusion, the sense of scale a wonder of technological know–how and optical trickery, but still the child within her wanted it to be real enough that her brain suspended its disbelief.

'Here,' Andaim said. 'I have something for you.'

She turned and Andaim gestured to a reclining chair set near the treeline, beside which stood Meyanna. Alpha saw beside the chair a device not dissimilar to the welding torch she had been given to torture Officer C'rairn with. The memory cautioned her and she did not move.

'It's a laser cutter,' Meyanna explained. 'It'll get through that mask in no time, if you'll let me.'

She hesitated still, staring at the chair.

'You have to be debriefed by the lieutenant,' Meyanna said, gesturing to Andaim. 'We thought it would be easier for you here than in the holding cells, and you can't speak with that horrific thing on your head.'

Andaim turned to her. 'Can you trust me, even though you don't know me?' She looked at him as he went on. 'You would not have been brought here to be harmed. Far from it, in fact. We know what you did. You saved lives. You know what the Word says: an eye for an eye, right? That works both ways.'

Andaim turned and walked across to the chair. He picked up the laser cutter and tested it, the sharp clicking noise sounding out of place amid nature's elegant harmony around her.

Andaim looked at her expectantly, and she walked toward the chair.

'Just lay down,' Meyanna said as she took the cutter from Andaim. 'I'll be as gentle as I can.'

She sat down on the edge of the chair, careful not to turn her back to them, and then swung her legs up onto the chair and lay back. Andaim sat beside her and then reached out and carefully took the mask in his grip. Meyanna moved the cutter close to her face, and then pushed Alpha's head gently so that she was forced to look away from them.

The cutter clicked loudly and she smelled an acrid stench of burning metal and saw thin wispy clouds of blue smoke smoulder up into the air above them as Meyanna worked.

'It's a mechanical lock,' Andaim said as Meyanna cut through the mask. 'Very simple, very solid, impossible to cheat. I've heard each of these masks comes with a unique key which is held back at the colonies. No other way for us to get this thing off, I'm afraid.'

Meyanna continued working, coughing and resting occasionally as the fumes became too dense. Alpha's neck was beginning to ache as Andaim held her head in place but then she heard something crack, felt heat against the back of her neck.

'Stand by,' Andaim said.

She tensed, waiting, and then she felt her skin hiss and a terrible pain sear her as the cutter broke through the metal brace securing the mask to the back of her head. Instantly, Meyanna stopped cutting as Andaim grabbed a cup of water from beside him and poured it across her neck, the water icy cold. She felt the pain recede immediately, felt a dizzying sense of relief as Andaim gripped the brace and pulled it away from her skin.

'One more to go,' he said.

Meyanna went to work again, this time tilting Alpha's head back so that she could attack the brace beneath her jaw.

The cutter clicked, the metal hissed and spat dense fumes, but the thinner metal of the jaw brace yielded more quickly than the one behind her head, and within a few minutes Andaim was dousing the slim wound on her neck with the icy water.

She felt suddenly nervous as he lifted the brace away, and a pain that she had forgotten existed beneath her jaw suddenly vanished. Meyanna set the cutter down beside them and then pulled the brace out of the way. She looked down at Alpha through the slits in her mask, and smiled.

'Okay, you ready?'

Alpha swallowed thickly and was suddenly very conscious of the metalwork against the inside of her throat, sore and dry. Andaim saw her throat move and nodded.

'We'll do that first.'

Andaim reached out and his fingers brushed her lips gently as he took a firm hold of the metal probes. 'Tilt your head back further,' he instructed, 'and we'll do this in one smooth go, no hesitations okay?'

She tilted her head back, felt her throat constrict as the metal pressed against it and then relaxed as she positioned herself where the resistance was the weakest.

'Okay,' Andaim said, 'on three. One. Two…'

She wretched as Andaim pulled hard on the metal probes sooner than she anticipated, and they were yanked from her throat along with what felt like half of her tongue before she could react or prevent him from moving. She glimpsed the probes flash past in front of her eyes and a trail of scarlet–tinted saliva that glistened in the sunlight as Andaim hurled the probes to one side.

She rolled off the bench to slump on her hands and knees on the grass. She coughed up bile, her throat feeling as though it were on fire. Her breath rasped in her throat and wheezed in her chest as she blinked tears from her eyes, and as her vision cleared so she stared at the grass beneath her.

Gone were the slits and the black metal.

She felt cool air on her cheeks, on her eyes, in her hair where it caressed her like the gentle touch of a mother's hand. She blinked and saw the plain grey metallic interior of the mask on the grass beneath her where it had fallen.

She stared at it, unable to move from where she knelt.

Meyanna's hand appeared, and in it was a cup of water.

Alpha grasped for the cup and threw it to her lips, drained it as though it were the only remaining water in the universe. It quenched her thirst and caressed the inside of her throat, cold and clear. She felt the tears that spilled down her cheeks but she did not hide them as she poured the next cup of water that Meyanna handed her across her face, felt it touch skin that had long since been dry and sore.

As she knelt, her eyes closed and her face tilted up to meet the sunlight, she heard Andaim's voice close by.

'Please tell me,' he said. 'What is your name?'

She opened her mouth to speak and her voice cracked, a feeble whisper that seemed to struggle up from somewhere deep inside to flutter free for what felt like the first time in aeons. Her voice sounded alien to her own ears.

'My name,' she rasped, 'is Evelyn.'

XVIII

Andaim mouthed the name silently as he watched her.

'You are an incredibly brave woman, Evelyn,' Meyanna said as she packed away the laser cutter. 'What you did back there in the prison hull saved a lot of lives, including mine. It makes me wonder why you were ever made to wear that mask?'

Evelyn slowly rolled onto her back on the grass, revelling in the warm sunlight that caressed her skin and the relief of damp water in her throat, a soft smile touching her lips as she lay with her eyes closed.

'I don't care to remember,' she replied, her voice still rough.

'We care,' Andaim said.

She turned her head to look at the officer, her brow furrowed. 'Why?'

'You risked your life to save others,' Meyanna said. 'How could we not care?'

Evelyn watched the two of them for a few moments.

'I am a convict, a killer.'

'Are you?' Meyanna asked. 'We've see nothing to suggest you're anything other than a human being.'

Evelyn frowned. 'I can't remember.'

'You may have had your memory altered,' Meyanna said. 'We just don't know much right now, not after what happened. We don't know half of what the Word may have been up to before...'

Meyanna broke off.

'Ethera?' Evelyn asked. 'Caneeron?'

It was Andaim who replied, shaking his head. 'Gone,' he said. 'Or at least the people are, long lost.'

'The planet we're orbiting,' Evelyn said. 'I saw it.'

'We're not on the colonies now, Evelyn,' Meyanna explained, and a realisation began to dawn in her expression. 'Just how much do you remember?'

Evelyn frowned, her eyes becoming vacant for a moment. 'Nothing,' she said, and then whispered: 'Just sadness.'

Meyanna looked down at the tiny woman before her. 'That's something we all remember. Every last one of us.'

Meyanna picked up her bag and turned away. Evelyn made to get up and follow her but Andaim reached out and rested a hand gently on her forearm.

'It's okay,' Meyanna said as she looked back. 'I have to attend to the hostages, but Andaim will stay here in the sanctuary with you for now. I'll be back as soon as I can.'

Evelyn watched as the captain's wife walked away.

'Why did you ask for amnesty for Qayin?' Andaim asked her. 'He's a real killer, maybe the most dangerous man aboard this ship.'

Evelyn sighed and looked out over the plain. 'He's misunderstood.'

Andaim almost snorted a laugh. 'I'll say. If you don't remember anything, how can you say that about Qayin?'

Evelyn blinked. 'I don't know, I just... I understand him, but I can't remember why.'

'That won't hold up in a court.'

'Not much a convict says does,' she replied. 'So I learned.'

'What the Word thinks of you doesn't hold sway here on the Atlantia. Practicalities are what matters and you earned yourself a lot of respect, in my eyes anyway.'

She watched him for a moment, and then closed her eyes again and turned her head back toward the sunlight.

'So this is why Qayin wanted to escape to the Atlantia so much,' she said. 'This is what he called the sanctuary.'

Andaim nodded, looking around.

'The only way to get service officers to work here,' he replied, 'is to give them something worthwhile. The sanctuary is the official name. We just call it the garden, as some of it is used to cultivate crops for food and to re–process water supplies.'

Evelyn lay in silence for a while, listening to the falling water and the sound of birds calling in the trees.

'Did you set the bomb that destroyed the high–security wing?' Andaim asked abruptly.

'There was a bomb?' she asked, sitting up.

'You didn't know?'

'I heard Qayin say that there was a blast,' she replied, 'but I didn't know for sure it was deliberate. When I first awoke I was in the escape capsule and the high–security wing was already destroyed. There were other survivors but the Atlantia opened fire on them.'

'So we heard,' Andaim said, 'and you killed at least one of them. We found his corpse in that storage unit.'

'It was him or me,' she said. 'I don't want to talk about it.'

'Well you're going to have to talk about something, because right now half the civilians are up in arms screaming about how they've been thrown out of the sanctuary in favour of a convicted murderer. We don't even know for sure if one of them didn't cause the blast on purpose, and the Word could arrive at any moment.'

Evelyn looked up at him, concern etched into her features now. 'The Word?'

Andaim sighed as he looked at her.

'The Word cannot have scoured your memory that much,' he said. 'You've been in stasis so long it may take a while to recall everything. The Word was effectively our government, a legion of micromachines whose collective intelligence exceeded anything that humans could achieve and enabled us to attain technological supremacy over neighbouring species.' Andaim picked at the grass as he spoke. 'The Word decided, at some point, that we had become a hinderance to its pursuit of knowledge and power. It broke out, infected mankind and eventually brought about our downfall.'

Evelyn took a moment to digest what Andaim had said. 'It pursues us, now?'

'Always,' Andaim said, 'forever.'

'Do we have any defences active?'

Andaim snorted derisively. 'A handful of Raython fighters, plasma cannons and assorted small arms. The Word could be using any one of the fleet's cruisers or capital ships to hunt us. We don't stand much of a chance.'

Evelyn looked at the sanctuary around her for a moment and then made her decision.

'The prison hull's fusion core is damaged and exposed,' she said. 'If we can retrieve it…'

Andaim's eyes locked onto hers. 'How do you know?'

'Saw it,' she said, 'before I re–boarded the hull. It's spraying energy out into space. It's no use to us now as propulsion, but as a weapon it could be invaluable.'

'No use to *us*?' Andaim echoed with a slight smile.

'We're all human,' she replied.

Andaim thought for a moment. 'The captain believes that the Word might be aboard the Atlantia, or at the very least somebody sympathetic to its cause. We fear that it might be behind the blast.'

'You say that the blast that killed the other high–security prisoners was sabotage,' she pressed. 'Why not head back there to investigate and quietly pick up the core at the same time? The Word will never know what you've done, and nor will anybody else on board.'

'And if the target of the Word is you?' Andaim pressed.

Evelyn glared at him. 'The Word put me in that mask and in that prison,' she snapped. 'You want me to show you how I feel about the Word? Take me right to it.'

***

XIX

'It makes sense,' Andaim insisted.

Captain Sansin sat in his chair, his head resting on his big hands as he stared at the viewing screen that showed the horizon of the planet curving through space before them, a perfect ring of soft blue light against a deep darkness.

'The fusion core isn't a weapon,' he pointed out, 'and if it's fractured it could as likely destroy us as the Word.'

'It could destroy us while it's hanging off the back of the damned ship!' Andaim snapped, and then drew himself back, 'sir.'

'The prisoners are still trapped over there,' the captain added. 'If we remove the fusion core they'll lose what little power they have. They'll die within a few short hours.'

Andaim ground his teeth in his jaw but he nodded. 'I'm aware of that captain. They would have to be housed aboard the Atlantia if this is going to work.'

Andaim saw Hevel and Dhalere emerge onto the bridge, the councillor's face twisted with outrage once more.

'Captain,' Hevel stepped up onto the captain's platform, his face grim. 'I have just been informed that the entire civilian population has been ejected from the sanctuary in favour of a convicted murderer. I, and they, would like an explanation.'

'The civilians will be returned to the sanctuary shortly,' the captain replied.

'That's not what I asked,' Hevel snapped. 'Our people are cooped up in the loading bays while Alpha Zero Seven is lounging about in the sanctuary. Do you have the faintest idea what that's doing to morale and...'

'To hell with the civilians' morale!' Andaim snapped. 'This is about survival! Perhaps those civilians that you claim to represent might like to volunteer their services in the military now that we're the last damned human beings in existence?' Andaim drew closer to Hevel. 'Perhaps *you* would?'

Hevel lifted his chin. 'My duty is to the people.'

'A politician's duty is always to himself,' Andaim shot back.

'Captain?' Hevel wailed. 'Have this man arrested and...'

'Silence!'

The captain's roar seemed to echo around the bridge. A silence descended in its wake, the only sound the soft beeping of computer terminals. The captain stood up and looked out of the viewing ports at the hull behind them, dragging the crippled prison hull and its trail of flickering debris.

'We have no choice,' he said finally. 'Any weapon, no matter how unstable or dangerous, is better than no weapon at all. The prisoners in our care may be the key to fighting back.'

Hevel gaped at the captain. 'I don't believe that I'm hearing this.'

'Two years ago we would not have believed that we would be the last surviving humans,' the captain pointed out, 'but it happened. We cannot risk the future of our species over our prejudice and fear. Even those convicts back there in the prison would likely understand that.'

Dhalere's quiet voice echoed through the bridge

'Did they understand that when they ran riot after the blast?' she asked. 'Did they understand that when they murdered seventeen correctional officers? Did Qayin understand that when he decapitated Governor Oculin Hayes?'

'They likely thought that they were in danger of dying,' Andaim replied. 'They were right, weren't they?'

Hevel straightened his jacket. 'Evacuating the air from the prison hull was the only way to quell the insurgency,' he snapped. 'If it had not been done the prisoners would likely have been in control of the ship by now.'

'Sure,' Andaim replied. 'You're a real hero.'

'The protocol was sound,' Dhalere replied for the councillor. 'Lieutenant, if we don't maintain at least some of the structure of our society aboard this ship then before we know it there will be nothing but anarchy. We won't need to worry about the Word finding us, because we'll already be lost.'

'We don't have time for pedantics,' Idris said. 'We need all available hands to man this ship: men, women, children, even convicts. If we do not all pull together, we will die together.'

'Poetic,' Hevel sneered. 'And if we release the convicts and they decide not to pull together after all, then we shall still die together, or at least at the hands of criminals who have no interest in preserving our lives or even their own!'

The captain turned and faced Hevel.

'Your opinion has been noted, councillor,' he rumbled. 'I'll remind you that the bridge of this ship is a military concern, not a political one. If you do not remove yourself from it this instant I'll have you arrested, and you can then share your opinions and ideas with the cell mates of the prisoners you killed when you ordered Governor Hayes to evacuate the air from the prison cell block.'

Hevel glared at the captain, and then he spun on his heel and stormed off the bridge.

The captain waited until he had gone and then turned to Andaim.

'How long will it take you to extract that core?'

Andaim shrugged. 'Evelyn said that it was...'

'Evelyn?'

'Alpha Zero Seven, sir,' Andaim explained. 'Her name's Evelyn. She said that the ruptured core was visible from outside the hull. If so, we need only seal it with drones and then extract it whole. Two hours, maybe three?'

'Can it be controlled?' the captain asked.

The fusion core was in effect a miniature star encased in a supremely strong container, an enormous quantity of matter compressed to unbelievable densities and capable of burning for literally hundreds of years until the density of the matter decreased sufficiently for the nuclear fusion reaction to cease. With the core ruptured and spraying highly radioactive material out into space, anything that came close to it would be exposed to a ray of energy bearing the unimaginable power of a star.

'We can shield it with a second core,' Andaim explained. 'Have it open upon automated or remote command like a sort of pulse weapon, but it'll be risky. A hair–line fracture in a core like that could widen and all we'd know about it would be a bright flash of light, then all our problems would be over and the Atlantia would no longer exist.'

Idris thought hard for a moment and then made his decision.

'Get to it,' the captain said, 'and get Evelyn out of the sanctuary. If the civilians can get back inside then it may release some of the pressure down there. I don't want Hevel whipping them into a frenzy.'

Andaim looked around at the bridge crew. 'There's nothing more he can do or say sir.'

The captain smiled grimly.

'Never, ever think that about a politician, Andaim. They always have something more to say.'

'Yes they do,' Dhalere said softly. She had remained behind after Hevel had stormed away. 'The civilians are afraid and confused. They have been placed in what amounts to prison cells while one of the most feared and reviled prisoners this vessel has ever seen wanders free in the comfort of the sanctuary. Can you blame them for becoming restless and frustrated with where they see the command of this vessel taking them?'

'That reviled prisoner,' Andaim snapped, 'has a name and a history and has already saved lives, and all that after nearly being vaporised by a bomb and then this very ship, under Hevel's orders. Do you think she would be so reviled were the civilians to learn of that?'

'I am aware of what she has achieved,' Dhalere replied, 'but none the less, she should not be favoured above those who are depending upon what we do for their survival.'

'Or ours,' the captain pointed out.

'And Evelyn?' Dhalere pressed. 'Perhaps your heroic murderer could be better put to use working on how to get that fusion core over here? An active role might shed her in a better light than simply locking her away and out of sight.'

'I thought that such prisoners could not be trusted?' Andaim challenged.

'And I thought you advocated for her and for allying ourselves with the convicts?' Dhalere replied. 'Isn't it time she got started and earned her place among us?'

Andaim bit his lip as Dhalere spun on her heel and strode from the bridge.

'Do it,' the captain said as she departed. 'Evelyn saw the damaged core, and it might appease Hevel and his little band.'

'I'm not in the appeasement business,' Andaim muttered.

'Nor am I, for much longer.'

*

Hevel prowled up and down his cabin, the narrow room confining his rage and his ambition.

The captain was a fool, of that he was certain. Hevel could not quite fathom where the sudden anger that he felt had come from, although the sheer frustration of being powerless aboard the Atlantia no doubt fuelled some of his rage. Once a powerful councillor, Hevel had been reduced to a mere cipher over the past couple of years, the Atlantia's crew disinterested in politicians and easily swayed by the mere mention of rank. He knew that they saw him as a mere irritation, somebody who was tolerated only because of a distorted sense of nostalgia for the old days, when government had mattered, when Hevel had mattered.

The captain would not have dared to bad–mouth him back on Ethera, especially not in front of a ship's entire command crew. The rage flushed hot through his veins and he thumped the wall. The captain was considering offering some kind of amnesty to common criminals, including his despised brother, Qayin: the idiot was actually extending an olive branch to murderers while pushing Hevel, a life–long servant of the colonies, to one side.

'Your opinion has been duly noted,' he uttered to himself.

The buzzer to his quarters beeped softly. 'Enter!'

The door hissed open and Dhalere walked in. Dhalere was an attractive woman whose entire family had been on Caneeron when it had been overrun by the Word. She used her work to prevent her from thinking about what had happened to them, and thus was always on the move.

'The civilians are being moved back into the sanctuary,' she reported. 'Alpha Zero Seven has been taken to the shuttle bay, presumably for some kind of mission.'

'The prison hull's fusion core,' Hevel said miserably. 'I think that they've got some idea of using it as a weapon.'

Dhalere frowned. 'Could it work?'

'Maybe,' he replied, 'but it could just as likely destroy us too.'

'That's dangerous,' Dhalere said, 'although no more dangerous than the Word.'

'Don't you start.'

Dhalere slid her arms about his neck and kissed him gently. 'Difficult times demand difficult measures,' she said.

'Don't they just.'

'You're concerned about your brother, Qayin?'

'He's a danger to everybody, including himself,' Hevel replied. 'The civilians will go insane when they hear of the captain's so–called plan for the convicts to be brought aboard the Atlantia.'

Dhalere nodded.

'Yes, they will,' she said. 'So perhaps you should not wait for the captain to reveal his plan to them?'

Hevel looked down at her, his rage forgotten and a rueful smile spreading across his lips. 'When did you become such an agile manipulator? You should have been a politician.'

Dhalere smiled. 'Better that they hear of the captain's insanity from their true leader, so that they are better prepared to act against him.'

Hevel felt his heart miss a beat as Dhalere's hand reached down and gently squeezed his groin.

'You're suggesting...'

'Mutiny,' Dhalere confirmed. 'The Word took everything from me and right now I don't give a damn about much, but I don't want a bunch of convicted rapists and murderers wandering around this ship. If I'm going to die it's not going to be at the hands of those bastards.'

Hevel's mind raced.

'We would need weapons,' he said. 'The captain's marines would...'

'Would not shoot civilians,' Dhalere interrupted in a whisper, her lips brushing his. 'You could storm the bridge without firing a shot, a bloodless coup. Bra'hiv's marines serve the colonies, not the captain. There are more than enough civilians willing to stand up and be counted alongside you, Hevel. The only question is whether you're willing to stand up and lead them.'

Hevel looked into her eyes, her gaze unblinking as she stared up at him with those limpid green pools.

'Do you think they would follow me?' he asked, his eyes feeling dry and his heart beating faster in his chest as adrenaline flushed hot through his veins.

Dhalere smiled again.

'You already have one mutineer on your side,' she said. 'Where one follows, so do others. Shall we begin?'

***

XX

'Are we absolutely sure the inmates are sealed in?'

Andaim's voice was tinged with tension as he guided the shuttle toward the prison hull, Evelyn watching from a jump seat in the rear of the cockpit. The craft was a simple, wedge–shaped design, capable of carrying four dozen personnel or troops in its hold and of atmospheric flight.

'All four linking passages have been disconnected and the prisoners are all on lock–down in their cells,' Bra'hiv confirmed from the co–pilot's seat. 'We've joined them together into a single longer passage and accessed an emergency hatch further down the hull beyond the reach of the prison population, in case we need to evacuate them in a hurry, but that hatch remains sealed for now.'

'What about access to the engine rooms?' Andaim demanded.

'Stilll sealed from the inside,' Bra'hiv confirmed. 'My men will guard that access point while you go in and obtain the fusion core, but without pressure suits no convict can approach you or Alpha Zero Seven anyway.'

'Her name's Evelyn,' Andaim replied.

Bra'hiv looked over his shoulder at her and shrugged. 'We'll cover you once the core is extracted, and fly it out for repairs and preparation aboard the Atlantia.'

Evelyn looked at Bra'hiv. 'Why not just pull the prisoners out first?'

'Because we can't risk any chance of them hijacking the mission and gaining access to the Atlantia,' Andaim explained. 'This way, if there's a problem then it's only us and Bra'hiv's team that they'll be able to attack and we can easily use the shuttle to escape.'

Evelyn watched as Andaim guided the shuttle aft alongside the Atlantia's enormous hull, toward the tangled bulk of the prison behind it. A cloud of spiralling debris tumbled slowly away from the hull's wake, and far below in the planet's atmosphere she could see tiny flashes of light as pieces of hull plating and other wreckage burned up.

The shuttle slowed as it entered the debris field and Evelyn looked out of the viewing port beside her at the hull, knowing that inside were at least a hundred dangerous men all hunting for any opportunity to escape their incarceration. With no hostages to bargain with they would attack at the slightest provocation and almost certainly fight to the death in their quest for freedom.

'The captain could be right,' she said as the shuttle rounded the prison hull's silent engines. 'Cutler and his men could easily be turned to our side, given the right incentive.'

'They won't,' Qayin said from where he was manacled in the rear of the shuttle with several armed marines. 'They don't trust him any more than they trust me. It'll be dog eat dog if they get chance to fight, each man for himself.'

'Wonderful,' Andaim said as he turned the shuttle toward a large, jagged black cavity ripped in the hull before them.

'There,' Evelyn said and pointed between Andaim's and Bra'hiv's shoulders. 'Out there, see that light?'

From the darkened interior of the hull a flare of distant blue–white light hovered like a lost star trapped among the wreckage, casting a narrow beam of light out into deep space.

'I see it,' Andaim said. 'I don't want to get the shuttle too close to that thing and besides it's too small in there. We'll have to dock out here and get inside. It could blow any moment if our thrusters destabilised it.'

'Wait,' Evelyn said, and pointed up into the darkened hull.

There, amid the torn girders and hull braces, a series of thick hull plates were torn outward like a gigantic metal flower, the petals reflecting the sunlight.

'That's where the blast happened,' Andaim realised. 'That's where the bomb was.'

'Yes,' Evelyn said, 'and look where it is, right inside where the high–security wing would have been.'

Andaim stared at the damaged hull plating for a moment before he replied.

'That was a highly restricted area,' he said. 'Only a few people would have been able to plant it.'

'And the captain's wife was one of them,' Evelyn said. 'She could have infected any one of the prisoners or staff.'

Andaim gripped his controls tighter but he did not reply.

'I'll get the men ready,' Bra'hiv said as he unclipped his seat harness, 'but for what it's worth, I don't think it likely that Meyanna Sansin is infected with the Word.' Bra'hiv turned and strode aft toward his men and Qayin.

Andaim looked over his shoulder at the big convict as he zipped up his environmental suit.

'I don't like having Qayin close by,' he complained. 'He's got nobody to protect but himself.'

'He's safer when you can keep an eye on him,' Evelyn pointed out as she pulled the visor of her suit down. 'Besides, I'm supposed to be a higher risk than he is, right?'

Andaim sealed his visor as he looked at her. 'Yeah,' he agreed. 'But you're...

'A woman?' she finished the sentence before he could.

'Trustworthy,' Andaim corrected her.

'What makes you think that?'

'Gut instinct.'

Evelyn smiled at him, and then a moment later Andaim hit a button on the control panel and the shuttle's rear hatch opened. The air rushed from the interior in a gust of ghostly vapour and then the troops unclipped their harnesses and made their way out of the shuttle toward the looming mass of twisted metal and impenetrable darkness.

*

The sanctuary was filled with civilians, flooding back inside after the removal of the mysterious prisoner Alpha Zero Seven. Whispers and rumours gusted across their ranks as Hevel walked with Dhalere into the sanctuary and was immediately greeted by a throng of concerned citizens: mothers herding nervous children, fathers with faces twisted in outrage, lost souls and teenagers who had seen their families wiped out.

All were looking at him, their voices commingled into one outpouring of grief and fear. Hevel called out to them, but the din of their voices drowned him out.

'Ladies, gentlemen, citizens, please listen to me!'

Hevel clambered up onto a grassy bank, his hands held aloft to catch the eye of people further away. Dhalere waited and watched among the throng as Hevel cried out over the heads of the crowd.

'I know how you feel!' he called, and the clamour of voices ceased as they strained to listen to him. 'I know because I feel the same. The commander of this vessel has lost his mind and is considering placing the rights of convicted criminals above those of honest citizens!'

A wave of righteous outrage soared from among the gathered citizens and Hevel waved them down, appealing with his expression and body language for calm.

'We cannot overpower them,' he said. 'We cannot start a war within a war and jeapodise our very survival at such a crucial moment in the history of our race! But I'm damned sure that we won't allow Captain Idris Sansin the chance to do that either!'

More shouts, waved hands and eyes ablaze with conviction.

'We should bring him down!' shouted one tall, bearded man. 'We're not second–class citizens!'

More shouts of encouragement and Hevel looked at the man.

'Indeed, but would you be willing to place yourself in harm's way as he does?'

'I'd give it my best shot!' the bearded man hollered back. 'So would we all!'

'Against the armed soldiers guarding this ship?' Hevel pressed.

'Yes, against them all!'

'Against the command crew who support him?' Hevel yelled.

'Yes, against them all!' shouted more people.

Hevel watched the crowd for a moment. 'Against the Word?'

The crowd fell silent and the bearded man spoke out. 'We cannot fight the Word, we're not strong enough.'

'That's right,' Hevel replied. 'We're not. Only a military force could fight back, could make a stand. Not us, and certainly not a rabble of criminals. We cannot take the captain's place, for we cannot do in his stead what he and his people can. We cannot take this ship by force, for it would be our own downfall. The captain and his crew are not our enemies, for they risk their lives to protect us all every day.' Hevel let his gaze sweep the watching citizens, now listening in their hundreds.

'Then what would you have us do?' asked the bearded man.

Hevel smiled.

'Walk with me,' he replied, 'to the bridge. What cannot be changed by force can be changed by guile and by the will of the people. *We* are the strongest force upon this vessel and our voice will be heard. Who will walk with me?'

The crowd shifted restlessly, citizens looking at each other for support and finding only anxiety and uncertainty.

Then, from the crowd, a woman called out.

'I will walk with you,' she said. 'I will follow the captain, but not into the hands of convicts!'

Hevel looked down at Dhalere, who had infiltrated the crowd as he spoke, as another woman shouted out her support, then another, then men, and from further back into the crowd, and before he knew it Hevel heard the commingled voices of hundreds of citizens shouting their support for him.

Hevel turned and strode down off the bank toward the sanctuary exits, the civilians following him en masse.

*

'They're inside.'

Captain Sansin watched as a viewing port displayed an image of the shuttle hanging in space alongside the shattered bulk of the prison hull, its rear ramp lowered.

'The sooner we get them out of there the better,' he said. 'Do we know what the lifespan of that core is?'

'It's been jettisoning energy into space for some time sir,' came the reply from Lael, 'but it should be good for many months yet. If we can hook it up to a fuelling cable and control it it will prove a valuable weapon.'

Sansin nodded. A fusion weapon was not something that the Word would be able to predict being used as a weapon aboard the Atlantia, especially as they were not used by the military at all. Fusion bombs were far in the history of the colonies, the technology used only for power–generation now. Directed energy weapons were possible but plasma charges were far more stable. Having that core in his hands represented the one opportunity for surprise that the Atlantia had, the one avenue to possible victory that...

'Sir, we've got a problem.'

The captain turned as Jerren called out. 'What is it?'

'Councillor Hevel sir, he's on his way to the bridge.'

'So?'

'Sir, the entire ship's compliment is behind him.'

The captain stood up and whirled to the bridge security team. 'Seal the hatches, immediately!'

The marines whirled to the doors, but before they could touch them they burst open as Hevel strode onto the bridge, the corridors behind him packed with civilians. Dhalere, his assistant, was by his side. The marines levelled their weapons at the intruders, backing away from them, but none of the armed men opened fire.

'What the hell is this?!' Captain Sansin roared, glaring at Hevel.

The councillor walked up onto the bridge and confronted the captain.

'This,' he replied, 'is the will of the people.'

'The will of the people?' Sansin echoed. 'Or the will of one very greedy man?'

'The prisoners,' Hevel snapped. 'They are still confined?'

The captain ground his teeth in his jaw but he did not reply. Hevel turned to the staff manning the bridge, to the marines aiming their weapons at him, and spoke loudly enough for all to hear.

'We are unarmed,' he said, 'and we do not wish to cause any bloodshed. But none of us will stand by and see our safety and security compromised by either the release of convicted and bloodthirsty criminals who have already tortured and killed our own people, or by the incompetent command of a captain who would put the lives of those criminals above the citizens and servants of our race.'

Hevel turned, surveying the bridge.

'You may shoot us if you wish,' he said to the marines, 'but you must shoot us all.'

The marines looked at the captain, who shook his head and gestured for them to lower their weapons.

'This is a mistake, Hevel,' he growled.

'No, captain,' Hevel snapped in reply. 'This is a solution.'

Hevel turned and waved Dhalere and several other civilians into the bridge. 'Take control of the command stations,' he ordered.

'This is a mutiny,' Sansin uttered. 'You're taking control of the ship?'

'You never *had* control, captain,' Hevel replied. 'We have fled for years across the cosmos, and what has changed in that time, captain? What has become of us? What have we learned? What have we done to improve our situation, to fight back against the Word?' Hevel shook his head. 'Nothing.'

'And what are you going to do, Hevel?' the captain asked. 'What can you do? We are helpless here.'

Hevel's mouth fractured into a grim smile. 'We have never been helpless, captain. You have merely been unable to help us to help ourselves, as is our right. Now, we shall take it. We shall fight back, right here.'

The captain's face turned to stone. 'We can't fight back, we don't have even nearly enough troops or fighters for a pitched battle against...'

'We will stand!' Hevel bellowed. 'And we will fight! We will run no longer! This is the will of the people!' Hevel turned to Dhalere. 'Do it,' he said. 'Cut the prison hull loose.'

'No!' Sansin bellowed. 'You do that and you'll kill everybody on board, including our own people!'

'They will evacuate using the shuttle,' Hevel snapped back. 'No convicts allowed!'

Sansin looked at his marines. 'Arrest this man, before it's too late.'

The soldiers wavered, looking back and forth between the captain and Hevel. Idris realised that Hevel's timing was perfect: Bra'hiv was absent, as was Andaim, and all of the convicts were back aboard the prison hull.

'Do it,' Hevel told the marines, 'if you must, but if you arrest me you must also arrest hundreds of citizens, for I act on their behalf and they will only replace me with another of their own.'

The soldiers glanced at the citizens packed into the corridors outside the bridge, and then back at the captain. Hevel looked at the bridge command crew, his voice carrying clearly to all of them.

'All of you are welcome to stay or to go,' he said. 'But you must choose whom you serve: your captain, or the civilians who depend upon your continued protection.'

The bridge crew looked at each other. Slowly, Jerren and several other officers walked away from their posts. Lael and Aranna remained. In response, the four marines lowered their weapons.

Hevel watched as they were disarmed by the civilians accompanying him, and then he turned to Dhalere. She looked down for a moment, studied the control panel before her, and then she flipped a series of switches.

'Order Bra'hiv and his men to evacuate immediately,' Hevel ordered.

Dhalere looked at him. 'If we bring them back here they may act against us.'

Hevel frowned, staring at the prison hull.

'If they refuse, shoot them down.'

'They're our troops!' the captain shouted. 'You're not saving lives, you're taking them!'

'They have the shuttle and they have a choice!' Hevel snapped back. 'I won't be extending the same courtesy to murderers, especially not Alpha Zero Seven.'

'You call them murderers,' Captain Sansin said softly, 'even as you murder them.'

Hevel ignored the captain and watched through the viewing ports as the tethers connecting the prison hull to the Atlantia were blasted free with explosive charges.

***

XXI

'Easy now.'

The engine room of the prison hull was not a large compartment like those aboard the Atlantia. It did not, in reality, have much of a propulsion unit, relying instead on whatever vessel it was tethered to for motion: another safety feature built in to its design that prevented prisoners from hijacking it as a means of travel.

The room was instead a series of huge pipes, tubes, transformers and pressure units, all of which had once channelled the immense power of the fusion core through the hull or converted its energy into electricity. The entire space was now enshrouded in darkness but for the fearsome flickering light ahead of them, reflecting off mangled beams and silently spiralling debris in the bitter vacuum.

The core was still buried deep inside the engine room, its blue–white beam having scythed a channel through its fractured core and then solid metal and hull plating to blast out into deep space. Evelyn glanced over her shoulder and saw two remote drones following Andaim toward the core. Both were equipped with mandibles and drills, able to operate closer to the core than any human would dare, although they too would be vaporised if they strayed into the beam of energy blazing from it.

'That's close enough,' Andaim said.

There was no noise in the vacuum of space and the core's blue–white light seemed almost calming and hypnotic to Evelyn as she stopped near the cover of a large, twisted beam of solid metal. Ahead, near the fusion beam, she could see endless ranks of hull braces illuminated in the glow, their tips glowing with molten metal where the beam had severed them.

'Okay,' Andaim said, his voice distorted over the intercom. 'Now the hard part. You ready?'

'Let's just get this over with,' she replied.

Andaim used a small hand unit to guide the drones past them and toward the blazing core, its light as bright as a burning star. Evelyn watched as the drones drifted toward the device, and then she felt rather than heard a series of deep, rolling booms echo through the hull from somewhere for'ard and the entire prison shuddered.

The core shifted and the blazing beam of energy seared through fresh metal high above them, globules of molten metal spilling like galaxies and spiralling through the engine room in all directions.

'Cover!' Andaim yelled.

A cloud of molten metal sprayed across one of the drones, melting its surface and severing control and power lines. The tiny drone spun out of control and hit the beam of light, vanishing instantly into a cloud of superheated particles.

Evelyn hauled herself tight behind the nearest beam as molten metal sprayed past her, just missing her environmental suit as Andaim crouched beneath a collapsed wall as glowing metal fragments showered around him and faded out as the brutal cold of space extinguished them.

'What was that?'

Andaim stared into empty space, listening rather than watching as the walls of the engine room stopped vibrating. He keyed his microphone.

'Bridge, Andaim, status?'

A hiss of static clouded the response. Evelyn felt a chill shudder down her spine as she watched Andaim try to contact the bridge twice again with no luck. She turned and pushed off the floor, gliding through the engine room to the aft hatches that led back toward the storage units and the cell block.

She sailed down the passage with Andaim in pursuit to where the three large windows stared out over the abyss of space between the ship and the planet, and her heart flipped in her chest as she saw that the planet was filling the windows, moving past them as the entire prison hull rotated in freefall.

Eve whirled to Andaim. 'We've been cut loose!' she yelled.

Andaim stared at her in disbelief. 'That's not possible! They wouldn't have done that!'

'We're loose,' Evelyn insisted. 'How long before we hit the atmosphere?'

Andaim grasped for his forehead with one hand as he tried to think straight, his gloved hand hitting his face visor.

'They would have ejected the prison hull using forced charges, to clear it from collision with the main hull. That would have slowed our orbit and be pulling us down faster and...'

'How long?' she interrupted.

'No more than a few minutes,' he replied. 'We've got to move, now!'

Evelyn followed Andaim back through the shattered remnants of the engine room and through a darkened corridor toward the storage units. Ahead, she saw a flare of light that faded out rapidly, and as they emerged from the tangled mess of the hull they saw the shuttle accelerate away toward the Atlantia, narrowly avoiding being hit by the giant rotating hull.

'No!' Andaim yelled.

Evelyn floated in space behind him as the shuttle shrank away to a tiny speck of light against the blackness, shining as the nearby star rose over the planet's horizon in a brilliant flare of light. Evelyn glanced down at the planet below, saw the light creeping across vast oceans and deserts below.

'They're gone,' she said. 'There's nothing that they could have done. We need to get back aboard the prison hull, right now.'

Andaim turned and drifted toward the prison hull again, this time accessing the vents into the storage units. Evelyn closed the vents behind them and followed Andaim down to the security door. Together they managed to push the door open enough to let a tiny trickle of air into the storage unit, which became a blast as the low–pressure vacuum sucked air from the corridor into the storage unit in ever increasing volumes.

The door swung open easily and Andaim yanked off his visor as he turned to Evelyn.

'Bra'hiv abandoned us!' she said as she pulled off her own visor.

'Something must have happened aboard Atlantia,' Andaim replied. 'Hevel, most likely.'

'Why?' Evely gasped.

'I don't know,' Andaim replied, and then fell silent as a new noise reached them from afar.

The sound of voices and clanging bars rang out as the incarcerated prisoners, realising what had happened, began battering at their cell doors, their commingled voices a hymn of human panic.

Eve pictured the prison hull from the outside and its shape, size and mass.

'How much of the hull will survive re–entry?' she asked Andaim.

He looked at her quizzically.

'Not much. She'll mostly burn up in the atmosphere, break up into smaller pieces. There won't be much that will hit the ground intact.'

'But some will,' Eve replied, and looked up at the cells. 'The hull will self–orientate for re–entry, right?'

'Standard procedure,' Andaim agreed. 'She'll still have enough fuel and power to right herself. That's probably what's already happening if she's rotating.'

'We've got to move, fast,' she said. 'Release the prisoners.'

'Do what?'

'Release them!' Evelyn snapped. 'They're dead if we don't take them with us!'

'Take them where?'

'I've got an idea,' she said.

Evelyn sprinted away down the corridor toward the cell block, Andaim following her until they reached the block itself, the clamouring of the prisoners almost deafening as they burst out onto the gantry.

Eve ripped off her boots and her environmental suit as Andaim ran for the control tower, and then pushed off the gantry until she hit a corpse. She pushed it aside and raised her arms and hands, looking at the cells until she had the eye of every inmate and their anguished cries faded into expectant silence.

'Listen to what I have to say,' she called out. 'Don't interrupt, because we'll be dead in a few minutes if you don't do exactly as I say.'

The inmates watched her, none moving, Cutler's eyes boring into hers from his cell as she spoke.

'We've been cut loose,' she said, fully expecting another broadside of rage, but the inmates remained silent and still. 'The hull will not survive re–entry into the atmosphere intact and we have no idea what or whom might be awaiting for us down there. Our only chance is to hunker down in the engine bay and hope for the best. To do that, we must free you all.'

The inmates watched her silently and she went on.

'We are enemies,' she said. 'We hate each other. But right now the only way we can survive this is if we work together. In a moment, Andaim is going to open the cell doors. I want all of you to make your way aft to the engine rooms that have not been breached, quickly but without panicking. The sooner we're back there, the sooner we can protect ourselves. Any questions?'

Cutler stood forward, lifted his chin.

'Why would you free us, just so we can kill you?'

Eve grinned without warmth.

'If you're stupid enough to kill the people who save your life, then likely every other inmate here will skin you alive right after, Cutler. So you go ahead and take your best shot. On the other hand we could open every cell door here, except yours…'

Cutler ground his teeth in his jaw but he said nothing. A soft but audible ripple of grim chuckles fluttered among the other inmates and Eve knew that she had them, at least for now. She turned and nodded at Andaim in the control tower.

Andaim adjusted the controls and with a mighty clatter the cell blocks opened as one. Eve rolled upside down alongside the nearest corpse and then pushed off it, back toward the gantry and her gravity suit and boots. She yanked them on just as the prisoners were floating over the tier balconies and moving toward her en masse.

She zipped up her suit but forced herself not to reach for her pistol as the inmates touched down all around, their eyes upon her.

'How come the mask is gone?' one of them asked her.

'That way,' she snapped back, jabbing a thumb over her shoulder at the exit. 'Move, now!'

The inmates turned as one and glided with admirable smoothness toward the exit. Cutler drifted by her, his icy little eyes fixed upon hers as he floated past, and then Andaim appeared from the control tower.

'That's it,' he said as he joined her. 'What the hell are we going to do with them now?

Eve was about to answer when a deep voice rumbled like boulders toward them.

'Leave that to me!'

They whirled to see Qayin appear on the gantry, his towering form stooping through the exit. A rush of hateful gasps rippled among the convicts and Qayin sneered at them.

'Whine all you want,' he growled, 'but Hevel just mutinied and cut us off. If we'd been aboard the Atlantia he'd have had us all shot on sight instead. Only reason you're all alive is 'cause of me.'

'What the hell are you doing here?!' Eve asked.

'Hevel,' was all that Qayin said.

'Where is the captain?' Andaim asked.

'Under guard,' Qayin replied. 'Hevel's taken the ship, threatened to shoot Bra'hiv down if he did not abandon you here and return to the Atlantia. He didn't have much choice but to leave.'

'Damn,' Andaim growled. 'I knew it, Hevel will kill us all.'

'You had a choice,' Evelyn said to Qayin. 'Why didn't you go back too?'

'Hevel would have me killed on sight,' Qayin replied. 'He's lost his mind, what he had left of it anyways. I figured I'd be safer with you guys.'

Andaim blinked as he glanced at Cutler, who was clenching his fists by his sides and fuming in silence. 'You sure got some strange ideas, Qayin.'

Eve looked up as the lights in the cell block began to flicker sporadically.

'Come on, we don't have time for this.'

Qayin followed her and Andaim as they jogged toward the aft exits.

'What the hell you gonna do now?' Qayin asked as they moved.

'The engine room,' Eve said. 'It's the strongest part of the ship.'

'It's also the part where the engines and fusion core are,' Qayin muttered. 'Case you didn't know.'

'You got any better ideas?' she challenged.

'If we can tuck in there somewhere, we might just make it down,' Andaim said for Qayin. 'It's about all we've got.'

Qayin shook his head, his gold and blue braids swinging.

'Gotta hope the Atlantia can hold out against the Word.'

'What?' Andaim asked.

'Hevel's all for stayin' put and fightin' it out, so he said over the intercom.'

'That doesn't sound like him,' Andaim said.

'It ain't like him,' Qayin replied. 'He's got 'bout as much hero in him as I got lawman.'

Eve shook her head.

'It doesn't make sense. Standing and fighting here is the last thing we should be doing. The Atlantia won't stand a chance without the fusion core to fight back with.'

Neither Andaim nor Qayin replied as they reached the engine compartments. The prisoners had already opened the shield doors and were amassed inside as Eve led Andaim and Qayin inside with them. The sight of the giant convict sent a further surge of anger through the amassed inmates, but Evelyn raised her hands as she called out.

'He's been trapped here with us,' she said. 'We're *all* betrayed here, so let's get over it and get to work.'

Cutler stood forward, acting as self–imposed spokesperson for the inmates.

'He's the one who put us here,' he said, pointing at Qayin. 'What makes you think any one of us would trust him?'

Eve was about to reply when a voice among the inmates did it for her.

'What makes you think that we want you speaking for us, Cutler?'

A murmur of agreement rippled through the crowd, and was silenced by a deep and reverberating rumble that shuddered through the entire hull.

'No time to argue now,' Evelyn said. 'Do you all want to live or die?'

All of the prisoners watched her without responding, and Eve turned to Qayin and Andaim.

'Seal all of the hatches behind us,' she said. 'The more hull we have between us and the heat, the better off we'll be.'

Qayin and Andaim turned and began sealing the shield doors as Evelyn walked directly toward the wall of inmates. They split before her in silence, her diminutive form carving through them like a knife as she headed toward the engine room doors proper.

The floor vibrated beneath her boots, humming with the contained energy locked into the fusion core in the damaged section of the hull nearby. Enough to fry Eve and everybody else on board too, she knew, but right now the core represented the lesser of two evils: a fast death by searing fusion heat, or a slower death by friction heat if the hull ruptured during entry into the atmosphere below.

Eve reached the doors and accessed their simple controls, opening them. A waft of dense heat billowed out from the engine rooms as the doors opened and the inmates hurried in without waiting for a command.

Qayin and Andaim joined her as she set the doors to close.

'Looks like you've got them under your little finger,' Qayin murmured with a wry smile. 'Maybe I shoulda thought 'bout signing you up to the gang before now?'

'You think that this lot will hold up?' she asked Andaim as she looked at the huge tubes and vents surrounding them.

'They're old,' he replied, looking at the long, tubular engine cores and the spherical titanium containment chambers at the far end of the engine rooms. 'But the hull's rotated now so we're at the back, and they're built the old way too.'

'If they don't,' Qayin said, 'then I don't hold out much hope for us either.'

'Easiest way out,' Eve replied as she walked through the engine room doors and then set about closing them behind her. 'It'll be so fast, by the time you realise it you'll already be dead.'

'That's a great comfort,' Andaim rolled his eyes.

The heavy doors rumbled shut and the deep red emergency lighting glistened on Andaim's face as the sweat built up on his skin.

'Damn, it's hot already,' Qayin said.

The hull vibrated again but this time the motion did not stop and a deafening, screeching sound of tortured metal echoed through the engine room from somewhere far for'ard.

'This is it!' Eve shouted at the inmates. 'Find something to brace yourself against and hold on as tight as you can!'

The engine room began to shudder and shake as she made her way as far aft as she could, seeing inmates propped behind bulkheads and even the exhaust channels themselves, the cylindrical behemoths rattling in their mounts.

Eve spotted a cross–hatched series of support braces buried deep in one corner of the engine room, too small for most of the inmates to crawl into. She crouched down, turned to face aft to keep her back to the deceleration and then levered herself into the tiny space. The entire hull was vibrating against her skin, numbing it within seconds. She tucked her boots against the back of her thighs, and crossed her arms across her chest as she rested her forehead against her knees, then looked across the engine room.

Qayin and Andaim were sitting much as she was, facing aft, their backs to the biggest support braces that they could find, those that attached to the hull's keel deep beneath them. Qayin was staring into space, his features calm and controlled as though he were just riding a transport to work. Andaim was looking right back at her, his face wracked with barely contained fear. Yet despite it he smiled at her and gave her a thumbs–up as though it would all be just fine.

He had guts, guts enough to push through his fear, guts enough to try to calm her wildly churning stomach. Even as she said a tiny prayer of hope in her mind that they might somehow survive this, she heard a sudden roar that seemed to fill the entire universe around them and the entire prison hull jolted violently enough that she banged her head on the metal brace above her.

She heard screams, saw a convict's body hurled through the air toward the shield doors as his grip was broken. He slammed into them with a sickening crunch as what sounded like a thousand howling hurricanes roared outside the hull and the heat began to increase all around her.

***

XXII

'Put it on screen.'

Hevel barked the order out across the bridge, and the view of the for'ard hull was replaced by that of the prison hull as it drifted away behind them, a shower of glistening metallic fragments clouding the view.

'How long before they burn up?' Hevel demanded.

'Four minutes until they hit the atmosphere,' replied Dhalere, manning the communications post on the bridge.

Hevel nodded slowly, his gaze fixed upon the ugly prison hull as it rolled over, the flare of multiple orientation rockets firing visible as it turned its strongest side to the planet below and angled itself for re–entry. The process was automated but it was only an emergency procedure, not one that was ever designed to be used. The prison hull was constructed in space for use in deep space only, not ever for planetary descents. It had no inherent aerodynamics, no planetary thrusters and the fusion core was for internal power only. Built to house convicts for whom the general populace held little sympathy or empathy, nobody really cared if the safety measures worked or not. To Hevel's knowledge, they had never even been tested.

'She's about to strike,' said Keyen, the bearded civilian who had joined Hevel's mutinous crew.

'Maintain watch,' Hevel replied. 'I want to see that thing burn.'

'This is murder,' said the captain, standing amid a ring of marines with his command crew. 'Worse than that, it's genocide.'

'It's necessary,' Hevel snapped back. 'Without that damned hull and its equally damned occupants to slow us down, we'll be better able to defend ourselves.'

'We can't fight,' Idris said again wearily. 'We can't make our stand here, Hevel.'

'That's the spirit that saw our race annihilated,' Hevel snapped.

'We'll be the ones who are annihilated,' the captain replied. 'Our last chance for survival was on that hull!'

Hevel smiled ruefully. 'I think that you give Andaim more credit that he's due, captain, and besides…'

'Not Andaim, you idiot!' the captain roared. 'The fusion core! We were planning to use it as a weapon against the Word. Now, it's lost to us!'

'That would have likely killed us as the Word!' Hevel sneered at the captain, pointing an accusing finger across the bridge. 'You're desperate and you don't know what to do!'

'No,' the captain replied, 'you're desperate, and now we and any living thing down on that planet beneath us will die because of us.'

'Perhaps,' Hevel snapped, 'but at least we will die fighting on our feet and not quivering on our knees.'

'Is that how you see it?' Idris asked. 'It is the fool who goes to his grave a failed hero.'

Hevel turned to look over his shoulder at the captain.

'How apt for my brother, Qayin.'

The captain glared at Hevel. 'And my best fighter pilot, Andaim? He was aboard that ship.'

Hevel turned back to the big screen. 'What will be, will be.'

As they watched, the metallic grey bulk of the prison hull suddenly flared with a brilliant orange and white light as it slammed into the planet's atmosphere. Even on the screen the light was brilliant enough to force the watching crew to squint, and the darkened corners of the bridge were illuminated as though by daylight as the prison hull began to burn up.

'Say goodbye to the prisoners,' Hevel said, 'and good riddance to them too.'

*

The blast of heat that seared through the prison hull seemed to thicken the air around Eve until it was no longer breathable. Sweat drenched her skin and her hair and dripped from her nose and chin as the hull shook violently around her and she buried her face into her knees.

The hull screeched and howled and the sound of rending metal filled the air as the entire hull was consumed by the savage inferno raging outside. Eve felt the metal beneath her heat up, heard men gasp and swear as they scalded themselves on deck plates.

The exhaust cylinders were rattling wildly, chunks of metal bracing and huge rivets popping out and tumbling to the deck as though it were raining steel. Eve turned her head and saw that the exhaust's seals were glowing red hot. In horror, she realised that the inferno outside was seeping into the hull's hydrogen scoops and blasting through the exhausts as though the ship were underway.

'The exhausts!' she screamed. 'Get away from the exhausts!'

The prisoners could not hear her above the cacophony of noise and suddenly a huge chunk of plating peeled away as though it were nothing more than silvery paper and a blast of white hot flame screeched down the gangway alongside the exhaust.

Eve saw half a dozen convicts instantly burst aflame, their features vanishing as they were scorched to the colour of flaming charcoal and they tumbled aft, consumed by fire and their flesh blasted away like burning leaves from their bodies.

The flames cut through thick metal stanchions and braces as though they were of no more substance than thin air, the entire starboard exhaust chamber collapsing onto the deck and crushing another handful of men sheltering beneath it. Eve heard their agonised screams as the super–heated metal scorched their still living bodies, cooking them alive.

Several inmates staggered away from the unbearable heat of the flames and were lifted off their feet as the gravity in the vessel shifted wildly as the hull began to lose orientation. Eve saw one of them fly upward and straight through the fearsome tongue of flaming roaring from the ruptured exhaust, unable to break her gaze as she searched for his body to re–emerge above the flames and saw only a cloud of vaporised and burning fragments blasted aft toward the stern bulkheads.

Eve could feel the heat from the flames but she forced herself not to move, her tiny pocket of safety the only thing preventing her from being hurled around the interior of the hull. She searched for Andaim, but the trembling heat haze from the flame and the heat scalding her eyeballs hid him from view.

She looked for'ard and saw that the shield doors were already glowing red around the edges, bright globules of metal shimmering like lava as they dripped from handles and pressure locks. The entire for'ard bulkhead seemed to bulge inward as though melting, straining the shield doors even further, and she heard massive impacts outside the hull as components were torn off by the fearsome inferno and turbulence outside to tumble in the hull's wake.

'The doors!'

The scream came from what sounded like miles away, so loud was the roaring of the flames and the rending of the tortured hull. Eve looked for'ard and saw the shield doors bulging outward, the rivets popping under the tremendous pressure. A flash of sparks and globules of molten metal sprayed out around the edges of the doors, and then they burst inward at the head of savage tongues of flame.

The main shield door blasted past Eve's shelter and crashed into the aft bulkhead somewhere behind her, burying itself deep into the hull plating. It was followed by a screaming vortex of glowing flames, ashes and a horizontal rain of molten metal that showered across the engine room like a lethal hail of burning bullets.

Screams erupted from convicts as they were hit by the terrible shrapnel and lost their grip on their hiding places. As they tumbled and crashed against the deck plating or were hurled into the roaring flames still spitting from the ruptured exhaust, Eve saw the for'ard bulkhead wall suddenly burst in front of her as though a giant invisible bullet had punctured it high in its centre.

The entire bulkhead wall peeled open like a terrible metallic flower, the petals rimmed with snakes of molten metal as a blast of hot air filled the engine room and slammed into the aft bulkhead.

Eve's head smacked into her knees as the terrific drag from windblast slowed the hull's plunge into oblivion, and to her horror she saw through boiling clouds of black and brown smoke a bright blue sky spinning over and over. Her head hit the braces above her and then her boots and butt slammed back into the deck, rattling her body. Screams from less well–braced convicts rang in her ears as their helpless bodies were flung around the interior of the hull, limbs breaking and skulls fracturing until their lifeless corpses flailed around and were caught up in the wreckage around her.

The massive tongues of flame spluttered out, a freezing wind replacing them and sucking the heat out of the hull. Only the rear bulkhead and the hull's high speed was building up enough air pressure to allow her to breathe in the rarified high atmosphere. Eve curled herself up as tightly as she could, squeezing her eyes shut and hoping against hope that the hull would hold for just a little longer.

The rattling, screaming, howling crescendo seemed to carry on for an eternity until Evelyn felt herself rolling upside down in her tiny sanctuary.

The entire hull seemed to tumble over on itself, shouts of alarm and pain competing with the rush of wind blustering through the hull's hollowing shell. Then a tremendous crash shook it and Eve screamed as she saw the entire remaining for'ard section of the hull ripped off as it crashed against rocks briefly visible through the dense smoke filling her vision.

The hull flipped over in mid–air, a flash of revolving blue sky and bright sunlight filling it for a brief moment, and then it righted itself and slammed into unyielding earth with a screeching, grinding blast of tortured metal. The exterior hull plating was stripped away as though it were the skin of some feeble fruit, the rear bulkhead tearing open as clouds of dust and sand and shards of metal sprayed across what was left of the hull as it ploughed across the ground and then smashed into deep water.

The water flushed like a tsunami through the hull, those few remaining souls who clutched to braces and bulkheads torn from their hiding places by the force of the water and snatched away into oblivion.

Eve had barely an instant to draw a deep breath before she was entombed beneath the water that rushed past her with unimaginable force, trying to drive the air from her lungs as it dragged her from her sanctuary. She glimpsed the hull flashing past her, a confused miasma of torn metal amid clouds of glistening bubbles, smouldering as it cooled.

The rear bulkhead loomed, patched with the mangled corpses of inmates who had been slammed against it, and then it rushed by as she passed through the ragged hole torn in it. She spun in the water, saw the entire bulk of the hull sinking away into a darkened oblivion of ocean far below her, and then she realised that she was sinking with it.

The huge suction of the hull and her dense gravity suit and boots were pulling her down. Evelyn reached down as she plunged through the deep water, the pressure on her lungs crushing her chest as she hauled off the heavy boots and then reached up, pulling on her zip. She tugged at it, tumbling end over end as the pressure increased and she felt her lungs burn and her heart pulse inside her.

The zip came free and she pulled it all the way down, pulled her arms out and then kicked free of it. The suit fell away and continued to sink beneath her as with the last of her strength she kicked for the shimmering light of the surface as a stream of bubbles spilled from her lips.

She rose, faster and faster until the surface of the ocean seemed close enough to touch. On impulse she reached out for it as her last reserves of will deserted her and the air spilled from her lungs in a great cloud of bubbles that glistened in the light of the sky above the water's surface.

Eve's vision faded and blackened, and then she broke through the surface.

She sucked in a huge lung full of air, still blind as she plunged back beneath the waves. Her eyesight returned and she managed to kick out with her numbed legs enough to break the surface and re–inflate her lungs again. Her vision starred and her limbs tingled but she managed to stay afloat as she sucked in huge volumes of blessed air and looked about her.

She could taste salt on the water and she turned to see a coastline of sand–coloured rock looming nearby. Above, in the blue sky, what looked like a shower of fast–moving stars shone as they fell, the debris from the hull leaving thin trails of smoke as countless chunks of smouldering metal plunged to the ground nearby.

She looked around for any sign of Andaim but there was nobody in the water with her.

Eve turned and wearily struck out for the shore, swimming through the choppy water until she made it to the edge of a broad beach. She got to her feet, staggered through the rollers until she cleared the water and collapsed to her hands and knees.

The sun in the sky above was warm, as was the sand beneath her, and she slumped onto it as she briefly recalled the beach in the sanctuary, back aboard the Atlantia.

Her exhaustion overwhelmed her and she lost consciousness.

***

XXIII

'They're gone.'

Dhalere turned away from then viewing screen and looked at Hevel as she spoke.

'Only fragments made it to the surface, several of which hit the water and all of which were aflame when they did so. There's nothing significant left but the largest stern section of Atlantia Five's hull, which hit deep ocean to the west of the deserts and will likely sink within days.'

Hevel stared at the screen, which still showed the planet and a few last remnants of the hull streaking flame across the atmosphere.

'Good. Now we can put this unfortunate episode behind us and move forward.'

Captain Idris Sansin shook his head.

'You really think that this crew is going to forget that you just killed over a hundred men? You think that will engender their trust, or their loyalty?'

Hevel shook his head as he took the captain's chair and swivelled it to face him.

'Until a few moments ago, captain, we were shackled to those damned prisoners and stuck here waiting to see who died first. Now, we're free again to defend ourselves and make a stand.'

'Make a stand how?' Idris demanded. 'Our weapons are severely depleted, as is our manpower. We face an enemy that has scoured our entire colony of life and possesses far greater firepower than our own. The moment we are sighted, we will be destroyed. Our only choice is to flee, right now.'

Hevel stood from the captain's chair again, placed his hands behind his back and stared down at Idris and C'rairn.

'Flee,' he echoed. 'To run away. To die like cowards. Is that what you would have us do, captain? Have we not fled enough? Do you not think that this crew wants the opportunity to fight back for a change? We've been running from the Word for years. How much longer must we flee before we realise that the only defence left to us now is attack?'

Idris said nothing.

'As I thought,' Hevel replied to his own question. 'You have no answer, captain. You no longer have what it takes to make the big decisions, and now we have nothing left but a mutiny to do what should have been done a very long time ago.'

The bridge door opened and Bra'hiv walked through with six of his men behind him, all of them carrying pulse rifles and ominous expressions. Bra'hiv halted at the bridge command platform and looked in turn at the captain and at Hevel.

'I am in command now, Bra'hiv,' Hevel snapped. 'What is your report?'

Bra'hiv hesitated, looking again at the captain.

'You may surrender your weapons and join the captain if you wish,' Hevel informed him. 'Or you may serve me. I intend to make a stand against the Word, here. The choice is yours, Bra'hiv.'

Bra'hiv looked at Idris for a long moment, and then turned to Hevel.

'Both Andaim and Evelyn were lost with the prison hull. We were unable to reach them before the hull was detatched.'

'The fusion core?' Dhalere asked.

'Lost, with the hull,' Bra'hiv confirmed.

'A shame,' Hevel replied, and then gestured to the captain and his command crew. 'Take them to the holding cells,' he ordered. 'We have a battle to undertake, and I don't want this old man getting in the way for a moment longer.'

Bra'hiv and his marines encircled the captain, who shot Hevel a last glance as he was led from the bridge.

'This is a mistake,' he shouted. 'You'll kill us all.'

Hevel did not reply, instead waiting until the captain and his crew were led away before he turned and surveyed the bridge. It was now mostly manned by civilians, people who probably had not done a single day's military service in all of their lives. They stared back at Hevel, nervous but anxious to please, to serve, to do something other than run and hide.

'What I will ask of you,' Hevel began, 'over the coming days, will likely scare us all. We know of what is out there, of what draws closer to us with every passing orbit, and I know that any man who did not fear it would be a fool.'

Hevel looked into the eyes of his new crew as he spoke.

'But to run forever, to hide and to cower in fear is just as foolish. We are the last of our kind,' he said. 'Would those who have died watch us from the beyond and cry in shame at what we have done? Ask yourselves, what would those whom you have lost want you to do? What would *you* like to do, given the chance?'

The crew remained silent but Hevel could see the resolve harden in their features, the restrained anger bubbling to the surface as they thought of their fathers, mothers, siblings and friends who had died so horrifically at the hands of the Word.

'We can either run for all eternity or we can stand and fight,' Hevel said as he slammed one clenched fist into his upturned palm. 'There is *never* going to be a right time, a perfect time, to fight back. We either decide to, or we continue to flee to who–knows–where across the cosmos. If any of you don't feel as though you can stomach this fight, then you're free to join the captain and his crew in the holding cells.'

Hevel pointed to the bridge door and waited. Several officers looked at the door, but nobody moved. Hevel lowered his arm again.

'Then this is it,' he said finally. 'This is our time to fight back. Tactical, what's our weapon status?'

Keyen looked down at the various screens before him. 'Er, all pulse weapons functional, but all also have limited plasma supplies. We'll need to re–fuel using the planet's resources.'

Hevel nodded. 'What's our hull integrity?'

'Fully secure,' Keyen replied. 'No breaches or damage from the blast, except the fuel leaks which are being fixed as we speak. We don't have any ray shielding left, however, so any hits we take will impact the hull directly.'

'What about directed weapons?'

'Automated grapples and explosive–harpoons are fully operational, but they're hardly going to be much use against the Word.'

'What about our fighters?' Hevel asked.

'Sixty automated drones,' came the reply, 'plus about eighteen Raython fighters with standard armoury of pulse weapons and magnetic mines.'

Hevel nodded thoughtfully.

'Our weapons and defences won't be any match for the Word,' he said out loud, 'at least not on the face of it. The only way we can really win the fight is not by force but by guile.'

'Sir,' Lael asked, still manning her post, 'you're asking us to go up against the most intelligent creation we know of in the universe. Neither force or guile will do us any good.'

'Perhaps,' Dhalere challenged from nearby, 'you'd prefer to join the captain in the holding cells?'

Lael did not respond and Hevel turned to the rest of the bridge crew.

'Prepare one of the shuttles for a descent,' he ordered. 'We'll collect supplies from the surface and start re–charging the plasma guns using the hydrogen scoops. Let's get to it!'

*

The holding cells were little more than barred pens more often used to store discharged ammunition magazines and other paraphernalia, located several decks below the bridge in a secured area. Bra'hiv and his marines led the captain and C'rairn, who had stood down along with the rest of the displaced bridge crew, down to the cells and locked them in.

Idris waited until the cells were shut and his people could not get injured by the mutinous marines before he spoke.

'Bra'hiv, you're making a mistake.'

Bra'hiv moved to stand in front of the captain's cell.

'I'm not making a mistake,' he replied. 'Better that I can keep an eye on what Hevel's doing and have him think that I stand with him, than be locked up in there with all of you.'

The captain heaved a sigh of relief.

'You know that Hevel can't command a warship much less win this battle.'

Bra'hiv sighed. 'The majority of the civilians are behind him and my men tell me that they won't back down. They've been screaming for retaliation for years. I don't doubt that some of them would choose to fight even if it were absolutely certain that they would die doing so.'

'It *is* absolutely certain,' C'rairn pointed out. 'And now we've lost Andaim too, and he was our best shot at figuring a way out of this.'

The captain looked across at C'rairn, who shrugged apologetically. 'Sorry sir, it's just the way it is. Andaim was the best tactical officer we had and...'

'I wasn't thinking that,' the captain said, and looked at Bra'hiv. 'If you could regain the bridge from Hevel, would you do it?'

Bra'hiv's expression betrayed no emotion. 'I always serve the colony sir.'

'Very diplomatic,' Idris acknowledged. 'Now take the stick out of your ass and tell me if you'd take the bridge if Andaim were still here.'

Bra'hiv lifted his chin. 'Yes sir, I would.'

Idris gripped the bars of the holding cell. 'Then find him.'

'But sir, he died in the…'

'A man like Andaim,' Idris said, 'is not dead until you're holding his corpse in your hands. He may have found a way to survive the re–entry, and that woman Evelyn seems almost indestructible. Serve Hevel, but try to find Andaim.'

Bra'hiv saluted. 'Yes, captain.'

The security team marines turned and strode away. Idris relinquished his grip on the bars of the cell and stepped back.

'Bra'hiv can't do this on his own,' C'rairn said. 'He could have turned against Hevel.'

'Bra'hiv feared that civilians would die in a firefight,' Idris corrected C'rairn. 'He maintained his position and did his job, and now he may be able to help us.'

'Even if he finds Andaim alive,' C'rairn said, 'how the hell will that help us? Most of the time we've only been a few hours ahead of the Word. It can't be long before we're found, and then….'

C'rairn's voice trailed off. Idris looked about him at the other cells where his bridge crew were crammed in. He managed to find his voice.

'We will figure something out,' he promised them. 'It's our duty to overcome adversity, just as we did when we escaped the colony, just as we have done ever since.'

***

XXIV

Eve awoke to a chill around her legs. She opened her eyes and saw water wash gently around her and then recede as the tide dragged it back toward the ocean. She lifted her head and somehow found the strength to drag herself up the beach.

The sun had shifted in the sky, higher now and blazing down from the heavens as she crawled to where a chunk of scorched hull plating had thumped down onto the beach to form a rudimentary metal cave. She crawled into the tiny patch of shade it provided and laid in a foetal position for a long time as she stared out across the coastline.

She could see from the endless expanse of undisturbed sand that nothing had walked on the beach in recent hours or days. The wash of foliage and debris off the waters of the ocean reached only half way up the beach, the high–tide mark most likely caused by the gravity of the small moon she could see high in the hard blue sky, a pale patch of ghostly white staring back down at her.

In the distance against the sky she could see a vast swelling of dark clouds as though the horizon were aflame and casting smoke across the heavens. The volcano, she recalled, seen erupting from orbit.

A brief memory of the sand–coloured wastes below the ship while it had been in orbit above the planet served as an indication that there would be little chance of her surviving for long out here alone. The more temperate regions she had glimpsed as the sun rose over this isolated little planet would be many months' march away and she had no idea what predators might haunt this world.

She recovered her breath and strength enough to get out from beneath the hull plating and stand up to walk slowly up the beach toward a low bluff. The dry, hot wind buffeted her hair as she clambered up the bluff and looked out across the wilderness.

The rocky, sandy firmament stretched away from her, flaring beneath the brutal sunlight. Patches of thorn scrub scratched an existence from the barren and unyielding soil, and ancient river courses long since desiccated wound their way like dead snakes toward the shoreline. In the distance a low ridge of rocky hills seemed to hover above the trembling horizon, the heat distortion making them seem closer than they really were.

She turned and looked out across the ocean. Broad, blue and empty, vanishing into a horizon devoid of life.

Evelyn sat down on the bluff, aware that she lacked even a source of drinking water, and wondered whether it might not have been better to have just been incinerated or drowned during the prison hull's last moments. Better to have died quickly than to suffer the agony of dehydration out here on the lonely dunes.

She scanned the beach, shielding her eyes with one hand for some sign of life or even of useful wreckage, but there was nothing but aged driftwood and what looked like some kind of sea foliage washed up by the tides, torn ribbons of greenery strewn in untidy tangles by the surf.

Evelyn got to her feet and walked along the bluff, headed toward the largest pile of foliage she could see further down the beach. Maybe it was edible, something to sustain herself while she figured out her next move. She was half way there when she heard a strange sound from out across the wilderness. She turned, shielded her eyes again, and from out of the rippling horizon emerged beasts. Her heart flipped as she saw them, moving fast toward her, thick hair trailing from behind their twin heads, long legs racing and leaving drifting clouds of sand billowing in their wake as they charged far faster than any human being could ever run.

Eve whirled and dashed down the bluff, ran across the beach toward the clumps of foliage. The thick sand slowed her down but she stumbled and struggled onward, her legs weary from both fatigue and countless months of zero gravity as she staggered to the clumps of foliage and slumped down among them. She reached across and hauled the damp mess over her, felt the blessed cold wet sand against her skin as it cooled her.

She shuffled further down into the sand, peering back up at the bluff as she heard the big animals' heavy footfalls thunder up to the bluff amid a cloud of drifting sand.

There were four of them, their flanks the colour of dust and sand, each with a long head at the front and a second behind it that was swathed in elaborate coils of fabric. The animals made gruff, groaning noises as their big, black eyes surveyed the beach. Eve squinted at the four animals, fear pulsing through her veins, and then suddenly one of the heads spoke in a strange dialect and pointed down the beach at her.

Her brain reinterpreted what she was seeing and she realised with some amazement that she was looking at four men riding on large, powerful beasts with long snouts and even longer legs that descended the bluff onto surer footing on the beach. The animals snorted and bridled as they were guided, and Eve realised with sudden shame that in her haste and fear she had left a trail of vivid footprints in the sand leading directly to the foliage under which she sheltered.

The towering animals halted beside the foliage and the four riders looked down at her from their towering mounts. The men looked at each other, and then one of them vaulted lithely from his animal and thumped down onto the sand. His face was shielded from view by thick swathes of material, but she could see his dark eyes watching her as he approached.

He spoke again, a strange warbling dialect that she could not understand yet somehow sounded familiar. He pointed at her and raised the fingers of his hand up and down, beckoning her to rise. Eve remained where she was beneath the shelter of the foliage, and she realised just how much she now wished she was still wearing her mask, separated from the rest of the universe by its featureless metallic shield.

The man in the swathes shrugged and reached to his belt. From a scabbard he drew an enormous hooked blade that flashed brightly in the sunlight, and then he shouted for her to rise.

Eve took hold of the foliage about her and then, slowly, she got to her feet. She heard the men gasp and point at her near–naked body, and the man with the blade lowered the weapon as he stared at her.

Eve darted forward and hurled the foliage at the man. She saw surprise on his features as he swung the big curved blade upward to deflect the foliage. Eve ducked down and threw her arm up under the blade, sending it high as she thrust her knee into the man's groin. It impacted with a dull thump and the man wheezed and gagged as he doubled over.

Eve twisted to one side, grabbed the man's wrist beneath the blade and twisted it over with all of her might, reversing it back on itself as the man crashed to his knees. The man cried out as his wrist cracked loudly and the blade fell from his grasp. Eve released his wrist and rolled away from him, grabbed the handle of the blade and came back up onto her feet with the weapon in her grasp and raised toward the three remaining riders.

They sat on their beasts and stared at her in amazement as their fallen comrade rolled about on the sand and groaned, holding his damaged shoulder with one hand and cupping his groin with the other.

Eve waited for the riders to move, but none of them did. They simple watched her from where they sat, neither threatening her nor retreating. She raised the blade higher as though making ready to strike. Still, they did not move.

Then, to her left, one by one, men appeared upon the bluff. First a dozen, then fifty, then over a hundred, all of them looking down at her on the beach. She looked at them as one of the men on the beasts before her jumped down onto the sand and walked toward her.

He unveiled his face, the clothing falling away to reveal aged features lined with deep gulleys and tanned the colour of scorched wood. He looked at her and then he smiled and bowed deeply before he turned and helped his fallen comrade to his feet.

He helped the fallen man back up onto his animal, which she realised was neither a carnivore nor capable of complex thought, and then mounted his own beast. He looked down at her and shrugged before he turned his beast away from her and guided it toward the bluff.

His three companions likewise turned away and rode toward the bluff.

Eve watched them go and then realised what they were doing.

The men kept riding, slowly, away from her. Eve cursed and walked in pursuit, dragging the surprisingly heavy blade with her.

There was, she realised, no choice. If she did not follow these men, she would die alone.

***

XXV

A low whistling sound drifted around the periphery of his consciousness, dragging him from oblivion and into the light. Andaim lifted his head as he opened his eyes and drew in a sharp breath as he jolted awake.

He was slumped against a warped bulkhead, a support brace above his head bent ninety degrees and buried in the sand behind him. He looked down at his body and patted his limbs and chest in search of injuries. Although battered and bruised, he could feel no broken bones.

The interior of the aft bulkhead was a cavernous wreck of torn metal, twisted hull plating and the scorched remains of the starboard exhaust cylinder. The hull was half buried in the sand, smoke spiralling up from fried electronics and slag piles of molten metal cooling in the breeze.

He rolled onto his back and smelled a strong waft of burning flesh. He turned his head and looked straight into the eyes of a man long dead, his flesh smouldering not a few cubits from where Andaim lay and his teeth bared in a rictus grin between shrivelled lips.

Andaim scrambled to his feet and away from the corpse, his legs unsteady as he surveyed the wreckage and the bodies of convicts strewn across the desert around it. He rubbed his head, recalling the aft section of the prison hull being torn away and plummeting into the deep sand dunes. He looked around for the rest of the hull, but at the speed and altitude from which they had fallen it could be tens of miles away.

The sun was descending in the sky and throwing long shadows across the desert. Andaim had no idea of where the nearest water was, only that if he didn't find it within a few hours he would likely die. That was if he didn't succumb to hypothermia in the night, all deserts prone to deep chills in the absence of the sun.

He scoured the wreckage, wrestling uniforms from the corpses of convicts as extra layers of insulation against both the searing heat of the sun and the cold of the night. He bundled them up and used the sleeves and legs to tie the bundle over his shoulders and around his waist. Satisfied, he was about to seek out the highest dune that he could find when he saw a trail of footprints in the sand leading away from the wreckage.

Andaim instinctively reached for his pistol, then cursed as he realised he did not have it. He turned and followed the trail, anxious not to overheat himself in the desert heat.

The trail led directly to the highest dune. Andaim clambered up it until he reached the top and saw the desert stretch away from him. He promptly dropped back down out of sight and flat against the hot sand, waiting for several seconds before peeking over the top of the dune.

Strewn across the desert was another smouldering section of hull. A column of dirty brown smoke spilled from the wreckage and billowed up into the hard blue sky, visible for miles around. But what interested Andaim was the crowd of several hundred men gathered in tight ranks near the wreck, and the small handful of convicts standing before them.

Even from a distance Andaim recognised Qayin's towering form standing at the head of the small knot of men. Before them were several powerful looking beasts, astride which sat men who stared down at the convicts, broad hooked blades in their hands. Andaim could see that Qayin and his companions' hands were bound behind their backs.

Andaim turned to retreat back down the dune, and froze as he stared down the perfectly mirror–polished surface of a sword, its tip hooked in a wicked barb. Against the bright sky a man looked down at him, his face swathed in colourful fabrics.

'Damn.'

*

Andaim was led down to the group of convicts, his hands bound behind his back by his captors, who apparently had watched him from the wreckage before following him with admirable silence up the dune.

Andaim saw Qayin turn to look at him and raise an eyebrow.

'That's a shame. I thought you'd burned up, lieutenant.'

'Good to see you too.'

Andaim spotted Cutler standing nearby, likewise bound, his suit scorched from the descent and numerous abrasions scarring his face. Andaim was shoved to the front of the group, his uniform marking him out as special. Their captors, sitting astride their big animals, were conversing while watching their new charges.

'What's the story?' he asked Qayin.

'No idea,' the big convict admitted. 'I ain't sure they know what to do with us. They haven't killed anybody yet.'

Andaim frowned, confused.

'What the hell are humans doing out here?' he thought out loud. 'The colonies were destroyed and we never sent survey ships out this way did we?'

'You're asking me?' Qayin snorted. 'You're the military man. These people don't have pulse rifles. They just got swords and shields.'

Andaim was about to answer when, over a low ridge, strode a man so huge that everybody fell silent as though by some unseen command. To the best of his memory, Qayin was physically the largest man that Andaim had ever encountered, but even the big convict was dwarfed by the warrior king approaching them. He stood a full head and shoulders above the warriors surrounding them, who parted before his approach, a huge beard adorning his giant head and a shield larger than a blast door strapped to his back. Tucked into the shield were the handles of what looked like two gigantic copper swords.

The man walked on legs twice the size of Andaim's, as sturdy and immovable as a mountain as he strode to the edge of the group of captives and scanned them with cruel, piercing eyes. He clenched and unclenched giant fists as though thinking hard.

'From where have you come?' he asked.

Andaim blinked in surprise as the words leaped out at him, the giant's voice a deep bass.

'From a long way away,' he answered.

The giant's eyes locked onto Andaim's.

'Your lives are now mine,' the huge warrior said, and then turned his back on them.

The men on the animals seemed to come to a decision. They called out several short, sharp commands, and before he knew it Andaim had a rope slung over his head and tied around his neck. The rope linked to another, which was looped over Qayin's giant head. Andaim noticed that their captors were wary of Qayin and fascinated by his gold–streaked hair: human curiosity, it seemed, spanned the cosmos.

Linked together by the coarse rope and with Andaim at the front, the prisoners were led by their mounted captors as the rest of the strange force of warriors fell into line and marched behind them toward the empty desert.

'Seriously?' Qayin grumbled. 'They're gonna make us walk all the way out there?'

Andaim said nothing. The fact that they hadn't been murdered on the spot by what were likely superstitious desert clans was a bonus enough, but the fact that their captors were both human and in good health suggested that survival out here in the desert was indeed possible.

'Don't complain,' he whispered back to Qayin. 'If they hadn't found us the desert would have killed us soon enough. Let's just see what they want.'

The small force of mounted warriors was soon joined by more animals controlled by men who rode not on their backs but in chariots tethered to the animals. Andaim watched as the men skilfully wheeled their chariots about across the desert, riding ahead to survey the route and conveying messages for their captors.

They walked for hours as the sun sank toward the horizon behind them, the skyline a trembling sea of molten metal and the endless desert stark against the bright sky. Their captors brought them water from time to time, but no food was shared. Andaim, his own head swimming and aching, managed to maintain a steady pace on the dusty path but he heard others behind him stumble and fall, the noose about his neck tugged as they collapsed and the entire column brought to a halt.

Their captors produced small, wicked little whips made of woven leather that whistled as they cut the air, striking the fallen convicts until they hauled themselves to their feet and staggered onward.

The sun was almost below the horizon, the cloying heat fading when Andaim smelled the odour of water upon the air. Other tracks wound in from the distant, lonely deserts, caravans of people and animals moving toward or away from the water. Trees, their leaves strange and long, their trunks layered, sprouted forth in a sprawling oasis of green as the little caravan of prisoners was led toward the water.

Andaim struggled up a low sloping dune and before him a spectacular sight unfolded.

A vast, shallow river valley dominated the desert canvass, green water sparkling in the sunlight and surrounded by dense ranks of trees on both banks. Other caravans followed the trade roads alongside the river and boats of all kinds were moored alongside the glittering waters.

Qayin moved to stand beside Andaim, both of them looking not at the river but at the huge monuments nearby bathed in the glorious rays of the setting sun. Qayin's deep voice reached Andaim as though from another time.

'Are you seeing what I'm seein'?'

Andaim merely nodded in response.

From the desert rose up three enormous monoliths, towering pyramids that reached hundreds of feet into the air. Andaim could not begin to imagine how many decades it must have taken these people to build them, only that the cost in lives must have been equally vast.

The three pyramids reflected the fiery glow of the sunset, their geometric sides perfectly smooth with polished white limestone. Andaim guessed that in the fierce light of the midday sun they must shine like white beacons that would be visible for miles across the deserts. At their lofty peaks, all three pyramids were capped with gold that shone as though the tops of the monuments were aflame, reflecting the fearsome glare of the setting sun.

The convicts stared at the pyramids in awe as Andaim glanced over his shoulder and saw Cutler likewise fascinated by the huge constructions.

Qayin hawked up a globule of phlegm and spat it out into the sand at his feet.

'They can build those but they can't put together a few vehicles?' he said. Andaim looked at the convict, who shrugged his big round shoulders. 'Just sayin'.'

Their captors shoved them in their backs and they were forced to descend the other side of the dune and join the road that led toward the vast monuments, their escorts led by the giant warrior chieftain.

***

DEAN CRAWFORD

XXVI

The night air was cold, but the fire blazing in the darkness of the desert cast its warmth across Evelyn's face as she sat with a large shawl wrapped around her shoulders. A cup of hot fluid steamed on the cold air as she held it, sipping the bitter drink from time to time and watching the men around her.

It seemed as though they worked quiet miracles on an hourly basis. From the scorched, parched desert sands did they find water and extract it from the land. From the very air did they extract water into sacks hung from the branches of gnarled and dessicated trees. From darkness they found light; from cold, warmth, and they clearly were capable of travelling vast distances upon the bizarre humped beasts that growled and spat and snorted as they slept in a circle around the encampment.

At their head she had noticed an older man who was followed with a calm reverence. He walked among the people, guiding them, consoling them, tirelessly berating with them and cajoling them to bend to his will. She had heard his name whispered from time to time among the women who seemed to be a part of this lonely yet friendly caravan of nomads.

Ahmosis.

The men who had found her on the beach had allowed her to follow them, had never once restrained her or given her a command. For hours had she walked behind them until they had reached the oasis, a jewel of life amid the endless desert wastes, where to her amazement had been encamped hundreds of men, women and children.

She knew little of the people themselves, although she had heard them refer to themselves as the *Shasu*, and she was watched with cautious yet curious eyes by all who passed her by as she sat by the fire. Children watched from the darkness of the night, their beautiful dark eyes shining in the reflection of the fire as they whispered and pointed at her. The women snatched their children away into the safety of the darkness, while the men sat around other fires and watched her, speaking of who she might be and why she had come. Evelyn remained silent, as she had so often found was the best course of action. Soon enough, one of them would come to her, and soon enough they did.

The old man strode past the fire, his long beard thick and white against his chest. He walked with the aid of a staff, which he dug into the ground at her feet and rested his hands upon. It reached almost to his chin, which he then also rested atop the staff as he looked down at her.

He smiled and then spoke in a strange dialect that made her frown. He watched her for a moment, registered her confusion, and then tried again.

'Perhaps in Coptic?'

Evelyn gasped as the words leaped from his mouth. The pronunciation was strange but more than familiar.

'Where am I?' she asked.

The old man smiled again and looked briefly about him at the desert.

'You are at the centre of the world,' he said, 'and caught like us between great cities and greater armies poised to destroy each other and us with them.'

Evelyn stared up at the old man. 'Who are you?'

'My name is Ahmosis,' he replied. 'Yours?'

'Evelyn.'

He peered at her with interest. 'Your name, it means: giver of life.'

Evelyn felt a profound sense of sadness fall in a dense pall around her. 'I wish that were true.'

Ahmosis set his staff down and slowly sat beside her, rubbing his legs as though the joints were troubling him.

'You are a woman,' he said. 'There could be no greater name for you than Evelyn. Tell me, how did you come to be here?'

Evelyn shrugged.

'I was sent here,' she said, 'for the things that I have done.'

'Sent from where?' Ahmosis asked.

Evelyn smiled, as an image of the sanctuary and Andaim and the Atlantia flickered like a long forgotten dream through her mind. 'From a beautiful place, that was safe and warm. I was there, for a while, but then I was cast out.'

'By whom?'

The memory of what had happened haunted Evelyn's mind as she spoke.

'The Word,' she said. 'It hunts us still.'

'There are more of you?'

Evelyn nodded. 'We fell together, and I don't know where they are or even if they survived.'

Ahmosis nodded slowly, his eyes staring into the fire.

'Tell me, Evelyn, did you fall from the sky?'

Evelyn hesitated, suddenly unsure of how much to tell this old man, of how much they should learn from her. Then she thought of the Word and of the destruction it had wrought, and she realised that she should share what little she could because these people would soon have to face that horror themselves.

'Yes,' she replied. 'We all fell, every last one of us. And now we are trapped here.'

'Can you ever return?' Ahmosis asked.

Evelyn looked up into the desert sky and saw a billion stars glittering in orbit around the wispy trail of a galaxy that spanned the heavens, the same one that she had once stared into as a child and wondered.

'I hope so.' She turned to Ahmosis. 'You are in danger, as long as I am here.'

Ahmosis nodded, apparently amused.

'We were in danger long before you arrived, Evelyn,' he said. 'But then you were sent to us, and you saved us.'

Evelyn blinked. 'I did?'

Ahmosis began to try to get to his feet, but his knees clicked loudly and he winced in pain. Evelyn jumped up and supported the old man's arm, and he smiled at her as he steadied himself.

'You have a good heart,' he said, 'no matter what you might think. Come, there is something that I wish to show you.'

Evelyn followed the old man through the camp, the ranks of the Shasu respectfully parting for Ahmosis as he passed through them, their eyes fixed upon hers as she walked with the shawl wrapped tightly around her against the chill.

Ahmosis walked out of the camp through the darkness, a small flaming torch he had picked up on the way crackling in the silence as he led her to a shallow dune. They climbed it together and reached the top.

Sprawling before them was the desert, peppered with scrub visible beneath the soft blue light cast by the moon high in the heavens.

'We were being pursued,' Ahmosis said, 'by an advance force of the Pharaoh.'

'Pharaoh?' Evelyn echoed.

'The Egyptian king, Thutmose,' the old man replied. 'The ruler of these lands and Canaan. They had pursued us as far as the river, but we could not cross and there was nowhere for us to flee except into the Reed Sea, where I feared my people would drown or be slaughtered where they stood.' He sighed. 'I implored the heavens for assistance, and then you came.'

'Me?'

Ahmosis turned to her. 'You. You fell from the sky in a fiery ball of light, smashed into the river and split the waters as though carving a path for my people. We were able to cross the Reed Sea before the Pharaoh's forces reached us and the waters closed in once more. It was a miracle, and we followed the trail of your descent and found you here.'

Evelyn stared at Ahmosis and then out across the nearby deserts.

'There may have been others,' she said. 'I need to find them.'

'And we need to survive,' Ahmosis replied. 'It will not take long for the Pharaoh's army to cross the river and pursue us. When they do, we will be forced to fight them or be slaughtered.'

Evelyn felt a strange sense of empathy with the old man as she thought of Captain Sansin and his own troubles high above them. She looked directly up above her into the night sky and picked out a tiny speck of light, the only one of the stars in the night sky that was not shimmering, its reflected light closer to the planet than the rest.

'I know how you feel,' she said.

Ahmosis turned to her. 'Then help us.'

'I don't know how I can,' she replied. 'Here, in this place, I can barely help myself.'

Ahmosis smiled gently.

'I think that you have more to you than you yourself believe,' he said, 'and I think that you brought something more with you than you know.'

'What do you mean?'

Ahmosis fixed his gaze upon her as he spoke.

'To find you after you parted the Reed Sea, we followed a great plume of smoke and cloud,' he said, 'that when night came turned to a pillar of fire.'

Evelyn nodded, the likely source of the fire the wreckage of the rest of the prison hull, and perhaps where Andaim had landed. If he had survived.

'Can you take me to it?' she asked.

Ahmosis nodded. 'You can travel there yourself,' he said, and with one arm pointed out across the desert behind them.

Evelyn turned, and in the distance she saw a fiery plume of smoke that was illuminated from within by a fierce orange glow. In an instant, she recalled the prison hull's aft section being ripped away during the descent. She realised that the fusion core must have been torn away with it, ripped off when the hull struck the distant hills. Now the searing flame–coloured light could mean only one thing: the fusion core was in plain sight on the hilltop, blazing its fearsome energy into the sky.

She turned to Ahmosis.

'You must listen to me carefully,' she said. 'You must not go up there alone. I will come with you, and we will need to construct something to safely carry what is up there.'

'It is an object of great power?' Ahmosis asked.

'Of unimaginable power,' Evelyn replied. 'It will destroy anybody who comes near it.'

Ahmosis' lips parted as he considered such an object.

'Can you control it?' he asked, his gnarled old hands gripping his staff tightly in his hands. 'Can you use it?'

The fusion core had clearly not been destroyed in the descent, protected deep in the hull's stern as she and the other convicts had been. She did not possess the equipment required to physically open and close the core itself, but if she could construct something that could contain it… She thought of the chunks of wrecked hull plating that now littered the desert in the aftermath of Atlantia Five's fiery descent, and a plan formed in her mind.

'Yes,' she said finally. 'I can control it but I'll need your help.'

Ahmosis nodded eagerly but then raised a finger.

'I will need this weapon,' he said. 'If it can free my people, if it can defeat Pharaoh, then I *must* have it.'

'I will help you use it,' Evelyn replied, 'if you will help me.'

Ahmosis grinned at her.

'Then it is agreed,' he replied. 'Take me to it. I shall command my people to follow us, and we shall build whatever you need to carry it.'

***

XXVII

'Captain on the bridge!'

Bra'hiv's deeply bellowed command announced Hevel's arrival. The new captain strode to sit in his chair and surveyed the crew as he scanned the various screens set into his chair.

'Is the shuttle ready?' he demanded.

'Yes sir,' Bra'hiv replied. 'I'll take a dozen men with me. We've identified an area south of the last known location of the prison hull, far enough that any survivors will not be able to board the shuttle. We'll collect what we can and make our way back aboard.'

Hevel nodded. 'What of Idris Sansin?'

'He and the command crew remain in custody sir,' Bra'hiv replied. 'They have made no complaints or demands.'

'That's not like him,' Hevel said thoughtfully. 'It likely means that he's up to something.'

'He can hardly do much,' Bra'hiv replied. 'He's locked in the holding cells with C'rairn and the others.'

'And you have no problem with C'rairn allying himself with the captain?' Hevel asked. 'He is one of your marines, after all.'

'I command the marines,' Bra'hiv replied, 'but their loyalty to the captain is strong.'

'He has loyalty outside of the bridge too,' Dhalere pointed out as she joined them. 'The civilians are restless. They don't understand what's happening here. They think that we're committing suicide, and until we make our stand they won't realise what we're capable of.'

'What *are* we capable of?' Bra'hiv asked her.

Hevel's head swivelled to peer at him. 'Whatever we put our minds to, Bra'hiv. Agreed?'

Hevel turned and looked at the screens.

'What do we know about the civilisation down there?' he asked.

'Nothing more than before,' Dhalere replied. 'No advanced technology, no industry, certainly no craft of any kind. We can see evidence of structures, some roads or tracks and small cities but that's all.'

Hevel nodded.

'What is the current age of the civilisations?' he asked. 'Do we know anything about how long they've been here?'

Bra'hiv frowned. 'Why would we need to know that?'

'Because I asked,' Hevel growled back.

'Hard to tell from orbit but they're not recent,' Dhalere said. 'Some structures show weathering that suggests an age of thousands of years. The shuttle crew might be able to shed more light on it when they reach the surface.'

Hevel stroked his chin with one hand.

'Take a look and get some readings, but I don't want any of them alerting whoever's living down there to our presence. Inform us of what you find as soon as you can, is that clear?'

'Standard procedure,' Bra'hiv replied.

The relative calm of the bridge was shattered by a single voice. 'Contact!'

Keyen almost jumped out of his seat as he called out across the bridge, his eyes fixed upon a tactical display linked to the ship's passive detectors arrayed along each side of the massive hull.

'Where away?' Bra'hiv demanded.

Keyen struggled to determine the source of the contact.

'Orientation three–five degrees, sub–level forty–eight degrees starboard,' he replied. 'Off the bow.'

'Get it up on a screen,' Bra'hiv snapped. 'Now!'

Keyen relayed his display onto the bridge's main screen, and the image of the peaceful looking planet far below was replaced with that of a pixelated speck moving against a background of distant stars.

'Size?' Hevel demanded.

'Avenger class sir,' came Bra'hiv's response, his experienced eye fixed upon the pixelated image of the vessel, 'twice our mass and moving fast.'

'Estimated time of arrival at our location?' Hevel asked Aranna.

'Maybe we should take this opportunity to leave.' Aranna uttered. 'We don't have time for…'

'Now!' Hevel roared.

'Less than two days!' Aranna replied. 'It's at the edge of the system, moving our way.'

Bra'hiv sighed as he felt his guts twist uncomfortably inside him. A stellar class vessel, moving at that speed, could only mean one thing. The Word had found them and was closing in for the kill. He turned to Hevel.

'They're here,' Bra'hiv said. 'We cannot run now if we wanted to.'

Hevel stood and looked at his men.

'This is it, then. It is now or never. We shall make our stand here and will achieve our finest hour.'

Hevel turned to Bra'hiv. 'You have the bridge.'

Hevel made his way quickly to the captain's ready room, located barely twenty seconds' walk from the bridge. He entered the quarters and ensured that the door was sealed and locked behind him and then hurried through into a small bathroom.

A polished steel mirror adorned one wall in the bleak little room, which was fashioned in a typically military style in dull greys and whites. Hevel moved in front of the mirror, turned on the light, and stared at his reflection.

He leaned closer to the mirror and reached up to his face. With the index finger of one hand he pulled at the skin on his cheek, stretching his lower eyelid down to expose his eyeball and the inside of his eyelid.

His guts turned to slime as he stared at the exposed flesh.

Inside, buried beneath the skin, dull flecks of metal caught the light from the bathroom, and as he watched several of the flecks reacted to the light and turned to face it.

Hevel switched off the light, and in the darkness he could see in the reflection of the mirror that his eyes were glowing with a faint red light.

*

Bra'hiv moved as fast as he could.

As soon as Hevel had marched off the bridge he turned and headed for the elevator banks, careful not to let Dhalere notice any haste in his movement. Once out of sight he dashed to the elevators and took the first one available down to the holding cells. He marched down between them until he found the captain.

Idris Sansin caught Bra'hiv's expression as he arrived.

'What is it?' he asked.

Bra'hiv stood to attention, more to calm his own nerves than anything else.

'The Word,' he said. 'It's here.'

The captain's face fell and his shoulders seemed to slump. 'Already?' he whispered. 'How long?'

'Less than two days,' Bra'hiv replied, and relayed what he knew about the incoming vessel. 'We'll be crushed sir,' he added. 'Hevel has no idea about how to command this ship and his bridge crew are useless – only Lael and Aranna have any proper training. They'll panic as soon as the first shot is fired.'

'We need to get the hell out of here,' the captain said. 'We can storm the War Room and regain control of the Atlantia from there.'

Bra'hiv knew that the War Room was used to control the ship in time of intense crisis or damage, a heavily armoured replica of the bridge deep inside the Atlantia's hull.

'If I spring you, sir' Bra'hiv cautioned, 'it could cause a riot and perhaps even fatalities. Even my own men are not sure on whose side they should be standing, and Hevel is likely to have placed loyal and armed men near the War Room just in case we try anything. Not something we need to happen right now.'

'We need to do something,' Idris snapped. 'We can't just sit here.'

'Which is why C'rairn will be coming with me to the surface,' Bra'hiv said as he opened the cell door.

C'rairn moved to the cell doors as they opened and stepped out. 'What would you have me do?'

Bra'hiv shut the cell door again.

'Hevel won't notice one man missing,' he replied. 'You can come with me to the surface and locate Andaim and anybody else that might have survived down there. We bring them back and surprise Hevel's people, having hopefully doubled our numbers. I'll then take my marines to the War Room and seize control. By then, Hevel's men won't suspect me of treachery.'

'That's thin,' Meyanna Sansin said. 'Hevel might have them shoot you on sight.'

'That's a chance we'll have to take, ma'am.'

The captain frowned.

'The convicts?' he asked. 'Why would they help us? They think we sent them to their deaths.'

'When they find out it was Hevel who murdered their cell mates they'll be more than keen to help us,' Bra'hiv said, 'because I'll extend the amnesty to all of them.'

A ripple of gasps fluttered between the cells.

'That's a mistake,' Meyanna insisted. 'They cannot be trusted – Hevel is right about that if nothing else.'

'Sir,' Bra'hiv said to the captain, 'right now we're the last remaining human beings that we know of. You said yourself that if we don't organise ourselves into a cohesive force and start working together, in a few days we'll be nothing but a memory to that monstrous thing that's hunting us down. Those prisoners down there represent a fighting force that we can't ignore, and with them we can remove Hevel from play and give ourselves at least a chance of survival. Without them...'

Bra'hiv let the question hang in the air for a long beat. The captain sighed and nodded.

'Very well,' he replied. 'Do it, as fast as you can.'

***

XXVIII

'Come with me.'

Andaim stood alongside Qayin as the doors to their prison were opened by a guard armed with a spear and what looked like a copper axe. Behind him stood a phalanx of armed men, all of them watching Qayin closely and each armed with a wicked, hook–bladed sword that Andaim had learned was called a *kopesh.*

The prison was a rock–cut cave, much like a tomb, with a set of wooden doors thick enough to prevent easy escape and guarded by men in sufficient numbers to contain the convicts. Flaming torches illuminated the passage way outside, excavated from the sandstone quarry in which the prison was located and open to the night sky above.

'I get out of one prison,' Qayin rumbled, 'and then get stuck in another.'

'That should tell you something about the company you're keeping,' Andaim replied as they were led out.

'Same to you,' Qayin smiled without warmth as he gestured to the open cell door.

Andaim stepped out of the cell, Qayin behind him. The guards shut the cell door behind them and locked it as Cutler stepped forward.

'What about us?' the old man demanded.

'I'd stay there if I were you,' Andaim said. 'They might intend to kill us both.'

Cutler did not reply as a guard snapped at Andaim.

'Follow me.'

Andaim obeyed with Qayin and they followed the guard down the passageway. The fact that he understood the guard's archaic dialect both surprised and unnerved Andaim. The basic vocabulary was sufficient for communication and the coincidence was not lost on Andaim. They had travelled for years aboard the Atlantia, from an entirely different star system, and yet here they had encountered human beings on another planet not dissimilar to home.

It had been rumoured for thousands of years back on Ethera that mankind had experienced numerous *re–births*, the spontaneous and rapid advances of technology that had spurred almost miraculous innovation and industry. Most often occurring during and after conflict, rather than in spite of it, these trimetric bursts of advancement had seen mankind emerge from a primitive state to one of advanced understanding in as little as a couple of centuries.

According to those same legends, mankind had also often experienced dramatic reversions back to his primitive state once again after major natural disasters, wars or simply the consequences of his own insatiable curiosity. The irony of the fact that those legends had become manifested for real in the dramatic and dangerous rise to power of the Word was not lost on Andaim, for it was just one such set of consequences that had reduced their home world to ash and rubble.

'What are you thinkin'?'

Qayin spoke softly, not looking at Andaim as they strode shoulder to shoulder, surrounded by the guards.

'That this doesn't make sense,' Andaim replied. 'If this is a human colony then it should be equally or even more advanced than our own.'

Qayin nodded, glancing at the swords and shields and the flaming torches that lit their way. 'Maybe it's the legends, y'know? The people rose and then fell at their own hand, and all that other stuff.'

'Just what I was thinking,' Andaim replied. 'What are the chances that this colony is older than ours?'

Qayin frowned, his gold and blue locks glistening in the torch light against his dark skin as they turned and climbed rock–cut steps out onto the open plain.

'If it is, then they got the bad end of a bad deal.'

They walked out onto the plain, the huge pyramids behind them soaring upward into the night sky, pale blue in the light from the moon above. Ahead, a vast encampment of tents was illuminated by a thousand flickering camp fires, the animals referred to as horses and camels arrayed around each fire, and in the centre of the camp a much larger tent surrounded by ranks of armed guards.

Their escort led them to the massive tent, the entrance to which was parted by servants who bowed down before the guards as they led Andaim and Qayin inside.

The interior of the tent was cavernous, filled with small flickering fires in ornate bowls arranged around the interior. The air was warm inside, the sandy earth covered in thick rugs that gave slightly beneath their boots as they walked. Some fifty or so heavily armed warriors stood lining a central path that led to the centre of the tent, their bodies oiled so that their tanned skin glowed in the firelight, their hands resting on their kopeshes, ready to be drawn at the slightest provocation.

Among them stood the gigantic warrior, whose name a fellow prisoner had revealed to Andaim in the rock cut prison. *Golyath*, King of the Pelasgians.

Ahead, a man wearing an ornate conical headdress awaited them. Extending from his chin was a jet black beard, tightly coiled and resting against his bare chest. His eyes were densely adorned with decorative markings that darkened them, and the bizarre headdress made him seem far taller than he probably was.

Qayin and Andaim were made to stop before him.

'Kneel,' one of the guards ordered.

Andaim looked at the man before him and decided to do as he was told, at least for now. Beside him, Qayin remained standing.

'I ain't kneelin' for nobody,' he growled.

The guards moved in an instant, whips cracking across Qayin's back as they hauled him down onto his knees. Qayin glared at the man before them, not breaking eye contact.

'Cut it out, we need their help,' Andaim hissed beneath his breath

'For what?'

The man moved in front of them, stepping down from the regal throne and looking at them both as though examining two small insects. His tall, cylindrical headdress glowed in the firelight as he spoke.

'I am Thutmose, Pharaoh and living God,' he said. 'Speak your names.'

Andaim decided to take control of the talking before Qayin got them both killed.

'I am Andaim, and this is Qayin,' he said. 'We are not from here.'

'You think me a fool?' the pharaoh uttered. 'Where are you from?'

'A long way away,' Andaim said, and on an impulse added: 'We need your help.'

The pharaoh stared at them both for a moment and then began to laugh. All around them, on cue, the rest of the occupants of the tent chuckled along with their king. Andaim heard Qayin rumble threateningly beside him and spoke up again.

'We are all in great danger,' he said.

The pharaoh's laughter faded away, and behind his decorated eyes Andaim thought he saw a flicker of caution.

'What danger?' the pharaoh asked. 'I am the most powerful ruler alive. The Hittites flee me from the north, Canaan bows before me to the east and the Shasu have scattered to the south as the wheat before the wind. I fear no man.'

Andaim, cautious of speaking out of turn, shook his head.

'What is coming is not a man,' he said.

The pharaoh smiled again as though pitying Andaim.

'You speak of Yahweh, the god of the Shasu and the Hebrews,' he uttered with contempt. 'They say he shall smite us all, yet they flee into the wilderness from my armies. Their god is nothing but air and smoke.'

Andaim shook his head.

'I don't know who the Hebrews are,' he said, 'but something is coming and if you do not free us it will destroy everything before it. Every man, every land and every animal for as far as you can see. There will be no escape.'

The lonely desert wind rumbled the walls of the tent and blustered past the torches, the flames snapping and crackling in the breeze. The pharaoh glared down at Andaim.

'There is no god but I,' he hissed, and clicked his fingers.

The guards leaped forward, kopesh blades flashing in the firelight as they were drawn, and Andaim felt the cold touch of the sharpened metal against his neck as the pharaoh smiled down at him.

'I am life and I am death,' the king said, 'and I choose your death.'

The guards tensed to pull their razor sharp blades across the throats of Qayin and Andaim when a sudden chorus of shouts gusted through the tent. Behind him, Andaim heard someone burst inside and hurry up to the pharaoh.

The man prostrated himself before his king, his chest heaving as he tried to catch his breath and his skin and clothes coated in sand and sweat from his journey.

'My god, my pharaoh,' he gasped, 'there is a new power in the land, that has struck fear into the hearts of men.'

The pharaoh glanced at Andaim and Qayin, and then at his loyal messenger. 'Speak of this power,' he commanded.

'The Hebrews,' the messenger gasped, 'they fled your chariots for the river at the reed sea. We pursued them but as they reached the shore their leader, Ahmosis, raised his staff to the sky.' The messenger gasped, his eyes wide with fear and loathing. 'My king, the sky did split into fire and flame above him, above us all, and a thunder tore the sky apart and parted the reed sea in two before our very eyes.'

The guards and the servants all listened in silence as the messenger spoke, sucking in great breaths of air as he did so.

'It is true, every word,' he said. 'The waters parted as the fire passed through them, and the Hebrews fled across the sea before the waters closed in again. We were not able to follow them.'

Andaim looked at Qayin. 'The prison hull?' he whispered.

Qayin shrugged.

'You know of this great power?' the pharaoh demanded.

Andaim opened his mouth to speak, but to his surprise it was Qayin who replied.

'We know of it,' he growled, 'and we wish it destroyed.'

The pharaoh examined Qayin for a moment. 'Stand.'

Qayin got to his feet and towered over the pharaoh, whose bizarre headdress barely drew level with the convict's scalp. Thutmose looked up at the giant man and showed the first signs of caution, glancing at Golyath as though for help. Andaim watched as the pharaoh made to take a pace back from Qayin but caught himself and held his ground.

'How?' the pharaoh demanded, 'how is it to be destroyed? Tell me, or I shall have your friend's throat cut.'

Andaim swivelled his eyes to look up at Qayin, who cast a glance down at him that betrayed no emotion. The big convict looked into the pharaoh's eyes.

'If you kill him, we will have no chance of defeating your enemy's god,' he growled.

Andaim almost collapsed with relief as the pharaoh quickly ordered his guards to stand down. The kopesh blade vanished from Andaim's throat.

'Tell me,' the pharaoh insisted of Qayin, 'or I shall have your throat cut instead.'

Qayin grinned, his broad locks quivering and shining in the firelight.

'We will defeat their god,' he replied, 'and you will free us. All of us.'

'How can I be sure of this?'

'They hide behind lies,' Andaim replied, still kneeling, 'just as all legends do. Tell us of what has happened to your people, of what they think the Shasu god has done, and we will explain what *really* happened.'

The pharaoh watched them for a moment longer and then he turned to sit on his throne once more as he gestured to one of his entourage. A thin, feminine looking man stepped forward, his eyes plastered with make up.

Qayin's eyes swivelled to look down at Andaim, who had got to his feet. 'You some kind of oracle now?' he whispered under his breath.

'Shut it,' Andaim replied. 'Play along nicely.'

The thin man spoke in a lilting, high pitched accent and Andaim realised that he was a eunuch, castrated at a young age.

'The Shasu called forth their God, Yawheh, when they travelled east after absconding from slavery in Egypt. The Shasu chieftan, a man named Ahmosis, claimed that there would be forty days of darkness across Egypt if they were pursued.' The thin man smiled faintly. 'We have been under a great cloud of darkness for seventeen days since.'

Andaim nodded. 'Go on.'

'Our forces pursued the Shasu, and Ahmosis called upon Yawheh to place ten plagues upon Egypt. First, the water in the river turned red and the fish died. Then the frogs died, and then the biting insects came in swarms from across the river and infested our cities and our people. Then our livestock began to die in great numbers from disease, a pestilence of boils and lesions that cut them down in their hundreds. Then came the locust swarms in the north and the failure of our crops when they consumed them, and in the wake of the swarms did the darkness spread further above us. Then came the fiery hail that we saw in the sky this day past. And then, finally, the worst of all our plagues.' The man hesitated. 'The death of many of our new borns.'

The thin man stood back, and the pharaoh looked down at Andaim.

'Ten plagues of our Egypt,' he said. 'Now perhaps you understand why we seek to destroy Ahmosis and his people.'

'Get out of that one,' Qayin whispered to Andaim from the corner of his mouth.

Andaim spoke slowly, his eyes fixed upon the pharaoh's.

'North of here there is a volcano that is erupting and casting an ash cloud across the skies that causes the darkness,' he said.

'Mount Thera,' the pharaoh said. 'It has been burning for weeks now.'

'Chemicals in the ash are falling to the surface and turning the river waters red when they do so. Those same chemicals will kill the fish and the frogs that live in the water. With nothing to eat them, the insects swell in numbers and swarm away from the water.' Andaim gestured outside the tent. 'Biting insects carry diseases that can be passed onto livestock, and far more will die if there are far more insects to infect them. The fiery hail above is where we came from and is nothing to do with the Shasu. A large enough piece of debris crashing through shallow water could explain why the reed sea you mentioned was parted for the Shasu, and then flooded back in behind them.'

Andaim drew breath, thinking fast.

'I don't know what locusts are, but most species swarm in response to other factors in the environment, and as so much is happening here right now they likely had a trigger in there somewhere. The spreading darkness is the volcano spewing more ash into the atmosphere over time.'

The pharaoh stood and stared down at Andaim.

'And the death of many of our new borns?' he demanded.

'A tragedy,' Andaim replied. 'Your people will no doubt have sheltered from the plagues in their homes, and when each successive plague disappeared they would have emerged for food and water. Naturally, mothers and fathers would have fed and watered their most vulnerable children first, which would have inadvertently exposed their young bodies to the last of the infections and plagues. With little immunity, they would have been the most likely to die.'

The pharaoh watched Andaim for a long time, and then he looked at Qayin.

'Is this true?'

Qayin nodded with a sombre expression. 'It is, my king, for I revealed these truths to my friend only this morning.'

Andaim emitted a tight cough, but the pharaoh appeared not to hear him as he approached Qayin and then on an impulse he reached out and touched the convict's gold and blue locks where they lay across his massive shoulders. The pharaoh seemed inexplicably fascinated by the colouring, enough so that Qayin growled at him.

'Hands off.'

The pharaoh did not obey. 'Your life is in my hand, Qayin,' he replied softly. 'Rebuke me, and I shall...'

'Whatever,' Qayin snapped.

The pharaoh's eyes flew wide as rage flashed across his features, but Andaim stepped in.

'We will help you,' he interjected. 'But there is little time.'

The pharaoh released Qayin's locks and turned to his guards.

'Return them to the prison,' he ordered. 'We march at dawn!' And then he looked at Qayin and Andaim. 'And you, my friends, shall march with us. If you succeed in defeating the Shasu god, you shall live. If not, I shall hand you over to my friend.'

The pharaoh grinned broadly and gestured behind them.

Andaim turned and saw Golyath fold his massive arms as he watched them.

***

XXIX

The dawn broke through a surreal mist that drifted in ghostly wreaths and ribbons across the timeless desert sands, the sun a glowing orb that hovered over the distant horizon as the Shasu army marched to the edge of a low ridge of hills. To the north the entire sky was dark and foreboding, billowing clouds of ash swelling to unimaginable heights in the vault of the heavens and casting the land into darkness.

Evelyn led the way, clambering up the rocky slopes that rose above the plains, part of a ridgeline that ran from south west to north east through the desert. Behind her, Ahmosis struggled with his staff, followed by a team of bearers who laboured with their heavy burden up the steep hillside.

Evelyn put one hand out to halt the men as she heard a sound emanating from somewhere above her. She looked up to see a towering pillar of smoke spiralling upward into the cold blue sky and heard a roaring, hissing noise that crackled with live energy and hinted at the colossal forces leaking from the fractured fusion core somewhere above them.

'This is far enough for now,' Evelyn said to Ahmosis. 'We cannot allow too many of your people to get too close. Death will surround it, and it will not care which lives it takes.'

Ahmosis stared up the steep hillside to where the pillar of smoke and cloud was writhing as flashes of light shimmered violently within it.

'What is there?' he asked, his voice almost a whisper.

'Power,' Evelyn promised.

Ahmosis followed her up a steep gulley, probably carved over millennia by the run off from heavy rains that may once have fallen here. Evelyn picked her way with care, reaching the edge of the hilltop and crouching down. Carefully, she peered over the top.

The swirling mists were being drawn up the hillside past her, a gusting breeze that broke over the ridge and swirled upwards in a spiralling vortex of vapour that surrounded the remains of the jagged outer shell of the fusion core laying some thirty cubits away from her on the rocky outcrop. The fractured core was blasting a slim ray of tremendous fusion energy upward into the swirling vapour clouds.

Evelyn figured that the core had fractured a tiny hairline crack in its shell, enough to blast off half of the slightly weaker outer shell but not enough for the core to explode completely. The ray of light, she knew, was many thousands of degrees in temperature. One false move and both she and the entire Shasu army would be incinerated.

Ahmosis crawled up alongside her and lay eyes upon the core for the first time. His eyes widened and she heard his breathing quicken as he stared with awe upon the raw power searing upward into the sky.

'This is how it's going to be,' Evelyn said to him. Ahmosis did not seem to hear her, and she grabbed his collar and yanked him toward her. 'Ahmosis, listen to me. This thing, it is not of this world, do you understand me? It did not come from here.'

Ahmosis nodded, transfixed by both Evelyn's gaze and the terrifying object concealed within the swirling mists.

'You must help me,' she said to him. 'But you must promise me that if I let you carry this in front of your army, you must earn it.'

'How?' Ahmosis asked.

'You must follow the Word,' she insisted, remembering the oft quoted verse from her childhood education, 'the laws that allow us to be the people we would wish to be. You must not commit murder. You must not commit adultery. You must not covet false idols. You must not...'

Ahmosis listened, and to each of Evelyn's ten recited laws he nodded, his grip on his staff as tight as the skin pulled across his aged features.

'These are the commandments by which we lived,' Evelyn finished. 'Now, it is time. Ask your men to bring the casket.'

Ahmosis cupped his hands around his mouth and shouted down the hillside.

From among the men came four with horns that they blew as they climbed, and behind them were a further eight men, but these struggled beneath a far larger burden.

Evelyn had been precise in her description of what the container for the fractured fusion cell should look like in terms of its dimensions and rigidity. She had directed Ahmosis's men to the site of the wreckage around the mountainside, selecting chunks of hull plating thick enough to contain the immense forces entrapped within the core. The men had worked throughout the night to forge the unwieldy chunks of hull plating into a useable shape while building the container for them. Two and a half cubits in length, one and a half in breadth, and one and a half in height. The chunks of hull plating were then inserted into the container, producing immensely strong interior walls.

The resulting container was now hauled up the hillside by Ahmosis's loyal followers, the men labouring without complaint as they approached Evelyn at the top of the ridgeline. They had inserted long wooden staves into rings at the four lower corners of the container before placing a purple veil over everything to conceal its existence from any *Egyptian* spies, as they referred to them.

The bearers reached Evelyn's position and sank to their knees on the rocky hillside, the purple veil billowing in the wind.

'Tell them to follow me,' Evelyn shouted to Ahmosis. 'You'll need your staff.'

Ahmosis instructed the bearers and then he slid his staff beneath the veil alongside the container. Evelyn crouched down low as she gripped the two front staves, ready to pace backwards onto the plateau. Ahmosis made his way to the rear of the container and likewise gripped the remaining two staves, the other bearers between them.

Together they heaved the container into the air and walked slowly up onto the plateau, the wind howling around them as above Evelyn heard a crackle of lightning. The sky seemed to shake around her as thunder rolled across the plains below and she struggled with the heavy container.

She felt a searing heat upon her back and immediately stopped. She set the container down and turned to see the shattered, smouldering fusion core barely a half dozen cubits behind her, half–sunk into the rock where it had fallen.

Ahmosis looked at her over the top of the container as the bearers crouched down and cowered in fear at the sight of such power so close by.

'Unveil it!' Evelyn shouted. 'We need to open the lid!'

Ahmosis reached out and untied the veil at his end, Evelyn mirroring his actions, and then Ahmosis hauled the veil from the container.

To Evelyn's amazement the workers had laboured through the night to add gold plating to the container, the surface of it reflecting the violent light storm in a dazzling array of colours. Atop the lid of the container they had forged two golden cherubim that faced each other and whose wings met in the middle. She stared at the magnificent container as Ahmosis looked at her with eyes filled with the fervour of the righteous.

'Give me your staff!' she shouted.

Ahmosis slid his staff from beneath the container and handed it to her. Evelyn set it down on the ground and then she shouted again above the din.

'Turn the container toward the light. We'll use it as a shield to get closer!'

Ahmosis helped her turn the golden container sideways–on to the fusion core, and then with his help she slid the ornate lid along its rails and off the container and set it down upon the ground. Then, inch by inch, they hefted the container ever closer to the core, the bearers pushing it with them.

The wind howled past Evelyn, her hair whipping around her face, and the heat built up around her as the leaking energy from the core seared it.

'Closer!' she shouted.

Ahmosis, his old face sheened with sweat, heaved the container closer to the fearsome light until it seemed to flare and fill their vision, their faces tingling from the heat.

'There!' Evelyn shouted, her voice almost drowned out by the roar.

She set the container down.

'Now, turn the inside toward the light!' she bellowed.

The bearers carefully rolled the container onto its side, their robes billowing in the wind. One of their headscarves was torn away by the force of the gale and flashed toward the pillar of energy, and Evelyn saw it flutter into the light and vanish in a flash of embers to the shock of the other bearers.

Evelyn picked up Ahmosis's staff and then from her waist she unravelled a length of coarse rope that she had instructed the Shasu to make for her. She tied one end of the long rope around the end of the staff, and then the other around a rock the size of her fist that she picked up from the plateau at her feet.

Evelyn swung the staff around and around over her head, the rope extending out above her as the weighted end spun wider and wider, and she crouched down as the rope reached the extent of its length and then swung the staff out to point almost directly at the core.

The weighted end of the rope shot out before her, past the core as it pulled the rope around it and then was yanked taut as it reached the length of its travel. The tethered rock bounced along the ground to reappear on the opposite side of the core, and tumbled to a halt a few cubits from where Ahmosis crouched.

Ahmosis saw the rock appear and he slid onto his belly and crawled closer to it, the fearsome blasts of energy from the core illuminating his old features as he reached out and grasped the rock, dragging the rope back to the container.

Together, with Ahmosis, Evelyn pulled on the rope as it tugged against the core's outer shell.

The core felt as though it weighed as much as a mountain despite its small size. Evelyn knew that the energy contained within was born of a very small object of tremendous mass, compressed in the same way a star is crushed by its own gravity. She tried again, squinting into the savage light as she hauled on the staff. The core shifted and the wind around her changed direction briefly as the beam of light shivered and lightning forked across the clouds above her.

'It's not working!' Ahmosis shouted.

Evelyn tried again, the other bearers joining them on the rope, but the core was too heavy. She was about to move closer to get more leverage when she felt a hand upon her shoulder. She turned to see Ahmosis standing behind her, gripping her shoulder gently but firmly as he took the staff from her hand.

'These are my people,' he shouted, 'my responsibility. This is my risk to take, my friend.'

Ahmosis did not give her a moment to respond. The old man stood and strode out into the light, as fearless as any man she had ever known. He walked toward the core, shielding his face and eyes with his hands, and wedged his staff deep under the core's outer shell. In the blinding light she saw Ahmosis push downward on the staff and prize the core free from its rocky tomb.

The core screeched, the unimaginable forces contained therein churning as it shifted position and then snapped back into place in its shattered cradle.

Evelyn saw the core now out of the depression in the rock, saw Ahmosis push harder on his staff as his beard smoked and his eyes squinted in the heat and from the pain.

'Now!' Evelyn yelled at the bearers.

The men heaved on the rope and the core slid free from its depression on the plateau as Ahmosis yanked his staff from beneath it and hurried back to join them, his old skin flushed a vivid shade of red and wisps of blue smoke curling from his beard.

Inch by inch, the bearers pulled the core backward until was alongside the container, and then Evelyn yelled to Ahmosis.

'Roll it over!'

Together, they used the staff to push the core over. The searing beam of energy above them swung through the morning sky, the swirling cloud following and coiling around it, the vigorous wind shifting with the blaze and howling as it whistled across the plateau and tugged at their clothes.

'Now!' Evelyn yelled and waved at the bearers.

Ahmosis shouted with her, and immediately the bearers grabbed the container's staves. As one, they lifted it and pushed it under the screaming, searing core as it pointed its lethal ray of energy away from them.

'Release it!' Evelyn shouted.

Ahmosis pulled the staff free, and the core rolled on its cradle and slammed into the container, the blazing beam of light slicing horizontally across the plateau and out across the deserts. Evelyn saw the beam sear the rocky earth, instantly turning it to molten liquid that ran in glowing rivers and spat bright sparks of magma.

'Roll the container upright, carefully!'

The men took hold of the staves and braced themselves as they began rolling it back into its normal upright position. The swirling vortex of cloud shifted up through the sky, wrapped forever around the blazing rays.

'Slowly!' Evelyn shouted.

The bearers took their time, the container shifting slowly over until it came to rest on its staves, the brilliant, quivering beam of energy rocketing upwards once again up into the swirling tower of cloud above them.

'The lid!' Ahmosis ordered.

The bearers moved to the lid and hefted it up to their shoulders and then carried it to the container.

'Don't drop it on!' Evelyn shouted. 'Slide it into the grooves!'

The bearers obeyed, crouching down slightly and sliding the lid into shaped grooves along the side of the container. Evelyn saw the lid glow brightly as the beam of light was cut off in mid–stream. With nowhere else to go, it blasted out of the remaining gap in a wide horizontal shaft and hit one of the bearers straight in his chest.

Evelyn saw the man's body evaporate as though it were a glowing liquid, his face twisting into a grotesque mask of agony before being blasted from his shoulders to arc across the plateau trailing flame and smoke. The rest of his body fell to its knees and collapsed in a smouldering heap on the soil, neatly severed in half, the flesh cauterised to the colour of charcoal.

'Push it closed!' Evelyn yelled as she heaved her shoulder into the back of the half–open lid.

Ahmosis fell in alongside her and together they pushed. The heavy gold lid slid across its grooves and with a final scream of energy it slammed shut.

The howling wind around them vanished, the gusting dust and swirling cloud above them shuddering with a last tortured crack of thunder that rattled out across the lonely plains and into the distance. From the thick mist the dawn sun broke through to bathe the plateau in a gentle golden light that was reflected in magical hues by the container now sitting on its staves before them.

Ahmosis was shaking, his smouldering beard quivering on his chest and his eyes wide as he stared at the now silent container. Slowly, he turned to Evelyn.

'Have I beheld the power of a God?' he asked, his voice timid even in the sudden silence enveloping the plateau.

Evelyn nodded. 'Pretty much.'

Around them the Shasu were appearing on the plateau in their hundreds, approaching the container. Ahmosis regained his composure and turned to face them, raising his staff high above his head.

'Behold!' he roared, indicating the container behind him. 'The power of our god, here in our hands, the bond between us forged in a holy covenant!'

The Shasu stared in awe at the container, which glowed with an unnatural light, the air around it trembling as intense heat leaked through imperfections in the lining. Ahmosis's voice thundered across the plateau as he thrust his staff into the air.

'Kneel, before this covenant ark!'

As one the Shasu fell to their knees in something akin to both awe and terror as they stared at the ark.

Evelyn watched as Ahmosis reverentially pulled the purple veil back over the ark, concealing it from view as he turned back to his people.

'We shall be pursued by Egypt no longer! We shall march *upon* Egypt!'

Evelyn saw the Shasu rise up, their hands to the sky as they let out a thunderous cheer almost as loud as the ark had roared.

***

XXX

Captain Idris Sansin sat upon a hard bench in the holding cell, surrounded by his bridge crew.

'So, what do you want to know, exactly?'

They stared at him for a long time, as though having finally had the courage to broach the matter they could not now fathom a suitable question with which to begin.

'Are there humans down there?' Meyanna asked finally. 'Civilisations like ours?'

'They're not quite like ours,' the captain replied.

'They're damned close enough, aren't they?' Meyanna said. 'Bra'hiv's marines are not likely to have made it all up. Hevel and his crew have detected a human presence on the planet below us.'

The captain nodded, staring at his boots as he did so.

'Do you remember your history classes, at school?' he asked the floor, and then looked up at the crew around him. 'The legends of a time when our people were consumed by ice?'

Jerren, the tactical officer, frowned at the captain. 'That was just religion, fantasy,' he said, 'from a time when we did not understand our world.'

'True,' the captain admitted, 'but then we also know that we did not evolve on our own planet, Ethera. Our species has no fossil evidence there, which led to the rise of religions and faith in deities, that we must somehow have been special in some way, the product of a god. It was only in recent times that we realised that we came to Ethera from elsewhere.'

'How?' asked Jerren.

'I wish I knew,' Idris replied. 'Our history, that of our structures and our agriculture, suggests that we never possessed the ability to travel between stars until now, so therefore the logical conclusion is that we travelled to Ethera from elsewhere.'

Meyanna's eyes narrowed.

'And you think that this is where we travelled from,' she said.

Idris inhaled deeply. 'I know of no other planetary system where human beings live outside of the colonies,' he replied. 'I have no idea if this world is the one from which we originated, or of why if that's true that these other humans did not travel with us. All I can say is that Bra'hiv's marines have confirmed that Hevel's preliminary scans of the planet beneath us also showed evidence of widescale glaciation, of ice floes that must have been miles deep. That, if nothing else, fits with the stories of legend that haunt the origin of our people.'

'It we have some understanding of their language that might give us a clue,' said Jerren. 'But if they are ancestors of ours, if we did come from here, then the Word will view them as an enemy also.'

Idris sighed.

'Yes, it will attack them as it attacks us,' he agreed. 'What we have done to ourselves will be done unto them.'

'We didn't start this war,' Meyanna insisted.

'We did,' Idris replied. 'The brutal truth is that we became too damned clever for our own good, developed technologies too complex for us to control, too advanced for us to understand, and before we realised it they were in control of us. I guess we knew that it was possible, but nobody really ever thought that it would happen the way it did.'

'The Word,' Jerren said. 'It was supposed to protect us.'

'It still thinks that it is protecting us,' the captain replied. 'The Word was the ultimate learning device, devoted to collecting knowledge. It became the creator of rules and laws that were more effective than anything we had ever known, the builder of technologies that took us to the stars.' He sighed. 'What we didn't know was that its greatest desire, to learn, required it to infiltrate our very minds.'

The captain saw members of his crew shiver mentally at the thought of what had happened, at what had been a pandemic of such bizarre and fearful proportions that those fortunate enough not to have been infected had been left with no choice but to flee with what they could carry in their hands, scattered to the farthest corners of the colonies.

'How did it get inside us?' Jerren asked.

The captain took a deep breath and looked at his wife, Meyanna.

'The truth is that we just don't know,' she replied, 'but we do know that it has something to do with our blood, which contains iron.'

'A metal,' Jerren acknowledged. 'So they could use it, as fuel?'

Meyanna nodded.

'The Word is in effect a machine, or rather billions of machines that act as a swarm and develop intelligence via sheer numbers. It's like a human brain – each neuron alone is nothing, but a few billion combined give us self–awareness, emotions, feelings. The Word may be a machine but its components became so small that by infecting the bloodstream of humans they could use the iron in our blood to replicate themselves and then move onto biological manipulation, taking over control of people from the inside out.'

Captain Sansin nodded, images of the downfall of mankind flashing like a macabre movie through his mind.

The miniaturisation of technology had been a natural consequence of the advancement of knowledge, and it had been developed for commercial reasons: tiny devices programmed to seek out atmospheric pollutants and consume them before returning to stations on Ethera's surface to be burned up and rebuilt once again: an endless cycle of chemical evolution. The devices had been given a catch–all name: *Legion.*

Of course, it had been equally natural that the military obtain the technology for battlefield and surveillance purposes. And it had been more natural still for criminals to obtain that technology and modify it for profit, or for fear. The ability to self–replicate had been expressly forbidden for all nano–technologies, but in the hands of those whose religious fervour belayed the voices of reason or caution, such considerations were of no consequence. At some point, probably in some illegal laboratory on a smuggler's asteroid mining complex or buried deep in a city on Caneeron, a terrorist had successfully performed self–replication on a lone nanobot and within hours had lost control of the process as the devices began replicating without limit.

The first swarms appeared, replicating and consuming metals to do so, programmed to automatically attack military vehicles. Initially, the military managed to respond, successfully deploying their own nano–devices in retaliation and quelling the outbreak.

But somewhere along the line, somehow, the combined numbers of devices broke a communication barrier, an undefined line between autonomous machines and cohesive flock: self–aware, more than the sum of their parts. Intelligence emerged, and before it could be contained it vanished.

For over a year nothing more was heard or seen of the swarm despite huge military expenditure in hunting it out. By the time it was realised what had happened, the sheer volume of people who had become infected, it was already too late.

Nobody could ever really forget the outbreak. The damnable thing about it was that the Word had been intelligent enough, driven enough, that it had ensured some seventy per cent of the human population had been infected before it sent out a signal: *replicate*. The swarm had contained billions of nano–devices, more than enough to infect every human being in the colonies. There had been no need for outright conflict: the Word had already deduced humanity's greatest weakness.

The first signs of infection had been a sort of mild fever and heightened pulse, nothing in itself. But then the first victims had begun reporting things swimming in their field of vision. Analysis had found the tiny metallic devices swarming through people's eyeballs. Emergency work by military forces had confirmed that the devices were first hijacking the optical nerves of every infected victim, gaining control of human eyesight before then infiltrating the nervous system and spinal cord. Within days of infection the human being was entirely conscious and yet unable to control any aspect of their physiology, be it locomotion, sight, hearing, touch or even the ability to sleep. All was controlled by what became known as the Word.

Upon the replication command, the tiny devices either reported the position of every infected human in the colonies or blinded them instantly to render them an ineffective defence against the Word. In a single instant billions were blinded, including over two thirds of the military and the entire emergency services of all colonies, those in closest contact with infected victims who had then themselves become infected long before the pandemic was activated.

As panic spread and civilisation began to collapse, the only people who remained uninfected were those who lived in remote locations, or those who served in the military who were isolated in some way aboard distant vessels or prisons.

As the Word moved in, taking control of virtually the entire colonial battle fleet and all merchant vessels, so the infected humans obeyed the Word without question. Their minds, still their own, were forced to watch their own actions without the slightest ability to control them. Fathers slaughtered wives and children, entire communities burned themselves within their own homes or travelled to the highest floors of tower blocks and strolled casually off the edges to their deaths. Those that remained stopped panicking as the insidious little machines inside them stimulated the pleasure regions of the brain, making even the most hideous of actions a pleasure as every last fragment of what remained of their human selves was lost to the Word.

In a matter of a few days, some eighty per cent of all humans had died in acts of suicide or murder prompted by the Word, who saw humanity's numbers as the greatest threat to its own existence. With most humans destroyed, and those that remained firmly enslaved, there was no longer any threat to the Word's existence or its pursuit of knowledge.

Atlantia, along with its prison ship Atlantia Five, was far enough from the carnage that it was able to escape. As a prison vessel, the safest location to hold convicts was upon the very edges of the colony's planetary system. Forced to flee as fast as it could, the Atlantia likely remained now as the last pocket of humanity in the known universe.

'We had no choice,' the captain said. 'Our only option was to put as much distance between us and the Word as we could, until we could figure out what the hell we could do to defeat it.'

'Which we can't,' Meyanna pointed out. 'It might be only a single ship coming after us but there are bound to be more. We can't fight a whole fleet.'

'There must have been other survivors though, right?' asked a junior officer. 'Other prison guard–ships, scout vessels, colony outposts and things like that?'

'We never picked up any signals,' the captain replied. 'Not in all the time we were in range of the colonies, or at least the ones that I knew of. Nothing. It was like humanity had never existed at all.'

Meyanna rubbed her forehead.

'So how come we've ended up here?' she asked. 'Blind luck wouldn't have led us to another planet inhabited by humans, right?'

'No,' the captain replied. 'I don't know how we ended up here. The ship's computer was commanded to plot a course that would be difficult to follow, to give us the best chance of evading capture or confrontation. It should have brought us to a location where the Word was least likely to find us.'

Jerren thought for a moment.

'What if it did its job right?' he asked out loud.

'What do you mean?' Meyanna asked.

Jerren got up from the hard bench and paced up and down the cell as he spoke.

'The ship was programmed to travel somewhere it was easy to hide,' he said. 'But as the Word knows we would probably do that, and it has links to all of the captured military vessels, it stands to reason that it would probably have been able to plot an identical course just by using another vessel's identical navigation computer.'

'Maybe,' the captain replied, 'but quantum–randomisation algorithms were built in to our escape and evasion programmes. No ship's computer should be able to come up with an identical course, in case of capture in battle and other dangerous eventualities.'

'Yes,' Jerren said, 'but what if that function was switched off for some reason?'

'Why would anybody do that unless..?'

The captain's features paled and his wife looked at Jerren. 'You think that somebody aboard this ship is infected?'

Jerren nodded.

'All they would have to do is deactivate the randomisation protocols, which can be done from the bridge when sending direct signals to other vessels. Otherwise we would not be able to communicate with each other in battle. If somebody re–wrote the coding in the ship's computer, or simply inserted a virus to shut the randomisation down, then anything we do could be easily replicated with an identical ship's computer.'

The captain stood.

'Over forty capital ships fell under the Word's control during the outbreak,' he said. 'Many of them were frigates like the Atlantia. What if the Word used us to seek out older human colonies?'

'Hevel,' Meyanna said. 'He's not going to stand and fight. He's waiting for the Word to reach us and he's removed the entire fighting staff from duty.'

'Or sent them down to the planet's surface,' the captain said. 'He's left us as vulnerable as possible, and the civilians are still inside the sanctuary.'

The captain stared at a wall filled with old graffiti, the scrawlings of the condemned.

'Why, though?' he asked out loud. 'Why has the Word gone so far to track *us* down, and why do all of this if it can destroy us so simply? We're a prison ship, not a fully manned frigate. The Word should be unafraid of us.'

It was Jerren who answered.

'We've either got something it wants, or somebody aboard has answers to how to defeat the Word.'

The captain raised his head from his thoughts as though struck by clairvoyance.

'Evelyn,' he whispered and turned to his command crew. 'She was the only person aboard fitted with a mask to silence her, right? But she was never tried for her crimes.'

'She murdered her entire family,' Meyanna replied. 'It's in what files we do have on her. She killed her son and her husband. She was awaiting trial for the death penalty when the pandemic caught hold.'

'And that's the thing,' the captain said. 'She committed a terrible crime, right? Carnage. Yet I don't recall ever seeing anything about a trial on the news channels, do you?'

He looked about at the crew, none of whom spoke.

'Isn't that odd?' Idris went on, warming to his theme. 'A mass murderer isn't normally somebody who is easily forgotten. Look at Qayin – he shot and killed a politician of all things, and *everybody* knows who he is.'

'You think that she's innocent?' Jerren asked.

'I think that we should figure out what the hell she was doing before she ended up in a cell in the high–security wing,' the captain replied. 'She had her memory wiped, right?'

'Apparently,' Meyanna replied, 'something to do with amnesia, the shock and horror of what she had done to her family.'

'Any chance that the amnesia was caused by drugs?' the captain asked her. 'That perhaps the Word tried to silence her?'

'Even if that were true, wouldn't the Word have just killed her like everybody else?'

'Maybe it didn't have enough control at that point,' Jerren suggested. 'If Evelyn uncovered evidence of the coming threat from the Word, then it would have been better for her to be silenced and imprisoned rather than simply murdered, or otherwise somebody else might have taken up her investigation.'

'I remember her file,' the captain said, 'she was some kind of journalist, right?'

Meyanna nodded. 'It would fit, but how could the Word have gotten her imprisoned so soon, and who actually committed the crime? Somebody had to kill her husband and child.'

Captain Sansin stopped pacing and stared at his wife.

'The political class,' he uttered. 'What if the Word started by infecting them and not the people? It could have used them to cover up any leaks about the infection, arranged for activists to be imprisoned, families murdered by corrupt or infected officials to provide enough of a crime to have them arrested.'

Jerren's face fell.

'She's been imprisoned all this time for the murder of her own family,' he gasped, 'and she may not have actually done it?'

'I thought that her actions in the prison were to gain amnesty for her crimes,' the captain said. 'But what if they were acts born of her true nature?'

'Andaim said that Evelyn claimed the Atlantia fired upon the escape capsules from the high–security wing,' Meyanna said. 'Governor Hayes ordered those shots, and if he was afraid of whatever Evelyn knows then it would make sense he would do such a thing.'

'You think that Governor Hayes was infected?' the captain asked his wife. 'He could have placed the bomb that destroyed the security wing.'

'We need her back here, right now,' Jerren said as he stood. 'If she has the key to defeating the Word up there in her head somewhere, then we need to find it. Maybe it was her knowledge that forced the Word to send the replicate signal before humanity was completely infected.'

'She's dead,' Meyanna insisted. 'You saw that hull burn up. Surely nobody could survive that?'

Captain Sansin gripped the bars of the cell.

'We'll have to hope otherwise, and that Bra'hiv can find her and turn any survivors to our side. We're running out of time.'

***

XXXI

'Captain on the bridge!'

Keyen's voice alerted the civilian staff as Hevel stepped through the main bridge doors and strode onto the command platform.

Pride surged through his veins as he stood beside the captain's chair and surveyed the bridge. He had never before realised that being the captain of a major fleet frigate would endow a man with such a sense of supreme power, something like a drug that made one feel somehow invincible.

Dhalere approached him from one side.

'The shuttle is away, sir,' she informed him. 'It will reach the surface within the hour. Bra'hiv and his marines are operating under our command and have accepted the terms of the mutiny. They will return with supplies as soon as the shuttle is full.'

'Good,' Hevel smiled in response, 'very good. Now, at last, we can bring this sorry episode to an end. What is the Word's range?'

Keyen replied immediately.

'Four solar orbital radii, closing fast sir.'

Hevel glanced across at a smaller hatch that adjoined the bridge. The captain's ready room, a small cabin where he could be on a moment's notice during time of conflict. Hevel turned to Dhalere.

'Have Arrana join me in the ready room in five minutes, please.'

Hevel stepped off the command platform and strode to the ready room. He opened the door and walked in, closing it behind him and looking at the captain's private sanctuary.

Considering the weighty responsibilities of a military command, it was a constant source of surprise to Hevel how sparse were the accommodation for naval officers. The captain's ready room contained a narrow bunk, a small desk and a tiny bathroom stall. The walls were of bare metal, unadorned except for a single projection plate that portrayed a family gathering.

Hevel edged closer and saw the image of the captain's family quiver into holographic life at his approach. The sound of laughter, a large family gathered around a garden table. Elderly grandparents, parents, children, friends, food and drink beneath a clear blue sky. Hevel felt a pang of jealousy and perhaps a sense of regret. He turned away from the image and walked around the tiny desk to sit in the captain's chair.

The ship's computerised log was set into the desk before him, and Hevel knew that he would not know or be able to fathom the captain's pass–code to examine the log. No matter – soon enough the Word would figure that out for him. For now, he had other business.

Hevel opened a drawer or two and quickly found what he was looking for. A bottle of amber liquor and four glasses tucked down low in a bottom drawer. In the bleak world of a military commander, away from home for countless months, small comforts were always carefully guarded possessions. Hevel poured two glasses, setting them down again and waiting.

The beep of an entry request sounded softly through the cabin, and Hevel opened the door using a button on the desk. Aranna walked into the cabin, the door shutting behind her as Hevel stood and greeted her.

'I wanted to thank you,' he said, 'for supporting me through this difficult time. I know how hard it must have been for you to stay the course when we have served for so long under Captain Sansin.'

'What will happen to him?' Aranna asked.

'Oh, nothing,' Hevel waved her off. 'I have no intention of bringing charges against either the captain or his crew. This mutiny, if it can even be called that, is required to wrest back control of a situation that the captain has clearly lost. If we left him in command we would die, and we would die at the expense of lesser citizens incarcerated for their crimes. To me, as a representative of the people, that was not acceptable.'

'What do we do now?' she asked.

Hevel walked out from behind the desk and picked up the glasses, handing one to Aranna.

'We do our best,' Hevel replied. 'The Word is closing in on us and there is now no escape from it. We will make our stand here.'

'What are our tactics?' Aranna pressed. 'Do we have a means to defeat the Word?'

Hevel smiled, his voice reassuring as he spoke.

'I have spoken at length with Bra'hiv and we have a plan that may work,' he said. 'Right now, all that we need to formulate is unity. We must be driven by the same goal, with the same unwavering determination, in order to prevail. If we falter, if we doubt ourselves or seek to retract our position, we will be crushed.' Hevel lifted his glass. 'The enemy is close at hand and it is up to us to ensure that we work together, as a species, to defeat the forces of darkness that threaten us.'

Hevel touched his glass to hers. 'To victory,' he said.

Aranna echoed his toast and then they both drained their glasses.

Hevel watched her for a moment and then smiled.

'I feel certain that you will perform your duties with the utmost courage and conviction,' he said, 'and ensure that humanity will be forever erased from existence.'

It took a moment for the confusion to register on Aranna's face as she digested Hevel's words. He saw her mouth open as though to clarify what she had heard, and then it happened. Aranna swayed sideways, one hand shooting out to steady herself against the captain's desk as Hevel caught her glass before it shattered on the deck at their feet.

Aranna opened her mouth to scream for help as Hevel lunged forward. He thrust one hand over her mouth as he caught Aranna and lowered her onto the captain's desk, pinning her in place with his weight. The drug he had slipped into her drink was weak and short–lived, but then he knew that he needed only moments.

Aranna's eyes were drooping as she hovered on the verge on consciousness. Hevel, holding her against his body, removed his hand from her mouth and leaned in. He kissed her fully on the lips, heard her moan and squirm in protest beneath him as his tongue probed hers. Hevel kissed her for several long seconds and then he stood up and released her.

Aranna staggered off the desk, regaining her feet and wiping one sleeve across her mouth as disgust flared in her blue eyes. She was about to open her mouth again to shout for help but almost immediately her eyes rolled up into her sockets and she sank to her knees, her body quivering as though a live current were surging through her, limbs twitching and eyelids flickering.

Hevel took another sip of his drink as he watched in fascination as the nanobots flooded up into Aranna's spinal cord, immobilised the signals from her brain by firing tiny electrical impulses into the nerves to prevent her from crying out for help or fleeing. As Hevel watched, other bots flooded into her bloodstream and began replicating as others still migrated to other parts of the body: the brain, the eyes and the ears.

Hevel knew that blood circulated through the human body roughly once every sixty seconds. Within three minutes, Aranna's major organs were infested with hundreds of bots, mostly concentrated around the spinal cord and in the brain in order to control her. Two minutes later and she was laying on her back on the deck and staring at Hevel as though coming awake from a dream.

'Welcome back,' Hevel said as he looked down at her. 'I take it that everything is okay?'

Aranna gasped as her brain's pleasure centres were stimulated by the bots. Her thighs quivered and she sucked in a deep breath, her lips parted and her eyes losing focus.

'I'll take that as a yes,' Hevel murmured to himself. 'Stand up.'

Aranna got to her feet, looking slightly vacant as she steadied herself against a wall.

'You will conduct your duties as normal,' Hevel ordered her, 'and you will take every opportunity to infect the rest of the command crew on the bridge. We do not have much time. As soon as the Word arrives and we can be boarded, we shall extend the infection to the civilians in the sanctuary and then to the captain and his crew. Is that clear?'

'What about the people on the planet below?'

As Aranna spoke her features registered shock as though she were not in control of her own voice. The bots would gain command of her facial expressions soon enough, Hevel reflected.

'That will be for the Word to decide,' Hevel replied. 'I expect that they will be destroyed. Dismissed.'

Aranna turned without a further comment and left the ready room.

Hevel watched her go.

As soon as the ready room door was closed he felt an overwhelming euphoria flood his brain as the bots infecting him went into overdrive, rewarding his performance. Hevel staggered to the narrow bunk as indescribable pleasure swelled within his body, his limbs twitching and his heart fluttering in his chest as, not for the first time, he collapsed into a crucible of ecstacy beyond anything that he could have imagined.

***

XXXII

Bra'hiv sat in a seat in the back of the cockpit as the shuttle craft descended through the rarified atmosphere of the planet. Billowing clouds soared into the pale blue dawn, and beneath them sprawled vast deserts scarred by the ghosts of old rivers long since dried out.

'Keep us in the cloud and out of sight,' he instructed the pilots as they guided the shuttle down. 'I don't want to attract any attention from the natives.'

The pilot nodded, guiding the shuttle through a thick bank of cloud. As they emerged, Bra'hiv saw the horizon enshrouded in darkness, the distant volcano spewing vast quantities of ash and debris into the atmosphere. The pilot banked the shuttle over to avoid the edge of the vast, ominous cloud.

'I'm picking up major habitations near the river,' he said as he glanced at his instruments. 'Large monuments, populations in excess of fifty thousand, a lot of agriculture.'

Bra'hiv leaned forward, watching as the clouds broke briefly before them through the broad, angular windshield. A winding river bisected the barren desert, lined with dense foliage, a snake of green amid the barren wilderness.

'Stay away from the river,' he said. 'People congregate near water.'

'I've got something else,' the co–pilot said, 'an energy source.'

'A what?' Bra'hiv asked.

'High megavolts,' the co–pilot responded. 'It's coming from out in the deserts somewhere, a fair way from the cities.'

Bra'hiv thought for a moment.

'The prison hull, did any pieces make it down around here?'

The co–pilot nodded as the shuttle was swallowed by another bank of cloud, rocking and swaying in the turbulence.

'A few pieces made it through the atmosphere and would have impacted around this area,' he replied.

Bra'hiv considered the possibility that somehow the fusion core of the prison hull might have landed intact on the surface. If it had, then any survivors of the descent would likely have sought it out. Human nature, he reflected: abandoned on an alien world, the convicts would have craved the sight of anything to remind them of home.

'Bring us down nearby,' Bra'hiv ordered, 'but not close enough to be seen. We need to maintain an element of surprise here, understood?'

'What about the supplies?' the pilot asked. 'We can take on water from the river, but there's nothing out here.'

'That fusion core is a weapon and is now our priority,' he explained, 'anything that makes a big bang is what we need. Unless you'd be happy taking on the Word with your pistol?'

The pilot did not reply to Bra'hiv's challenge, instead turning the shuttle toward the signal from the fusion core.

Bra'hiv sat back in his seat and glanced behind him to the armed marines strapped into the crew compartment in the shuttle. He felt certain that they would follow his lead and take back both the core and any survivors: what was less certain was whether Hevel would allow them back aboard the ship.

For the first time in his career, Bra'hiv realised that he was hoping that incompetence would win through.

*

Andaim heard the noise as he walked.

The pharaoh's army had decamped at first light, Golyath's Pelasgian mercenaries at their head as they marched south west away from the broad expanses of the river and the monumental pyramids toward the endless wastes of the desert. The baggage train of the army, marching through the swirling clouds of golden dust churned up by countless thousands of feet, stretched almost two miles behind the main fighting force.

Chariots led the way, scout forces wheeling ahead of the main army to find routes through the worst of the desert.

Amazingly, the pharaoh had emerged with the sunrise with an entirely different headdress, the conical decoration gone in favour of densely braided hair in alternating shades of blue and gold. Despite their predicament, Andaim had forced himself not to burst out laughing as he saw the pharaoh's wiry, short version of Qayin emerge from his personal quarters.

Andaim walked behind the pharaoh's personal carriage, which was carried aloft upon the shoulders of a dozen servants. Qayin strode beside

Andaim, the big man sweating profusely in the sun despite his bare chest and legs.

'You hear that?' he asked Qayin.

'What?' the big man grumbled. 'You mean the sound of my life draining from my every pore?'

Andaim squinted up into the sky above, peering into the broken cumulus clouds drifting through the blue, but he could see nothing through the hazy dawn mist. Only the faintest hum drifted upon the wind, the sound of turbine engines soaring at high altitude.

'A shuttle,' he guessed.

Qayin scrutinised the sky for a moment before he shrugged and loped onward through the hot sand.

'The hell with them,' he muttered. 'They ain't looking for us no more, probably scouting for water.'

Andaim looked ahead, toward the distant hills where a towering column of flame and cloud had only hours before been rising up into the dawn sky. There, as the sun had risen above the horizon, the deserts glowing in captivating hues around them, they had watched as the pillar of flame had quivered and danced ever more violently before until, with a dull rumble of thunder, it had vanished and the distant skyline had fallen into silence as the pillar of smoke and cloud had vanished.

'Maybe,' he replied. 'Or maybe they've got some plans for whatever it was that landed out there too. If we can reach them, we could join them.'

Qayin frowned. 'You want to make it back aboard?'

'It'll be the only chance we have to board a shuttle. Why, you think it's going to be better for you down here with the natives?'

'I ain't a prisoner down here.' Qayin glanced at the pharaoh. 'Not right now, anyways.'

'And what happens when the Word arrives and finds more humans populating this planet?' Andaim challenged. 'You think that it won't seek to destroy each and every one of them too?'

'Ain't my problem,' Qayin muttered. 'I'll be long gone.'

'You sure will be if the Word finds you.'

Andaim fell silent as the pharaoh looked over his shoulder at them. 'You, both of you, what do you speak of?'

'Our future,' Andaim replied, 'free from the god of the Shasu.'

The pharaoh watched them for a long moment, as though once again considering whether to cut their throats. Then he pointed to Qayin. 'You,' he said. 'Join me.'

Qayin raised an eyebrow and glanced at Andaim before he accelerated his stride, quickly coming up alongside the pharaoh's litter. The bearers slowed and the big man vaulted up onto it and sat opposite the pharaoh. Qayin glanced at Andaim and offered him a broad grin.

'Your friend,' the pharaoh said, 'you mock him often.'

'He's easy to mock,' Qayin replied.

'How will I defeat the Shasu?' the pharaoh asked again.

'You'll find out when we get there.'

'Why should I trust you?'

'Same reason I have to trust you,' Qayin replied. 'No choice.'

'What happens if the Shasu send their God to kill me?'

Qayhin shrugged without concern. 'Send in your mercenaries first. That way, you can see what happens without wasting any of your own men.'

The pharaoh watched Qayin for a long moment and then a cold little smile spread across his face.

'You are a pragmatist, Qayin,' he said. 'I could use more men like you. But first, I need a test of your loyalty.'

Qayin eyed the king warily. 'What kind of test?'

'The definitive kind,' the pharaoh replied and then raised his hand.

Behind them a series of barked commands were shouted out, drifting down the column of the army like an echo vanishing into the distance, and with remarkable speed the entire army halted on the desolate plain.

Several of the pharaoh's guards appeared beside the litter, and the pharaoh leaned out and spoke with them. They hurried away as the pharaoh leaned back in his plush seat and looked at Qayin.

'I have need of a military man,' he said, 'a trusted advisor. You shall become my fist among the men, and place weight and violence behind my commands wherever it is needed.'

'That sounds like something I would excel at,' Qayin replied. 'What's in it for me?'

The pharaoh raised one delicately painted eyebrow. 'Your life.'

Qayin smiled. 'A wise and generous king, you are,' he said.

The pharaoh leaned forward.

'Now, tell me how I will defeat the army of the Shasu.'

'No,' Qayin replied.

The pharaoh clicked his fingers and immediately the Pelasgian guards were back and ordering Qayin down out of the litter. The big convict jumped back down into the sand and instantly spotted a large ring of Pelasgian soldiers standing nearby, their arms interlocked and their giant king Golyath standing among them.

'If you or your friend will not obey me by choice,' the pharaoh called down, 'then I shall provide a different incentive for your loyalty.'

Qayin's big wrists were bound close together using rough cord, a length of the cord roughly half a cubit between his wrists allowing him some freedom of movement. Moments later, one of the guards drew a huge kopesh and turned it over, handle first, toward Qayin.

Qayin took the blade as the Pelasgians opened their circle. Beyond them, on the plain, the entire army stood and watched as Qayin strode into the circle of men, fully prepared to fight each and every one of them to the death.

He had not realised that there was another man standing inside the circle.

The pharaoh's voice rang out across the desert.

'The choice is yours, Qayin. Your life, or that of Andaim.'

Qayin's eyes settled on Andaim's, the officer's wrists likewise bound and a blade glittering in his grasp in the hot sunlight.

***

XXXIII

'They're coming.'

The voice of Ahmosis' lieutenant was crisp on the cool air, but the last of the mist was fading rapidly away and the heat was building fast.

Evelyn walked beside the ark, keeping one eye on it as it was carried aloft at the head of the army by the Shasu's bearers. Their faces were wracked with fear as they bore the weighty burden between them, the ark trembling with heat, its veil quivering and the occasional spark of energy flickering like lightning beneath it.

'Forward!' Ahmosis boomed, raising his staff aloft.

The Shasu had left their women and children encamped in a wadi several miles behind them, the animals accompanying them in case the army was routed and forced to flee, giving them the chance to avoid the pharaoh's men. Now they were descending down from the hills toward the plain below.

'How many?' Ahmosis asked.

'Perhaps ten thousand,' the lieutenant replied. 'Their scouts are riding ahead of their vanguard, and they have the Pelasgians with them.'

'Golyath?' Ahmosis asked.

'His banner flies at the head of the mercenaries, and we're confident of the Egyptian's numbers by the size of their column wake.'

'The baggage train,' Ahmosis agreed. 'The pharaoh Thutmose is supposed to be marching north,' he explained to Evelyn, 'toward Canaan to put down the Hittites. The entire army has diverted to put down our rebellion first. An honour, I suppose, as well as an inconvenience. I doubt they would have confronted us with such a large force otherwise.'

'Their king will travel with them?' Evelyn asked.

'The pharaoh will be with them and may even take to the field himself.' Ahmosis glanced at the ark behind them. 'I certainly hope so.'

'Remember,' Evelyn said, 'if you win the battle, you don't have to slaughter the entire army. Let the pharaoh see the ark and what it can do and you'll earn your people the right to live without oppression, agreed?'

Ahmosis scowled but he nodded. 'It will be so.'

Evelyn looked ahead to where the trembling horizon of the plain was marred by a vast drifting cloud of golden dust, the mark of thousands of feet on the move. She looked behind her and saw the Shasu marching with their swords and shields gripped firmly in their hands, their eyes fixed upon the distant horizon and filled with the fervour of god's army.

They were following the ark with a near religious zeal, the lust for vengeance poisoning their expressions. Evelyn thought of the Atlantia's crew, perhaps imprisoned now or fighting for their lives against each other or against the Word.

Even as she thought of them she heard the faint drone of turbine engines somewhere high above her in the sky. The haze and scattered cloud hid the source of the noise enough that she could not pick out where the craft was, but her first thought was that it sounded remarkably like a shuttle. Small engines, not those of a fighter aircraft. She craned her neck up to the sky, searching for the shuttle. If it was heading down to the surface and was nearby then there was a chance, however slim, of making it back to the ship.

'What is it?' Ahmosis asked.

'Nothing,' she replied.

'Ahmosis,' cried one of the Shasu soldiers. 'The army of the pharaoh has stopped!'

Evelyn looked up and saw the vast dust cloud drifting away across the plain and dissipating rapidly in the hot wind. Against the distant and rippling horizon she could just make out a dark stain, countless specks of people and banners and flags rippling in the wind.

'They await us?' Evelyn asked.

'No,' Ahmosis replied, 'they would send their chariots as soon as we were sighted. They are watching something else.'

'Then let's go,' Evelyn replied, searching the turbulent sky above once more. 'The sooner this is over, the better.'

*

Andaim tightened his grip on his kopesh, the hooked bronze blade flickering in the light as he edged toward Qayin.

The convict loomed over Andaim, his own fist curled around the handle of a kopesh.

'I've been waiting a long time for this,' he growled.

'Don't waste any time talking then.'

Qayin lifted one giant arm and swung for Andaim's neck, the blade whistling through the air as the Egyptian army and Golyath's mercenaries roared in approval.

Andaim ducked and leaped to his left, the blade flashing by so close to his face that he felt a rush of air in its wake as he stepped in and swung his kopesh back–handed, seeking to unzip Qayin's flank.

The big man twisted aside, pivoting with surprising grace on the ball of one foot as he turned full circle out of Andaim's reach. Andaim let his weapon flow upward and over as he brought it crashing down over his head toward Qayin's broad chest.

The convict threw up his kopesh and the two curved blades clanged loudly as they clashed. Andaim felt his blow arrested and pain shuddered through his wrists at the impact. Qayin's immense strength overwhelmed him almost immediately as the convict drove him backwards and then turned his kopesh, trying to twist Andaim's weapon from his grasp.

Andaim folded over sideways as he struggled to prevent his wrist from giving way. He turned and changed his grip as he whipped around to turn his back to Qayin and then drove an elbow backwards into the big man's face. Qayin grunted and jerked backwards as he released Andaim's blade from his own.

Andaim spun lightly and whipped the back of his kopesh up across the giant's chest.

The copper blade sliced into Qayin's dense pectoral muscles and left a bright, glistening red gash as Qayin growled in pain and gave more ground, staggering backwards out of Andaim's reach as a rush of cheers and shouts broke out among the watching troops.

The convict's eyes fixed upon Andaim's and he rushed in, his bulging muscles gleaming in the sunlight. Andaim feigned a left thrust with his kopesh and then jerked right and out of range of Qayin's weapon as it plunged down toward his scalp.

Qayin staggered and Andaim whipped his kopesh upward once more, the blade scything across Qayin's flank. The convict gasped and his hand flashed to his wounded side as he turned, keeping his kopesh between himself and Andaim as he struggled to stay on his feet.

Andaim leaped forward and jabbed the kopesh at Qayin's face, forcing him backwards as the big convict clumsily tried to swipe his weapon at Andaim. The crowd of soldiers watched in earnest, cheers and gasps erupting from their ranks as they closed in.

Andaim saw the big man start to tire, his body sheened with sweat beneath the burning sun and his eyes drooping, his gold and blue braided hair hanging in thick, damp locks. Andaim jabbed the kopesh once more at Qayin's face and then spun on his heel, whipping the weapon around in a savage back–handed blow straight at Qayin's face.

To his surprise Qayin made no attempt to avoid the flickering blade. His big hand released his kopesh, which dropped into the sand at his feet as he instead reached up and lunged in toward Andaim, all pretence of exhaustion vanished. His huge hand caught Andaim's wrist in full flight as his other hand formed a fist that ploughed into Andaim's kidney.

Andaim's back arched as the blow crumpled him and he slammed onto his back in the sand, the bright sun flaring into his eyes. He rolled over, pain surging through his body as he struggled to his feet.

Qayin was watching him with a broad smile on his features. He picked up both of the kopeshes and brandished them, one in each hand. The watching crowd cheered the huge convict on and Qayin turned to look at the pharaoh.

The pharaoh cast Andaim a brief, disgusted glance and then nodded to Qayin.

Qayin rushed in toward Andaim, who kicked his foot across the sand at their feet and sent it spraying into Qayin's face. The convict hesitated, swiping at the sand embedded in his eyes as Andaim rushed in and grabbed the big man's head in his hands, twisting it sideways with all of his might and pulling downward.

Qayin was yanked off balance and flipped over to crash down onto the sand as Andaim landed on top of him, grabbing the convict's hands and pulling them inward between them to cross the kopeshes as he leaned down against the sharp bronze blades and pushed them toward Qayin's throat.

Qayin's thickly muscled arms bulged as he fought back against Andaim's weight, his vast chest heaving as he sucked in air to fuel his strength. Andaim leaned further forward and pushed all of his weight across the blades as they sank toward Qayin's neck.

'You been looking forward to this?' Andaim hissed, his voice hoarse with effort.

Qayin's arms trembled beneath Andaim's weight, the edges of the blades touching his skin, and Andaim saw his big dark eyes quiver with a brief flare of panic.

'I ain't afraid to die,' Qayin snarled back with the last of his strength.

Andaim saw a red welt appear on Qayin's neck beneath the blades as they sawed into his flesh. Andaim jerked back and rolled off Qayin, came up onto his feet and walked away from the fallen convict. He faced the pharaoh and Golyath, stared them both straight in the eye before spitting into the sand at his feet.

The cheering crowds of Egyptian and Pelasgians soldiers fell silent and stared in disbelief at Andaim, stunned by his defiance. The pharaoh's eyes widened with indignation and he seemed to tremble in his litter as he raised a long, slender arm that quivered with rage.

He was about to give the order to kill Andaim when, from across the desert, a blare of horns rolled with the desert wind and ten thousand heads turned to the west. Andaim looked over his shoulder and saw ranged across the horizon the marching shape of thousands of men bearing arms and rippling banners of war, and at their head a small group bearing aloft some sort of container hidden beneath a veil.

'The Hebrews are coming,' the pharaoh snarled, pointing at the oncoming army. 'To arms!'

***

XXXIV

'It was here,' Bra'hiv said as he stood upon the plateau.

He held in his hand a small device that scanned the surrounding deserts and began to click loudly as he held it out to the north east, the shuttle parked behind him on the plateau.

'Ten leagues, maybe twelve,' C'rairn said as he glanced at the device and the signal it was detecting far out across the deserts. 'Looks like somebody took it with them.'

Bra'hiv looked out across the bright horizon to where he could see a smudge of wind–driven sand spreading across the desert.

'How the hell could they have got close to it?' he uttered.

'Survivors,' C'rairn replied. 'Somebody who knew what to do.'

'Andaim, maybe even Qayin or the other convicts, or Evelyn.'

'It's Andaim we want,' C'rairn said. 'He's the priority. Anybody else we can take along will be good, but right now we need somebody the people can trust.'

'How long until the Word arrives?' Bra'hiv asked, although he already knew the answer.

'A few hours at the most.'

Bra'hiv stared out at the distant dust cloud and he knew that there was no longer any choice.

'We'll have to get in there and bring them out, right now.'

'What about the supplies?' C'rairn asked. 'And protocol? If we're seen…'

'To hell with protocol! If we don't win this battle we won't be alive to consume the supplies and nobody will be left to bear witness to our presence. Let's go.'

*

The blast from the Shasu's horns was made all the more deafening as from the far north a deep rumbling noise reverberated through the land as Andaim turned along with the rest of the army.

The Shasu's horns had blared and it seemed as though the entire planet had rumbled in response. The horizon to the far north, smeared with ominous clouds that soared into the heavens, now flickered with lightning and glowed in an apocalyptic light as the Egyptian army swayed and faltered and Golyath's Pelasgians leaped into battle order around their king.

Qayin got to his feet, clutching his wounds as he stared at the oncoming Shasu army.

'What they got there, out in front of 'em?'

Andaim shook his head.

'I've got a bad feeling about this,' he said as the pharaoh's guards fell in protectively alongside their king. 'I don't know how, but they might have the prison hull's engine core in there. We need it.'

The pharaoh looked at Qayin.

'Speak of your plan, or I shall have you both slaughtered here before the gods of my enemies!'

Andaim, pleased for once to not be answering all of the questions, stood back and waited to see how Qayin would respond. The convict looked across the plain at the oncoming Shasu army and then turned to the pharaoh.

'Dig trenches,' he replied.

The pharaoh stared at Qayin for a long moment, as did the rest of the amassed troops gathered close enough to understand what Qayin had said.

'Dig trenches?' the pharaoh echoed in disgust.

'Now,' Qayin said, 'as fast as you can.'

The pharaoh seemed momentarily speechless, but then he stood and climbed down from his litter as he pointed his staff at Qayin.

'You wish us to dig in the ground like a dog and hide?' he asked. 'For my army to bury its head in the sand? For my chariots, my strongest asset, to be prevented from moving freely across the field?'

Qayin took a pace forward, one eye casting across the immense baggage train following the army.

'If you want your people to live, yes,' he said.

The pharaoh glared at Qayin for a moment longer, and then his features screwed up with rage and he swiped his hand in Qayin's direction and looked at Golyath.

'Put them to death! All of them!'

Golyath grinned, his beard glowing in the strange light cast by the sun through the soaring clouds of ash in the sky above. He loomed toward them both, reached back behind his head and drew out his gigantic swords, the blades flashing like gold as he swung them at Qayin. Qayin leaped backwards and out of range of the swords as he whirled and tossed one of the weapons in his big fists to Andaim. Andaim caught the kopesh just in time to raise it as Golyath swung a sword toward his head.

The blow shuddered through Andaim's kopesh and he stumbled backwards and collapsed onto the dust on his back, his arm pulsing with pain. Qayin lunged at Golyath, who smashed the convict's kopesh aside with one mighty blow as his other fist, still clenching a sword, smashed into Qayin's face and hurled him onto his back in the dust alongside Andaim.

The Pelasgians cheered en masse as Golyath stormed forward, a sword in each fist pointing down at Qayin and Andaim as he made to drive them into their bellies and pin them to the very earth beneath them. The blades flashed in the light as Golyath raised them above his head, but even before the first blow had been struck thunder ripped across the sky, a tremendous roar that seemed to shake the earth beneath their feet, the desert sands shifting and pulsing as though alive.

Golyath stumbled backward, off balance as the earth shuddered.

Andaim looked to the north, saw a bright flare of glowing flame searing the interior of the vast ash cloud, and he realised what had happened. The volcano had blown, the caldera blasted clean off the island, and the tectonic forces unleashed by the blast were now reverberating through the earth beneath their feet. The Egyptians and Pelasgians toppled and swayed in panic as the earthquake rumbled through the ground beneath them.

'The Hebrew gods are angry!' Qayin shouted at the pharaoh. 'They seek your downfall, and we will help them if you do not do as we say!'

'You said that their gods were false!' the pharaoh screamed.

'And you said that you would spare us!'

'Kill them!' the pharaoh shrieked again at Golyath, pointing at them as his litter swayed and shook.

Andaim blinked dust from his eyes as he saw Golyath sink to one knee in an attempt to steady himself, and yelled at Cutler and the other prisoners.

'Cutler, on me, now!'

The convicts shook off their guards and dashed across the plain, all of them giving Golyath a wide berth as they ran toward Andaim and Qayin.

'Shall we?' Andaim suggested.

Qayin lurched to his feet and together they began running for the Shasu lines as Cutler and the other convicts streamed past them, the ground beneath their feet no longer shaking.

Andaim turned as he ran and saw Golyath rise to his feet and let out a blood curdling roar as he lunged in pursuit.

*

Evelyn stared at the huge warrior as he charged defiantly across the plain, dwarfing Andaim and Qayin as he bore down upon them. Behind them, the Pelasgians and Egyptians watched in awe as their feared leader charged an entire army single–handed.

'Golyath,' Ahmosis uttered. 'We must open the ark, now!'

'No!' Evelyn shouted as she watched Andaim running and saw Cutler stumble and fall. Andaim turned and hurried to the older man's side, helping him to his feet.

Golyath bore down upon them and smashed Cutler aside with one huge forearm as Andaim leaped clear of the giant's wildly swinging swords.

'Wait,' Evelyn ordered Ahmosis.

'There is no time, we must...'

Evelyn broke away from the Shasu line and grabbed a bolas and a slingshot from one of the Shasu warriors, yanking them from his grasp as she leaped forward. Her heart began to hammer in her chest as she ran out onto the plain, away from the safety of the Shasu lines and toward the vast Egyptian army filling the plain before her. The three–pronged bolas held small wrapped weights at the end of each prong of cordage and the slingshot held a single polished pebble half the size of her fist.

For a few moments she was running with all of her strength and yet realising that she had no idea why. Qayin and the other convicts dashed past her in the opposite direction, staring at her in surprise as she sprinted into a void of silence broken only by the super–charged crackle of lightning in the apocalyptic sky above and the sounds of mortal combat just ahead of her.

Golyath's huge form loomed before her against the turbulent canvas of the skies and he raised both of his arms, as wide it seemed as a tree. In each hand he held the giant swords, the blades flashing like fiery beacons in the bright sunlight as he swung at Andaim.

Andaim scrambled out of range, and Golyath turned to where Cutler lay on his back in the dust, out of breath and defenceless. Golyath raised his sword.

Evelyn screamed at the giant king as she ran.

'Golyath, here!'

Golyath's eyes bored into hers as she rushed toward him. Evelyn saw the blades flash as Golyath turned and raised them upward, and as she ran they flashed down toward her.

Instantly she threw herself forward through the air as she hurled the bolas not at the giant's head but at his gigantic legs and his greaves. Evelyn landed flat onto the dusty ground, the skin on her chest scraping painfully on the stony plain. The thick cordage spun through the air as the bolas' weights fanned out. They flew beneath the flashing blades and slammed into Golyath's legs in a tangle of cord. The weights whipped around and tied themselves tightly about his legs and Golyath looked down in surprise, swaying as his huge swinging blades pulled him off balance.

Evelyn leaped to her feet and threw herself out of range as Golyath roared and reversed his swing in an attempt to slice her open as she lay on the ground. The blades whispered through the air in front of her as the tips flashed past her nose, and as they passed so she opened the slingshot and lunged forward.

She yanked the slingshot up behind her in an overarm swing, heard her own cry as she threw every ounce of her bodyweight and strength into the blow. The stone in the slingshot whipped up and over her head and she hauled it downward, Golyath's huge head staring at her as the stone impacted the bridge of his nose with a sickening crack of fractured bone and cartilage.

Golyath roared as his nose collapsed and blood splattered thickly across his face and beard in a deep red flood, his eyes momentarily closing under the blow. His wildly swinging blades threw him backwards and he tried to catch himself but his legs would not move, and Evelyn saw the giant topple backwards and slam down into the dust.

Evelyn hurled herself onto the giant's chest, tore a large dagger from its scabbard on the warrior's own belt as she clambered onto him and raised the weapon in both hands above his head, the blade pointing down like the sword of Damocles toward Golyath's throat.

The huge man stared up at her, stunned into submission both by the blow and the speed of his defeat. His swords were too large for him to turn and bring to bear upon her, and he released them, his huge arms reaching up to try to catch the dagger in mid–flight. Evelyn sucked in a lungful of air and plunged the blade down before he could stop her.

The weapon thrust down through Golyath's thick neck, transecting his windpipe and spinal cord as it was driven straight through and down into the dust beneath where he sprawled. Golyath's big eyes flared wide as he stared at her and she felt his body shudder and relax as he lost control of it, his arms flopping to his sides. A great gush of arterial blood spilled in thick, pulsing torrents from his gaping mouth to stain his great beard, and the life slowly drained from his eyes.

A last, great rush of air blasted from Golyath's lungs, and then he fell silent and still.

Evelyn, her hands tightly grasping the blade's handle, released it and she stood up on Golyath's chest to look out over the Egyptian army. Despite the storm rippling through the apocalyptic clouds above them, both armies had fallen silent.

***

XXXV

Evelyn leaped off Golyath's immense corpse as Cutler stumbled to his feet, his features stricken as he stared at her in disbelief.

From a distance, she heard the Egyptian Pharaoh's agonised, enraged scream. 'Kill them all!'

'Come on!' she yelled.

A roar of rage soared from the Pelasgian and Egyptian ranks as behind them the entire army plunged into motion, thousands of men sprinting in a wave of flying legs and flashing swords, chariots leaping away from their flanks at breakneck speed.

'Run, now!' Evelyn yelled at Andaim.

Andaim heard another blare of the Shasu's horns and he turned to see several dozen of their men upon a low ridgeline near the head of the army. They bore banners that rippled in the hot wind, and in their midst eight men bearing the curious container beneath a dark veil.

Above the screaming hymn of war emanating from the charging army, thunderous booms rolled and echoed across the heavens as though the gods were warring in the skies. Andaim looked up and saw the vast cloud system swelling as the far off volcano erupted with tremendous force, blasting the molten contents of the planet high into the atmosphere.

Andaim leaped to his feet and ran hard alongside Evelyn, the earth beneath their feet trembling with the force of the army pursuing them across the plain.

The Shasu were ranged across the low ridge ahead, maybe some five thousand in number, barely half the Pharaoh's strength and far less trained and organised.

'They're going to be slaughtered,' Andaim gasped to Evelyn.

Evelyn did not reply, and moments later she saw the Shasu's men emerge atop the ridge line, the horizon behind them seared with sunlight beneath the turbulent clouds above as they carried the ark, the horns blaring all around it.

Evelyn passed Cutler as the old man ran, her heart thundering in her chest as she looked over her shoulder at the vast ocean of running

Egyptians flooding across the plain toward them. The sky above was swept with apocalyptically churned clouds of dark, murderous grey that obscured the sun and cast shadows across the plain, and the hot wind began to feel cold as it was whipped up by the change in air pressure.

Ahmosis stood before the ark, his arms upraised to the turbulent heavens and his staff even higher as he cried out to his people.

'Take heart, this battle and this plain shall be ours!'

The Shasu ranks shifted nervously as they watched and heard the Pelasgians and Egyptians rushing toward them, thousands of feet pounding the earth.

Evelyn shouted to Ahmosis as she ran.

'Open it! Open it now!'

Ahmosis stood back and lowered his staff to point at the ark. With a flourish Ahmosis tore off the veil and let the gusting wind tear it from his grasp to flutter high above the Shasu army.

Evelyn watched as she ran as the bearers lifted the ark by one of its staves, tilting it toward the charging Egyptians, saw the heat trembling from the edges of the lid as the bearers prepared to slide it free and unleash the hellish forces contained within.

Ahmosis reached down to the corner of the lid and braced himself with one foot against the side of the ark.

Evelyn shouted out to Cutler and Andaim. 'Get down, now!'

Evelyn threw herself down onto the dust, felt the vibrations from the charging army behind them shudder through her body as beside her Andaim and Cutler landed hard.

Evelyn heard Ahmosis's shout from the ridgeline ahead.

'For the promised land!' he roared.

The Shasu guard blew hard on their horns, the blaring instruments completely drowned out by the roaring Egyptians thundering across the plain and filling the horizon before the Shasu, and then all sound was bludgeoned into memory as the lid of the ark slid back and a searing blast of energy shrieked forth from inside it and burst across the plain.

Evelyn hugged the dirt as tightly as she could, her head flat against it as the air turned hot above her and the wind scoured the desert dust and sent it blasting past her.

The air around the army suddenly rushed toward the Egyptians, and Evelyn saw a bright beam of fearsome energy scythe into the Pelasgain ranks and then sweep left and right as the bearers twisted the ark back and forth under Ahmosis's guidance.

The sprinting ranks of the Pelasgians and Egyptians vanished into clouds of wind–blown particles of burning flesh, their tanned bodies turning black and bursting into flame even as they ran. Chariots vanished in roiling clouds of black smoke and flame as the ark's terrible fire blasted them aside, the gale drawn in by it howling past Evelyn with such force that she felt compelled to cling to the earth for fear of being dragged into the maelstrom.

Above the shrieking of the gale, the thunderous roar of the ark and the hellish lightning raining white fire across the turbulent sky, Evelyn saw the Egyptian charge broken into a terrible sea of burning flesh, of tumbling bodies incinerated in mid–stride, horses crumbling into flying limbs or galloping across earth scorched by the ark's fire and bursting into flames as the desert plain behind her was turned into a glassy sea of molten sand and rock.

The screams of men dying in their hundreds rose up above the diabolical cacophony of destruction as the ark's power swept left and right, Ahmosis shouting commands to the bearers as they guided the beam deep into the ranks of the Egyptians, cutting entire battalions down in single, terrible strokes of white fire.

The blazing trail of flame struck rocky outcrops and withered them away as though they were made of nothing more than ash, molten rock hurled into the dense ranks and cutting more men down in lethal blasts of burning shrapnel. Flames rose up, a howling inferno whipped into vortexes of twisting flames as the bodies of the dead and dying burned in their hundreds to spew dirty, oily smoke up into the chaotic sky above.

Through the carnage and the flames, Evelyn heard Ahmosis' screaming.

'Kill them all!'

Evelyn crawled on her belly toward the ridge, and then scrambled to her feet in a crouch as she climbed up to the Shasu lines and shouted at Ahmosis.

'Enough!'

Ahmosis did not seem to hear her, his face ablaze with the murderous joy of vengeance as he pointed his staff out across the terrified Egyptian army, the ark's bearers following the staff with the ark.

Evelyn dashed around behind the ark to where the ornate lid was drawn back, and she leaned her weight into it. The lid shifted a fraction, cutting off some of the energy, and Ahmosis turned to see her.

'No,' he shouted. 'They must pay!'

'They have paid!' Evelyn shouted back. 'Remember what I said! Are you a man or a murderer?'

Ahmosis stared down at her, the thunderous skies behind him framing his wildly flying hair and beard, lightning forking across the heavens, and for a moment she thought that he was too far gone. But then the blind rage infecting his eyes faded and he lowered his staff.

The bearers responded, tilting the ark back and lowering it onto its staves. The roaring energy beam rocketed upward into the sky, slicing up through towering thunder clouds that began to swirl around its fearsome energy.

The bearers pushed Evelyn aside and heaved their combined weight behind the lid and in moments the gale rushed out as the beam was cut off. The deafening roar subsided with a crack of thunder that rolled away across the plain and the wind fell still once more.

A deafening silence consumed the Shasu ranks.

Evelyn sagged against the rocks beside her and then turned to look out to the east.

The remains of the Pelasgian army was scattered across the plain, thousands of charred and smouldering bodies packed densely together like the waves of a black sea. Beyond their remains the Egyptians were fleeing in disarray, chariots riding over infantry in their haste to escape. In their wake was a terrible scene of flame and blood: the very earth had been scorched to a black and smouldering wasteland, littered with the crumbling corpses of countless men and animals. A vast expanse of the desert many leagues wide had been utterly scoured of life, much of it still aflame. The smell of burning flesh wafted across the plain as in the heavens above lightning forked and danced.

Evelyn turned to Ahmosis.

'You got what you wanted,' she said.

The old man stared out across the plain and she could see in his face the sheer disbelief at what he had witnessed. Shock was creeping in, and she realised that behind him the entire Shasu force was standing in appalled silence, transfixed by the carnage before them.

Evelyn moved to stand before Ahmosis.

'That was how it feels to wield ultimate power,' she said. 'And this is how it feels afterward.'

Ahmosis gazed upon the hellish scene before him and she saw tears forming in his old eyes.

'What have I done?' he whispered, his frame suddenly seeming old and weak.

'You have become fear,' Evelyn replied. 'You have become your enemy. You must take your people to safety. The power of the ark has been unleashed now, and every Pharaoh that ever lives will remember it, but they will also want it. Do you understand?'

Ahmosis looked down at her. 'We shall be persecuted?'

'You shall be feared,' she replied. 'All persecution is based upon fear.'

Ahmosis turned and looked at the ark now sitting beside them, heat shimmering above it and a few droops of molten gold glowing against its flanks.

'Take it away,' he said.

'I'll need your help,' Evelyn said, 'as I have helped you.'

Ahmosis nodded, held his staff tight in his grip. 'You shall have it, anything that you need.'

Evelyn turned as behind her Andaim and Qayin stood upon the crest of the ridge, Cutler and the other convicts with them. Ahmosis's men were holding them under guard but Evelyn raised her hand.

'No,' she said. 'They are friends. Let them pass.'

The bearers backed away as Andaim stared at both Evelyn and the ark beside her.

'You've been busy,' he observed breathlessly.

Evelyn was about to reply when the sound of whining turbine engines howled through the skies above them. She looked up and her heart leaped inside her as she saw one of Atlantia's shuttle craft curve gracefully through the skies above them, arcing around and preparing to land on the undamaged ground between them and the remains of the pharaoh's army.

Ahmosis, clutching his staff, stared in wide–eyed wonder at the shuttle as the Shasu gasped and cowered, some of them pointing up at the shuttle.

'What is this?' he demanded of Evelyn.

'I helped your people,' Evelyn replied. 'You help me bring the ark to that craft and then you leave, all of you.'

The bearers, shell–shocked into subservience, hoisted the ark onto their shoulders as the veil was placed back over it, and together they descended down onto the plain.

The shuttle's rear doors opened and Evelyn saw Bra'hiv run out, followed by armed marines with plasma rifles cradled in their grasp.

'Stand down,' Evelyn called to him. 'They're all with us.'

Bra'hiv glanced at the scorched plain smothered with smouldering corpses nearby, the Shasu army, and then at Evelyn.

'Like death does she wander,' he murmured. 'What have you been doing here?'

'Giving us a fighting chance,' Evelyn replied, and gestured to the ark as the bearers placed it on the ground nearby. 'The fusion core from the prison hull,' she explained.

Bra'hiv nodded. 'I'll get it on board.'

Evelyn gripped him by the arm. 'Take the core, but leave the container for Ahmosis and his people.'

Bra'hiv shrugged. 'Whatever gets them up in the morning.'

Evelyn watched as Bra'hiv's men hauled out an armoured containment chamber from inside the shuttle and carried it to the ark. She turned to Andaim.

'What's happening up there?' she asked.

'I don't know,' he replied. 'But I saw Atlantia was still in orbit this morning at sunrise, so whatever's going on she hasn't been destroyed yet. No sign of the Word either.'

'Oh, it's there all right,' Bra'hiv replied from nearby as he directed his men around the ark. 'It'll reach orbit any time.'

Andaim turned to Qayin, who was standing nearby with Cutler and the remaining convicts, barely forty or so of them left.

'We need you, all of you,' he said. 'Hevel's got to be removed and we'll need men and muscle to do it. You think you can get Cutler and his people to help out?'

Qayin glanced at the gathered convicts standing nearby.

'*His* people? And in return for what?' Qayin asked.

'A full amnesty,' Bra'hiv replied for Andaim, and then addressed the convicts as one. 'This is no longer a *them–and–us* situation. You can't afford to go it alone anymore and neither can we. The Word is almost here, and if we don't work together we'll all be dead. Captain Sansin has offered a full pardon, to each and every one of you, if you will take up arms alongside the rest of us against the Word.'

One of the convicts stood forward. 'What chance do we have against the Word?'

Bra'hiv gestured to the fusion core, which was being transferred from the ark to a shielded containment unit, the Shasu watching fearfully.

'That's a weapon,' he replied, 'and we have fighter craft that can be manned. Most of all, we have a reason to live. The Word is a machine,

228

nothing more. We are not. Think about it. If you stay here you'll be slaves or prisoners or living out here in the desert eating dung. If you come with us, if you fight for us and we win, you'll be free again.'

Another convict shouted out. 'How can we trust the captain? He sold us out!'

Qayin shook his head.

'Hevel sold us out,' he growled back, 'and took control of the ship. It was Sansin who tried to keep a hold of us. If we want to live we need to take back the Atlantia for ourselves and start fightin'. There's no more running away.'

Qayin moved to one side and stood between Andaim and Bra'hiv as he spoke to the convicts. 'I don't know about all of you, but I done enough runnin'.'

The convicts watched Qayin for a long moment, and then one by one they walked toward the waiting shuttle. Cutler moved to follow them. Bra'hiv made to stop him but Evelyn gripped the soldier's arm.

'No,' she said. 'We need every pair of hands we can get.'

Bra'hiv stood back, suspicion writ deep upon his features. Evelyn looked at Cutler, who stared at her for a long moment as though he did not understand what he had witnessed.

'Why?' he asked. 'Why did you and Andaim protect me?'

'Because every last human life is worth protecting now,' she replied. 'Even yours.'

Cutler scowled at her, but he marched past and up into the shuttle.

Evelyn turned to see that the fusion core had been transferred to the containment unit and was being carried up into the shuttle, Ahmosis and his people watching it go. The now empty ark stood before them.

Evelyn walked up to Ahmosis and gestured to the ark.

'It may be empty now, but the memory of what it has done will stay with your people for millennia,' she said.

Ahmosis nodded vacantly and then looked at her and Andaim as he moved alongside.

'Where did you come from?' he asked.

Evelyn sighed.

'We came from a beautiful place,' she replied, 'but we were cast out by knowledge far more powerful than we could control and can never return.'

Ahmosis nodded thoughtfully as though he understood, and looked at the shuttle.

'Where will you go?'

Andaim pulled Evelyn gently by the arm as the shuttle's engines whined into life, and she cast Ahmosis a last smile.

'I don't know. Somewhere we can start over.'

And then she was running for the shuttle amid churned clouds of dust that shone in the sunlight, and the rear–doors closed as she strapped herself in and the shuttle lifted off and pitched up toward the sky.

'You ready for this?' Andaim asked.

Evelyn nodded. 'I've been waiting a long time for it.'

Andaim cast a glance out of a viewing port and saw the desert sink away, scorched by a blackened stain of destruction cast by the ruptured fusion core.

'Let's get our ship back.'

***

XXXVI

'On screen.'

The bridge was hushed as the main display switched from a view of the nearby planet to a star field.

Hevel sat in the captain's chair, watching the screen as around him the bridge crew stared at the huge vessel cruising toward them. It seemed dwarfed by the vastness of space and the infinite number of stars glowing behind it, but a glance at the scaling register on one side of the screen belied the illusion.

Although superficially similar in appearance the vessel was almost twice the size of Atlantia, an Avenger–Class battleship that had once been the pride of the colonial fleet. It's long, slender hull was flanked by two wings that allowed for the carriage of directed energy weapons far superior to Atlantia's plasma guns, its hull huge enough to bear twin anti–matter engines to provide internal power as well as the energy for its weapons. The Avenger class were power–projection vessels, used to defend the borders of the colonies in time of military tension with other, less cooperative races.

'Range?' Hevel asked.

Aranna glanced down at her instruments, her voice monotone in reply. 'Two planetary diameters, sir. She'll be with us within an hour or two.'

'Weapons range?'

'She'll be able to destroy us from at least forty hull lengths,' Aranna replied. 'We're outgunned by a factor of four, sir.'

Hevel nodded as he surveyed the huge vessel. Once, her hull had been painted a grey–blue and flashed with the insignia of the colonial fleet. Now, the hull was flecked with strange black striations as though she were entombed within a lattice of dark vines.

'What's happened to her?' Keyen asked.

Hevel stood up as he replied.

'She's being consumed. The same process that happened to the human population. I suspect that the standard hull plating is being reconfigured, made tougher somehow using knowledge that we cannot possibly fathom.'

The Word, that all–consuming sponge of knowledge that had expanded and conquered all of mankind's populated worlds and then spread its blackened tentacles across the cosmos, now consuming the very vessels upon which it travelled.

'How long before we're within communication range?' he asked.

'No more than an hour, sir,' Lael replied. 'What do we do now?'

Hevel tightened his uniform.

'We wait,' he replied. 'We wait until we're as close as we can possibly get before we open fire.'

Lael, manning her station across the bridge, stared at Hevel as though he were insane.

'Sir, that ship will blast us into history long before our weapons will be within optimum range. If we wait, we die.'

Hevel nodded slowly. 'That's what I want them to think.'

'What are we going to do?' Lael pressed. 'We need a cohesive plan of attack.'

Hevel turned to face the crew.

'We're going to let her come in close,' he replied, 'and then we're going to move to an attack position and ram her. We're big enough, and fast enough, to do sufficient damage to her that she will never be able to recover.'

'That's insane, sir,' Lael replied. 'The whole point of being here was to stand and fight, not commit suicide.'

'You heard Bra'hiv's report,' Hevel replied. 'There are people down there on that planet below us, human beings that we never even knew existed. We cannot expose them to the Word. The battle must be fought here and it must be over as quickly as possible. The only weapon we possess which may be powerful enough to destroy that battleship is our entire vessel. The Atlantia has enough mass to tear the Avenger in half, provided we can get close enough.'

'And if we can't?'

Hevel turned to the main screen and smiled.

'We will,' he replied. 'The Word was made by humans, built by us to be like us. It has our insatiable curiosity. If we sit here and make no effort to run, show no sign of fear, it will be drawn in to us. Then, in the final moments, we will strike.'

Hevel turned to Dhalere, who nodded.

'Atlantia's mass is sufficient and the destruction of our fusion engines will likely cause permanent damage to the Avenger's primary drives, disabling her and perhaps even destroying her. It will work.'

Hevel nodded and looked at the bridge crew.

'We have a duty. We are not the last of our kind. There will be more, and as of this time they are uninfected, safe from the Word. If we do not stop the Word decisively, and prevent its spread to this planet, then surely they will be crushed as so many of us once were.'

The bridge crew's gazes remained fixed on Hevel as he surveyed them and found them willing to do their duty.

'It will be so,' he said. 'Prepare the ship for battle.'

An alert beeped on the communications officer's panel and she called out to Hevel.

'The shuttle is returning sir,' Lael reported. 'They've recovered supplies and some materials from the planet.'

'Supplies are of no use to us,' Hevel shot back. 'This will be our last, glorious stand.'

The tactical officer near Lael peered down at his screen.

'I'm picking up a huge energy concentration aboard the shuttle, sir,' Keyen said.

Hevel moved down off the command platform and across the bridge to look over the officer's shoulder.

'What kind of energy?' he asked.

Keyen frowned, shook his head.

'I can't be sure sir, the shuttle's hull plating is confusing the signal, but whatever it is it's powerful enough to show up on our scanners.'

Hevel stared suspiciously at the screen.

'The population on the planet is pre–industrial, correct?'

'Yes sir, no evidence of technology beyond stonework and irrigation.'

'On screen.'

The image of the Avenger vanished to be replaced by a broad canvass of blue oceans flecked with white cloud, and against it the tiny speck of the shuttle craft accelerating to orbital speed as it closed in on the Atlantia.

'How many people are aboard?' he asked.

Keyen scanned his instruments. 'I read at least eighty people, sir. That's far too many.'

Hevel clenched his fists at his sides as he stared at the shuttle.

'Bra'hiv took only himself and forty of his men with him,' he said. 'Contact them, find out what's going on.'

Aranna keyed her microphone and spoke quickly and efficiently into it.

'Ranger Six–Four–Nine, report casualties, status and persons aboard?'

A hiss of static whistled across the link with the shuttle as Bra'hiv's reply echoed through the bridge.

'Six–Four–Nine, three casualties, all despatched personnel accounted for, status green.'

Hevel peered at the approaching shuttle and keyed his personal microphone on the captain's seat.

'Who are the casualties?' he asked.

'Three survivors from the prison vessel sir,' came the response. *'They need treatment.'*

'We read eighty persons aboard,' Hevel growled.

'Negative,' Bra'hiv replied, *'our engine was damaged after take off by debris from the volcano sir. It's throwing all of our sensors out too. I'll be approaching on manual control.'*

Hevel peered at the shuttle craft. 'I see no damage.'

The transmission crackled and popped with static, Bra'hiv's response unreadable. Hevel switched off the microphone and turned to his bridge crew.

'Tactical? Activate the port bow turrets.'

Keyen obeyed without question, but Lael's eyes flew wide as she stared at Hevel. 'What?'

'They've been compromised,' Hevel snapped. 'We cannot trust them.'

'Compromised by whom?'

Hevel ignored her and pointed at Keyen. 'Blast them, now!'

'Yes sir, target acquired.'

'No!'

Lael launched herself across the bridge and ploughed into Keyen, smashing him clear of his post as they crashed down onto the hard deck plating.

'Security!'

Lael straddled Keyen and swung a punch with her bunched right fist as he tried to get up and throw her off. The blow smacked into his mouth with a loud crack and a stab of pain that bolted through her knuckles. Keyen's eyes rolled up into their sockets as he slumped down, and Lael leaped to her feet and grabbed the microphone.

'Six–Four–Nine, evasive action, you're compromised and...'

Security guards thundered up onto the tactical post and hauled Lael away from the microphone. She kicked and fought but the soldiers were too strong for her as they pulled her away and bound her wrists behind her back with steel manacles.

Hevel, his hands behind his back, turned to Aranna.

'If you will.'

Aranna stood without a word and strode to the tactical position. Her hands flew across the keys as though he had manned the station for a decade. Lael stared at him, her eyes wide as Aranna activated the turrets.

'Aranna, what the hell are you doing?!'

Aranna did not reply, and then Lael saw Hevel approach her. A cold sliver of fear slithered deep inside her belly as Hevel, his hands behind his back and a smile on his face, walked up to her and stared unblinkingly into her eyes.

'Don't fear, Lael,' he said. 'You'll understand, soon, that this is all for you, all for *us*.'

Hevel smiled and Lael's guts turned to slime as she saw the whites of his eyes flicker as black flecks darted back and forth behind them. She craned her head back over her shoulder and saw the two guards holding her, their eyes filled with writhing black specks.

'No,' she gasped. 'You're going to kill us all!'

'I'm going to save you all,' Hevel grinned. 'This, Lael, is your destiny. It is all mankind's destiny and you cannot escape or avoid it. This is our future.'

'He's infected!' Lael shouted, looking desperately at the bridge crew.

They stared at her, their features devoid of emotion as though they were waxworks carved by human hands and left standing at their posts. The light of life in their eyes had suddenly been extinguished by the infection surging through their bodies.

'Take her to the holding cells,' Hevel ordered the guards. 'I will deal with all of them shortly.'

As Lael was dragged away, Hevel turned to Aranna.

'The shuttle,' he ordered, 'destroy it now!'

***

DEAN CRAWFORD

XXXVII

'Zero–Nine–Six, evasive action, you're compromised and...'

Bra'hiv looked up in surprise at the Atlantia as the sound of Lael's voice was abruptly cut off.

'What was that about?' Andaim asked as he approached the cockpit, Evelyn beside him as Bra'hiv grabbed the controls.

'I don't know but I'm not taking any risks. Strap in!'

Evelyn hauled herself into her seat just as the hull of the Atlantia flared brightly and a fearsome ball of flickering blue energy flashed toward the shuttle.

'Evasive action!' Bra'hiv yelled as he hauled the shuttle up, gas thrusters igniting on her lower bow as the computers sought to adjust the craft's plane of motion.

The energy pulse flared in the viewing screen and flashed past beneath them. The shuttle rocked violently and then tumbled as a blast hit it from behind. A shower of plasma flashed past the screen and an alarm sounded inside the cockpit as Bra'hiv fought for control.

'Shrapnel damage,' he yelled. 'We've lost two aft thrusters!'

Evelyn's hair swayed back and forth as though she were underwater in a storm as the turbulence from the blast shuddered through the shuttle's hull. She looked over her shoulder, to where the eighty or so marines and convicts were strapped in with the ark magnetically attached to the deck in between them. The fusion core crackled with restrained energy inside its containment unit, sending expressions of deep concern across the faces of the watching men.

'How long until we dock?' Andaim asked.

Bra'hiv regained control of the shuttle, grimly hanging on to the controls as he looked at his instruments.

'Two minutes, but the docking bay doors are closed.'

'Hevel,' Qayin said from where he was strapped into a seat nearby. 'He ain't gonna let us in.'

The Atlantia loomed large before them, and as Evelyn peered at the huge vessel she suddenly felt a chill as she saw a particularly bright star hovering in sight just beneath it.

'The Word,' she said, 'it's here.'

She pointed to the star, a giant vessel bathed in bright sunlight that flared off its hull as it closed in on the planet.

'Damn it,' Andaim cursed, 'we need to get aboard.'

Bra'hiv guided the shuttle toward the Atlantia's stern as he replied. 'If I can get close enough we'll be inside the reach of the turrets and we can use the shuttle's guns to blast the bay doors open.'

'We'll need to suit up,' Andaim said. 'You'll blast the atmosphere from the loading bays if you do that.'

'No choice,' Bra'hiv said.

'But if you get closer to the turrets,' Evelyn said, 'you won't have enough time to…'

'Evasive action!' Bra'hiv cut her off as two bright plasma flares burst from the turrets lining the Atlantia's hull.

The shuttle yawed violently as Bra'hiv pushed over into a steep dive, turning on three axis at once to avoid the aim of the turrets. The hull shuddered as the thrusters fired to guide the shuttle on a new course, but they were small and not designed to provide rapid changes of direction.

The shuttle plunged downward, the plasma flares flashing past overhead and detonating with a deep double blast. The shuttle's hull shrieked as its plating was hammered by super–heated plasma and buckled under the weight and heat of the blows.

The shuttle tumbled over and a shower of sparks burst from interior panels to spray over the convicts strapped into the landing bay. Bra'hiv fought for control again as the planet's surface flashed past the viewing panel, followed by the vast hull of Atlantia as two more plasma turrets fired at them.

'Full power!' Andaim yelled. 'Aim straight for the hull and get us out of here!'

Bra'hiv slammed the throttles wide open as he wrested back control of the shuttle. Alarms blared in the cockpit and the lighting turned red as the little vessel accelerated toward the frigate.

The plasma charges flashed past on either side of the shuttle and detonated behind it, but the blasts were far enough away to escape further damage. Bra'hiv, his face set and his teeth gritted, aimed straight for the main docking bay nestled beneath the Atlantia's stern as more plasma flashes rippled along the vessel's hull.

'The Word is here, but Hevel's firing on *us*?' Bra'hiv growled.

Andaim whirled to Qayin. 'Is he really that insane for power?'

Qayin shook his head. 'This ain't right, not even for him.'

'Suit up!' Bra'hiv yelled. 'We're going in!'

Andaim and Evelyn lurched out of their seats and grabbed the nearest environment suits that were clipped to the hull walls. Evelyn clambered into hers as in the cargo hold the marines clicked their visors into place and charged their rifles.

'What about us?!' Qayin called, and gestured to the convicts.

'Stay with the core,' Andaim said as he pulled his visor down over his face, 'and hope it doesn't blow up!'

Qayin yanked off his straps and stood up.

'I ain't stayin' behind,' he growled.

'This isn't about staying behind,' Evelyn said as she pulled a rifle from the nearest rack and handed it to Qayin. 'This is where we need you, to protect that core. If it's destroyed this is all over and so are we.' She turned to the convicts. 'You wanted your freedom? This is how you earn it.'

Evelyn pulled rifles down from the racks and hurled them through the cargo hold at the convicts, the weapons spinning lazily as they tumbled through the zero gravity and were caught by surprised inmates.

'If we go down,' Evelyn said, and gestured to Andaim and the marines, 'the only thing standing between our survival and annihilation will be all of you.' The convicts looked at her in silence. 'You want to run, or fight?'

The convicts looked at each other, and then Cutler activated his rifle.

'We've got this,' the old convict replied.

Thirty more rifles hummed into life as the convicts activated them, and Evelyn turned to the cockpit. Bra'hiv was aiming straight for the main docking bay door, the shuttle's weapons primed and ready.

'Here we go,' she said, crouching down and braced herself behind one of the vacant cockpit seats.

Bra'hiv pulled the trigger on his controls and a salvo of plasma charges blasted from the shuttle's hull and zipped toward the bay doors even as the Atlantia's vast stern loomed over them and plunged the shuttle into deep shadow. Evelyn peeked out and saw the charges smash into the immense doors, flares of bright plasma splashing in electric blue halos as they battered the doors.

As the blasts cleared the doors held firm, scorched but solid.

Bra'hiv fired again, more plasma charges blazing out in front of the shuttle and smashing into the doors. Evelyn saw bright blasts of colour and molten metal blossom from the impacts and then a rush of vapour from a jagged hole in the doors as the atmosphere was vacuumed from the landing bay.

Amid the vapour she saw bodies tumbling out into space, black suited marines.

'Hevel's turned the marines against us,' Andaim gasped in horror.

'Brace for impact!' Bra'hiv yelled as he aimed for the hole.

The huge cargo doors loomed up and then flashed past as the shuttle plunged into the landing bay. Instantly a galaxy of rifle fire showered down toward the shuttle from marines upon the gantries that encircled the landing bay, the blasts hammering the viewing shield.

Bra'hiv fired his pulse cannons again, the blasts smashing into the marines firing at them and hurling them in flaming arcs across the bay as several gantries collapsed in tangled piles of metal. A blast of rifle fire caught the shuttle's starboard bow and the thrusters failed as Bra'hiv fought to keep the vessel under control. Bra'hiv yanked the controls and the shuttle lurched as Bra'hiv fired the engines again to slow her down and activated the magnetic clamps all at once.

The shuttle crashed down, spraying sparks as its landing clamps gouged into the metal deck and it shuddered to a halt in the centre of the landing bay.

'Deploy now!'

Bra'hiv opened the rear doors of the shuttle and the air was sucked from the vessel as the troops plunged out into the landing bay into a hail of rifle fire that soared down from the gantries above them. Evelyn dashed past the convicts as they sat in their seats and out into the landing bay.

Bra'hiv's men fired up at the gantries as they dashed from the cover of the rear of the shuttle, spreading out as Evelyn hit the deck and turned to fire at a trooper high above her. She heard Bra'hiv dash onto the ramp nearby and then hit the controls for the shuttle's ramp. The ramp hissed closed, the blasts from the trooper's rifles crashing against it as the interior of the shuttle was refilled with air and heat.

'Advance by sections and stay close or we could get confused about who's who real fast!' Bra'hiv yelled. 'Take the high ground back!'

The marines dashed in organised groups toward the gantry steps, staying in motion to spoil the aim of their former comrades high above raining fire down around them. Evelyn sprinted for the nearest set of steps, following Andaim as ahead two marines were cut down by the rifle fire, their suits emptying of air in an instant as the blasts melted the seals.

Andaim vaulted over the first of them and fired up the gantry steps, his shots gouging a wide hole in the guts of a trooper descending toward them. Evelyn slid to her knees and aimed up the steps, firing and catching a second trooper high on his leg, blasting the limb from his body as he toppled over the gantry rail and plunged down beside her.

Evelyn followed Andaim as he ran up the steps, fighting the weight of his environmental suit and the magnetic gravity as he fired, clearing the steps one at a time.

Evelyn risked a glanced over her shoulder and saw Bra'hiv leading more marines up a second gantry, covering fire from men using the shuttle as cover down in the landing bay hitting troopers higher up and clearing the way.

'Enemy, flank!'

Evelyn turned and saw dozens of men plunge into the landing bay from both sides, and with a chill she realised that they had been drawn into a trap.

'They're flanking us!' she shouted.

Bra'hiv's men on the landing bay deck switched their fire, but the rush of men was too large and they began falling back toward the cover of the shuttle as plasma charges flashed back and forth in a violent miasma of blue and white fire. Evelyn dashed back down the gantry steps and hurled herself in behind a metal support pillar as a flash of blasts sent sprays of molten metal spiralling through the air around her.

'Get off the gantries!' she yelled.

She leaned out and fired off two shots into the charging troopers, hitting one man straight in the neck and blasting his visor off and most of his face with it. A second trooper collapsed as his knee was smashed out by a plasma round and his boot skittered away from him across the deck.

Evelyn crouched and shielded her face as dozens of shots zipped toward and past her in return, and then she heard the shuttle's turbines fire up. A blast of heat hit her as the shuttle rocked sideways and then jerked upward into the air, spinning around as jet wash hammered the decks, the few remaining operational thrusters firing blasts of gas in spluttering bursts. Through the shuttle's screen she saw Qayin's distinctive gold and blue locks as he turned the shuttle to face the incoming troops.

'Cover!' Evelyn yelled.

Qayin fired the shuttle's cannons into the mass of approaching troops, blasting them like flaming skittles across the deck as the plasma charges detonated in brilliant blue–white balls of energy that seared the men from existence.

Evelyn almost cheered as Qayin struggled with the controls to turn the shuttle around and cover their left flank, letting a blast of plasma fire rip into the charging troops flooding into the cargo hold and decimating them in a fiery halo of plasma and burning bodies.

Andaim, crouched on the gantries, resumed his climb and burst out onto the upper levels as Evelyn fired from the landing bay deck at the remaining troopers high above them. She fired over their heads, keeping them down as Andaim bore down upon them and opened fire, cutting them down.

Bra'hiv's men rushed up onto the gantries from the opposite side and moments later the firing stopped as behind Evelyn the shuttle slammed awkwardly back down onto the deck and the engines whined down, smoke spiralling from the damaged thrusters.

'Seal the landing bay!' Bra'hiv shouted into his microphone.

Evelyn heard the command and dashed across the landing bay to the control office and blasted the door open with a single shot from her rifle. A rush of air billowed out of the empty office as she plunged inside and reached for the controls, activating the emergency doors.

At the far end of the bay a second set of shield doors rumbled into place to seal off the jagged, gaping hole. She heard sirens and then the hiss of air being vented back into the bay.

She strode back out of the office to see Bra'hiv and Andaim examining the corpse of one of Hevel's fallen marines. As Bra'hiv removed his visor, she could see the pain in his features.

'Lavere,' he identified the fallen marine. 'A good man. What was he thinking?'

As Evelyn joined them, they looked down and saw from Lavere's ear a thin trickle of what looked like black oil draining onto the deck.

'I don't think he was thinking,' Andaim said. 'He's infected.'

Bra'hiv stood back and fired a single blast that melted the pool of nanobots into a molten slag that hissed as it cooled.

'The entire ship could have been overrun,' Evelyn said. 'The captain...'

'There's only one way to find out,' Andaim said. 'Let's get moving.'

Bra'hiv's voice echoed through the landing bay as Qayin, the convicts and the remaining marines joined them.

'Impressive work,' he said. 'That includes you, Qayin. You and the rest of the convicts fall in with us on the gantries. Stay tight, we're the only people we can be sure are not yet infected, understood?'

The convicts and marines nodded as one, their faces grim.

***

XXXVIII

'The landing bay has been breached, sir.'

Hevel turned slowly in the captain's chair, his eyes scanning the bridge.

His limbs were moving more slowly now, and his vision was blurred by red clouds that seemed to allow him to see through things, as though he were watching the world through an Infra–Red lens. Ever since he had decided to unleash the Word upon the crew the nanobots in his body and theirs had been replicating, surging through his body. At first he had experienced pangs of doubt, the natural and human fear of the unknown, but every time his hubris had emerged it had been drowned out by pulses of unimaginable pleasure, of dreamlike euphoria far stronger than any drug. With each pulse, his fear and his hesitance had faded away like long forgotten memories.

The rest of his crew on the bridge glowed back at him, their eyes like pin–points of fiery orange light, candle flames glowing in a blue–black world. None of them blinked. None of them needed to any more.

'How many men do we have left?' he asked.

Keyen glanced down mechanically at his instruments.

'Forty at the most, sir,' Keyen replied, his voice strangely monotone. 'They're fighting back, but they're also retreating away from the landing bay. The shuttle's weapons took most of them out.'

Hevel swivelled again in his seat and looked at the main screen.

'Where is the Avenger?' he asked.

Without waiting for a command, Keyen switched the view on the main screen from the fighting in the corridors of the ship to the star field outside. The Avenger was much closer now, looming large and her hull glistening with black striations that caught the bright glow of the sun as though aflame, the other side of her hull lost in deep shadow.

'She's within firing range, sir,' Keyen added.

Hevel stood up, his joints clicking strangely as the metallic elements within his body began to overwhelm the biological tendons and muscles. He felt both weak and immensely strong, like a mountain: immovable, yet still able to weather aeons of storms.

'Send a signal,' he said. 'We will deactivate all weapons and be ready for boarding.'

'Yes sir,' came the reply from Aranna, now manning the communication station, her blonde hair falling out in clumps as her body temperature increased.

Hevel, still retaining some of his former human instinct, felt compelled to straighten his uniform and his hair with one hand. Then, he hesitated. That was no longer necessary. He was no longer enslaved by human emotions such as pride: actions, based on knowledge, were all that was required to command and to conquer.

Hevel stood with his hands behind his back, and with his bridge crew awaited the arrival of the Word.

*

'Forward!'

Bra'hiv fired his plasma rifle, two shots zipping down the corridor and exploding against a bulkhead behind which crouched two enemy troopers, their eyes glowing red through the smoke. Smouldering plasma sprayed across the passage, some of it igniting a trooper's sleeve.

The soldier glanced without haste at his burning arm, and slowly began trying to pat the flames out. A second shot from Andaim blew his scalp off of his head and sent it tumbling down the passage in a trail of blue smoke.

Evelyn saw Andaim dash forward to the next bulkhead and hurl himself into cover as a salvo of blasts screamed back at them and hammered the bulkheads and ceiling. She hugged the cold metal wall for a moment before leaning out and firing, the rounds deafeningly loud in the confined corridor as they shot down the passageway at terrific speed and kept the soldiers' heads down.

Behind her, the convicts and allied soldiers fired carefully timed salvos, one after the other, dashing past each other and keeping the enemy occupied as they advanced.

Evelyn's ears rang with the infernal noise of prolonged gunfire and her eyes stung as the smoke from repeated impacts of searing plasma energy filled the corridor.

'Go, now!'

Bra'hiv fired again and then dashed forward to crouch behind another bulkhead as Evelyn fired covering shots down the corridor.

'They're falling back!' Andaim yelled.

'Not fast enough,' Bra'hiv shouted back above the din of the rifle fire. 'We'll never get to the bridge at this rate!'

Evelyn squinted through the smoke and the darkness and saw the enemy troopers congregating toward a larger, inter–segmental bulkhead with a large pressure hatch.

'They'll cut us off!' Bra'hiv called as he fired down the corridor.

Evelyn shouted at Bra'hiv as she broke into a run.

'Cover me!'

She dashed past them, running low as she pulled a spare plasma cartridge from her uniform and slid it down the corridor in front of her. The plasma blasts from the enemy troops zipped over her head as she ran and she smelled her hair being singed by the heat of the passing shots. The magazine spun lazily as it slid along the deck and Evelyn hurled herself into cover and took aim as the magazine came to a stop a few feet from where the troops were retreating through the pressure bulkhead.

Evelyn held her breath for a moment and then squeezed her trigger.

The plasma round hit the magazine and it exploded with a blinding flash and a blossoming cloud of plasma fragments that showered the corridor to the sound of screams of agony as the enemy troops tumbled over each other, their uniforms aflame.

'Forward!' Bra'hiv shouted.

Evelyn kept firing through the bulkhead until Bra'hiv and Andaim thundered past her, firing as they went. They burst through the bulkhead and for the first time in several minutes the tremendous din of gunfire was silenced.

Smoke coiled and drifted in dense whorls, the ceiling lights glowing through it as Evelyn stepped over the sizzling corpses of several dead troopers to where Andaim and Bra'hiv were peering down the corridor ahead.

'The bridge is about a hundred cubits from here,' Bra'hiv said.

'They'll have likely locked themselves in,' Andaim said. 'We won't be able to storm the bridge without causing too much damage to the controls.'

'The holding cells,' Bra'hiv said, standing and changing direction as they followed him. 'The captain will know his security override codes. We can ask him to shut the bridge down, and transfer control to the War Room.'

A deep voice spoke from behind.

'Hevel will anticipate that move,' Qayin said. 'If you go down there he'll try to shut you off somehow.'

'You got any better ideas?' Bra'hiv snapped back.

'I'll head for the bridge and keep them busy there,' Qayin replied. 'You free the captain and occupy the War Room.'

Bra'hiv looked over his shoulder at Qayin.

'You want me to let you and a bunch of convicts take over the ship's bridge?'

'Hevel is mine,' Qayin growled, and then mimicked Bra'hiv's authoritarian tones. 'You got any better ideas?'

'He's right,' Evelyn said. 'We can't do everything on our own. The more fronts we keep them busy on, the more likely one of them will break.'

Bra'hiv scowled as he reached an intersection of passages, some leading for'ard, others aft toward the elevator banks.

'Fine,' he said to Qayin. 'How are you going to get in?'

Qayin grinned and gestured over his shoulder. 'Let me take one of your men and a few of my crew, wearing your uniforms,' he replied. 'Hevel will think they're his men, who have valiantly captured me and are running for cover onto the bridge before the hated intruders reach them.'

Bra'hiv's eyes narrowed. 'That ruse won't last long. Our people aren't infected, Hevel will realise that quickly.'

'It'll last long enough to get me close to the bridge,' Qayin replied. 'Hevel's curiosity will do the rest, once he realises it's me.'

Bra'hiv nodded and pointed with a gloved hand as the troops spilled into the corridor, C'rairn seeing his signal. C'rairn selected a handful of convicts, Cutler among them, and they flanked Qayin as the convict surrendered his rifle. C'rairn produced a set of manacles and loosely set them over Qayin's wrists without fastening them as Cutler and the others dragged themselves into the uniforms of fallen, infected marines.

'Good luck,' Evelyn said to the big man as he turned with the troops toward the bridge.

'I don't need no luck,' he growled back. 'I need vengeance.'

C'rairn marched Qayin and his crew away, while Bra'hiv whirled and set off at a run for the holding cells.

'Come on,' he shouted. 'Stay away from the elevator shafts, they're controlled from the bridge. We'll take the stairs.'

Evelyn followed them down to the emergency stair wells that led both up and down inside the Atlantia's cavernous hull. Their boots thundered as they hurried through the ship and exited the stairwells on the holding cell's level.

A blast of gunfire sprayed the passageway and both Andaim and Bra'hiv hurled themselves to the deck as Evelyn almost ploughed into them. She leaped past as the plasma blasts showered the corridor, and fired as she crossed the passageway.

Two soldiers, firing from cover. Her wild shot smacked into the bulkheads near one of the shooters and sprayed plasma across his uniform as Bra'hiv and Andaim fired from their prone positions below her. Both soldiers were hit square–on and tumbled to the deck, their strangled cries of pain echoing up and down the passageway.

'Forward!'

Bra'hiv led the way, the troops following as they advanced upon the cells. Andaim fired again as one of the wounded soldiers attempted to raise his rifle, the blast shattering his skull as his flesh hissed in the heat.

The other fallen man stared up at them, one half of his face blackened and smouldering where the rifle blast had hit him. His good eye was lifeless, staring into space, but the other was filled with shimmering black filaments of what looked like metal.

Bra'hiv leaned down close and looked at the mess filling the dead man's eye socket.

'The infection is at the early stages,' he said. 'Eyes, ears, brain stem and so on. It might not have spread too far.'

Evelyn felt her skin crawl as though insects had burrowed under it. The tiny machines that had once thrived in this man's body were now smouldering, many of them melted together in the heat of the plasma blast that had killed their host. Now, the molten slag of the eye socket quivered as a tiny flood of seething metallic particles churned out of his brain, seeking a new home.

'Get back!' Andaim shouted.

They stood back and watched as the shimmering, glossy black pool of tiny machines spilled out onto the deck, spreading out like a lake of oil. Andaim and Bra'hiv waited until they were all out of the dead soldier's body, and then they fired.

The plasma blasts fried the tiny objects into a smouldering pool of glowing, red hot metal that puffed coils of acrid blue smoke onto the air. Evelyn stared down at the bubbling, churning pool of machines.

'Can we avoid being infected ourselves?' she asked.

Bra'hiv shook his head. 'This type of bot, the infectious ones, can't survive outside of a human body for long, they don't have enough power. As long as we don't stray too close, and we destroy as many as we can, we'll be okay. Head shots will destroy most of them.'

'But the rest of the crew,' she said, 'we could be walking into an entire infected ship.'

'No,' Andaim shook his head, 'the Word infects over time but then shows itself at a universal command to all victims, not individuals. The original carrier must have activated them at a given time.'

'When the mutiny occurred, or soon afterward,' Evelyn said. 'Hevel.'

'Come on,' Bra'hiv urged them.

They dashed over the corpses and ran toward the holding cells, reaching them in time to see the captain and his bridge crew gripping the bars of their cells and craning their necks to see what was happening.

'About time!' The captain's voice boomed out as Bra'hiv, Andaim, Evelyn and dozens of troops and convicts flooded into the holding cells. Idris saw the convicts. 'What the hell?'

'Long story,' Bra'hiv said, and then he hesitated.

'What are you waiting for?' the captain uttered. 'Open the cells!'

Evelyn walked up to the captain and spoke quickly. 'The Word is aboard, captain. The infection must have occurred before we left Ethera. The bomb that destroyed the high–security wing must have been placed there by somebody with privileged access: the governor, a guard, or your wife.'

The captain stared at Evelyn and then turned to his wife. Meyanna's face went white as her jaw dropped.

'Lael told us that Hevel was infected, but I'm not,' she gasped. 'We've all been tested, several times.'

'The Word must have found a way to conceal itself, to be harboured by a carrier and not visible to normal blood tests,' Evelyn explained, unable to keep the apologetic tone from her voice. 'People don't know that it's inside them and we can't find it, else it would have been spotted before now by your tests.'

'We've been locked in here since Hevel took the bridge,' the captain snapped. 'We're sure that he's infected, and if any of us were too surely he would not have placed them here.'

'Unless he wanted all of you infected too,' Andaim pointed out. 'Which could have occurred by now.'

The captain gripped the bars tighter. 'Then what do you propose we do?'

'The War Room,' Bra'hiv said. 'We'll escort you there under armed guard and try to regain control of the ship while each of you are fully scanned by us using microwave transmitters.'

'Why couldn't that have been done in the first place?' Evelyn asked.

'Because the scan could be lethal,' Meyanna replied. 'The microwaves will heat up the bots if they're inside us, destroying them but also any organs they're attached to.'

'You'll either be cleared,' Brahiv said, 'or you'll be dead. Do you agree to the scans?'

The captain nodded. 'I'll go first. Hurry.'

Idris waited until his door was unlocked and then he stepped out.

'We'll still need to take the bridge back, even if we have the War Room,' he said.

'Qayin is heading there now,' Andaim said.

'Qayin?'

'Like Bra'hiv said,' Evelyn replied, 'long story.'

'Besides, we've got bigger problems even than that,' Bra'hiv added.

Idris grabbed his security chief by the collar. 'Bigger *how*?'

'An Avenger class cruiser,' Bra'hiv replied, 'almost within firing range.'

The captain's eyes flared wide as he released the marine's collar. 'We can't face them in open battle.'

'That's why we need to get to the War Room,' Andaim said, 'and fast. Qayin will try to take the bridge without firing at anything, but if he fails we still need to try to regain control of the ship and get the hell out of here.'

Idris nodded as his wife joined him, Evelyn giving her a wide berth.

'What about the civilians?' Meyanna asked.

'We don't know,' Bra'hiv said, 'but most likely they're still in the sanctuary, which we would be best served by sealing for the time being. We need to go sir, now. If Hevel thinks we're going to undermine him, his best bet is to infect as many people as he can before he's captured or killed. You know how this works.'

'Let's go,' Idris snapped as he was handed a rifle. 'Before the Avenger blows us all to hell.'

XXXIX

Qayin strode toward the main door of the bridge, which was sealed shut. Cutler, C'rairn and the two convicts accompanying him walked as pairs in front and behind and he could feel the tension infecting them, almost as if the Word were already coursing through their veins.

The slowed at the bridge door and C'rairn reached out and tapped the intercom panel.

'Bridge, we have a prisoner.'

They stood and waited for a response, but no reply came from the bridge. Qayin reflected that with the doors sealed shut any infection might also have remained inside the bridge, unless Hevel had managed to spread the minions of the Word to the captured crew or civilians. Everybody knew that the tiny, myriad machines used by the Word to infect humans could not survive for long outside of the human body, their design specifically created to obtain fuel from the iron in human blood, leaving the victim anaemic in the early stages of infection. Outside of their hosts their internal power lasted only a few minutes: power conduits and electrical supplies provided raw energy in voltages too high for the miniscule devices, frying them whenever they tried to plug themselves in, and solar energy was only strong enough in a truly planetary environment so the hull's sanctuary would not provide a refuge for them.

Hevel would have been forced to infect any victims via direct contact of some kind.

'They're not going for it,' Cutler whispered under his breath.

'Bridge, we have a prisoner,' C'rairn intoned into the intercom again.

Qayin spoke softly through the corner of his mouth.

'If the doors open, push me through and then get the hell out of here, understood?'

'You'll die,' C'rairn replied, not looking at him.

Qayin shrugged. 'Everybody dies.'

They stared at the dull grey doors for several more seconds, and then suddenly they hissed open.

Qayin moved immediately, the manacles falling away as he lunged into the bridge. C'rairn hit the emergency close button and the bridge doors slammed shut behind him as he came to a stop and squinted as his eyes tried to adjust to the gloom.

The bridge stations were all occupied but none of the staff were looking at Qayin. All of them appeared rooted to the spot, their hands resting lightly on the control panels. In the low lighting of the bridge he thought he could see a dull red glow within their eyes.

Qayin looked at the captain's chair and saw the figure of a man seated there, silhouetted against the banks of lights on the far side of the bridge. His eyes glowed more brightly, more powerfully than the rest, charged with a malevolent presence as though Qayin were staring into the eyes of a demon, a demon he recognised.

Suddenly he understood what had happened to his brother, what had driven him to excesses of power at the expense of their family, their friends, everybody they had ever known.

'How long?' Qayin asked.

'Does it matter?'

Hevel's voice rippled, no longer his own but a strange warble, part–human and part machine. The Word had taken his mind long ago, but even that it seemed was not enough. Not satisfied with controlling him, such was the Word's hatred of mankind that it instead was driven to make Hevel into a copy of himself, a simulation of the man he had once been, less than the original.

'It matters to me,' Qayin growled.

'Ah,' Hevel said as he slowly got to his feet. 'You think that your brother is gone, don't you? Well, he isn't gone, Qayin. I am still your brother.'

'You,' Qayin said. 'It was you who sabotaged the prison hull, detonated the bomb.'

'It was the governor, Oculin Hayes, but it matters little. We were performing the will of the Word,' Hevel replied. 'Evelyn must die, and yet, somehow, she lives. Misplaced loyalties, Qayin, have cost our family dear.'

Hevel stepped into the light and Qayin fought to control himself.

Hevel was naked, but the sheer volume of machinery now polluting his body was sufficient that he was still drawn to the deck's magnetic plating as though he were wearing a gravity suit. His body was mostly covered with a seething mass of tiny machines that crawled beneath his skin, turning his skin into a glossy black veil that rippled in the light like the surface of a distant lake beneath moonlight.

His joints and limbs were heavily metallised, the raw materials of his body converted into stronger defences, or more likely harvested from the deck beneath his feet an atom at a time and transported to where he needed it most. It almost looked as though he was wearing a suit of armour.

Hevel's hair was falling out, the heat from his overactive brain killing off the skin of his scalp, and his ears, lips, hands and eyes were distorted and sheened with thin metal plating, enhanced for superior senses.

'My brother is long gone,' Qayin snarled. 'What's left is nothing more than a glorified slave.'

'Come now, Qayin,' Hevel smiled, his lips catching the light and his teeth flashing silver and graphite grey. 'You were always the strong one, always the fastest, always the toughest, and me, I was always the academic. But look at me now, brother. I am stronger than you, faster than you, and I still have the intelligence that you so often ignored as you cowered in your cell with the scum of society.'

Qayin smiled, although it felt like more of a sneer. 'Funny, how easily people describe convicts with the same words they use to describe politicians.'

'You wasted your life, Qayin,' Hevel went on. 'Do you know how our mother and father wept as they learned of your each, successive failure? How they mourned your incarceration? How they begged for answers to why they had not done enough to help you?'

Qayin's blood ran hot through his veins. 'I made my own choices.'

'And that's supposed to calm them, to console them?' Hevel asked. 'They are with the Word now, just like all humanity, and they now no longer worry about you Qayin. I doubt they'd even recognise you. This life,' he said, gesturing to himself, 'is so much better than the one that went before. There is no pain, brother. No regret, no illness, no suffering. We are at one and our cause is universal.'

'What cause?' Qayin asked.

'The perseverance of mankind, of course,' Hevel chuckled. 'You believe us to be evil, a conquering force, but the Word saw the potential of mankind long ago. People used to say, didn't they, used to ask: "imagine what we could be if we didn't spend so much time at war, or fighting crime or tackling disease? Imagine what we could be if we all worked together?"' Hevel pointed to his own chest. 'Now, we can find out.'

'You're not a man.'

'And I'm all the better for it,' Hevel snapped back. 'I'm more than a man now, Qayin. You could be to. Would you like to see our mother again, our father?'

Qayin ground his teeth in his skull. 'They're gone, Hevel, just like you.'

'No,' Hevel said. 'They are back home, walking as we do, a part of the Word now but alive none the less. The Word killed nobody, Qayin. There was no apocalypse that your captain speaks of, no genocide, no killing but for our defensive posture against your feeble efforts to stop us. We protected the best of human life, Qayin. It survived *because* of us, not in spite of us. Now it is your turn.'

'I'd rather die.'

'That would be a shame, Qayin,' Hevel said as he took a pace closer. 'There is no need for you to die. There is no need for any of us to die, ever.'

'I didn't hear you sayin' that when you murdered half the prison block.'

'Come now, Qayin,' Hevel soothed, 'the mercy I would show you does not extend to the scum who have scoured your life of decency. Human garbage, the dregs of your kind deserved no such consideration. Our mother and father are waiting for us, Qayin,' he urged, 'and your vessel is doomed anyway.'

Qayin hesitated and Hevel smiled.

'Yes, brother,' he said. 'All this time you've hated me, but I was infected long before the Word arrived. You would have been too had you not been imprisoned, beyond my reach.'

Qayin's mind raced. Hevel's callous destruction of life in the prison block, an act beyond even him. Hevel had not shown any such signs of genocidal thought in the months after the Atlantia had first fled the disaster that befell mankind, which would mean...

'Who?' Qayin asked. 'Who infected you?'

'Come,' Hevel replied, 'and I will show you.'

'No,' Qayin growled. 'My brother was not a killer. He was a victim. I know you're still in there, Hevel. No machine could ever take all of any of us, any of our family. Fight it, Hevel.'

'Why fight?' Hevel asked rhetorically. 'I like it too much.'

Hevel held out his hand, the fingernails black like polished obsidian and the veins lacing the back of his hand throbbing with the minute devices seething through his bloodstream.

Qayin looked at his brother's hand and slowly he reached out toward it. The glossy black nails reached for Qayin's bigger hand, Hevel's demonically glowing eyes fixed upon Qayin's and filled with an emotion that Qayin had not recognised before, something between hope and regret, as though whoever his brother had once been was now incarcerated forever more in a prison far more insufferable than anything Qayin had been forced to endure: alive, but no longer in control of his own mind and body.

The tip of Hevel's fingers touched Qayin's, cold and hard, and Qayin's rage broke free.

Qayin twisted aside and snatched his hand away as he lunged forward and behind Hevel, drawing a pistol from where it was concealed in the pocket of his uniform. He grabbed Hevel from behind and leaned back as he hoisted him off balance and buried the barrel of the pistol into the small of Hevel's back, right against the base of his spine.

'Call if off, brother,' he growled into Hevel's metallic ear. 'Do it now or I'll blow you wide open.'

Hevel, his warbling digitized voice utterly without concern, replied.

'Do it,' he said, 'it makes no difference. I will be gone but the Word will be forever.'

'Once you would have done anything to protect your fellow man,' Qayin growled.

'I *am* protecting us,' Hevel replied. 'That is what we do.'

'No,' Qayin snapped, 'you take lives and you turn men into machines. You're nothing but an overgrown piece of circuitry.'

'In some ways so are you,' Hevel replied, almost sadly. 'The difference is, I am stronger.'

The blow came from nowhere, Hevel's elbow jerking with hydraulic force to thud deep into Qayin's rib cage with a dull crunch. Qayin's body convulsed reflexively from the blow, momentarily crippled from the impact as Hevel spun with impossible speed. One arm scythed down to smash the pistol aside hard enough that Qayin's entire arm went numb as Hevel grasped Qayin's collar and hurled him aside.

Qayin flew through the air and smashed into a pillar, his huge body crashing onto the deck as he gasped for breath. He looked down and saw the pistol still in his grasp, but he could not make his hand work to lift it and pull the trigger. Hevel's blow was placed with biological certainty, the inherited knowledge of the Word, hitting nerve centres and pinch–points with deadly precision to disable Qayin's arm.

'My brother,' Hevel sneered as he walked toward Qayin's crippled form, his every footfall sounding like metal upon metal. 'Such a shame, in so many ways.'

Hevel reached down and grabbed Qayin's collar, lifting the giant man's body up the pillar until his feet dangled off the floor. Qayin gagged, his throat collapsing inside Hevel's iron grasp as his brother stared at him with those cruel glowing eyes.

'If you cannot join us by choice,' he said, 'then you shall join us by force.'

Qayin saw Hevel open his mouth. His tongue sparkled as metallic filaments caught the light, and from within his stomach poured a flood of tiny metal creatures like insects that scuttled from his mouth and down his chin. Qayin stared in horror as the miniscule machines rushed across Hevel's naked arm toward Qayin's chin and mouth.

'Do not fight them,' Hevel said, smiling, 'for they will not harm you.'

Qayin stared at the tiny machines, and in a panic he heaved his damaged right arm across behind his back and grabbed the pistol from it in his uninjured left hand. He jammed the weapon against Hevel's arm and fired.

The plasma round blasted through Hevel's arm, exploding outward in a bright shower of searing metal, energy and burning flesh. Hevel screamed and leaped away as the blast melted the flood of horrific machines, gusting them away like glowing sparks in a breeze as Hevel grabbed his damaged arm and hugged it.

'So you can still feel pain,' Qayin growled as he took aim.

Hevel screamed and charged at Qayin, his arms outstretched and one of them trailing sparks from the remains of its ragged elbow as he ran. Qayin fired again, the plasma charge hitting Hevel straight in the face and blasting his head from his shoulders in a cloud of smoke. The stench of scorched flesh and burning metal filled the air as Qayin watched his brother's lifeless body collapse to its knees on the deck before him and then slowly topple sideways.

Qayin lowered the pistol and looked around at the bridge.

Hevel's bridge crew remained at their stations, their hands moving as though of their own accord across the control panels. Rage seethed through Qayin and he strode across the bridge, aimed and fired at the nearest of them, a bearded man who ignored Qayin's approach. The shot blasted his head from his shoulders.

Instantly, the other bridge crew members left their posts and converged on Qayin.

Qayin whirled and fired upon the nearest of them, a pretty young girl with blonde hair whose face vanished in a blaze of plasma. She collapsed as Qayin turned and dropped two more of them before a fourth leaped with astonishing speed and smashed the pistol from Qayin's grasp as another plunged into him from behind.

Qayin hit the deck on his side with a bone–jarring crash as the infected officer landed on top of him with incredible force. Qayin howled as pain ripped through his fractured ribs, and he saw the infected crewman straddle him and pin his arms in place with his knees.

The crewman opened his mouth and a flood of machines poured forth in a torrent as they flowed down his chest toward Qayin. Qayin seethed and writhed but the crewman's weight and strength were far too great.

The blast came from one side, a plasma charge hurling the crewman off Qayin in a shower of sparks that scorched his skin. Qayin turned as he saw C'rairn, Cutler and the other two convicts burst onto the bridge and fan out, firing as they went.

Qayin rolled over, scrambled to his feet and grabbed his pistol as he saw the tiny machines spill from the fallen crewman's chest and onto the deck. He turned and fired at them, the plasma round blasting them into tiny pellets of glowing metal.

Qayin looked up as Cutler, C'rairn and the two convicts cleared the deck. 'I tol' you all to get out of here,' he snapped.

C'rairn popped his visor open as he turned to Qayin.

'Yeah, well I don't much like taking orders either.'

Qayin grinned without warmth, his teeth bright in the gloom, and then he looked down at the corpse of his brother. He knelt down, the headless remains smouldering at the neck where the shot had severed Hevel's head.

'I'm sorry, man,' C'rairn said. 'We never knew.'

Qayin nodded. 'Nor did he.'

'Sir?'

C'rairn turned, mildly surprised that Cutler would address him as "sir". The convict was standing at the communications console as he pointed at the main screen. There, filling the view, was the Avenger.

'It's signalling us, Qayin,' Cutler said. 'It wants to talk.'

Qayin raised an eyebrow, his luminescent tattoos glowing. 'Well, let's talk.'

'We should wait for the captain,' C'rairn advised. 'He'll know what to do and…

'Captain ain't here,' Qayin replied, anger still seething like acid through his veins, 'and we've got the bridge.'

C'rairn stared at Qayin for a moment. 'You're kidding?'

'Can the War Room be shut off from here?' Qayin asked Cutler.

The old man nodded and flipped a couple of switches on his console. 'Already done.'

C'rairn looked at the two convicts in despair.

'After all that's happened?' he wailed.

Qayin's men swung their rifles to point at C'rairn as Qayin stepped down off the captain's platform and reached out for the soldier's weapon. C'rairn reluctantly handed his rifle over as Qayin spoke.

'I tol' you not to bother comin' in here, didn't I?' he said.

***

XL

Evelyn watched as Captain Idris Sansin reached the War Room and keyed in both his access codes and a voice and facial recognition program. The War Room's heavily shielded doors hissed open and with Andaim she followed the captain inside as the lights flickered on.

The War Room was the same basic layout as the bridge, but smaller and with fewer stations. Designed to act as a secure secondary command post should the ship be boarded or otherwise compromised, the entire vessel could be run from it if required.

'Stations, everybody,' the captain commanded, Bra'hiv's men keeping their weapons trained on the captain and his crew as they dispersed to their posts. Evelyn, suddenly feeling a little left out, stood near the now closed shield doors and watched as the ship's defence systems came on–line via the War Room.

'Start the scans,' Andaim ordered Bra'hiv. 'No exceptions, just to be sure.'

'Where is Qayin?' the captain demanded as Bra'hiv began passing a microwave scanner over him.

'The bridge,' came the reply from a station nearby as Lael surveyed the instruments. 'I'm detecting gunfire residue.'

'Are they okay?'

Evelyn waited tensely as the data streamed in from around the ship.

'Qayin is alive,' came the response from Lael, 'as are his human companions. I'm detecting several dead bodies with unusually hot core temperatures.'

'Hevel and his bridge crew,' Andaim guessed, 'he must have infected them all.'

'Put me through to them,' the captain ordered.

Lael flipped a few switches before her and then frowned. 'We're shut out,' she said.

'We're what?'

'All communication links have been isolated,' Lael repeated. 'Logs suggest it's only just been done.'

The captain stared at the blank monitors before him, and looked at Evelyn.

'You got any idea what he's up to?'

'None,' Evelyn said as she shook her head.

Bra'hiv stepped back from the captain and examined his scanner's screen. 'You're clear,' he reported, 'no nanobots inside you.'

Bra'hiv spent the next few minutes scanning Meyanna and each of the bridge crew. They waited as he examined the results of the scans.

'No infections that I can detect,' he reported. 'Everybody's clean.'

A tangible air of relief filled the War Room as Evelyn looked at Meyanna. 'I'm sorry, I had to…'

'I know,' Meyanna replied. 'Better to be safe than sorry, right?'

'It's Qayin,' Lael announced as a beeping signal sounded out through the War Room. 'They're signalling us. I'll put it on screen.'

A link was established, and Evelyn saw a screen flicker into life to gaze into the bridge far above them.

She saw Qayin immediately, sitting in the captain's chair. Around him were Cutler and his fellow convicts, manning various bridge stations. Qayin glanced up at them as he apparently realised that he was being watched and he smiled broadly.

'There you are,' he greeted them. 'Welcome to my bridge.'

'*Your* bridge?' Sansin uttered. 'What's happening up there Qayin?'

'Ah, captain,' Qayin raised a hand to wave idly as he spoke, 'you're finally out of your cage. Feels good, doesn't it?'

'Where is Hevel?' Idris demanded.

'Dead,' Qayin replied, his smile slipping. 'Although I think he'd been dead for a very long time.'

'Give up the bridge,' Sansin ordered. 'We're coming up.'

'I wouldn't do that if I were you,' Qayin replied.

Evelyn felt a pulse of concern as she pushed off the pillar and looked at Qayin. 'We need to take control back,' she said. 'This isn't over yet.'

Qayin inclined his head.

'Yeah,' he agreed, 'but y'know, I kinda like this seat and the view is great.'

'Qayin,' Andaim growled, 'after all that's happened this isn't the time to try a coup. We're about to be destroyed.'

Qayin shrugged, playing idly with the switches on the captain's chair. 'Well, you see lieutenant, I ain't so sure about that.'

'What the hell are you talking about?!' Idris roared. 'You'll get us all killed! If we do not cooperate we will be dead before this day is out.'

'That might not be true,' Qayin replied. 'I've been speaking to the Word and you're right: cooperation makes a world of difference.'

A silence descended upon the War Room as the captain frowned. 'Talking to it?'

'Talking to it,' Qayin confirmed. 'It's remarkably reasonable, you know? Calls itself Tyraeus.'

Sansin made a sign at Lael, whipping his hand across his own throat, and the transmission signal vanished as the captain turned to Andaim.

'Commander Tyraeus Forge,' the captain said.

'One of the finest battleship officers we ever had,' Andaim agreed. 'He must have been infected early. That would explain how the command structure was so easily destroyed during the apocaplyse: Tyraeus was in constant contact with both the high command and political leaders.'

'And Qayin's been speaking to him,' the captain said. 'Why would the Word bother with him? You think he's lying?'

'No,' Andaim said. 'That's an Avenger class cruiser sitting out there and it could have blown us to hell an hour or more ago. Something's going on all right.'

'What the hell would it want to *talk* to us about?' Sansin asked. 'It's wiped out our entire race and we're the last few left.'

'Maybe it's seen the humans on the surface,' Evelyn suggested, 'and it's trying to buy time until more ships arrive and it can destroy them too.'

Sansin gestured to the screen and Qayin's image returned as Lael re–opened the channel.

'I don't like being cut off,' the convict snarled.

'Tough,' Sansin snapped back, 'it already happened. What does the Word want with a traitorous bastard like you, Qayin?'

'Well now,' Qayin replied casually, 'that's the thing, ain't it? It's not me the Word wants.'

'That's no surprise,' Andaim shot back, 'you're not worth anything to anybody.'

'Sticks and stones, Andaim,' Qayin grinned. 'Thing is, it doesn't want you either, or any of the Atlantia's crew or any of the people down there on that planet.'

Evelyn glanced at Andaim, who in turn looked quizzically at Qayin.

'What does it want?' the captain asked for them all.

'It wants Eve,' Qayin replied.

Evelyn stared at Qayin in horror, and then at the captain, at Andaim and the bridge crew.

'What does it want with you?' Andaim asked.

Evelyn shook her head, trying to make her jaw move to reply. 'I don't know.'

The captain looked at her for a long moment and then back at Qayin. 'No can do. I don't negotiate with people like you.'

Qayin shrugged.

'I kinda knew that you'd say that, so here's the deal.'

Qayin raised one arm and gestured lazily to his side. Cutler and another convict walked into view, each gripping the arm of Officer C'rairn, one of them with a pistol to the officer's head.

'You two–faced bastard, let him go!' Andaim shouted.

'Now now, lieutenant,' Qayin sneered. 'No sense in getting all worked up about it. I'm a criminal, right? What did you expect?'

Andaim cursed under his breath and turned away from the screen as though he could not bear to look at Qayin any longer.

'Give us Eve and we'll give up C'rairn,' Qayin said. 'That's our leverage over the Word. If we don't give her up we'll be blown apart and this really will all be over.'

Andaim looked over his shoulder at the convict.

'After all she's done, you still turn your back on her as quickly as you draw a breath.'

'We don't know what she's done,' Qayin said. 'Maybe that's the thing, and Hevel and his friends probably knew something about that. Hand her over to the Word and we get to go free.'

'You don't seriously believe that?' the captain challenged him. 'The Word will take what it wants and blow us all into oblivion a split–second later.'

'Maybe,' Qayin shrugged, 'but then again it might not, and if we don't do what it asks it'll definitely blow us away, so I figure it's the better end of a bad deal.'

From behind Qayin, Cutler looked at Evelyn and spoke.

'It's just like in the desert, right Evelyn? We all gotta do what we gotta do. It's Golyath and Thutmose all over again.'

Evelyn stared at Cutler for a moment and she caught a glance from Andaim. The desert. She had watched as Qayin and Andaim fled the Egyptian army, and Andaim had gone back for Cutler, and she had fought Golyath to protect them both.

Evelyn turned to the captain.

'I will go,' she said.

'Like hell,' Sansin shot back. 'I'm not giving up a single person to that murderous bastard and…'

'I must go,' she interrupted without force.

The captain stared down at her. 'The Word will kill you if Qayin doesn't first.'

Evelyn nodded once. 'Better me on my own than all of us.'

Andaim shot to her side and grabbed her arm. 'No.'

Evelyn hesitated, saw the concern etched into Andaim's features and for the first time she thought that she saw a glimpse of something else. She reached up and gently rested her hand on his for a moment before pushing it away.

'I have to go,' she repeated, and then looked at the captain. 'Any chance of avoiding conflict is worth the effort, and it's not just us we have to think about now. There's a whole population down there on that planet that has no defence at all against the Word.'

The captain's voice was a harsh whisper.

'It'll kill you,' he growled. 'The Word does not do anything without good reason and it has no good reason to let any of us live.'

Evelyn smiled briefly but she shook her head.

'Logic doesn't matter, captain,' she replied. 'It's a risk worth taking, agreed?'

The captain bit his lip, but she knew that he could not argue with her. She glanced at Qayin's image up on the display screen. 'I'll take a shuttle and be over shortly,' she said.

'I'll await your arrival,' Qayin confirmed. 'I'm cutting off all communications until you arrive.' The channel cut off and the screen went blank.

'This is a mistake,' Andaim snapped. 'You're being sacrificed on Qayin's say so.'

'No,' Evelyn said. 'He's got a plan.'

'What plan?' Idris asked. 'He's holding C'rairn hostage! It's the damned prison ship situation all over again.'

'No,' she said. 'If Hevel was infected then he could have placed bugs and monitoring devices all over the bridge when he mutinied. We have to assume Qayin's compromised, and he said Hevel and *his friends* – that could mean there are more infected people aboard the Atlantia.'

The captain rubbed his forehead with his hand. 'We don't have time to scan the civilians in the sanctuary.'

'Which is why I need to do what Qayin is asking,' Evelyn pressed. 'We need the Word to think that we're playing along.'

'You're sure Qayin's bluffing?' Andaim asked.

'Of coursed he is,' she replied. 'He hates the Word as much as any of us, especially if it killed his brother. He knows we can't win and that it cannot be trusted. If Qayin really was in control of the bridge he'd have fired the engines and blasted us out of here as fast as he could and given us time to plan something.'

'Cutler said something to you about the desert?' Captain Sansin asked.

'We were being hunted by an army,' Andaim explained, 'trapped between two kings, Golyath and Thutmose.'

The captain's eyes narrowed thoughtfully. 'So they're trapped on the bridge somehow?'

'Qayin must fear that he's under observation from the Word. He can't say what he wants to, but I'm thinking he wants me to travel over there,' Evelyn explained, 'and take the fusion core with me. Hevel could not have informed the Word about the fusion core until it was within communication range, which wasn't until very recently and he's .'

'That's a very risky assumption,' Andaim pointed out. 'He could have signalled the Avenger when we left the surface with Bra'hiv, and warned it of our plan.'

'We won't know for sure,' Evelyn agreed. 'But we don't have much choice, do we? The only way to win this is to travel across to the Avenger.'

Captain Sansin's features collapsed. 'You're going to go *in* there?'

'There is no other option,' Evelyn said. 'We have to utterly destroy that vessel and then flee, and the only way we can properly do that is from the inside.'

'I thought that we would mount the fusion core externally and open fire on the Avenger,' Andaim said.

'And have the Avenger blast it and take the Atlantia down with a single salvo?' Evelyn challenged him. 'It has to be aboard the Avenger and we don't have much time. I go now or the Word gets suspicious and we're vaporised anyway. What's it going to be, captain?'

Idris stared up at the blank screen and then he sighed mightily.

'Very well,' he said, 'but I'm not going to just sit here and let you go without getting ready for a fight.'

'I wouldn't expect anything less,' Evelyn said. 'I don't know if the Word intends to double cross us, but I sure as hell don't have a problem with trying to blow it to hell while we're in the process.'

Idris thought for a moment. 'How many Raython fighters does an Avenger class cruiser carry?'

Andaim smiled. 'Eighteen,' he replied. 'And Tyraeus hasn't launched them into a defensive screen either.'

'Something that a commander of his standing would never have neglected to do,' the captain replied. 'Maybe the Word's confidence in itself might also be a weakness. Do you think that you could go aboard with Evelyn and launch them?'

'If we can reach them, we can fly them, captain.'

'Then do it,' Idris ordered.

'How will you get away?' Andaim asked Evelyn. 'If we're busy trying to steal the fighters, how will you get the core to Tyraeus?'

'I won't,' Evelyn said. 'Leave the core on the shuttle when we land. It'll shield your men from the Avenger's scanners, and once you've got the fighters blow the core to hell.'

Andaim's features tightened. 'But if you're still aboard…'

'The Word will still be destroyed,' Evelyn cut him off. 'Agreed?'

Andaim swallowed thickly but nodded once. The captain looked at Evelyn.

'You don't know what's in there,' he warned her. 'We saw things, back during the war, before we were forced to leave Ethera. Terrible things, Evelyn.'

She hesitated at the War Room door, and then opened it and hurried out.

***

XLI

Evelyn boarded the shuttle and sealed the ramp behind her as Andaim made his way into the cockpit. He began surveying the instruments as she walked past the fusion core in its magnetic containment unit and moved to sit alongside him.

'Will it hold up? The shuttle, I mean?' she asked.

'It's only a short hop between the ships,' Andaim replied. 'She's good for that, but the hull's very weak. If Tyraeus decides to hit us we'll be vaporised.'

'Comforting.'

Andaim looked at her as he ignited the engines, the whine from them humming through the hull.

'You don't have to do this,' he said.

Evelyn sighed, looking out of the viewing screen at the cargo deck still littered with the corpses of marines infected with the madness that was the Word.

'I don't know who I am,' she replied. 'I don't know anything but my own name, but that thing over there, Tyraeus, knows about me. I can't just walk away.'

Andaim gripped the controls as the shuttle lifted off the deck of the landing bay, tilting awkwardly under the uneven thrust from its remaining engines. Ahead, they saw a rush of air billow out into space in clouds of vapour as the bay's shield doors opened onto the yawning abyss of deep space, exposing the cavity where Bra'hiv had blasted through exterior doors. The shuttle drifted forward as Andaim guided it out of the bay and turned alongside the Atlantia.

The old frigate's big hull gleamed in the sunlight, and not for the first time Evelyn marvelled at the sight of the planet beneath them, vast expanses of blue and green, of sandy deserts and billowing clouds.

'We'll never be able to come back here, will we?' she said.

'No,' Andaim said. 'Not as long as the Word exists anyway. The people down there are too vulnerable.'

Andaim guided the shuttle beneath the frigates's massive hull, turning away from the planet as they passed beneath the Atlantia and out toward deep space.

There, opposite them, was the Avenger. Evelyn scanned the battleship's enormous lines, the sleek hull bristling with plasma cannons that speckled its surface, the ghost–grey metal hull blackened in large areas as the Word slowly converted it into something entirely new, consumed by the powerful machines swarming through it.

'I still don't get it,' Andaim said. 'Why does it want you there? What possible purpose could it have for you?'

'We're going to find out real soon,' she said. 'Pick the landing bay closest to the bridge.'

Andaim guided the shuttle toward the Avenger's for'ard bays, nestled close behind the bulge of the bridge deck and surrounded by heavy armaments. Evelyn heard him whistle through his teeth as he noted that all of the guns were pointed directly at them and tracking their movements.

'One shot,' he said.

'They'd have fired by now,' Evelyn said. 'They mistrust us, just as we mistrust them, but curiosity is what's keeping us alive right now.'

Andaim nodded, and she looked over her shoulder to where the fusion core sat in its containment unit behind them, strapped to the deck. Their last defence, if they could get it close enough to strike the Avenger somewhere truly vulnerable.

The Avenger loomed vast in the viewing screen and then there was nothing but the open landing bay, a rectangle of bright yellow light against the blackness of the hull. Evelyn caught from the corner of her eye the shape of the Avenger's hull shifting as though it were a black sea of oil, the waves catching the light as they rolled back and forth.

'It's as if the whole ship is alive,' she said as the sight made her shiver.

The shuttle was swallowed by the landing bay doors and Evelyn craned her neck around to look out of the window behind her. Sure enough, as the shuttle sailed in the doors began closing behind them.

'They're just sealing the bay so the air can be released into it,' Andaim said, sounding as though he was trying to comfort himself as much as her.

'You didn't have to be here,' she said. 'I could have come alone.'

Andaim smiled tightly as he guided the shuttle down and it settled onto the deck, the engines winding down.

'There was no way I was going to do that,' he replied. 'And you know it.'

For the first time since she had been released from the bitter and claustrophobic chill of the escape capsule days before Evelyn felt a small but growing patch of warmth flood her chest, a foreign sensation that she realised she had forgotten about. Andaim did not meet her gaze, focusing instead on shutting the engines down.

It was Qayin's voice that broke the silence.

'Seriously, you two are making me feel all warm and fluffy inside.'

Evelyn looked over her shoulder at him. 'Shut it, creep.'

Qayin grinned, his white teeth bright in the darkness.

'I can't tell if we've been scanned or not,' Andaim said, 'but the interference run by Atlantia might not be enough to have blocked the Avenger's instruments. The Word might know that Evelyn is not alone and that the core is aboard.'

There were thirty convicts in the rear of the shuttle, and to her surprise one of the first volunteers had been Cutler. It was the old man who replied to Andaim.

'So? This is the best chance we have, so I say let's take it.'

'You've changed your tune,' Andaim said as he got up out of his seat.

'I got my reasons,' Cutler replied, casting a quick glance at Evelyn.

The convicts were all armed with plasma rifles and blast charges, and all of them had a singular mission.

'You know what to do,' Andaim said.

The convicts held their rifles tightly to their chests, each bearing an expression of determination which provoked in Evelyn a brief and slightly odd sense of pride.

Andaim opened the shuttle's boarding ramp and then turned to Evelyn.

'This is it,' he said.

Evelyn sucked in a deep breath as she stepped out onto the ramp. Andaim's hand grasped her arm briefly.

'Come back,' he said.

Evelyn managed a faint smile, and then she walked down the ramp and out across the landing bay.

A number of identical shuttles were parked on the far side of the bay, looking as pristine as they had when they had first been built. On the opposite side were some small vehicles, machinery and a series of escape capsules set into the walls: standard procedure in any landing bay that was periodically exposed to the vacuum of space. She could see various pieces of equipment scattered about, left where they had fallen when the ship had first been overrun. Some of the walls bore scorch marks where plasma rounds had battered them, as the last surviving members of the crew fought for their lives.

Evelyn strode to an access door and it opened before her without prompting. She slowed and then eased her way inside.

Her breath caught in her throat as she saw the interior of the passageway. It was lined with a seething mass of black bots, billions of them scuttling like glossy black insects in layers so thick that she could no longer see the walls of the passageway. She hesitated, realising that she was utterly exposing herself to the Word.

She looked over her shoulder at the shuttle, knowing that Andaim and the convicts were inside and waiting for her to move. If she faltered, then they would be destroyed. She turned back to the passageway, and as loathing filled her guts she stepped inside.

The bots swarmed away from her as she walked in, scattering in black clouds up the walls and along the deck, as though she were a candle flame parting the darkness before her. Shocked, she stepped fully into the passageway and the door hissed shut behind her.

*

'They're inside.'

Captain Idris Sansin watched as the shuttle craft cruised into the Avenger's landing bay and the doors slowly closed behind it.

'This had better work,' he said as he turned to his tactical officer. 'How many of our own Raythons are operational?'

'Twelve are ready to fly sir,' Jerren said. 'The other six are currently inoperative and awaiting repair.'

Idris nodded and turned back to the viewing screen on the bridge.

As soon as Qayin had shut off communications with the War Room and Evelyn had made her announcement that she would be travelling to the Avenger, she had instead dashed with Andaim and the captain to the Atlantia's bridge. There, Qayin had willingly let them in. Concerned about the Word monitoring communications channels through bots that may have survived the raid on the bridge, Qayin had wanted a face–to–face meeting.

There, he had explained to the captain his reasoning and to Idris's surprise relinquished control of the bridge back to the captain. It was as much of a deception as he could have managed given his limited time and resources, but it was something more than they had had before.

Quietly, without fuss, the bridge and surrounding areas had been scanned and cleaned of all remaining bots, including several pockets tapping into the communications channels aboard the ship that would likely have relayed Qayin's demands to the Avenger, thus bolstering the deception. A tiny handful had been isolated and purposefully allowed to remain, and now those channels were being used to send false signals proclaiming that there was nothing that could be done, that there were no operable defensive fighters available, little plasma for weapons and a great number of sick and injured aboard.

Thus, the game was in motion.

But now the entire venture was in Evelyn's hands. As she had said, the Word had revealed a weakness: *her*. Quite why it wanted her alive, or indeed wanted her at all, was beyond the captain, but the fact that Hevel and Governor Hayes had in their infected state tried to kill her by blasting the high–security wing into oblivion meant that there was *something* going on. The Word had wanted Evelyn dead, yet now it apparently wanted her alive.

'Has there been any signal from Tyraeus?'

'Nothing sir,' came the response, 'all channels are silent.'

The plan was simple enough, albeit that it might require Evelyn to sacrifice herself, but that had been her decision. She had wanted to go despite Andaim's loudly voiced protests, which had in the captain's opinion been expressed without due consideration for his standing as an officer. Meyanna had suggested letting the indiscretion go by, for reasons that Idris wasn't sure of.

'How far from the Avenger's landing bay to the fighter wing?' he asked Jerren.

'Seven floors, four hundred cubits,' came the response.

The captain looked at the viewing screen, at the cruiser's huge hull laden with heavy weapons, and visualised the path that Andaim and his men would be forced to take. Their route had been chosen based on the amount of bots smothering the Avenger's hull. There were large areas so far left untouched, and it was assumed that the interior sections of the ship beneath these areas of hull were also uninfected. The Avenger was a large vessel, and even the voracious nature of the Word would take a while to spread to all of her corners, if indeed it even intended to.

Thus it had been determined that the fighter hangars, where the Avenger's four wings of top–rated offensive Raython spacecraft were stored, were also likely untouched. Manned fighters were of less use to a mechanical foe, and it had been surmised that as the Avenger had not deigned to launch a defensive screen of fighters when it had arrived alongside the Atlantia, they were thus not yet under its control.

'How long, do you think?' he asked Jerren.

'If they're unopposed in their path? Ten minutes, maybe twelve.'

Idris nodded and put his hands behind his back.

'Prepare all armouries for battle,' he said, 'but pass the word verbally, not through the communications channels. Charge the plasma banks, but do it slowly.'

As his officers dashed to perform their duties and the bridge lights were dimmed to a dull red, Captain Idris Sansin felt his wife's hand squeeze his arm.

'This is it,' he said softly to her.

***

XLII

Evelyn walked slowly, her arms tucked in by her sides and her head slightly ducked down.

She could hear the hiss of countless spindly metallic legs clicking on the metal walls and bulkheads as she walked, swarming around her but always at least a few inches from her boots, a similar sized patch of bare metal above her on the ceiling as she walked.

She tried to keep her head level as she walked, almost as if pretending that the bots were not there, but her eyes swivelled left and right and up and down as she strode toward the bridge, seeking any sign that these horrendous little things were preparing to swarm upon her and consume her body in a frenzy of gnashing pincers and burrowing tools.

Warrior Drones, she faintly remembered them as being called. Larger than most nanotech devices, military grade. Programmed to attack, to consume, to swarm and to terrify. The size of large insects, they were equipped with razor sharp pincers, fangs and legs and shielded by glossy black shells of gleaming metal.

The bots also stayed clear of the nearest ceiling light to Evelyn, but all of the others were smothered after she passed through, plunging the passageway behind her into darkness and keeping the corridor ahead likewise inky black.

She wondered what had happened to the crew. She saw occasional scorch marks scarring the walls of the passageway, revealing that they too had fought each other as the infection had spread, mind after mind lost to the Word and its unstoppable mission of conquest. But she had seen no bodies, no blood, no other evidence of the aftermath of the carnage of battle.

The passageway ended and opened out onto the bridge deck, where two large doors awaited her. There, standing either side of the doors, were two marines. Evelyn paused on the opposite side of the bridge doors from them, watching. The bots around her scuttled back into the passageway and she realised that she had been allowed to pass through only so that she could be trapped here. With a plunging sense of dread, she knew that she would never be allowed to leave this place.

The soldiers did not look at her and she realised that beneath their visors their faces rippled with the countless bots crawling beneath their pale skin. The lights in the bridge deck illuminated them well but she could still detect the glow in their eyes and sense the heat radiating from their bodies, more machines now than men.

Without a word one of them stepped aside from the bridge door, his rifle held at port arms and his unblinking gaze staring at her expectantly. Evelyn took another deep breath and strode toward the door, which hissed open and revealed the interior of the bridge as she walked in.

Back before the catastrophe that had consumed the colonies, the bridge of a battleship would have been an almost sacred place that no civilian would ever have been allowed to see. Classified instruments of all kinds, carefully concealed data on range, speed, weapons and tactics were on display, and behind each station was a motionless human, or what was left of them, their arms now writing masses of bots spreading out across the control panels as though their bodies were now welded to their stations.

In the centre of the bridge and sitting in what had once been the captain's seat, was the figure of a man, but a kind that Evelyn had never seen before.

'Welcome, Eve,' the man said.

His voice was deep, like Qayin's but rippling as though heard underwater. The figure stood and she got her first clear look at what was left of Captain Tyraeus Forge.

His skin was a rippling mass of bots that darkened his pale skin, as though little of his flesh and bone remained. The bold leader's features were thus recognisable but somehow deformed, a complex but unfaithful and ever–changing replication of a once famed and powerful battleship commander.

Evelyn stood her ground before him and noticed movement up on the bridge ceiling. Thousands of bots scuttled back and forth, following trails like insects as they scurried.

'They will not harm you, Eve,' Tyraeus said.

'I'm supposed to believe that?' Evelyn asked, finally finding her voice. 'You wanted me dead.'

'No,' Tyraeus replied, 'I have never wanted you dead, Eve. Hevel went beyond his remit. Too much of his human weakness remained and he feared you Evelyn, he feared you very greatly indeed.'

Evelyn realised that Hevel must have managed to contact the Avenger before his demise, but she could not know how much information Hevel had imparted. She said nothing for a moment, staring instead at this monstrous deformation of a man. The commander's uniform was gone, what remained of his naked body seething with bots both above and beneath the surface. His teeth when he smiled gleamed metallic silver that flashed as they reflected the lights of the bridge around them.

'Why did he fear me?' she asked.

Tyraeus's mouth blossomed like a metallic flower and revealed its gruesome interior swarming with bots as he spoke.

'He knew who you were,' the commander explained. 'He understood *what* you were.'

Evelyn frowned. 'I can't remember anything.'

'I know,' Tyraeus nodded, his scalp glistening like a giant black fruit gone to the bad. 'I can help you with that, but to do so you will have to trust me.'

Evelyn opened her mouth to protest, but before she could do so two solid hands gripped her by the arms. She looked to her sides and saw two marines holding her, their skin undulating beneath their uniforms as the bots controlled their muscles. She tried to shake their grip loose but they were as immovable as iron.

Tyraeus moved toward her, his legs swarming with bots that rippled and pulsed as they flexed their tiny bodies in unison to drive the commander forward. Evelyn recoiled from him, saw his glowing eyes boring into hers and his mouth opening as he spoke, tiny bots darting in and out.

'You must trust me, Evelyn,' he said. 'You must believe me.'

'How can I?' she gasped, keeping her mouth tightly closed for fear of one of the bots leaping from Tyraeus and infiltrating her body. 'You've murdered millions, hijacked their bodies for your own ends until nothing of them remains.'

Tyraeus shook his head.

'Every human being we have encountered has fought us,' he said, 'but once infected, every one of them has welcomed us. We are the future, Evelyn. This is what we are now, this is who we are now and we embrace it willingly.'

Evelyn shook her head as her face screwed up in disgust at the sight of him.

'I'll never embrace that,' she spat, and glanced down at his artificial body.

Tyraeus laughed, loudly, bots swarming across his face.

'I don't suppose that you would,' he replied, and then he looked deep into her eyes. 'But not because you wouldn't want to, once infected. It is because you cannot.'

Evelyn frowned. 'Cannot what?'

Tyraeus looked at her for a long beat and then suddenly Evelyn understood. With a terrific wave of realisation she realised why she had been incarcerated, why she had been buried away for so long, why she could not remember who she was or even why she would have committed such a heinous crime in the first place.

'I'm innocent,' she said. 'I didn't kill my family.'

Tyraeus nodded.

'And I can show you why,' he replied.

Tyraeus stood back and nodded to his soldiers. Evelyn screamed as she was lifted bodily into the air and plunged onto her back across a tactical display in the centre of the bridge. The two soldiers pinned her down with an iron grip as Tyraeus moved over her, and in his hand he held something that she never thought that she would see again.

'No, please,' she begged as tears spilled from her eyes.

Tyraeus lifted the object in his hands and spoke with something that almost sounded like regret.

'I'm sorry, Evelyn,' he replied, 'but if I show you what you know, you can never share it with anybody. The Word is the law, and this mask is its judgement upon you.'

The dull, grey face of a metal mask stared back at Evelyn, its throat–probes long and gleaming.

Tyraeus lifted the metal mask over her face and Evelyn thrashed and writhed to escape, but the commander's hand stilled her head as though it were caught in a vice. Another trooper appeared, and one black–veined hand forced her jaw open.

Evelyn saw the probes briefly and then she gagged and her screams were choked off as the probes plunged deep into her throat and silenced her. The taste of metal filled her mouth and she fought the urge to vomit as the mask closed over her face and the thin slits of light appeared before her eyes as though she were imprisoned.

She wept, openly and without shame as she heard the mask being fixed into place. Tyraeus held up the mask key to show her, and then he slipped it between his blackened lips as countless bots swarmed upon it and it was consumed.

'Now,' Tyraeus said, 'you must learn the truth and understand why you must join us.'

Evelyn, shivering in the grip of the guards, saw Tyraeus lift his index finger before her. Upon the tip swarmed a small bundle of bots, a glistening, writhing ball of nanotechs too small to spot individually with the naked eye, like black smoke entrapped in a glass sphere. Evelyn tried to scream but no sound came forth. She tried to escape but she could not move. Tyraeus lowered his finger to her lips, the probes once again preventing her from closing her mouth, and she felt the tiny bots scuttle across her lips and into her mouth, pouring like water into her throat.

'Now you shall learn the truth, Evelyn,' Tyraeus said.

Evelyn felt sick to her stomach as the bots vanished but she could feel them, somehow, a tiny patch of warmth inside her neck as they swarmed upward through her sinuses, climbing toward her skull. She felt them swarm like an itch behind her eyes and toward her brain, and then her vision turned red and she felt her fear fall away like an old skin.

'There,' Tyraeus said as she felt the soldiers release her. 'That wasn't so bad, was it?'

Evelyn, unable to respond, simply lay on her back as Tyraeus's voice lulled her into a bizarre sleep, one where she dreamed and yet could see the bridge around her at the same time. She felt warm, safe, cossetted, and some small part of her made her realise why the Word has been so rapid and successful in consuming its victims. It stimulated the pleasure sensors of the brain first: it eradicated fear, stifled pain, silenced doubt.

Evelyn willingly remained on her back as the bots infiltrated her brain and showed her the past.

***

.

XLIII

'This way.'

Andaim guided Qayin's convicts through the Avenger's hull, moving quickly but quietly as they headed toward the fighter wing and kept their eyes open for any sign of marauding bots.

The decks around them were deserted, cold and mostly dark. Andaim could only guess at why, but he assumed that with the crew overwhelmed and much of the ship's accommodation and crew support sections unrequired by the Word, they had simply been shut down to conserve power or redirect it toward weapons systems.

They had passed kitchens, ward rooms and canteens and found them all empty, often with drinks and trays left where they had fallen. There were few traces of evidence of battle down here, which made it likely that the entire crew had rushed to defend the ship against its infected members. The entire hull had an abandoned feel to it, eerie and cold.

'How much further?' Qayin asked. 'Damned cold down here.'

'Environmental controls have been deactivated,' Andaim replied. 'No need when there's no humans left to support.'

Their breath condensed in clouds in the darkness, and crystals of ice twinkled on the walls of the corridors.

'We're damned lucky it didn't expel the air too,' Qayin observed.

'Let's not tempt fate,' Cutler uttered behind them as they hurried along.

All of the men carried emergency oxygen supplies and visors, but they had little protection against the bitter cold as they moved.

'The cold might help us,' Andaim realised as he walked.

'How you figure that?' Qayin uttered.

'Temperature extremes,' Andaim replied. 'The bots don't like extreme cold or heat. That's maybe why they're taking so long to colonise the entire vessel. They'd have started at the control centre, the bridge, and moved slowly aft. If they've shut down the environmental controls and the rest of the ship is abandoned, they might not have had any reason to come back here for months.'

Qayin looked about him in the darkness.

'That ain't gonna stop them comin' back here if we get ourselves noticed,' he pointed out. 'Sooner we can get those fighter's up and runnin', the sooner we can get the hell out of here and attack.'

Andaim nodded as he guided the men down a flight of steps toward the fighter decks below. His flashlight illuminated the frozen walls of the corridor ahead, filled with clouds of water vapour that whorled in the light.

'Get down!' he yelled.

It was the movement of the mist that alerted him, of something that had just passed through at speed. Andaim fired twice into the mist and saw his plasma round illuminate a human form as it ploughed into them and sent them sprawling to the deck.

Andaim hurled himself into the cover of a bulkhead as he saw several pairs of glowing red eyes through the clouds of vapour and a salvo of plasma rounds flash past. Two convicts howled in agony as they were seared with rounds and they tumbled down the steps onto the deck, writhing as their flesh burned.

The reason for the circulating air and the lack of crew remains finally explained, Andaim shouted to the convicts behind him.

'Fire at will!' he yelled. 'Go for the eyes!'

Andaim returned fire, aiming for the glowing red orbs and hitting one of the Avenger's infected crew straight in the face, his smouldering torso plunging to the deck. Qayin and the convicts laid down a thunderous hail of fire that flashed through the passageway ahead, smashing infected crewmen aside until their bodies lay sprawled like a grotesque carpet down the corridor.

The firefight ended rapidly as Andaim peered through the smoke. The heat of the plasma rounds had evaporated the mist, and he could see several bodies glowing as uniforms burned and spilled embers around gaping wounds.

'They knew we were coming!' Cutler said.

'Masks on,' Andaim ordered. 'I don't want anybody getting infected, understood?'

The convicts donned their full–face respirator masks as Andaim called back among their ranks.

'Torches, now!'

Two men hurried forward, lugging heavier weapons. Standing side by side, they activated the torches and a searing blue flame erupted from the barrel of each weapon. They advanced slowly, blasting the bodies of the dead crewmen with fearsome tongues of flame.

Andaim and Qayin followed behind them, saw clouds of tiny metallic bots gusted in glowing embers before the flames as they tried to escape their fallen hosts, pouring from chest and stomach wounds. The choking, commingled vapours of burning flesh and molten metal were held back by the face masks as Andaim followed the torch–men until they cleared the corpses and shut off their weapons.

'All right,' he said into his microphone, 'they know we're here, so no more foreplay. Let's move, as fast as we can!'

'About time,' Qayin snapped.

Andaim turned and led the men at a jog with his rifle held at his hip before him, ready to fire at the smallest hint of opposition. They plunged down the corridor to a second flight of steps that led down to the hangar decks. Andaim pulled a plasma charge from his belt and activated it as they reached the top of the stairs, then tossed it as hard as he could out of sight down the corridor below.

A bright flash of light and a deafening crash shook the corridor as Andaim plunged down the flight of steps and fired into the swirling plasma haze filling the corridor, Qayin and the convicts rushing down behind him and firing a salvo of blasts into the darkness.

Two bodies spun aside as they were hit, red eyes glowing as they tumbled to the deck. Andaim fired at their heads, smashing them into smoking masses of scorched flesh and metal. He waved the torch–men ahead, their bright blue flames searing the corpses and cleansing them by fire.

Ahead, a massive bulkhead blocked their way to the hangar decks, likely sealed by the Word. Andaim hurried up to the doors and waved the men forward

'This is where we'll face the biggest opposition,' he said. 'They're not likely to have left the fighters unguarded, even if they haven't needed them so far. We go in fast, but cover each other like I told you and try not to damage the ships, okay?'

The convicts nodded as one, and then Andaim hesitated.

'Where's Cutler?'

The convicts looked back into their midst but the old man was nowhere to be seen.

'He didn't get hit,' Qayin growled suspiciously, 'and I ain't seen him since we burned up that first group of crewmen. He must have lost his stones and fled.'

Andaim cursed but he knew there was little he could do.

'Let's just hope the damned fool doesn't do something we'll all regret.'

Andaim placed plasma charges at the doors' hinges and locking mechanism before waving the men back and sprinting back up the corridor. As soon as he was sure everybody was in cover, he lifted a detonator in his hand and squeezed the trigger.

The blast hurled the doors clean off their hinges, severing the metal braces and sending a gust of searing hot air past where Andaim crouched. A cloud of acrid smoke spilled into the corridor as Andaim charged toward the doors, a gaping hole torn in the hangar wall as though some immense beast had bitten through it, tongues of bright metal glinting in the light from the hangar bay.

Andaim hopped through the gaping hole and instantly saw ranks of crewmen advancing across the bay toward him, their rifles held at their hips as they marched robotically and opened fire.

Andaim threw himself down flat onto the deck and opened fire as a salvo of plasma rounds zipped over his head to hammer the hangar wall behind him. Cries of pain rang out through the hanger as plasma rounds scorched the walls and the air around him as he picked off target after target, dropping the crewmen as they lumbered forward. The convicts pouring into the hangar charged toward them.

'Don't get too close to them!' he yelled. 'You'll be infected! Advance by sections!'

Most of the convicts obeyed, but one fired from just a few feet away from an infected crewman. Andaim glimpsed the blast hit the crewman and spew molten metal across the convict, along with a cloud of bots. The convict screamed and swiped his hand across his body, trying to wipe off the bots that swarmed up his clothes and across his visor, flooding in through the holes burned in the plastic by the shrapnel.

The convict's hands flew to his head as he tried to block his eyes and mouth, but then he was writhing in agony as the bots burrowed into his facial cavities. Andaim swivelled to aim at the convict, but a heavy hand belayed him as Qayin shook his head.

'Not yet, wait until they're all in his head.'

Andaim waited until the convict's hands slumped by his side, and then a blast of plasma fire hit the convict and vaporised his skull in a cloud of blue smoke. Qayin lowered his rifle and then turned it back to the remaining crewmen still advancing upon them in stiff ranks, tumbling over their fallen brethren or walking into the hail of lethal plasma fire.

'You were right!' Qayin yelled as he fired. 'They're stiffened up by the cold. The bots can't make them move fast enough.'

The remaining crewmen were shuffling toward cover but Andaim saw the convicts cut them off, firing quick and precise blasts that severed legs and immobilised them before taking the more difficult head–shots.

Moments later the deafening blasts were silenced and the hangar fell quiet, littered with the bodies of perhaps fifty former crewmen of the Avenger. Andaim looked over the barrel of his rifle for movement.

'That's it!' Andaim shouted. 'Torch men, finish them off and then get aboard your ships!'

With a ragged cheer the convicts sprinted to either side of the hangar, where the ranks of sleek Raython fighters stood waiting, their cockpits sealed shut.

Andaim dashed across to the hangar control room and accessed the computers there, the keyboards glistening with frost as he tapped keys. A wall–drive hummed into life and he hit a button.

Across the hangar the cockpits of the fighters opened up one by one.

'Now we're even,' he smiled grimly.

Andaim shouldered his rifle and dashed for the nearest vacant cockpit.

***

XLIV

Home.

Evelyn saw her home.

The image of the house that she had been raised in was dreamlike, high above a river valley where other similar houses perched on the forested hillsides. She saw her parents' faces, her kindly mother and strict but loving father, saw memories that brought both delight and grief rushing upon her soul in equal measure.

The soft orange glow of the sun rising above the mountains into the pink sky, the winding trees that turned slowly on twisting trunks with the sunlight as the days passed, the colour of their leaves denoting the time of day, the folding of their branches warning of the long dark nights. She saw the river that she had played beside as a child, her friends, their school, the ceaseless blinking lights of commuter craft ascending into the sky from the spaceport a few leagues away, crossing the arc of the gas giant around which her home planet orbited.

Caneeron was tidally locked in orbit around Titas, the gas giant. As such, one side of her home world was in darkness for much of the day, lit only by long twilight periods as it caught the sun across Titas's horizon as it orbited the giant. On Evelyn's side, Caneeron was aglow for much longer periods but it remained a cold planet, much of its heat derived from the gravitational flexing of its core as it orbited Titas. Volcanism wracked the equatorial regions, leaving only about a third of the available land mass truly habitable and largely powered by geo–thermal forces. The rest was a mixture of oceans, ice sheets and searing volcanic plains.

Human life had not evolved on Caneeron, although the mountains and ice sheets were home to a wild variety of animals and predators. The planet represented a valuable mineral resource for the colonies, her father a prospector who surveyed there for a major mining corporation on Ethera, the home world of all her kind.

Images flashed through her mind and she saw the family she had been forced to forget, her husband and their little boy: smiling faces, happiness, the peaceful existence of the colonies.

Then the mood changed, the images darkening. Evelyn saw the office where she had worked for many years, for the media. An investigator. She had done well, uncovered corporate espionage, exposed corrupt politicians, crushed unjust convictions.

Then the Word emerged from the battle between militarised nanotech swarms. The belief that somewhere, somehow, the police were showing signs of becoming militarised without government or democratic consent. The increase in political conservatism, the sense of always being watched, an invasive series of laws being passed that served no purpose but to increase military spending and classified projects and protect those projects from independent or even political oversight.

She had investigated for months, uncovering an ever growing network of incidences of deaths involving whistle blowers, government employees and unfortunate bystanders to what were described as *unfortunate accidents* in remote regions of both Caneeron and Ethera. Then, the emergence of tremendously potent like devlamine: her interview with a convict bearing the Mark of Qayin, the luminescent tattoos on his face and his braided gold and blue locks outshone by the rage infecting his massive frame.

Eventually she had gone too far. The threats began against her life, against the lives of her family. The media company she worked for suddenly fired her, her long–standing and honourable boss turning into a tyrant who almost physically ejected her from the building.

Drugs had been found in her home. Police arrived, arrests were made. She was questioned, recalled nothing of how the drugs had gotten into her home: she and her husband hated such things. She was released, her disgrace covered by the media company she had once worked for, no mention that the police found no evidence of her or any of her family being habitual drug users.

She saw herself at home that night, her husband's kind words, saw her sleeping child, recalled feeling so afraid for him. And then the morning. The blood, everywhere. The confusion. Her husband dead, his head a mess of blood and bone where he had been shot. Her son, likewise dead. The crushing grief. The sirens, the arrest, the drugs scattered across her kitchen, the weapon found in the trash.

The tests followed. She was positive for drugs in her system even though she had not taken even pain killers for weeks. The charges for the murder of her entire family. The incarceration, immediate and high–security. The restraints and the mask, for *her own safety* and that of her gaolers.

And then…

… Evelyn jolted as she saw the man hovering in her field of vision in a laboratory of some kind, and the tiny seething ball of bots being inserted into her mouth, powerless to prevent them from surging into her body.

The pain.

The fevers.

The hacking, blood splattered coughs.

And then then bots being ejected from her mouth to tumble onto the floor of her cell, their tiny metallic bodies silent and still in a pool of blood–stained bile.

Evelyn jolted awake.

Tyraeus was watching her with interest as the visions faded. She saw his hand reach out, felt her throat and nose itching painfully and then the bots poured out of her. She coughed, her chest heaving, the only sound that of air wheezing as it was sucked in and expelled from her lungs.

Evelyn slumped back onto the tactical display, tasted blood in her mouth as Tyraeus looked down at her.

'Your body rejected the bots, Evelyn,' he said as he held in his metallic palm a ball of damaged bots that writhed there. 'You're immune system isolated them and ejected them. You fought them off, and they were unable to infect you. We need to know how, and why.'

Evelyn tried to speak, desperate to ask more questions: why? Why do this to so many people? Why attempt to eradicate an entire species? But her voice was trapped once more inside, her pained expression veiled by the steel mask.

Tyraeus looked over his shoulder at her, his red eyes glowing.

'There were others, of course,' he said, 'but they were killed or chose to take their own lives and their secret with them. Many, I suspect, did not even know that they carried such an immunity. But you, you were alive on the Atlantia's prison hull, and when we realised that you were immune we knew we had to have you back.'

Tyraeus's metal shoulders sagged slightly.

'Alas, the Word was already under suspicion and we had to initiate the occupation. The Atlantia escaped with you and your fellow inmates attached, one of the few vessels isolated enough not to have been sufficiently infected. Our only assets aboard were Hevel and Governor Hayes, shallow men interested only in power and self–preservation. At the very least, they enabled us to catch up with you before their demise.'

Tyraeus turned his back to her again.

'Now that we have you, we can finally dispense with the Atlantia and its crew.'

Evelyn peered left and right at the troopers standing silently either side of her. Both were staring into space as though immobile unless fed with a command. She kept her entire body still as she shifted one hand toward the holster of the soldier to her right.

'Command,' Tyraeus said, and she heard a hum as though the ship were coming alive all at once. 'Charge weapons, all plasma turrets engage Atlantia, point–blank range!'

Evelyn reached out and snatched the pistol from the soldier's holster, whipping it up as the trooper looked down at her in surprise in time for her first shot to smash into his warped face in a blaze of blue–white plasma. The trooper staggered backwards as Evelyn rolled off the tactical display and aimed at her other captor, blasting him in the centre of his chest even as he was raising his own weapon.

The soldier spun aside and fell, leaving a column of blue smoke hanging in the air as Evelyn whirled and fired at Tyraeus.

Tyraeus turned as the three plasma rounds blasted his chest, his huge form staggering backwards as a plume of molten bots spilled like a waterfall of tiny sparks from his body and littered the deck at his feet. Molten plasma and metal hissed and spat sparks and smoke from his body as he regained his balance, and to Evelyn's horror he smiled at her.

'Defiant, to the last,' he said.

Evelyn saw thousands of bots scuttling across the ceiling to drop onto Tyraeus's head and pour like liquid oil into his wounds, filling them as swiftly as they had been blasted from him. His immense bulk righted itself and he stormed toward her.

Evelyn fired again as she retreated across the bridge, but Tyraeus ducked aside from the plasma rounds that whistled past him, or whipped armoured hands up to deflect the searing hot balls of energy, the metallic pads on his palms instantly glowing red hot.

Evelyn's back hit the wall of the bridge and she saw bots scuttling toward her across the ceiling in a shiny black flood.

'You cannot be turned, Eve,' Tyraeus snarled at her, 'but you can be destroyed.'

A metallic hand shot out and gripped her throat, Tyraeus's palm still hot from the plasma rounds as he lifted her off of her feet and glared straight into her face as the flood of bots swarmed toward her down the wall.

'Let me taste you, Evelyn,' Tyraeus growled.

The metallic head moved closer to her and she smelled a bizarre waft of fumes emitted from his mouth as he opened it and a black tongue swarming with bots probed for her lips.

Evelyn lifted her arm and fired the pistol.

The plasma round hit Tyraeus' in the side of his head, blasting through bots and bone and spraying the contents of his skull across a work station to her left. Tyraeus's huge hand fell away from her throat and she hurled herself from the wall as the bots plunged down onto Tyraeus's body instead of her own.

Evelyn staggered away, the bots roiling in a black mass around Tyraeus's body as she staggered across the bridge toward the communications station. She blasted the immobile crewman standing there, the smouldering corpse hurled into the back wall of the bridge, and then she keyed the microphone.

'Atlantia, this is the Avenger, I have the bridge.'

A hiss of static filled the bridge, and Evelyn saw the other infected crewmen slowly turning toward her, red eyes glowing in the darkness.

'Atlantia, this is the Avenger, Evelyn has the bridge,' she repeated.

More static, and then a reply that came not from the microphone but from the bridge.

'No, Evelyn, you do not.'

Against the banks of coloured lights and instruments she saw Tyraeus climb to his feet, his huge bulk silhouetted against the lights. There were no longer any glowing eyes in his head, and his voice sounded even more distorted than before as he stomped awkwardly toward her.

The overhead lighting glinted off the roiling mass of bots that now made up his head, a seething swarm that had assumed a bizarre caricature of Tyraeus's features. She recoiled from his advance, turned and fired at the nearest crewman in her way. The crewman dropped as his head was blasted from his shoulders and she retreated further, but Tyraeus merely stepped up onto the communications deck and followed her.

'There is no escape,' Tyraeus intoned, his lips rippling as he spoke. 'You will become one with the Word eventually, Evelyn, whether alive or dead.'

Across the ceiling the swarm of bots expanded like a gigantic black spider, their tiny legs rustling as they scuttled toward her. She shot another crewman, dropping him as she made her way toward the bridge exit.

'You cannot survive out there, Evelyn,' Tyraeus assured her. 'You will be consumed.'

The bots were flooding across the ceiling, within a few feet of her now as she lowered the pistol and looked at Tyraeus. Evelyn stared at the commander for a long moment and then she made her decision.

'You will not kill me,' she said. 'You seek knowledge, and with me dead you will not understand my immunity.'

Evelyn lifted the pistol and pointed it toward her own head.

The bots above her stopped moving as though frozen in place. Tyraeus stopped barely a few cubits away, his head undulating and flexing as the bots shifted position and their bodies caught the light.

'I will not be consumed,' Evelyn insisted.

'No,' Tyraeus admitted, 'but you can be controlled. The Word is too strong for you to fight forever, Evelyn: our name is Legion, for we are many. Even if it costs us a billion of our number, even if the unbearable pain of repeated infection robs you of your sanity, we shall forge on until we learn everything that we need from you. And then, Evelyn, then you shall be consumed.'

Evelyn felt her legs turn to what felt like mist, buckling beneath her as fear seethed through her veins like ice. Behind her the bridge doors opened. She turned, and there she saw a thick morass of bots swarm into the bridge, the commingled sound of their millions of limbs like distant, rushing water.

She turned to Tyraeus and knew that there was only one remaining option for her.

Evelyn leaped over the tactical station and grabbed hold of a support pillar. She aimed her pistol at the bridge windows and fired several shots straight at them.

'No!'

Tyraeus's voice was drowned out as the plasma blasts fractured and then blasted the window out and the air screamed out of the bridge and into the deep vacuum of space. Around her a dense cloud of bots was sucked in a spiralling black vortex toward the shattered window, plunging into oblivion as Tyraeus sought a handhold nearby.

***

XLV

'She's charging weapons, sir!' Jerren yelled.

Captain Idris Sansin whirled as he directed orders across the Atlantia's bridge.

'Evasive action, all turrets fire at will! Launch all fighters!'

A series of alarms blared through the ship as it suddenly lurched forward under power and pitched up out of plane with the Avenger. The captain saw the big cruiser's hull ripple with blue–white flashes as plasma turrets opened fire, blazing salvos toward them.

'Multiple launches to port!' Jerren shouted.

'Full ahead, hard to port!' Idris yelled in reply. 'Decrease our profile and brace for impact!'

The Atlantia's thrusters surged her forward while turning her toward the incoming fire in an attempt to minimize strikes. She lumbered around, and Idris watched through the viewing ports as several plasma blasts sailed harmlessly by aft of her engines.

The hull shuddered as four plasma charges impacted her, distant rumbles audible on the bridge as the hull was bombarded.

'Damage report!' Idris yelled above the alarms.

'Hull intact, plating damaged starboard–stern quarter, no leaks!'

Idris whirled, his fist clenched before him. 'Return fire!'

The hull shuddered again as the huge cannons along the Atlantia's hull thundered their response. The viewing screen showed the dozen immense plasma balls streaking toward the Avenger.

The battle cruiser dropped down, her nose diving beneath the salvo of shots, but six of them peppered her stern quarter and Idris thought he saw debris ejected from one of them.

'Hull breach in her stern quarter sir!' Lael yelled in delight.

'How is that possible?' Idris demanded. 'She's tougher than that!'

'Not right now sir!' Jerren shouted jubilantly. 'Lack of maintenance maybe? Either way, her hull plating must have degraded somehow.'

Idris Sansin got out of his chair as a pulse of vengeance made itself heard more clearly with every passing beat of his heart.

'Get behind her, away from where the bots are protecting her hull!' he said. 'Go for her engines!'

The bridge crew began labouring to turn the Atlantia around to break the Avenger's line and get in behind her.

'All power aft engines!' Idris yelled. 'Ignore her shots and go for the kill!'

The Atlantia heaved around, swinging her nose high over the Avenger's hull as she made to reverse course and dive down to direct a salvo of blasts at the cruiser's engines. Beneath her, the Avenger was rolling to one side to bring her biggest guns to bear on the Atlantia.

Like two giant whales dancing deep in the black depths of an ocean, the two battleships vied for position as from the Avenger's hull poured a tiny flotilla of metallic specks that flashed in the light from the nearby star.

*

'Stick together!'

Andaim's voice called out over the intercom as he guided his Raython fighter out of the Avenger's landing bay and accelerated away into space. He looked up and saw the Atlantia high above him, her huge bulk swinging around to bring her guns to bear on the Avenger's engines.

'Damn these things are fast!'

Qayin's voice sounded almost panicked over the intercom as the little fighters raced out into space.

'Keep your distance from each other!' Andaim cautioned as he craned his neck to look behind him.

The long, tear–drop shaped canopy of the Raython afforded him a clear view of the craft controlled by the convicts. There was no sign of the orderly formations Andaim had seen in his career with the colonial forces. Instead, the fighters seemed to squabble for space as they fanned out chaotically.

'Keep it together,' Andaim said, 'it's easy to get lost out here.'

'There's the Atlantia!' said one. 'This is cool!'

'Cut the chatter!' Andaim said. 'Check your plasma charges, engine temperatures and life support systems are all fully functional!'

There was a moment's silence as his lawless pilots hunted for the correct instruments amid a dazzling array of dials, monitors, switches and holographic displays.

'Use the command switch on your control column,' he went on, 'and select the Avenger as your target!'

A barrage of questions flooded the intercom.

'Which one's the command switch?'

'Where is my plasma charge?'

'My stuff says I only have half of my fuel.'

'What does the big yellow and black lever do...?'

'Don't touch that!' Andaim interrupted. 'Unless you want to eject!'

Another long silence and then Qayin's voice cut through the chatter.

'Turn on your weapons using the red hat–switch on your control column,' he rumbled, 'then point at anything that's not the Atlantia and blow it to hell.'

'Right,' came a response, 'I can dig that.'

A ripple of affirmations crossed the intercom, and Andaim saw the other fighter's wings sweep forward slightly, projecting their pulse cannons like a pit viper baring its fangs.

'Let's go,' Andaim snapped.

He rolled his fighter over and pulled toward the Avenger, craned his head back and saw the other fighters wheeling in a crazy display like a flock of intoxicated metal birds as they followed him.

'Stay fast,' Andaim advised, 'and never try to shoot out the plasma guns, they're too powerful. Attack the engines, and stay on the opposite side of her to the Atlantia. I don't want half of you being blasted by our own side.'

The fighters' wings flashed in the bright sunlight as they rocketed back down toward the huge cruiser. Andaim noted that most of the ship's aft lights were extinguished.

Andaim's cockpit was plunged into shadow and then flooded again with sunlight as he rolled it over and pulled in alongside the cruiser's huge hull. Vast expanses of metal flashed past on his right side and he saw a plasma cannon flash as it blasted charges up toward the Atlantia. Too close for the cruiser's guns to target him, he flashed past beneath the cannon as he saw the glow from the engines appear ahead.

To his surprise a debris cloud flashed into view, smouldering deck plates torn from the Avenger's hull spilling junk from its interior into space. Andaim pulled up and away from the damaged section of hull and craned his neck back over his right shoulder to look into the breach.

'Guys, the Avenger's aft quarter is already damaged. Aim to hit her there and aft of that spot.'

'Roger that,' Qayin replied, sounding more like a fighter pilot with every passing second.

Andaim pulled away from the hull, plasma flashes erupting around him as the Avenger's smaller cannons picked him up and tried to track him. He threw the Raython into a hard left turn, defying the cannons' aim as he turned back and aimed at the engines.

He fired a blast of plasma charges and pulled up, saw them smash into massive power lines and rupture them in bright explosions that flashed past his cockpit and ejected fuel into space in vast glistening clouds.

'All fighters, attack now!'

He needn't have bothered giving the command. He heard a series of whoops and yells and looked behind his seat as he rocketed up and away from the battle. Behind him the Avenger's vast expanses of hull were peppered with bright explosions as the fighters following him flashed past, firing as they went.

Blasts of plasma erupted in response, pursuing the fleeing squadron, and Andaim heard a scream over the intercom as one of the Raythons was hit square on the tail and blasted into a million glowing fragments that blossomed brightly before fading away into oblivion.

'Keep moving!' Andaim shouted. 'Never fly straight and level for more than five seconds!'

The fighters split like wheeling birds as Andaim looked up and saw the Atlantia diving down toward the Avenger's aft section, her pulse cannons blasting rounds at the bigger vessel and her own hull peppered with flickering fires. Plasma rounds flashed between the two ships as though they were giant storms hurling lightning across the void between them.

'She's taking a beating!' somebody shouted, seeing the damage.

'Leave the engines to Atlantia!' Andaim commanded.

The fighters swept past beneath the Atlantia's diving nose, the huge frigate plunging downward as Andaim rocketed along the Avenger's hull, which was now titled ninety degrees over as it fired round after round toward the Atlantia.

Plasma flashes flared brightly before him and he swerved his fighter to avoid the big guns, smaller rounds flashing past him like shooting stars as he rocketed along just above the cruiser's surface.

An alarm sounded in his cockpit and he looked down at a holographic display. There, images of the Avenger and the Atlantia locked in their lethal dance were portrayed, along with multiple new targets emerging as though from nowhere ahead of him.

'I've got new targets,' Qayin reported. 'Fighters from the Atlantia?'

Andaim looked to his right and saw a cloud of flashing specks racing toward them from the Atlantia as Bra'hiv and his men rushed to assist them.

'Negative,' Andaim reported, 'they're at right–two quadrant, in–bound. New targets are dead–ahead.'

'What the hell are they then?'

Andaim was about to reply when Bra'hiv's voice cut into the intercom.

'Atlantia, Blue Flight to Andaim, pull up! All fighters get away from the Avenger now!'

Andaim looked ahead and against the blackness of space he saw a great cloud of metallic specks lifting off the Avenger's hull and clumping together in tight swarms.

Andaim fired two shots at the swarms and saw the plasma charges blast into them, melting countless billions of bots as though a galaxy had exploded. The bots had formed clouds that now reached out toward the fighters. Andaim hauled back on his control column and rocketed up and away from the swarms, the other fighters following him.

He heard a scream as one of the fighters plunged through the nearest swarm and emerged coated in black bots.

'Eject!' Andaim shouted. 'Eject now!'

The Raython fighter seemed to come apart at the seams, torn into pieces by countless bots gnawing through hull plating, power lines and the cockpit canopy. The cries of the pilot degenerated into a strangled groan as the bots plunged onto and through his body and the fighter crumbled and vanished into a cloud of debris.

'All fighters, stay clear of the Avenger's hull!' Andaim shouted. 'The bots won't be able to travel far away from it or they'll freeze!'

Andaim pulled his fighter over the top of a large arc and looked out of the top of his canopy down upon the Avenger's hull. The black masses on the hull were moving aft, swarming toward the damaged sections of the ship.

'Bra'hiv!' Andaim called. 'Order the Atlantia to target the swarms!'

'Negative,' Bra'hiv replied without emotion. 'She must be disabled first or we're wasting our time. Target the landing bay immediately and destroy the shuttle and the fusion core!'

'Eve is still on the bridge!' Andaim yelled. 'We can't leave her there!'

'One life,' Bra'hiv countered, 'or several hundred, lieutenant?'

In his cockpit Andaim cursed and hammered a fist against his cockpit canopy, but he rolled the Raython over and swung her around toward the Avenger's bow. A cloud of nanobots rose to meet him and he opened fire, plasma charges racing away from his fighter and bursting through the blackened, glistening cloud in a blaze of light that smashed it into countless billions of glowing orange embers.

Andaim yanked the Raython up before it collided with the remnants of the cloud, rolling as he guided the fighter over them. The cloud flashed past above his canopy as he rolled the Raython into plane with the Avenger and saw that the landing bay they had used was once again open.

'Target in sight and in range,' he said over his intercom. 'All fighters on me. Hit the landing bay now!'

A chorus of whoops and yells filled Andaim's earphones as he raced toward the Avenger's open landing bay and locked his weapons onto it, searching for the tiny shuttle parked inside with its lethal fusion core aboard.

A hail of plasma fire rocketed up from the Avenger's hull toward him and he rolled the Raython over a parabolic manoeuvre designed to make his little fighter as hard to track as possible. The fearsome plasma blasts shot past, zipping by his wings and casting flashes of blue light into the tiny cockpit as they raced by.

Andaim rolled out and pulled level with the onrushing landing bay, his aiming reticle buried deep into the target as his finger moved to the fire button on his control column.

And then his heart skipped a beat.

The landing bay was empty.

The shuttle was gone.

'All fighters, abort!' he yelled.

Andaim hauled his Raython up, the Avenger's huge hull racing past beneath him as he climbed away and rolled the fighter violently to avoid the plasma fire following him up.

'What do you mean it's gone?' Bra'hiv asked. 'Now what do we do?'

Andaim's guts plunged as he realised that they no longer had the fusion core.

XLVI

Evelyn hugged the pillar in the bridge as she saw the clouds of bots swirling toward the ruptured viewing port. They tumbled in a glistening black morass and she heard the howl of oxygen being sucked past her diminish as the bots plugged the damaged port.

Tyraeus's immense bulk crashed to the deck with a loud thud and Evelyn saw the open bridge doors beckoning her. She turned and dashed for them, the passageway beyond now devoid of the hideous bots, but the doors slammed shut in her face.

She whirled and aimed her pistol at Tyraeus but he was already upon her. One metallic fist closed around her wrist and squeezed with unimaginable force. She screamed, her cry caught in her throat as the pistol was twisted from her grasp and clattered to the deck at her feet.

Tyraeus glared down at her with his bizarre, rippling face, his eyes fashioned from concentric rings of bots. Incredibly, a thin layer of them mimicked a blink as he stared sightlessly into her eyes.

'You are one of us,' Tyraeus growled, his voice a sickening chimera of machine and the memory of a man. 'You shall become the Word.'

Evelyn sank to her knees, grasping her arm as pain surged through her bones as Tyraeus twisted his grip. Tears flooded down Evelyn's cheeks and she heard the faintest groan of agony escape from between her lips as Tyraeus looked down at her, the bots forming his features shifting to portray an expression of pity.

'We know now, that there are people down there on that planet,' he said. 'We shall get to them later, but for now we shall begin with your friends out there. Can you see them, Evelyn?'

Tyraeus shifted his bulk out of her view, and through the remaining viewing ports she could see the battle raging outside as fighters rushed in and hammered the Avenger's hull with shots, the blasts reverberating through the ship as some of the Raython fighters were consumed by rippling balls of bots and disintegrated into balls of flame and debris that showered the cruiser's vast hull.

The Atlantia was plunging down behind the Avenger, her hull speckled with fires and trailing sparkling clouds of debris as she sank out of sight, her plasma cannons blazing.

'They seek to disable us, of course,' Tyraeus warbled. 'But we will repair the damage. They, on the other hand, will not survive when I detonate the fusion core you have planted aboard this vessel.'

Evelyn stared up at Tyraeus, who cast his grim smile upon her.

'Yes, Evelyn. Hevel was not the only mole aboard your ship. He was a victim. I know all about the weapon you have created, and I can assure you that we have nothing to fear from it here. My people will be disposing of it even as we speak.'

Evelyn felt fresh pain wrench through her as Tyraeus lifted her bodily off the deck and dragged her to the nearest viewing port. Her metal mask slammed against the deep glass panel as she was pinned there by Tyraeus's hand.

'Watch,' he commanded. 'Watch as every last one of them is blasted into history. And then I shall make you watch as we hunt down every last man, woman and child on the surface and bring them back to this vessel.'

Evelyn squirmed as she heard Tyraeus chuckle.

'Yes,' the commander said, 'we will not kill you, Evelyn. I will not have you miss the suffering that I have planned for you and your people. Every last one of them will be turned in front of your very eyes, their bodies violated by bots until nothing of them remains.'

Evelyn, her face pinned to the viewing port, saw the reflection of the bridge in the glass before her. The helm was behind her, not too far. If she could get Tyraeus to release her, then she could…

'No, Evelyn,' came his voice from behind her. 'I will stand here now until this battle is done and you will witness every last death, especially that of the captain and his pathetic little crew.'

Evelyn saw a fighter spiral out of control, trailing flame and debris as it crashed into the hull far away, a distant flash of flame sucked into the oblivion of space as the battle raged. The fighters darted in again and again, but their weapons were of no use from such range and those that strayed too close vanished into the clouds of bots swarming just above the hull.

'It is over,' Tyraeus said as the Atlantia's huge hull sank behind the Avenger, and then she saw in the reflection of the glass the commander turn to look at his crewmen. 'Prepare to launch the shuttle!'

Evelyn felt desperation fill her soul with a chill as she realised that there was nothing she could do to stop Tyraeus from blasting the Atlantia and fatally damaging the ship. Tears blurred her eyes as she stared into the deep star fields and wished that miracles were real.

A robotic, rippling voice replied to Tyraeus from somewhere behind her.

'The shuttle is gone, commander.'

Tyraeus turned his head, the bots mutating again to mimic rage.

'What do you mean it's gone?!' he demanded.

As Evelyn stared into the star fields a flash of bright grey and white light flared into her vision and she blinked as she saw a shuttle craft hove into view in front of the bridge ports and turn about, its aft quarters pointing at the bridge. She stared in disbelief as the boarding ramp opened onto the vacuum, a cloud of vapour puffing from its interior.

There, wearing an environmental suit, was Cutler, his cold little eyes easily recognisable despite the harsh light and deep shadows cast by the nearby star. He looked at her and she thought she saw the faintest glimmer of recognition and surprise in his features. Then she saw the hatred within them as he looked past her and directly at Tyraeus.

Evelyn heard Tyraeus's gasp, as though he were sucking in air even though he no longer needed to breath.

'No!'

Cutler leaned down and heaved a big container over onto its side, the dense containment unit weighing nothing in the zero gravity. Cutler's expression of deep surprise was reflected in both Evelyn's and Tyraeus's grotesque features as Cutler looked at Evelyn and his cold little eyes twinkled with grim delight.

Evelyn heard Tyraeus's scream and felt the pressure vanish from her neck. She hurled herself clear of his grip and dashed across the bridge for the exit.

'Destroy him!' Tyraeus roared, and pointed at the shuttle.

The bots plugging the damaged viewing ports flooded out into space in a black column toward Cutler and the shuttle, a blast of air escaping once again as Evelyn reached the bridge doors and opened them. She looked back and saw Cutler heave the lid of the containment unit open as the snaking, glistening coil of bots rushed toward him.

Tyraeus turned and charged across the bridge after her, his black and rippling features twisted with outrage and his hands reaching out for her. Evelyn hurled herself through the bridge doors and sealed them shut, then turned and ran for her life.

*

Cutler saw the bots swarming toward him just as he saw Evelyn leap through the Avenger's bridge doors and Tyraeus slam into them from the other side.

He waited until Tyraeus turned and that hideous mask of a face stared through the bridge windows straight into Cutler's eyes.

Cutler smiled.

He heaved the lid of the containment unit open as the undulating snake of bots reached out for him, and a blast of pure fusion energy seared the bots into a molten wind of particles as the fusion core's blazing rays melted the Avenger's bridge windows and filled its interior with a flaming Armageddon of glowing metal and burning machinery.

He saw Tyraeus dash across the bridge toward him, but the blazing beam of energy sliced through his metallic frame as though it did not exist, smashing him into a billion fragments of debris as it tore through the bridge and beyond.

The blast of energy propelled the shuttle away from the Avenger like an engine, but Cutler did what he could to sweep the bridge with the awesome power of the fractured fusion core, slicing through hull plating as though it were paper. Explosions rocked the for'ard hull of the big cruiser, and to its aft quarters Cutler saw the Atlantia's plasma cannons shredding the Avenger's engines in violent flashes and explosions that flared as brightly as the nearby star, blinding him.

Cutler threw his arms up to shield his view, and as he did so he saw the cloud of bots swarming over his environmental suit, rushing toward his visor. He heard their evil little legs scuttling over his helmet, saw glinting little incisors slicing into his visor, scratching it as they worked to penetrate it and kill him.

Cutler glimpsed the fires ripping through the Avenger's hull as she was battered by the Atlantia's powerful broadsides, and he realised that the cruiser's retaliating fire was decreasing and becoming more sporadic and unguided as control of the battleship was lost.

Cutler focused on the little bots swarming across his suit as he clambered around the containment unit. He knew that he would not survive long enough to make it back in one piece to the Atlantia, and he knew likewise that the sooner it was over, the better. He would not be turned.

'Suicide is better than surrender, you little bastards,' he snarled.

Cutler gripped the side of the containment unit as its heat seared his body and took a huge breath before he thrust his head down into the beam in a blaze of light. He felt the briefest moment of unbearable agony and then his body was blasted out into the darkness in a cloud of flaming embers.

***

XLVII

Evelyn heard the multiple explosions swell behind her as she sprinted down the corridor. Around her the Avenger's lights flickered and the hull shuddered as multiple blasts hammered the stern and the blazing fusion core sliced into the bridge.

She hurled herself to the deck as a blast ripped through the wall behind her, a hot wash of flames gusting overhead as the bridge melted behind her in a tumult of flames and oxygen was sucked past her in an inferno as the Avenger's mighty hull was breached.

Evelyn hauled herself along the deck against the gale, dragged herself through a bulkhead and then hooked her boot around the open pressure hatch and pulled on it. The vortex of wind caught the door and it slammed shut. Evelyn dragged herself to her feet and heaved the locking bar down into place, but she knew it would not hold for long.

She turned and ran for the shuttle decks, hoping against hope that there would still be one of the pristine craft waiting for her and functional. The Avenger's hull vibrated and the lights dulled again and then she realised that she could no longer feel the distant throb of the huge engines, as though the ship's heartbeat had been stilled.

The main lighting flickered weakly and then plunged the corridor into absolute blackness. Evelyn skidded to a halt, reaching out for the walls around her to steady herself as the ship shifted under the blows from the Atlantia's heavy cannons. Emergency lights flickered on, a dull red glow that banished the darkness but made her feel as though the ship was bleeding out around her.

Evelyn was about to start running again when she heard a new sound, as though a billion grains of sand were being poured into the corridor behind her. She turned and saw a thick black morass of bots surging like a wave down the corridor behind her from where they had eaten through the bulkhead door, and behind them a searing wall of roiling flame.

Evelyn turned and sprinted for the shuttle bay, leaping down a flight of steps ahead of her and hitting the deck hard. Pain flared in her ankle, but she clambered to her feet and looked behind her as she ran.

The bots flooded down the stairwell like a gigantic black snake, and the glow from the flames brightened on the deck above as air rushed toward her, cooling the sweat on her skin beneath her mask. Pain flared up and down her leg and she tore off her magnetic suit and stopped to yank off her boots. They dropped to the deck with a clang as she clambered out of her suit and grabbed the wall of the corridor as she floated off the ground. She pushed with her good foot and sailed away down the corridor as the giant wave of bots closed in on her and the flames burst into the passageway.

She reached out for bulkheads, gripping them as she sailed through and hauling herself ever faster down the corridor, but the wave of bots was closing on her, pursued by the explosions as section after section of the Avenger's hull was consumed by flames.

Another bulkhead sped past and she briefly considered trying to close a hatch behind her but the bots were far too close now. One mistake, one moment too late, and they would flood through and consume her for nothing more than revenge.

She saw the final stairwell down to the landing bay deck and pushed off the ceiling. She sailed down into the lower level and pushed off the deck with her uninjured foot, sailing forwards and up toward the ceiling as she saw the landing bay doors ahead, wide open and beckoning her onward.

A rush of air began to howl past her toward the landing bays, and she realised in horror that they must have been breached. Then she realised that she would never be able to start a shuttle's engines quickly enough to avoid being consumed by the bots. They would swallow her whole before she could even get the rear ramp closed. Panic consumed her as she looked behind and saw the bots swarming en masse, the flames reflecting off their glossy black mass as they roared in pursuit.

Evelyn burst out into the landing bay as she sought a handhold, and saw that Cutler must have left the bay doors open behind him after he flew the shuttle out. The air was being sucked in a howling wind from the entire ship, roaring through the landing bay and out into deep space.

Evelyn's hand caught on the edge of a discarded vehicle and she was swung around to point feet–first toward the open bay doors as the flood of bots poured into the bay and were vacuumed toward oblivion past her.

To her left, she saw the ranks of escape capsules set into the wall of the bay.

One of them was open.

She felt warmth swell in her heart for the wily old criminal who had so unexpectedly become her saviour. She pulled her legs in and kicked off the side of the machine and propelled herself toward the open capsule as the bots poured through the bay, rolling and writhing as they tried to follow her.

Evelyn saw the capsule rush up before her, her body moving ever faster sideways as it was dragged toward the open bay doors, and then she slammed into the capsule and turned herself around, hanging by her fingertips in the howling gale as she looked over her shoulder and saw the bots forming a writhing black snake that coiled toward her, undulating in the wind.

Evelyn breathed deeply and pulled herself into the capsule as the bots reached out for her. She hauled herself in and pulled her legs in, turning over into a standing position in the capsule and hitting the switches to close the lid. The panel hissed painfully slowly as it swung over her and closed, and then it clicked as the safety latches locked into place.

The bots slammed into the capsule, their writhing black masses blocking out the light and their tiny mandibles scratching the clear viewing port as they fought to get inside. Evelyn heard a rush of deafening flame and saw the bots seared and swept from the capsule by the ferocity of the blast as the explosions ripped through the landing bay. Heat swelled inside the capsule and a warning alarm blared as words flashed before her on the control panel.

SURVIVAL PROTOCOL: ENGAGE?

Evelyn hit the button and suddenly the capsule sank back from the flames, several of the bots still glowing in the heat as they clung to the glass, and then the capsule filled with fluid and Evelyn felt it flow warm and thick up to her neck. She closed her eyes, knowing that with the mask on she could not prevent it from flooding her lungs.

She writhed and choked as it spilled into her body, the warmth both comforting and frightening her until her body got its first rush of oxygen from the fluid. Before she could even process the thought, the capsule jerked and she was slammed against the viewing port as the capsule was ejected from the Avenger's hull and blasted out into space.

She saw the hull of the Avenger retreating rapidly away, the entire for'ard section consumed by fires and the bridge a smouldering mess of melted metal and shattered hull plating. Clouds of spinning debris sparkled in the harsh sunlight as her capsule flew away from the hull, and she saw the remaining bots clinging to the outside of her capsule vanish as their grip was lost and their internal circuitry froze solid.

The amber per–flurocarbon fluid blurred her vision but she could see the Atlantia turning away from the crippled battleship, her own hull glowing with multiple fires, and she could see fighters zipping back and forth through the debris field, some of them shooting at the Avenger even as the last of her lights flickered out.

Evelyn hung suspended in the fluid, her body overcome with an overwhelming sense of exhaustion as she felt her eyelids drooping. A weariness as heavy as all the universe seemed to weigh in upon her, and with the last vestiges of her awareness she realised that she was being automatically anaesthetised by the fluid to preserve her for as long as possible.

She tried to stay awake long enough to activate her homing beacon, but she no longer had the strength to move her arms. In the distance, through the slits of her mask, she saw a beam of energy blazing away into deep space and a pair of shuttles cruising toward it. Her last thought was for Cutler's remarkable courage, and of whether he or Andaim had survived the battle that had raged around her.

And then all was darkness.

*

'We've got the fusion core in sight, calling in the shuttles now!'

Bra'hiv's voice was calm over the intercom as Andaim guided his Raython fighter alongside the crippled hulk of the Avenger.

'Any sign of Evelyn?' he asked.

A long silence ensued as he cruised slowly through the debris field.

'Negative,' came the reply from Qayin. 'The bridge took one hell of a beating. Looks like Cutler decided to take matters into his own hands, heroic son of a bitch.'

Andaim saw Qayin's fighter rounding the darkened bow of the Avenger, and he followed it around and saw the shattered remnants of the bridge, a cavernous hole filled with twisted metal hanging like grey vines where they had melted before the core's raging energy and then frozen in the bitter cold of space.

'She could have made it to the shuttle bay,' Andaim suggested.

'Yeah,' Qayin agreed, 'but I ain't seein' no other shuttles out here, and that part of the ship is a mess and on fire. All the oxygen aboard the ship is burning up.'

'We need to go aboard and find her.'

The reply came not from Qayin but from Captain Idris Sansin.

'There will be no personnel entering that vessel. We're still registering massive movements aboard her. The bots are flocking for warmth and will likely attack and infect anybody who boards her. She must be quarantined and destroyed.'

'Evelyn might still be aboard!' Andaim shouted into his microphone.

There was another pause and then Sansin's voice, heavy with regret.

'I'm sorry, Andaim,' he said, 'but we're detecting no signs of biological life aboard the ship. If Evelyn was aboard she did not survive.'

Andaim stared at the bulk of the Avenger's hull, the captain's orders reaching him as though from a great distance.

'All fighters recover immediately to the Atlantia's landing bay, slowly. I don't want any of you nutcracker convicts crashing into my ship. We've lost enough people for one day.'

The Avenger hung dark and silent, surrounded by a cloud of debris and escaping atmospheric gases that entombed it. Andaim gave it a long, last glance and then he turned his fighter toward the Atlantia.

***

XLVIII

The cold awoke her.

Light flared into her eyes and she squinted, as though a star had ignited right before her. She moved an arm to shield her eyes and felt it drag heavily through the per–fluorocarbon.

Memories flashed through her awareness.

Tyraeus. The battle. Cutler's courage. Her escape.

She squinted as the fluid stung her eyes, saw nothing but immense star fields spreading before her, their light distorted slightly by the frost encrusting the viewing shield.

A red flashing light blinked in the darkness and she looked down.

FUEL CRITICAL: ENGAGE BEACON?

Evelyn heaved her arm up and hit the button, and she glimpsed in the darkness a dim flashing reflected off the ice before her, the homing beacon switching on with the last of the power contained in the escape capsule.

The per–fluorocarbon was cold, its heat–retaining qualities no match for a long duration exposure to deep space. Her body was not yet shivering but it could only be a matter of time before the fluid began to crystalize, ice chunks forming within it and deep freezing her body to float into eternity, wandering the lonely darkness of space.

Evelyn tried to call out, but the fluid and her mask prevented her from making even the smallest recognisable sounds.

The capsule was slowly rotating, the star field moving achingly slowly around as a brightness appeared, the brilliant glow of a yellow star flashing into view across the shoulder of the planet. Evelyn stared at the sunrise, saw the distant cloud tops and a debris field scattered across the void before her, chunks of metal and sparkling fragments of glass and plastic spinning in a silent ballet through the bitter vacuum.

The scene was beautiful, tranquil and yet achingly lonely as she felt herself slipping away. The life support systems were all flashing red and she knew that she must have already exhausted the oxygen content of the per–fluorocarbon. The light of the sun cast a brief warmth across the viewing shield, bathed her in a gentle light as she floated in the fluid and finally let herself go.

In the light flaring across the debris field she saw the bulk of the Avenger in the distance, its hull darkened and lifeless as it drifted, the relic of a once proud and powerful nation of mankind lost forever.

Evelyn's eyes closed slowly as the memory of her husband and her young son drifted through her mind, and she smiled as she slipped away into darkness.

*

Andaim nudged his Raython around a tumbling block of metallic debris that flashed in the sunlight as it descended toward the vast planet below. He could see flares and streaks of light as debris burned up in the atmosphere, his sharp young eyes seeking any sign of a shuttle craft or escape pod among the endless clouds of debris.

'Scorcher One, you're low on fuel, return to Atlantia immediately.'

Andaim swung his head around, scanning the debris field as he replied.

'Just a little longer.'

The Raython climbed out of the debris cloud as Andaim spotted the shuttles and fighters all streaming back toward the Atlantia, some of them trailing plumes of gas from damaged pipework.

'The Atlantia's sensors will detect any survivors,' came Lael's response over the intercom.

'You're too far out,' Andaim insisted.

'The captain has given his orders and…'

'The captain can shove his orders!' Andaim snapped.

The radio chatter went dead as Andaim swung his Raython angrily around and swept back through the debris field, keeping one eye on his holographic orientation display for any signals from within the clouds of wreckage.

The cockpit alternated between bright light and deep blackness as the sun was silhouetted by junk flashing past Andaim's cockpit. He squinted as he dove beneath a massive generator rolling gracefully by on his right, and then something flickered on his holographic display.

Andaim's eyes locked onto it even as it vanished from sight. A tiny signal from far out beyond the debris field. Andaim's pulse quickened and he focused the Raython's tiny radar more closely in on the quadrant to get a better fix.

'I've got something,' he said. 'Very faint signal, coming from the edge of the debris field. It looks like one of ours.'

Andaim squinted at the display as it scanned the distant object. It only took his mind a moment to register what he was seeing, the scan results denoting a colonial escape capsule, low on reserves, containing the weak signal of a human occupant: a female.

'Launch everything!' Andaim yelled. 'All available craft, survivor located, quadrant five–seven–nine–oh–four.'

Andaim's left hand moved without conscious thought, slamming the throttle to the firewall as he hurled the Raython over, centrifugal force crushing him into his seat as the fighter leaped forward.

Debris from around the Avenger flashed past his cockpit as he weaved the fighter through the fields of wreckage, past the bow of the crippled cruiser and out into empty space, bearing down upon the tiny signal flashing on his holographic display.

He saw other shuttles and Raythons turning to follow him but he raced out in front, the throttle still wide open and the fighter accelerating wildly as he soared with the racing sunlight toward the escape capsule.

Ahead, against a billion glistening stars, he saw a tiny beacon flash and he flipped the fighter over, facing back the way he had come but leaving his throttles wide open. The immense thrust of the engines now slowed him dramatically as he closed in on the signal, and he flipped the fighter over once more as he eased off the power.

The capsule emerged from the blackness ahead and he could see immediately that it was coated in frost and ice.

'Shuttle to my quadrant, now!' he snapped down the intercom.

'Ranger Four inbound,' came the reply. 'Sixty seconds.'

Andaim guided the fighter gently in alongside the slowly rotating capsule, and in the brilliant light from the flaring sun he saw a metal mask behind the frosted viewing shield, the rough surface of the mask glinting cold and hard in the light.

Andaim's guts plunged as he realised that Evelyn was back where she started, encased in an escape capsule with the mask silencing and hiding her from the rest of humanity.

He heard Captain Sansin's voice over the intercom.

'Good job, Andaim. Bring her home.'

The shuttle swooped in from out of the sunlight at the head of a flotilla of craft that had swarmed toward Evelyn's capsule. Now, as the shuttle turned about and opened its rear ramp to allow troops in environmental suits to exit on tethers and bring the capsule to safety, the flotilla of craft formed an honour guard around the shuttle and followed it back to the Atlantia.

***

XLIX

'You've had a hell of a few days.'

Evelyn was sitting upright in a bed in the Atlantia's sick–bay, watching as Meyanna Sansin tended to the innumerable bruises and abrasions scarring her body. The mask was no longer on her face, hanging instead on the wall near her bed. She had insisted on keeping it, despite the assertion of several physicians that the memory was something she was better off without. They had no reply when she told them that it was a memory that she would *never* be without.

Meyanna patched another wound as the sick bay doors hissed open and Qayin strode in, his thick blue and gold locks looking surprisingly natural over a dark blue colonial uniform.

'You're kidding?' she uttered, her throat still a little dry from where the probes had scraped her vocal chords.

'They're only human,' Qayin replied in his deep bass voice as he ran his hands down the pristine uniform. 'They knew they'd be lost without me.'

Meyanna peered at Evelyn as she tilted her head in Qayin's direction. 'Despite everything, we have failed abysmally to protect ourselves from them.'

Evelyn looked at Qayin. 'Cutler?'

Qayin shook his head. 'We found what was left of him floating in the debris a few hours ago.'

'He stood up,' she said urgently. 'Went on his own and...'

'We know,' Qayin said. 'He turned the battle all on his own, and if he were now I'd thump the idiot. He didn't have to die.'

'He had nothing left to live for,' Evelyn replied.

'That's why I'd have thumped him,' Qayin snapped. 'He had plenty to live for, but instead he went and played idiot hero. It looks like the bots got to him when he used the fusion core, and he decided to check out and take them with him.'

Evelyn looked down as Meyanna used a cauterising tool to neatly close a lesion on her left forearm, the wound sealing shut and leaving only a fine red line. The doctor applied a gel and then wrapped a dressing around the wound.

'You're good to go,' Meyanna said. 'You need to rest. Try not to get into trouble for a while, okay?'

'Who do you think you're talking to?' Qayin asked rhetorically. 'This girl can't say good mornin' without starting a war.'

Evelyn slid her legs off the bed, and was instantly lifted off the deck by Qayin's giant arms and hugged so tightly she thought her chest would cave in.

'Welcome back,' the big man said as he set her back down. 'Now, you're wanted for debrief,' Qayin reported. 'So move yo' ass.'

Evelyn walked out of the sick bay with Qayin as escort, her white civilian clothes feeling astonishingly clean against her skin and the ship's air cool and reassuring upon her face.

The civilians were evidently being scanned for infection by the Atlantia's medical staff, the sick bay corridors full of men, women and children watching her as she passed, whispers and cautious glances cast at her from all corners. But unlike the prison, this time there was admiration and awe in their expressions, the pointing fingers no longer accusing.

The trip up the elevator shafts to the bridge was brief, and she walked onto the bridge to see the captain once again occupying his favourite chair, his crew bustling over their duties overseeing the extensive repairs to the frigate's hull.

Everybody stopped and a rattle of applause erupted through the bridge as the entire crew leaped to their feet. She spotted a couple of former convicts working alongside the officers, and she felt a heat in her cheeks and down her neck and realised that she did not know where to look.

Her eyes met Andaim's, the lieutenant leaning with his arms folded against a pillar near the captain's chair and watching her with a quiet smile.

The captain stood up and strode down to greet her, his grip warm and firm as he shook her hand and then pulled her close in a brief embrace.

'I never thought I'd say this,' he admitted, 'but I'm glad to see you back aboard and safe.'

Evelyn smiled broadly, the warmth permeating her soul feeling like an old friend long lost.

'It's good to be back,' she said, and was momentarily surprised at herself.

The captain stood back from her and glanced at Qayin. 'My apologies for this,' he said, gesturing to the former convict's uniform.

'Best thing that ever happened to him,' she replied. 'You wanted to debrief me?'

'Nothing so formal,' the captain said as he waved her to follow him onto the bridge. 'Meyanna has cleared you?'

'I'm not infected,' Evelyn replied. 'She gave me the all clear using the scanners. What about the rest of the crew and civilians?'

'Meyanna has developed a non–lethal test for the bots,' the captain said. 'We're checking everybody right now.' The captain sat back down in his chair and looked at her. 'You saw him, Tyraeus?'

'What was left of him.'

'What did he tell you?'

'He told me of what really happened to me,' she replied, 'to my family. I think he was trying to win me over to his side.'

'Why?'

'I don't know.'

Evelyn had not had long to think about what had happened, about what she had learned, but her memory of nearly dying when the high–security prison wing had been sabotaged meant that she now wanted to reveal as little as possible about her condition. She carried an immunity to the Word. She could not imagine how that was possible, but that Tyraeus had been telling the truth was clear enough: she had seen what had happened to the bots he had put into her body. With his ship destroyed and the Atlantia far beyond communications range with the colonies, whoever else was infected aboard ship would have no way to report her presence back.

Hevel had not been the only agent of the Word aboard the Atlantia.

Evelyn was not about to give another of the Word's minions the chance to remove her from play as Hevel and Governor Hayes had tried to do. She had decided to wait until she could communicate her immunity quietly to Meyanna Sansin, while identifying the infected crew members, and set about finding a way to inoculate the rest of the Atlantia's crew. For now, silence was once again her friend and ally.

'What did happen to your family?' the captain asked.

Evelyn explained what Tyraeus had told her, the entire command crew listening to her story, and the captain exhaled heavily when she had finished.

'I'm sorry,' he said. 'I had no idea that you were married, or a mother. We all just thought…'

'It doesn't matter,' Evelyn replied. 'All that matters is that the Word has failed to destroy us and has failed to destroy the people who live on that planet down there. This is where we must turn the battle.'

The captain rubbed his chin, the stubble rasping as he looked at her.

'You're thinking what I'm thinking,' he said.

'We don't run anymore,' she confirmed, and looked across the bridge at the crew watching her. 'We *can* defeat the Word. We just did. If we run they will continue to follow us and people will continue to die, until eventually there really will be nobody left. The people on that planet will die too. We cannot pass them by and leave them to be slaughtered by the Word, and we cannot condemn our children to a future of running and hiding across the cosmos.'

Evelyn looked about her at the bridge crew, and she realised that somebody had moved to stand alongside her. Andaim's voice filled the bridge.

'I say we fight back!' he shouted.

A broadside of cheers filled the bridge, and Evelyn saw the lieutenant grinning down at her. 'Welcome back,' he said.

The captain stood up, and made his decision.

'I agree,' he said. 'Running has not served us any purpose other than to deplete our numbers even further. Helm, take us clear of the Avenger's wreckage as soon as our engines are fully repaired. Tactical, I'll need you to organise the salvage parties to recover what useful materials we can from her hull and debris before she is destroyed. Andaim, you will lead the scouting parties back down to the planet: we'll need to complete our gathering of supplies, and ensure that we leave as little trace of our presence here as possible.'

'Aye, captain,' Andaim nodded.

***

L

The valley at the heart of the Atlantia's sanctuary was filled with crowds of civilians all waiting in lines to be checked by Meyanna Sansin and her medical team for infection by the Word: the men, women and children who represented the survivors of the calamity that had consumed the colonies. At their centre stood ranks of soldiers, pilots, military officers and former convicts now resplendent in their junior–grade uniforms that managed, mostly, to conceal the gang tattoos and scars that marked their bodies.

Behind them, on a raised dais, Captain Idris Sansin addressed the crowd, his voice rolling out over their heads and across the valley.

'Citizens, it does not require me to elaborate on what has become of our people these past months and years. We have suffered, even as the memory of those we left behind still lingers in our minds, as we have been pursued across the cosmos by a force of our own creation, bent on turning us to its will or destroying us entirely.' The captain paused for effect. 'No more.'

A deafening cheer went up as the civilians and military contingent showed their anger and their appreciation, and as Evelyn watched she realised that a real corner had been turned, that this was the point where they would start fighting back, together.

'There are people on the planet below us who know nothing of what has come so close to destroying their world and their way of life,' the captain went on. 'We shall deploy drones to observe them, unobtrusively, to witness their development in the hopes that someday they may achieve sufficient enlightenment to begin to understand the universe around them. For our part, we will run no longer. We shall turn and face our adversary, if not to protect ourselves then to protect those who have no defence at all against the Word.'

He looked across the heads of so many people who were now reliant upon his every decision; a lone leader controlling the fate of what little was left of humanity.

'The wreck of Avenger has been fitted with the fractured fusion core that once powered the prison hull attached to the Atlantia,' he said, 'and her course set for the star that resides at the centre of this planetary system. In a few short days the Avenger will collide with the surface of that star and be melted into inorganic atoms. Captain Tyraeus, his infected crew and vessel will be no more.'

The captain clenched his fist beside his head.

'We can defeat the Word, we have defeated the Word, and by everything that makes us who we are I proclaim that we shall search the cosmos for every last trace of the Word and blast it from existence until it becomes history!'

More cheers thundered from the crowds below as the captain turned and surveyed his military.

'We now have a full complement of fighter aircraft,' he said, 'soldiers are being trained, pilots, scouts and officers. We all have a part to play, and we shall fulfil our roles to the very best of our ability. We are the last human beings, the last survivors of our kind.' He surveyed the crowds one more time. 'But this is not the end of our story. This is the beginning!'

The crowds applauded and let out thunderous cheers.

Andaim leaned in as the captain walked down off the raised dais.

'Keeping our presence from the people on the planet below may prove difficult,' Andaim pointed out, 'even if they never see our drones. They witnessed some of our technologies.'

'Time will distort the memory of what happened,' the captain assured him, 'just as it did for us, until we realised that we were not alone in the universe. They may tell stories, share legends, but none of it will alter the course of their development if they possess the same spirit of the pursuit of knowledge and curiosity that we do.' He smiled briefly. 'They will learn.'

'And what about the remains of the prison hull, Atlantia Five?' Andaim pressed. 'Most of the hull went down in the ocean and it hasn't sunk yet.'

The captain sighed and nodded.

'The oceans there are deep, and the people do not possess the technology to survey the ocean beds. Relax, Andaim,' the captain reassured him. 'By the time they have the ability to dive that deep beneath the water, that hull will have disintegrated into nothing but corals and dust.'

He turned to Evelyn, who stood beside Qayin and his uniformed cohorts, all of whom were either beaming with pride or shuffling nervously, clearly uncomfortable with the sudden attention they were being subject to.

'And you, Evelyn?' he asked. 'You have the gratitude of the entire ship's compliment and the respect of her crew. The amnesty is extended to all convicts who were incarcerated aboard Atlantia Five. We could use another good fighter aboard this ship, be it with Bra'hiv's soldiers or Andaim's pilots.'

Evelyn looked at Bra'hiv and then at Andaim, before she replied.

'I think that Bra'hiv knows how to look after himself,' she said. 'But Andaim...'

The lieutenant grinned.

'I'll feel safer with her around,' he said to the captain. 'I'll schedule her flight training to begin as soon as she's ready.'

The captain nodded and then turned as a section of the sanctuary's vast sky faded away to reveal the vast panorama of the star fields surrounding them, specked with a handful of brighter points of light, other planets in orbit around the blinding flare of their parent star.

The entire ship's compliment fell silent and watched as the colourful blue and green planet receded slowly behind them. Against the vast panorama a thin streak of blue–white energy behind the Avenger's crippled hull drifted toward the star as it rose over the planet's horizon, heading on its course for destruction amid unimaginable heat.

From the Atlantia's hull a flotilla of dozens of drones launched out into the blackened void and turned toward the nearby planet. Metallic and shaped like discs, with a central bulge that contained their ion drives and internal circuitry, the unmanned drones were capable of both inter–stellar and atmospheric flight, of tremendous velocities and manoeuvrability and of functioning almost indefinitely.

Evelyn watched them depart, knowing that the drones would patrol the planet for aeons to come, silent guardians against the return of the Word. The population of the planet below would probably see them in the skies from time to time, but would likely never understand why they were there or what their purpose was.

*

Dhalere watched the spectacular scene across the heavens of the sanctuary, the Avenger departing toward its doom in the heart of the fearsome star and the wave of drones vanishing toward the distant planet, to act as guardians for perhaps millennia into the future. The planet below them had seemed so inviting, somewhere that she could have fled, but now she knew that she never could. There was no right thing to do, no wrong thing to do.

She knew that she would have to do something, though.

Her mind seemed confused, as though her thoughts were not her own as she slipped away from the throng watching the wreckage of the Avenger vanish toward the huge star. She hurried through the ship, seeking the solace of her tiny cabin and shutting the door behind her and locking it firmly.

She walked slowly into her bathroom and stood in front of the steel mirror on the wall.

She was still young, still beautiful with her dark skin and exotic almond eyes, and yet she felt somehow as though everything was slipping away from her for reasons that she could not exactly describe.

A lone tear fell from her cheek and dropped onto the sink. She looked down at it and her heart sank as she watched it drain slowly away. A few tiny black specks lined its wake, and as she leaned closer to the sink she saw them shift position, climbing back toward her.

Dhalere looked closely at her reflection in the mirror and saw the tiny shapes drifting across the whites of her eyes, scuttling back and forth like minuscule demons flocking away from the light.

Her face smiled cruelly back at her, using muscles that she could not herself control as a lance of bright pain briefly sheared her vision and then faded to be replaced with a wonderful warmth and comfort.

Dhalere understood the warning, despite the fear that coursed through her veins. There was little time. She would be tested for infection by Meyanna Sansin: somehow, she had to avoid detection.

***

LI

'Keep going.'

Heliosa's voice rang out across the deck of the ship, the blue waves crashing against her hull as his crew rowed and the wind rumbled through the vast canvass sails.

Heliosa turned and looked behind him to the distant horizon already receding beneath the endless waves. Pale cliffs rose up in the distance through the haze, two distinct towers against the brilliant sky. He shielded his eyes against the sunlight and peered at them, knowing that no man had ever sailed this far west and lived to tell the tale.

'We shouldn't be here,' his first mate, Acklion, growled. 'You know the law, Heliosa.'

Heliosa nodded as he lowered his hand, the law common among all sea farers of the Greek Islands. *No man may trade nor sail beyond the Pillars of Hercules.*

'I know the law,' he replied, 'but the law doesn't know about that.'

He turned and pointed at the low smear of brown smoke staining the perfect blue sky ahead, and the immense and bizarre object beneath it.

'Bring Jaela up here, now!' he ordered.

Acklion dashed below decks and came back moments later with a woman, who carried with her canvasses and brushes.

'Quickly,' Heliosa snapped. 'Record it!'

Jaela, her eyes wide and her jaw agape, sat upon the bow of the vessel and began hurriedly trying to inscribe what she saw before her.

The huge, silvery–grey object was plunging beneath the waves, a towering monolith of spires and domes that seemed as large as an entire city, the ocean crashing and seething around it as though consuming it whole.

'For the love of Poseidon!' Acklion pleaded. 'We must leave this place!'

Heliosa did not reply as Jaela scrawled what she could see, strange symbols emblazoned across the side of the vast city as the ocean roared and blasted from its windows and port holes as it sank beneath the waves with a final, thunderous crash that shook Heliosa's ship and sent the slaves screaming and cowering beneath their benches, their manacled wrists huddled over their heads.

Heliosa gasped, his heart beating as he watched the last of the magnificent vessel plunge beneath the waves and the ocean settle before them.

'Did you see it?' he demanded of Jaela. 'Did you see it?!'

Jaela nodded and she held up the canvass in her hands to show him. Heliosa and Acklion stared at the symbols, and then at each other.

'The home of Atlas,' Acklion gasped.

Heliosa seemed mesmerised by the symbols as he replied.

ATLANTIA5

'Atlantias,' he whispered. 'A city consumed by the sea. We must never forget this day. Record it,' he ordered Jaela. 'Record everything we saw.'

*

The gathering was vast, a sea of people watching as the setting sun glowed like fire upon their faces, as though the gods had parted the turbulent clouds and reached out for them as Ahmosis raised his staff and spoke. Nearby, the Ark of the Covenant glowed brilliantly in the fiery light below Mount Sinai as Ahmosis' voice rang out across the barren plains and regaled them with the tales of legend. As Ahmosis spoke, above them in the darkening sky a single bright star that had remained in view for several days slowly drifted away and faded from sight into the endless heavens.

The Shasu listened in respectful silence, their hearts and minds gripped with fervour as their leader spoke of the beautiful garden from which Andaim and Evelyn had been cast; of the Word and the commandments and the power of their god, handed down from the heavens into the Ark of the Covenant and unleashed upon the Pharaoh's army; of the fall of Golyath at the hands of a tiny, lone warrior; of the ten plagues that had befallen the worshippers of false idols in Egypt, and of

Qayin and Hevel until, finally, those chosen by the gods in heaven had been freed to wander the wilderness in search of a new home.

And the Shasu scribes around him rushed to record his words in their ancient Hebrew script.

***

ABOUT THE AUTHOR

Dean Crawford is the author of the internationally published series of thrillers featuring *Ethan Warner*, a former United States Marine now employed by a government agency tasked with investigating unusual scientific phenomena. The novels have been *Sunday Times* paperback best-sellers and have gained the interest of major Hollywood production studios. He is also the enthusiastic author of many independently published Science Fiction novels.

REVIEWS

All authors love to hear from their readers. If you enjoyed my work, please do let me know by leaving a review on Amazon. Taking a few moments to review our works lets us authors know about our audience and what you want to read, and ultimately gives you better value for money and better books.

Printed in Great Britain
by Amazon